EMP DEADFALL
Dark New World: Book 3

JJ HOLDEN
&
HENRY GENE FOSTER

Copyright © 2016 by JJ Holden / Henry Gene Foster
All rights reserved.
www.jjholdenbooks.com

This is a work of fiction. All of the characters, organizations, and events portrayed in this novel are either products of the author's imagination or are used fictitiously.

ISBN: 1537782649
ISBN-13: 978-1537782645

EMP DEADFALL

- 1 -

1000 HOURS - ZERO DAY +18

CASSY AND MICHAEL rode west on the only two horses their newly formed Clan had managed to scrounge in the week since they arrived at Cassy's small, self-sufficient farm outside Lancaster's hilly Pennsylvania Dutch countryside. It had been a dangerous trek under frequent attack by well-armed invading forces. They'd lost one of their own to the invaders only days before they arrived at Cassy's farm.

But the Clan was now settling in nicely, the formerly urban Clan members pitching in with more enthusiasm than skill as they learned the unfamiliar chores that would keep Cassy's uncommonly well-designed little farm going. They all knew that any sense of safety was a dangerous illusion, but work needed doing so there was little time for worry. There was no safety anywhere now, not in this awful new world made for them by the invaders.

Behind the two riders, wisps of smoke still rose from the burnt-out wreckage of the nearby Patterson family farm. It was direct evidence of raiding by vicious gangs, mostly people forced out into the country as cities eastward to New York and beyond were rendered unlivable. Cassy kept silent now, her jaw clenched. The once peaceful Patterson spread had been a scene from hell, every building burnt and the fields, laden with crops almost ready to harvest, torched.

They had found the mangled corpses of Mr. and Mrs. Patterson hanging side by side on a sturdy branch of the rugged old oak tree by the barn. Nearby, the corpses of their two teenage children sprawled in unnatural poses, partly carved up. The sight had almost made Cassy vomit. Around the farm, nothing of value remained. Cassy was thankful she'd had Michael, the Clan's resident Jarhead, with her today.

Michael interrupted her rage-filled thoughts. She thought she heard a volcanic anger in his voice, belying the mask of disciplined calm that Michael usually wore in battle. "What do you make of the sign they left?" he asked.

Cassy looked blankly back at Michael, her brain in a fog. It took a second for her to understand his words. Then she answered, "They didn't bring that sign with them raiding, I think. They probably built it using wood from the Patterson's farm buildings. The paint was probably Patterson blood. It's a warning, and a brag."

"Yeah. Makes sense, I reckon. What do you think it *means*, though? 'Red Locusts swarm, and the rats in the corn will flee or die.' It doesn't seem real."

"They're the locusts, and farmers are the rats in the corn. At least we have a name for them now. Red Locusts..."

And if she ever caught one of those monsters they'd truly be red, with their own blood. Cassy wanted to cut off their genitals and shove them down their throats, or do something equally horrific and satisfying. In the week since they'd arrived at her homestead, the bodies they found hacked up at nearby farms, many in traditional Amish farm clothing, had gone from being simply murdered corpses to showing evidence of cannibalism. The remnants of the Patterson barbecue proved that the raiders had progressed to slaughtering decent people for food. "Long pig." Cassy shuddered, overwhelmed with rage, fear, and disgust.

Michael grunted. "They're long gone—that scene looks about a day old—but I hope they left without hitting your friend's place. Karma's coming for them, I swear it. Call me 'Karma.' "

Cassy frowned. "Angie's an old lady, but a good farmer. We could use her knowledge. If she's alive I'd like to bring her back and make her part of our Clan, God willing." She didn't tell Michael how unlikely she thought it was that Angie would be alive; her place was too close to the Patterson farm to be so lucky. But she had to check.

They rode on in silence awhile, until they came in view of a small homestead. Cassy cried out a strangled scream as ahead of them, Angie's home blazed. Wordlessly, Cassy and Michael dismounted and readied their rifles. They hitched the horses to a branch and then crept forward to investigate. Cassy soon wished she hadn't. Angie, the happy and harmless elderly lady who traded her delicious preserves to Cassy in exchange for a bit of help now and then, lay spread-eagled on the hood of her car. She didn't have any real meat on her bones, so she'd thankfully been spared being carved into food, but those damn assholes had slit her throat. Nailed to the back of her head was a single board, torn from her house judging by the paint on it, and in her blood they had written on it, "Hoarder."

Michael spat. "Fuck these bastards. We gotta hunt them down. I've never seen anything like this, not even from those fuckin' barbarian ragheads in Crapghanistan."

Michael grew eerily quiet, and his intensity was frightening. Instead of flinching, however, Cassy reached over and put her hand on his shoulder.

Screw it. She needed comforting. With tears in her eyes

she buried her face against Michael's chest and wrapped her arms around his waist, holding on tight. If she just squeezed hard enough then maybe when she opened her eyes Angie wouldn't be dead...

Michael put his arms around Cassy, held her gently and let her cry. For now, he just stood and held her, shielding her however briefly from the horror. She cried it out. Cassy was grateful for his solid presence.

After several minutes Cassy regained her composure, let go of Michael, and wiped her eyes on her sleeve. "Okay, there's another family around here, but far enough away that they may still live," she said. "The Jepsons. If the raiders haven't killed them yet by the time we get there, I don't expect a warm welcome, but I just can't leave them for the Red Locusts. We need to try to talk sense into them. They'll be stubborn."

Michael nodded. "Okay... Why won't they give you a warm welcome? I thought you were friends with just about everyone around here."

With a shrug, Cassy said, "We go way back, to when I first moved here. I tried to do things right, and get permits for the things I needed to build. But Mrs. Jepson was on the zoning committee. They declined a few things, and it was Mrs. Jepson's fault. She claimed my ideas were unsound, not based in real-world experience. My prepper design for reclaiming wastewater really bothered her. She said the building codes don't allow that sort of thing and that the committee had no reason to grant a variance. So, I filed appeals and after a few months it went to trial. In the meantime, I just built what I needed and thumbed my nose at her because the court granted a stay on any action against me by the local government while they reviewed the case. Made her look impotent. Better yet, just about everyone around here hates big government, and they sided with me.

Bringing in the government like that hurt her husband's handyman business, too. She blames me, but it's her own stick-up-the-ass fault."

"Small town politics. Gotta love it," replied Michael. "Seems you're growing as a leader, Cassy. Frank ought to be happy about that. No matter how much you protest, the rest of us—including Frank—think of you as the Clan's real leader now." He smiled his crooked smile and added, "Frank says he knows just enough about farming to kill a house plant." His smile broadened into an open grin as he added, "Frank doesn't want people looking to him for advice when the green peppers start to molt, or whatever they do. He said that."

Cassy again thought about how Frank had kept them all fairly sane and in focus during the dangerous trip, while Michael guarded them against surprise ambushes and the like. Cassy had stumbled onto the group as a late arrival, and she wasn't sure she much liked her apparent promotion to "Clan leader," whatever that meant. But the farm was hers so she supposed it had to be that way. Her house, her rules. The Clan went along with it, decent folk that they were, and she knew she'd been lucky to join them.

"Shut up, Michael," Cassy smiled with a wink, her voice dripping with fake irritation.

Michael smiled to himself as their mounts wended their way down the hill. He always accompanied Cassy as protection on these outings, when she tried to reconnect with old neighbors. Their verbal exchanges were just how they bantered when no one was around, or the dark new world's vicious insanity wore them down. He needed pressure relief too, from time to time.

"Let's get this over with," he said as they neared the Jepson farm.

***

Dean Jepson pulled another half-basket of berries off the bush. His homemade berry picking tool was working well, and he smiled. It was a simple thing, just a length of PVC pipe he'd split at the end, then used heat to spread the two halves apart. These he'd twisted with more heat until they curved upward, and then folded back. The result looked like a plastic pitch fork with tines pointing back at the wielder. When he drew it down a bramble, ripe berries fell like sweet, soft hail into the bucket he held beneath. It showed the kind of simple genius Dean was known for around here. At the rate his new tool let him pick berries, he'd have the whole acre harvested by the end of tomorrow. Pie for weeks, and goods to trade...

The loud *crack* of a rifle interrupted his thoughts, and his head whipped toward the noise. Sonovabitch, it had come from the direction of his house, a half mile away. Why wouldn't everyone just leave his family and him alone? He dropped his tool, snatched up his rifle nearby—he never left the house without it these days—and sprinted toward home.

***

Cassy and Michael heard a shot fired up ahead and both spurred their horses into a full gallop, ignoring scrapes and bruises from brush and young trees they whipped by. They came to the top of a small rise, stopped, and looked down at a house just beyond the foot of the hill, a couple hundred feet ahead. Cassy saw four people in a rough semi-circle facing the front of the house, each behind a tree or shrub for cover or at least some concealment. From a front window of the small house, Cassy saw the barrel of a rifle protruding. A woman inside was shouting, but at this range Cassy couldn't tell what was said. She could imagine though. The four raiders took turns shooting at the house and then ducking back behind cover. Another shot rang out from inside the house.

Cassy said, "That's the Jepson home." Her voice was a flat monotone, because damn if she was going to lose her composure just now. Time enough for that after these bastard raiders were strung up and gone straight to Hell. "Let's kill these assholes, Michael."

Michael only nodded, slid off his horse with rifle in hand, and moved forward into cover. Cassy again marveled at the former Marine Scout's ability to almost disappear into the background when he wanted to. He seemed to glide as he prowled in battle mode, she thought. Then she dismounted and stepped forward as best she could. At the crest, she took aim at one of the raiders who, being between her and the house, all faced away from her. She lined up the center of his back in her M4's scope.

She was starting to squeeze the trigger when a dark mass burst from bushes nearby and plowed straight into the man Cassy had been sighting in on. A gleam of metal flashed in the sunlight, and Cassy watched as Dean Jepson plunged a knife into the other man's throat. He bolted to his feet, bloody knife in hand, and whirled to face the others. It all happened so fast that Cassy hadn't had time to redirect her aim.

Michael was faster, however; as the three remaining raiders turned to swing their rifles around toward Dean, Michael fired a single shot and the raider closest to Dean flopped over, most of his head missing.

Cassy again marveled at Michael's ruthless efficiency in battle. She'd seen it before during the Clan's violently dangerous trek to the hoped-for safety of what her mother called her "prepper farm." As she watched in her scope, Dean took a step toward the other two raiders. Another shot rang out from within the house, but missed its target.

The other two raiders briefly stared at the mostly-headless body of their companion and then turned and sprinted away into the patchy woodlands nearby.

"Nice shooting," said Cassy, and then climbed back atop her horse. When Michael mounted up again as well, she clucked her tongue against her front teeth, *tsk tsk*, and the horses began to walk down the hill. "Let's go see what kind of welcome we'll get."

* * *

Peter Ixin pursed his lips in frustration. He'd returned from tailing Cassy to her farm to White Stag Farms, or what was left of it, and taken over the place with a little bit of violence and a lot of solid promises. The supervisors who still lived—after Peter's demonstration of authority removed one of them from their midst—were compliant, showing no signs of resisting. Good, because he'd kill every last one of those morons if they ever showed the least bit of spine. No sir, Peter wasn't gonna take any of their crap. Not anymore.

But despite their compliance, getting his people ready to move out was taking longer than expected, and his irritation grew. How the hell could he lead them to the promised land, like Moses before, if these lazy bastards wouldn't work harder to get ready? Damn it, Moses never had to deal with people this lazy, why should Peter? It wasn't right. Selfish pricks.

Next to him his right-hand man, Jim, muttered, "Okay boss, we got twelve carts salvaged with enough horses to pull 'em, along with our own mounts, and enough left over for a couple scouts to take point while we travel. And we managed to get all the chickens that lived through the bombing caged up and on the wagons. We got enough flour and rice and shit to make the journey. So why aren't they ready to go yet?"

Peter grunted in agreement. "Seems they want to pack up their mementos. Sentimental bullshit. They need to make new memories in the place I'm leading them to, right?"

Jim chuckled for his boss. "Far as I see, the memories here sucked. Better off forgetting."

Peter knew he was just being a toady, and he relished his new power over Jim and everyone around him. Now that he had the power, he'd been able to whip everyone into action despite the losers who didn't want to go. Too fuckin' bad. Peter wasn't going to leave one damn lazy sumbitch behind. Not alive, anyway. He would need all the hands he could get to take over that sweet little farm they would journey to. More hands meant more guns, and an easier time killing that bitch spy and all her jerk-off followers.

"Moses is coming for you, bitch," Peter muttered, but he knew that Jim wouldn't ask what he meant or let anyone else ask without giving 'em a proper ass kicking. "Jim, if they aren't ready in the next hour, start showing them the folly of their ways, yeah?"

Jim grinned and tightened his grip on his baseball bat. It was covered with dark brown stains from previous teaching moments. "Me 'n my move-faster-stick got you covered, boss."

An hour later some people still dawdled, not ready to move out. A couple of kids cried, begging to stay. Mothers wasted time pampering their little brats. Ungrateful shits, all of 'em. Peter checked the magazine on his rifle, almost casually, and said, "Let the teaching begin, Jim. I don't want anyone really hurt, they'd just slow us down. But you know... Get my point across."

Jim showed none of the humor he had earlier. He pursed his lips. "Boss, I hate this part. You know? But they gotta learn. It's a new world now, and we have no time for the weak, the sentimental, the slow. So yeah, I'll do what we need to do—it's for the greater good."

Peter nodded once and wondered why it was important to Jim to be *right* about these punishments. It was sometimes amusing to see the man try to figure out how to justify doing what he wanted to. Still, Jim was a good man, a trait he'd have to keep an eye on. Good people sometimes lacked the foresight to see the *greater good* that Peter was leading them toward, especially if reaching it required sacrifices. But for now, Jim was on board. And as long as Jim was part of the program, Peter would let him bask in his reflected glory. The man certainly had no qualms using the privileges of his rank to take his pick of the pretty little fillies among Peter's people, willing or otherwise. Peter was more than happy to turn a blind eye to Jim's "eccentricities" so long as he remained an effective bulldog and as long as Peter could continue to feign ignorance of Jim's less savory "punishments" among the womenfolk. It was a small price to pay for the glory of the lands they would soon settle on.

He watched Jim move among the people like some medieval Inquisitor, judging each person's preparedness, being present and making them anxious. As a management technique, it worked. Peter, the Boss, watched Jim as he nodded at one man, then at a woman (but with a glower at her rambunctious child), frowned at a sweating man who had paused for a sip of water. Apparently, those people were packed and ready.

But then Jim came to a family still struggling to tie their possessions to what little room remained on one of the wagons. Their teen daughter was bent at the waist struggling to tighten a length of rope. Jim asked, looking at the man of the household, "Foreman Peter ordered you people to be ready an hour ago, mister. What's the delay?"

The other man had to be nearing fifty. Peter decided he didn't care what happened to him. Get in line or get what's coming, it didn't matter. Old horses had better work if they wanted to eat, right? Jim's posture was relaxed, open, friendly. But Peter saw that the older man wasn't fooled; he tensed immediately, and his gaze darted left then right, looking for friendly faces. The other people, however, found conspicuous reasons to turn their back to the unfolding scene. Good. They were learning.

The man, who Peter remembered was named Eric, looked at his feet, shoulders slumped. "Jim, we're trying, but my arthritis won't let me tie up, and my wife don't know knots. My daughter's working the line, but she's not strong enough. Too much other stuff on the wagon. She just needs another minute, I swear, Jim. I'll help her, okay?" he said, holding both palms up toward Jim placatingly. It didn't work, of course.

Jim snarled, then stormed toward the girl. She was no more than fifteen and squealed in fear when Jim approached. He snatched her arm, and Peter knew she'd have bruises when her squeal of fear turned to a screech of pain.

Her father, Eric, moved in a flash, leaping at Jim. "Get your hands off my daughter, you freak," he screamed. He led with a clenched fist and struck Jim in the back of his head. Eric's momentum carried him forward, and he smashed into the man hurting his daughter. They fell to the ground, Eric on top, and Jim's bat went flying away. Eric quickly straddled him and raised his fist to smash it into Jim's face. Jim snarled, but it wouldn't do him any good; Eric had the look of murder on his face, and Jim had let him get the upper hand.

Fuck this, thought Peter. Even an old workhorse, good for nothing but the glue factory, could get a surprise kick in, but Jim mattered a lot more than that asshole. In one deft movement Peter raised his rifle and, with barely a moment to sight in, squeezed the trigger.

Bang. The man's chest caved in, gore splattering the wagon behind him. His wife—Peter couldn't remember the old bitch's name—screamed and lunged forward. The daughter, however, leapt toward her mother and restrained her, screaming at her mother to stop. Smart girl.

Jim rose, face red with anger, and stalked to his bat and picked it up. Turning, he grinned at the two women. It was a wolf-like expression. Sometimes, Peter mused, Jim was more demon than angel, despite what the man tried so desperately to portray to the world. "Jim! Stand down," barked Peter.

Jim stopped and then froze in place, trembling with the effort of controlling himself. "Yes, boss," he hissed. Peter would overlook that mild insubordination, of course. One gave certain liberties to one's right-hand man, after all.

As the two women then fell upon their dead husband and father, wailing, Peter decided it was time to get things under control personally. "Dammit, you lazy sonsabitches! Get your fat asses in gear. If that load isn't tied in the next five minutes, you'll both join Eric. I hope you heard me because I'm not going to say it again. Get your asses up if you want to live. I don't give two shits either way. The rest of our people matter a lot more to me than you two lazy bitches."

Slowly, the daughter regained her composure then pulled her scrawny mother up and away from their old, dead dad. Or husband. Whatever. In two minutes they managed to get back to tying the load. In five, they were done. About freakin' time.

Peter let out a whistle, and the train of people and wagons slowly moved out. Eric's daughter and wife looked back on the body, which lay in the dirt unattended, with tears in their eyes. Peter nodded once, curtly. This was good; the rest of his people would remember this lesson well. With the entire body of people finally in motion, Peter rode forward whistling a cheerful marching tune. Of course Jim, riding a bit behind him, would take note of anyone foolish enough to chase Peter with hard stares. Yeah, Peter would clear those books eventually, but not until the time suited him.

* * *

Capt. Taggart, his combat promotion from Sergeant still feeling alien, grinned at Eagan's clowning. The buck private had marched stiffly into the makeshift safe house wearing the wreckage of another invader drone on his head. Loudly, the soldier proclaimed himself King of New York and dubbed Taggart, his commanding officer, Sir Bigshit of Rank.

"That's treason, Lord Shitbird," proclaimed Taggart with mock severity. "I shall indeed have you drawn and quartered."

Eagan held his nose in the air, standing nobly erect, and sniffed with disdain. "I'll have you know, *Captain* Bigshit, that as King of these here domains it is I, the King, who decides what's treason. 'Cause there's nobody else left with a crown." He looked briefly sad, maybe shadowed by personal ghosts, then squared his shoulders and added, "Besides, the Prez is probably dead somewhere, so who's gonna complain?"

Taggart replied, "Well, me, for one. You may be King, but you're still just a trench monkey private, shitbird. Now go get that fuckin' SITREP I asked for. We need intel on our ad-hoc half-company of troops."

Eagan laughed. "I can tell you without looking. The soldiers are squared away, except the lazy ones—mostly Mexicans. The Militia guys are leaking baby batter over the prospect of playing Real Soldier."

"First of all, we don't have any Mexicans here. They're mostly Cubans and Puerto Ricans. It's New York, for chrissake. And what about the gangbangers and civvies?"

"Well, the gangbangers are excited about comparing jail tattoos—they're giggling like girls at a pajama party. You could say their morale seems fine. And the civvies have food, so they'll be happy to go out and try to die for you."

Taggart frowned thoughtfully, impressed at Eagan's rapid but observant report. It wasn't like Taggart *wanted* these civilians to die. They just tended to die in combat, usually spectacularly and in the worst ways possible, because, as Eagan said, they lacked training. "Show some respect, Eagan. They're fighting for their country, at least. All *you* do is pretend to check up on them, and Jew them out of their rations at poker. They ready to fight?"

"They're all pissed as hell at the 'vaders," Eagan replied. "Most of them lost people, whole families sometimes, so yeah, they're ready."   He frowned at Taggart. "That Jew remark was racist, sir. Jews fight harder than Mexicans or a certain Irishman in this room that I could name. I, sir, am deeply offended. Deeply, and I wear the Crown of New York. Sir."

Taggart snorted, "Shut up and get me some November Juliet."

Eagan chuckled and walked over to the coffee machine, an ancient percolator they'd cut the cord off of and set on a small "rocket stove" to get to bubbling. "That's racist, too, Sarge. I mean Captain. I'm sure both our black soldiers don't much like that term."

"November Juliet? Eagan, shut up. No, wait—tell me what our friend, Mr. Black, is up to."

"He's busy reorganizing his Resistance supply network. We aren't the only ones hurt by that traitor Spyder's takeover of Black's territory."

"Good, he won't be around much. Make sure he's gone, and then get all our men and women together. I want to talk to them. We're just about ready to launch something awesome. On our own."

"How '80s of you, sir. Aye, Aye, I'll go gather the cannon fodder. I hope you have a rousing speech prepared, sir. If you don't, I'll look for a copy of that movie where General Patton says they're not supposed to die for their country, the other guy's supposed to die for *his* country. Helluva speech." He shrugged. "They're eager to fight, but maybe not so eager to be shot back at."

"Don't end your sentences with a preposition, shitbird. Get going."

Eagan stood tall and saluted, with a grin so loud Taggart could almost hear the "fuck you" behind it, but he didn't say anything. The private was wired tight when the bullets flew, so no room to chew his ass. Oh well, maybe next time. "Get the fuck out, Eagan."

Eagan left, and Taggart slid his hand under the desk to pull out a bottle of Wild Turkey 101 whiskey he'd hidden there. "Hello, darling," he said. Turkey was the best mass-produced whiskey on the market as far as he was concerned, and he licked his lips in anticipation of the mellow burn sliding down his throat. It was medicine, he figured, and he prescribed it for himself whenever he had to deal with his civilians. No doubt those unsat smokers and jokers would have *something* sarcastic to say when he gave his speech. Fuckers. And God bless 'em for stepping forward to fight for their country because most of the sheep out there were content to starve before they'd risk their necks right now to fight for America. Reverently, he poured two knuckles' worth of whiskey—now *that* was a proper shot!

Then the door opened and Black's sidekick, Chongo,

walked in looking none too pleased. Taggart let out a sigh, then said, "Hello, Chongo. What can I help you with?" Taggart eyed his shot glass longingly, but waited.

Chongo replied, "Sir, Mr. Black wants to know—and I'm quoting him, don't get pissed—when *the fuck* you are gonna do something useful with all the people we've gathered."

Taggart frowned. "You mean the people I gathered? Tell your boss that I'm totally on board. We're getting ready for a pretty major operation. I've got a platoon and a half with guns, and we've been coordinating with other Resistance groups through some guy out in rural Pennsylvania who's part of those 20s we keep hearing about. He's not the only one who knows the 20s anymore."

Chongo nodded. "You know I hate it when he sends me to ask you stuff, right? He don't like to come himself, on account of not wanting any conflict between you two roosters."

Taggart chuckled. "Yeah. Please tell him that I've got things in motion that will at least put a thorn in the side of our enemy. We're going to move out tonight on a series of raids, but I can't say where. I won't tell anyone until we're in the field and in motion."

"He ain't gonna like that, but I ain't about to tell you how to do your thing. You lay it down how you want, and I'll just pass the deets along as you give 'em to me."

Taggart said, "Ha! Yeah, it must suck to be the guy between us. Well, let him know what's up, okay? Tonight my group's hitting a warehouse of supplies, and other groups will be running interference and laying down confusion in the enemy ranks. At least, we will if our 20s guy has done his job."

- 2 -

1100 HOURS - ZERO DAY +18

ETHAN DOUBLE-CHECKED HIS work. A windmill needed a new slip washer to reduce drag on the blades. Once again, he wished Michael and Cassy were around. He already missed having their hands to help out as the rest of the Clan worked diligently to get "Camp"—the Clan's nickname for Cassy's farm—ready for winter, or harvesting the many varieties of fruits, vegetables, and herbs as they ripened. Fruits, nuts, and produce grew seemingly at random around Cassy's farm, and he hadn't yet asked her why she mixed everything up like that. Still, Ethan knew how important Cassy's mission was. Saving the neighbors not only built goodwill, but having more people might spare the Clan trouble from the raiders who increasingly ravaged the surrounding region. They'd already brought in a dozen people, who helped a lot around the farm.

Maybe raids only seemed to be increasing, Ethan reflected, because the people out there were dying in droves. But he knew that starvation and disease were a big part of the death toll; malnutrition and stress weakened people's immune systems, and once-rare treatable diseases were becoming rampant and often fatal as medicines grew scarce. Not to mention the damn diseases caused by so many unburied bodies...

But raiders, like parasites, killed their own hosts. With ever fewer available victims, raiders were themselves becoming desperate. Cannibalism was one early tactic, but that only worked when there were victims out there to eat. Ethan shuddered at the thought of falling into raider hands. One raider group, numbering at least twenty people, had already discovered the Clan's rapidly expanding farm. They had not attacked yet, and their attempt to scout the farm had cost the bastards at least three lives. Michael and the new Marines were so very good at killing when necessary. It was a damn shame it was necessary so often, and Ethan figured it would only happen more as things got worse outside of the farm's resource-rich borders.

With a grunt of approval, Ethan finished checking his work. The windmill would once again lift water on one leg of its journey to the top of the hill, where the animals were penned. Since it had ground to a halt yesterday, people had been forced to carry water to the animals—quicker than herding them to a pond—and that had taken lots of cursing plus priceless man-hours to accomplish. The Clan needed those hours on other projects, like finishing the first of the new earthbag houses, harvesting crops, canning extra food for the winter before it spoiled, mucking out the livestock pens, tending to the compost accelerator pits... The list went on and on. Shaking his head, Ethan muttered, "Time to find something else useful to do."

He made his way toward the field of spring wheat, where harvesting was underway. They were bundling the cut long stems into sheaths and taking them to a nearby shed for drying and, eventually, threshing by hand. It was labor-intensive, and he resolved to think of ways to make it more efficient. When he had time, of course.

Ethan grabbed a sheath in either hand and carried them toward a nearby wheelbarrow, then carefully lifted them into it. As he dusted off his hands on his pants he saw Amber approach and grinned. He hadn't seen her at all today, and his spirits rose as she smiled back.

He was about to say hello when Frank came up behind her and dropped four sheaths of wheat in the wheelbarrow. "Hey, Ethan. Can you load these up and wheel it to the shack? Thanks. Amber, give me a hand." He motioned for Amber to follow, and she shrugged to Ethan and hustled to catch up, with a single glance over her shoulder for Ethan. He realized he must openly look stricken and forced his face back to normal, hoping no one saw it. But damn!

There was no denying it; Amber was as attracted to him as he was to her. He hadn't even realized it was happening, this attraction, but there it was. It grew between them during the trek here, but she was taken then, and they both reined it in as best they could. Maybe he shouldn't have. But they were here now, and it was time to take it to the next level if he could. See what happened. Yes, she had to work out the conflict she felt between grief over Jed and guilt about her attraction to him. But he had his own ghosts to drive out. All the gods of HAM radios and little fishes must know the two were meant for each other!

Okay, Jed's death hadn't gone down quite the way he'd told the group it did, and he didn't know how to set that problem right. They'd been in combat when it happened, and he knew that no plan ever survived once a battle started. He knew—and kept telling himself—it wasn't his fault. It really wasn't, but the memory hounded him just about every night now. Good sleep had become rare. Sometimes he'd go reeling with mixed guilt about Jed, gratitude for Amber's interest, hunger to have her with him, and this damned frustration. And confusion.

Ethan paused and frowned as he dropped the last sheath into the wheelbarrow. Frank wasn't usually so terse. He was a friendly guy by nature, one of those steady people you know you can trust within five minutes of meeting him, and he'd try to do right even if he didn't like you. Ethan and Frank always got along fine. Of course a lot of work needed doing, that never stopped. But couldn't he take a few seconds to smile and say hello before getting down to business?

Frank must be grumpy and Ethan had an itchy feeling it involved him. Maybe Frank and his wife, Mary, were arguing, though there was no sign of that earlier. Ugh. Well, there was still work to do and lunch—and a much-needed nap after, for the hottest part of the day—and then more work.

Lunch was still an hour away, so Ethan loaded a six-pack of water bottles into the wheelbarrow for the people in the field and headed back. Cassy had been drilling into everyone that they should try not to waste any trips. There was always something to do, something to bring back and save someone else a special trip. She'd said that and, as usual, was right. So, water bottles this time.

A similar sequence happened each time he finished loading the wheelbarrow. Push to shed, unload sheathes, find something useful for the way back, return. Wash, rinse, repeat. There was plenty of time to work out the situation with Frank during the mindless routine parts.

So, okay. (Ouch! Damned hole almost jammed up the barrow's wheel this time. Gotta bring back a shovel and fill it in, next trip.) If Amber was near, so was Frank, sometimes conspicuously so. It was happening every time. He was being pushy. Was that just paranoia? Maybe.

As Ethan finished loading another trip's worth of spring

wheat, he saw movement from the corner of his eye and glanced toward it. Amber was coming toward him with two bundles of wheat and wore a welcoming half-smile on her face as she approached. Okay, here's the test...

When she had got to a dozen yards away, sure enough, Frank intercepted her. He spoke for half a minute, and the conversation looked heated. Amber's smile flipped into a frown, eyebrows furrowed and lips pursed, while Frank stiffened his stance; his back was turned so Ethan couldn't see Frank's face, but he certainly acted tense.

Then Amber turned her head to look at Ethan, looked away, turned, and stomped off into the field for more grain. She was radiating anger. Frank picked up her two sheaths and walked toward the wheelbarrow, eyeing Ethan, and stopped about six feet away. He looked at Ethan for what felt like a long time. It made Ethan damned uncomfortable. Yeah, Frank was a good guy, but this was getting weird. What on earth had Ethan done to earn this from Frank?

"Well? What's going on, Frank?" Ethan asked. His tension showed in his voice, and he didn't bother to hide his irritation. "You don't stop me from talking to anyone else, so what gives?"

After a long pause, Frank broke eye contact and looked up into the air as he let out a long breath, a sigh of resignation. "Okay, Ethan. Here's the deal. We like you, and you're one of us. No doubts about that, and I want to make darn sure you know it. But this thing with Amber, well, it's not right. Not yet, anyway. None of us who made this Clan during the trek are okay with it if you two go ahead. Not because we don't like you, or her. Be clear about that, it's important."

Frank clearly had to work hard to get all this out in a level voice. Ethan wondered if Frank thought Amber and he didn't have to struggle with this. Was he maybe just a bit ashamed? He should be! But he started up again. "Look. Jed's barely been gone a week. His kid still cries at night, I know y'all hear it sometimes. And even some of the new faces 'round here, who heard the story, have come up to me to jaw about it. They weren't even there, but they don't like it, either. Y'hear what I'm sayin', friend? Crank it back," Frank said with a weird, almost driven look.

Ethan felt his throat tighten as a sinking feeling washed over him. Almost, he felt sorry for Frank. But just as quickly, it turned to anger. Who were they to say who could do what? They weren't the morality police in this new world, dammit. And the newcomers sure as shit had no business saying a damn thing about any of it. Hell, they were lucky just to be here with the Clan. What made them feel entitled to have any say on two veteran Clan members' private lives? Screw that.

"Frank, I don't give a damn what the new people think and neither should you. They don't know us, we don't yet know them and they're here because *we, the Clan*, took mercy on them." He paused to blow out some air, breathe, try to get rid of some of the anger he was feeling. "But I'm really hurt that you'd go against us on this, Frank. We didn't pick this, it just happened, you know that." He glared for a moment but it felt uncomfortable. He liked Frank, dammit, so he added, "I thought we were friends."

Oh God, was that him whining? At Frank of all people? He felt a bit mortified. Try something else... "Amber likes me, and I like her, right? Why shouldn't we have the chance to see where that leads? In this crappy new world, a little bit of happiness is hard to find. So tell me what's wrong with that, Frank, or get out of our way. We can't worry about who's talking to whom."

Frank's tension eased a bit, and he smiled wanly. Like he got it. "Well, I *am* your friend, Ethan. And that's why I gotta stop you two from rushing into what you both want to do.

First, because of Jed's kid. She needs to mourn her dad without some guy she doesn't really know hovering around her mom. Believe me when I tell you, the whole rest of your life will be easier if you hold back for a while, until she's ready to let you in. Not even as just a good friend to her mom. Not yet. I hope that makes sense."

Ethan found himself slowly nodding. Unfortunately, it did make a good kind of sense, though it totally sucked. But that still didn't account for his friend turning on him like this. "There's more, right? Well, what's the other reason? You said 'first,' so what's 'second'?"

Frank looked startled for a moment, like a kid caught smoking, and then shook his head. "Yep, you're right, and it's more *important* than the first reason. The second reason is, both of you have to wait until *the Clan* is ready, because that's what makes us a Clan, respecting the Clan's wishes and expecting their help and support. It's a two-way street. And for now, at least, the Clan does include the new people, because they may fail but they haven't yet, and they're with us. We'd be stupid to make them outsiders for no reason. We all let them in, so they expect the Clan's help and support too, which means they matter. They have to."

He paused, looking thoughtful, before continuing. "Like you said, Ethan, we're in a different world now. It's a dangerous world. It kills people. And we're trying to build a new society, maybe better than the old one that stopped working when the lights went out. That world's dead and will be for a long time. Maybe forever. And here, now, in our chancy new world, things still can get dicey again. They probably will, actually. So if you want to survive, and you want Amber and her daughter to survive with you in whatever safety there might be, then you gotta fit in. You *need* to make an effort to show you're in the in-group, not an outsider. It's that simple. You follow whatever morals the group has as a whole until the Clan feels more secure about you and Amber, or whatever. Even if you don't agree."

He gave Ethan a worried look, and Ethan broke into a laugh. Frank's features turned angry until Ethan held up a placating hand, still smiling. "I'm sorry, Frank. I know you're right, and I'm not laughing at you. It's just that I was reading about evolutionary psychology the other day, and you just described it perfectly. I guess you're pretty smart, but that doesn't surprise me. You're a good leader, after all."

Frank looked uncomfortable. "Um... Okay. What the hell is evolutionary psychology, and what's it got to do with us? Sounds pretty useless outside a classroom."

"Not really. I'm actually glad you reminded me. It's a field where they figured out there's an evolutionary benefit to showing the other people in a tribe that you're one of them, that you share the same basic values. Every tribe—or culture —has a very clear bias on this, that, and the other thing they consider important. Showing you support their biases strengthens the group dynamic, and that's important to survival, or it can be. You just pointed out that it's important to survival right here, for us, if we want the tribe to pass on their genes and ideas from one generation to the next. That's what it's about."

Frank grinned at the Clan's resident intellectual geek. "That's a mouthful, Ethan. But it rings true, eh? Go along to get along, I guess that sums it up pretty good."

Ethan nodded, and replied, "Yeah. Nicely put. Okay, don't worry about me. I won't make any more waves about this until you or Cassy say so, just to be sure, because I'm not always good at being part of anything. But Frank... I don't think I can wait forever."

Frank nodded and chuckled, putting a friendly hand on Ethan's shoulder as the chow bell rang in the distance. "C'mon, Ryder-man. Let's go get some grub."

*　*　*

1300 HOURS - ZERO DAY +18

Frank looked up from digging up the last potatoes of the season as Michael and Cassy rode back into the farm's yard with two other people on horseback. Good, he thought. Her last trip had been disappointing and apparently gruesome. He stopped digging and stood straight, wiping his hands against each other then stretching his back and neck. That done, he smiled and waved. Michael was doing his eyes-everywhere thing, a scout being super-aware of his surroundings. Cassy saw Frank and waved back. When they came to a stop nearby, Frank walked over to help Cassy dismount and clasped her on the shoulder. "Welcome back, Cassy. Michael. Let's get you all some water, and you can introduce us to your new friends."

Frank caught an odd look between Cassy and Michael and a similar glance between the couple they had brought in. Well, that was odd. He'd have to keep an eye on that situation. If it was a case of "too many tomcats in one room," he and Cassy would have a decision to make. Frank just did not want to deal with it if he didn't have to.

Cassy nodded. "I could use some water, and the horses must be thirsty. Thanks. So, this is a couple I knew before the lights went out. Mr. Dean Jepson and his wife, Monique. Jepsons, this is Frank Conzet, the guy who put our Clan together and led us safely here."

Frank shook their hands. "Not just me, and not entirely safely. We lost one on the way, a good friend and a good man. And once we got here, Cassy's the boss, not me. No amount of money could get me to take that role again," he chuckled. "It's a pleasure to meet you both. How do you know Cassy?"

Monique stiffened at that while Dean glanced at her, with what Frank thought was apprehension. Interesting. Dammit, there better not be bad blood there. No one needed that, but Cassy was just the sort of person who'd bring in people in need even if they weren't a great fit for the group...

"Oh, we go way back," replied Dean. "And it wasn't always very friendly."

Monique pursed her lips, then interrupted. "I was on the code enforcement team at County. Cassy didn't like some of the codes. It went to an administrative hearing, and Cassy won. End of story, I guess. Anyway, that code doesn't mean much anymore. It was a different time."

Frank watched Cassy closely as Monique spoke, and was unsettled by the tense expression on her face. Yep, he'd keep a damn close eye on those two. "Well, that's all over now, right? No codes need enforcing, at least not until things go back to normal. If they ever do. You're very welcome here if Cassy says so; we can always use another set or two of hands. Got farming experience, Mr. Jepson?"

Dean nodded. "I reckon I do, a fair bit of experience. I'm sure we can earn our keep pretty good, yes sir. Thanks for inviting us. We'll see how this goes. I won't be anyone's burden, Frank. We'll earn our keep or go. But we're private folks stuck in our ways. I imagine it'll be an adjustment, but we'll fit in if we can."

Frank nodded and put on a friendly face, reflecting that now he knew the term, he could recognize evolutionary psychology when it happened right in front of him. Useful idea. That Ethan was proving his worth in more ways than just as their resident geek genius about electronic stuff.

* * *

1500 HOURS - ZERO DAY +18

Cassy walked through her house, checking it room by room. Not looking for anything specific, she just felt better after she reassured herself that nothing was wrong. She did it a couple times each day, when time allowed. The living room was fine, though cluttered with everyone's stuff. There was no way to keep it uncluttered with so many people in there, and she'd more or less given up trying. The kitchen too was in order, and *that room*, as her mother called it, she kept immaculate. The others had damned well learned quickly not to leave a mess in there, she thought with satisfaction. Until they finished the outdoor kitchen, all cooking had to be done either over an outside fire pit or in her kitchen, and leaving a kitchen messy took unacceptable chances with health. In this world, it just wasn't an option. There was a reason so many cultures put clean kitchens high on their lists of virtues.

So next, she headed upstairs and checked her bedroom. The door was slightly ajar. She hadn't left it that way, and Cassy tensed, approached the door with her hand on the grip of the .40 caliber she'd traded her .38 for, and flung the door open with a bang.

On the bed, Cassy's mom jumped in alarm, then realized it was her daughter. "Goodness, Cassy, you'll give an old woman a heart attack," she exclaimed.

"Yeah right, Mom. You're going to outlive us all," Cassy teased. But then Cassy saw what was on the bed, and froze. It was a box of small glass vials, all but a few of them empty. "Mom... tell me that's not your insulin. You have more, right?"

Mandy frowned and shook her head. "No, dear, this is all I have left. I figured I'd tell you in a day or two if the scouts didn't find any more while they're out and about looking for other survivors."

"But you're almost out, Mom," Cassy said, her irritation rising.

Mandy flinched at the harsh tone. "Calm down, sweetie. You know that the Lord will provide, if it's meant to happen. Either we'll find more, or I'll go to be with my husband, and that's a fine thing, too."

Cassy flashed at her mother. "Not yet it's not. Jesus, Mom, you can't get this low without telling me!"

Mandy pursed her lips. "Do *not* speak like that in front of me. Show respect for the Lord, or at least for me. You aren't too old for me to yell at you in front of everyone. Anyway, I raised you better than that."

Cassy took a deep breath and let it out. "I know, Mom. I'm sorry, and I know the Lord loves us. I just... You scare me when you get low on your insulin. For crying out loud, this place is overflowing with fruits and vegetables, and grains too. *Why* do you keep eating so much meat and bread, and putting so much honey in your tea, and—"

Mandy held up her hand, palm toward Cassy, and brought the interruption to a halt. "I'm an old woman, sweetie. I don't have your father anymore, so I take comfort where I can. If comfort is a bad diet, I'm okay with that. Why not? When I'm done here on Earth, I'll be with him again. All the rest is fuss and feathers and barking at nothing. Dying holds no fear for me, sweetie."

"Fine, I know you don't care. You say so often enough. But Aidan and Brianna care, and I care, and the whole Clan cares because without your help organizing things we'd lose precious time. We need all the time we can get to be ready for winter. We need you not to leave us just yet." By now Cassy's eyes had taken on a mischievous sparkle. She added, "But I guess you can thank God, because I thought to stockpile a bunch of it here, down in the bunker."

Mandy's eyes narrowed in thought. "Perhaps He gave

you that idea, Cassy. And just how, sweetie, did you get your hands on 'a bunch of insulin'? Do you have a prescription? Why didn't you tell me you have diabetes?"

Cassy smiled. "No, Mom, I'm fine. You don't need a prescription when you know people who can get on the Dark Web."

Mandy looked up with one eyebrow raised, and the confused look on her face made Cassy smile. "It's like a hidden internet that you get on with a special browser and a VPN..." Her mother looked even more blank so Cassy brought it back down a level. "Anyway, you could get just about anything needed before it all fell apart. That's where I got my stockpile of medicines. Antibiotics, insulin, and so on. I have months of insulin for you, because I bought enough for the neighbors when I thought the end of the world would be due to the dollar collapsing. We're well stocked now, even in this nightmare where everyone is starving to death. We have more than you need, for quite a while."

Cassy put on a happy face, but inside she seethed in frustration. The insulin wouldn't last forever despite what she told her mom, and if she couldn't get her mom to eat a more diabetic-friendly diet, it was just a matter of time until Grandma Mandy would be gone. She wished she could make that frustrating old lady eat right, but no one could force Mandy to do anything. A stubborn, strong old lady. It was probably where Cassy got it, come to think of it.

"Love you, Mom. Think about eating some kale, okay?" But she knew Mandy would do no such thing. Sighing, she made a mental note to put insulin on the scrounger's A-List of items to look for.

* * *

Taggart looked up at the hot afternoon sky and wished it

were cooler. But then again, winter would come all too soon, if they lived that long. He'd take summer discomfort over winter's whole different set of more lethal challenges. He didn't know how he'd keep his men alive. Well, one obstacle would be the same: Mr. Black and his goons, as always, were threatening to get out of control. Self-control, reasoning, and thinking beyond the next impulse? Not their strong suit. At least the Militia folks and Taggart's own soldiers were towing Taggart's line. The soldiers did already, and all it had taken to get the Militia forces under his chain of command was to tell them they were now in the regular military under the declaration of Martial Law, and the future depended on them. You could see them stand straighter when they heard that. No, they were almost all completely with the program now.

Some had resisted, of course. Barracks lawyer types claimed they were under State authority via the Posse Comitatus regs, until Taggart pointed out there was no State-level chain of command and they were superseded by the Enforcement Acts in the mid-'50s. In occupied territory, military regs for troops applied.

But what really brought them in was peer pressure by the other Militia troops. They hadn't been disorderly since. Taggart was happy, for once, to have received all that training about such issues in NCO school. He'd hated it at the time—useless civilian garbage—but it came in handy now...

Eagan stood beside him in silence for a while, but then broke into his thought. "Hey Cap, how come those gangbanger assholes get to do what they want? I mean, you're in charge of them too, right?"

Taggart grimaced. "It seems the gangbangers who follow Mr. Black don't want to obey the rules of Martial Law. Our problem with them is, Mr. Black takes every opportunity to undermine military authority. He told his 'bangers he was pissed at the Militia for 'betraying his trust.' Black's connections brought the Militia in, after all, so I can understand why he was pissed. Command Chain issues are *always* a pain in the ass, Eagan. Remember that if you ever shape up enough to hit NCO."

Taggart ignored Eagan's insubordinate chuckle, of course—this was just how they interacted in private. Eagan was a good soldier most of the time and could be counted on when it all hit the fan at once. He'd seen that when the 'vaders took out the rest of his troops. But Eagan had a point; sooner or later Black needed his comeuppance. Under the terms of Martial Law, he had potentially become treasonous, to say nothing of Black's role in getting Taggart's poor kid brother killed, long ago. Taggart smiled at the thought of applying comeuppance personally. But not before he tried it out on Chongo first. Now *there* was a case of treason no one would dispute.

Taggart continued, "Eagan, for now I have to go along to get along, because we need Black's forces, and his contacts. His resources have kept us alive. And he's been careful to keep his contact with the 20s a secret despite our best efforts to figure it out. We need his intel even more than we do his irregulars." He shook his head. "When the kitchen's on fire, you smile at the firemen dumping buckets of water on you." Frustration on top of more frustration... The day Black died would be a very good day. He sighed. "Our guys are more combat-effective with than without him, whether we like it or not. And safer, too, with Black's forces to lean on."

Eagan smirked. "I'm a shitbird, you always say, but *that guy* is just a beotch. I mean, a beotch, sir! So, um, when the time comes, can I shoot him?"

Taggart couldn't quite hold the smile off his face, and the kid saw it. He was getting to be almost like Taggart's lost brother. No, maybe more like a nephew. An irritating, pain-in-the-ass nephew you couldn't help rooting for. And face it, a damn good man to have at your side when bullets started to fly.

"Aw, shut up, Eagan," Taggart growled, dropping back into his customary gruff sergeant role. "Do some pushups, run around the block. Something not here. And don't worry, kid. The cosmos, or God, or Vishnu, or SpongeBob SquarePants will deal with Black someday. It's the nature of things. Let's just hope we're there to see it."

It didn't seem likely. Before anything else, tomorrow's raid had to succeed, with Chongo sniping from the sidelines and Black undermining every decision he made. He and the kid faced an impossible task. Well, they'd just have to take it a step at a time, and then another, and another, and not get killed.

"Yeah, good luck with that," he muttered to himself and reached for another shot of the good stuff.

- 3 -

0900 HOURS - ZERO DAY +19

CHIHUN GHIM'S FOOT caught on a rock, and he fell to his knees. Grunting from the pain, he sat and examined his legs. His khaki pants had a new hole over the left knee, and he saw that a bit of blood seeped into the torn fabric. Flexing his leg, however, he didn't feel too much pain. Nothing more serious than a scraped knee.

That was a relief, though there was still danger of infection like the one setting into the recent cut on his face. He'd received that a few days prior, just outside of Harrisburg, escaping another armed patrol of invaders. He could have killed the Arabic soldier who had found him, but that would go against everything he believed in. The result of that decision was a very close call with death, hours of running and hiding, and a bloody gash over his right cheekbone running all the way down to his chin. Yet, he'd found a way to live up to the precepts of his philosophy even in the face of an enemy who wanted to kill him.

As he sat clutching his skinned knee, he almost wished he'd decided to head north instead of south from College Township—home of Penn State, where he was a senior—but no, the foreign invaders were thicker to the north, everyone said, so he had taken the safer direction. "Not much safer," he muttered, considering how most of the people he'd met along the way wanted to kill him, thinking him one of the enemy.

Chihun had a vague idea of heading toward Scranton, where his parents had lived and where he might have some family left, but every time he tried to head north he ran into patrols, or hostile people. He'd been steadily herded southeasterly.

"Life is pain, but that pain comes only from holding on. Let Scranton go, and follow where life takes you, Choony," he told himself.

Once the pain in his knee subsided, he adjusted his wire-rim glasses and crossed his legs, then tried to clear his mind. Perhaps meditating would grant him some enlightenment about where to go next. His parents would have said so, but Chihun wasn't so certain. Still, meditating always made him feel better and focus his thoughts.

"I take refuge in the Buddha, the Dharma, and the Sangha," he began, but then a shot rang out in the east, and he threw himself flat. The gunshot was chased by dozens more.

Chihun calmed himself and simply observed. Okay, there were a few different weapons being fired, because the shots sounded different. And he couldn't be certain, but he thought whoever had been shot at was firing back. He frowned; that meant raiders, or invaders. But at least this time there was return fire. Most of the gunfights he'd heard since leaving Penn State had been clearly one-sided.

The sporadic gunfire continued, and with each report his heart ached. People were likely dying right now, all because some people wanted more than they had. Because some had more than others, death would come for some. And such was the case all over America, he realized. What other reason could there be for the invasion?

Chihun came to a realization, and it struck him with almost a physical sensation: he must go and see of what use he could be should anyone survive the attack. What else was his purpose for having wandered to *this* spot at *this* time, if not to aid his fellow victims? Perhaps only to bury them, though he hoped not.

"You asked for clarity of purpose, Choony. Do not turn away from the sign you've been given." He stood and then crept forward, careful to stay in cover as much as possible, heading toward the sounds of violence. It took only a couple of minutes to find the source.

As he crested a low hill covered in trees and bushes, he saw below him the terrible scene. A dozen men and women were scattered in a semi-circle around the southern side of a pair of houses. They all wore some sort of red clothing or headbands, bandanas or scarves, and were shooting at the occupants hidden within the houses; one house looked finished, and the other was under construction, with no roof as of yet.

Chihun was struck by the fact of the attackers' bits of red clothing. For a moment, he was lost in the memory of his parents describing the chaos of the war in their homeland, the civil war that had cost them most of their family, and which had made them flee to America for safety back in the early '50s, after the Americans pushed the flood of Chinese back across the border. His parents had described the terrible cruelty and torments brought upon their village by red-clad communist warriors, Chinese and Korean alike.

From inside those buildings came a flurry of return fire, bringing Chihun back to the moment. One of the red-clad attackers fell screaming, and the two nearest him fled southward. A shot rang out from the property, but it didn't come from the houses. He glanced around and saw that there was a makeshift tower, like a guard tower, and Chihun marveled that he hadn't seen it before. He'd just been so focused on the people in red.

The thought struck him that anyone in that tower who saw him would likely shoot at him at the moment. He threw himself to the ground ungracefully and hoped he had not been seen by the tower's defenders.

Below him, the fight was petering out. Another of the red attackers fell, this time without so much as a scream, and another fled. Seeing that, the other reds began to fall back, at first in an orderly way but as another fell to a defender's bullet, the rest fled in earnest. In moments, the fight was over.

Now Chihun considered a different problem. If the tower defenders had not seen him yet, they would see him if he tried to escape the area right now. Moreover, he decided, the red fighters had scattered and would likely stumble across him, or he across them, if he ran without a purpose in mind. For the time being, he was stuck. "Okay, Choony," he muttered, "just stay put a few hours, and then make your escape. The red bandits will be gone by then, and the tower people won't be on alert. Maybe you can get away unseen."

Having made a decision, he settled in to meditate again, more to pass time quickly than for any new enlightenment.

* * *

Spyder never enjoyed waking up early, but today he had no choice. That damn Colonel Ree had sent a man—at least, Spyder thought it was a man, you could never tell with those slant-eyes—to come summon him. Summoning! Him, King Spyder, *El Jeffe* of not one or two but of *four* city blocks. It was a damn insult, that's what it was. But today wasn't the day to get some payback on that *puto*. So, he had got out of bed and woke up Sebastian, his right-hand-man, and had to kick him in the ribs to get the asshole to wake up.

Ha, that's what Seb got for staying up all night drinking and entertaining a couple *chicas* with nothing to trade for food but some fine ass. Well, Seb always fed hoes pretty good, if they put out good and didn't complain too much about his screwed up fetishes. They always came back for more, next time they got too hungry.

The thought made Spyder smile, until he remembered where he and Sebastian were headed at nine in the damn morning. "So what you think Gook-Ree wants with me today, fool?"

Sebastian grunted. Hungover and tired, he wasn't much for conversation today. Normally that would be damn funny, but any time Spyder had to go meet Ree he wanted Sebastian on point, not slippin' like he was today. Ree probably knew Seb was crispy from partying, and that's why he hollered today for this stupid meeting.

"He better not want more 'volunteers.' It's getting hard to catch peeps. Yesterday we had to give Ree one of my own citizens to make quota," Spyder said.

"Let's just kill him," groaned Sebastian. "No one could get through our walls now. They gotta be ten feet high! Let him come at us. We strapped with his guns, too. Like goddamn Tony Montana himself, yo."

Spyder looked at Sebastian with a sneer. "Fool, don't you know Tony Montana dies at the end? He says some shit about his little friend, then gets caught slippin', *chingada*."

Sebastian pursed his lips at the insult but didn't reply, which was awesome. Sometimes Spyder just had to put him in his place like that. Good for morale. Spyder's morale, anyway.

The two finally reached the raghead base and walked in

without being challenged, which made Spyder feel important. But then they got to Colonel Ree's pavilion and they were halted and told to wait, which just pissed Spyder off. "*Why do they call us in but make us wait?*" he asked Sebastian in broken Spanish.

Colonel Ree kept them waiting almost an hour, and Spyder's frustration grew. He was about to complain to Sebastian for the dozenth time and was starting to consider murdering someone just to let out his anger, when one of Ree's guards came out.

"Colonel Ree wishes to see you now," said the guard, and then spun on his heels, opened the tent flap to Ree's chambers, and waited.

Spyder looked at the guard for a couple seconds, visions of slitting the man's throat dancing through his head. He took a deep breath to calm himself, then marched forward without a word to Sebastian, who followed along like the dutiful pitbull he was. At least *that* made Spyder feel a little better. Only a little.

He walked into the tent and saw Ree on his stupid folding chair, and six of the ragheads lined up on both sides of the tent, sitting cross-legged and watching Spyder enter. He and Seb came to a halt in front of Ree, and Spyder gave the expected bow, but only a half-bow—enough to avoid risking Ree's anger, but no more. Out of the corner of his eye, he saw Sebastian bow lower. Seb was dull as a hammer, but just as useful as one, and he was cunning. He knew how to inspire fear in Spyder's soldiers and the civilians alike, and how to play some games Spyder was just bad at. Like this crap here, bowing and scraping to Ree.

"You called us, we came," Spyder said simply, carefully trying to keep his anger out of his voice. "What can I do for you, Colonel?"

Ree's eyes narrowed, and a chill went up Spyder's spine.

Ree said through his translator, "I will assume you have not heard the glorious news. I am now General Ree. My commander was killed in glorious action in service to the Great Leader, when a terrorist sniper slew him. I have been elevated to his position."

Spyder understood immediately that Ree meant the Resistance, or those damn 20s, but whatever. If it made the puto feel better to call them terrorists, it didn't matter to Spyder. He was only mildly curious as to why they changed it up. "Congratulations, General," said Spyder with mock formality. Thankfully the interpreter must not have relayed that sarcasm to Ree, because he seemed to relax a bit. Asshole.

"I have been advised," said Ree, "that the Resistance fighters who escaped the territory you occupied last week remain at large. Were you not instructed to find them, and to kill them?"

It was Spyder's turn to tense up. This wasn't a good start to the conversation. "Well, yeah, but every time we figure out where they're at, they run and hide. It's like they know we're coming, yo. I mean, sir. But they ain't bothering us no more. I think they bounced out, ran away for good. We don't gotta worry about them, sir."

All of which was true. Angel and his pendejo followers were pretty good at hiding, and running. They were probably long gone. Spyder would have been long gone, in the same situation.

Ree said, "That is not what my agents have told me. They are regrouping, rebuilding. So they will return, and it will be more difficult than ever to locate their base of operations next time. I do not wish to hear your excuses, American. I have given you instructions, and if you will not follow them then I will be forced to reconsider our relationship. *You are dismissed.*" Ree's face might as well have been carved from stone; Spyder couldn't read it. But the edge of danger in Ree's voice was unmistakable. Shit was getting out of control, and fast.

Spyder and Sebastian backed out of the tent like good little lapdogs, but once they were out of earshot, Spyder turned to Seb. "We need to get this monkey off our backs, yo. Seb, get our homies ready. Maybe a day, maybe a week, but soon we're gonna remind Ree what's so dangerous about America. We gonna crash his party, you know what I'm sayin'? Him and his 'sandy' friends, yo, they gonna learn."

Oh, yes indeed. Spyder thought about the coming "party" and smiled. Yeah, Ree and his sandy buddies were gonna learn alright. And Spyder was determined to make it a short damn lesson, yeah.

* * *

1500 HOURS - ZERO DAY +19

Ethan walked beside Frank as they left the meeting. Everyone in the Clan had been required to attend the emergency get-together, save for the Jepson family and the other half-dozen people who had joined them in the past week. Cassy's brilliant idea had been to have these Clan meetings once each week or as needed, and it was a great idea. It reinforced Cassy's vision of the group being like a *real* clan, where everyone who earned it had a voice, and where the leadership—Cassy and Frank, mostly—were only the "first among equals." But, you had to prove yourself to the Clan to earn that privilege, and the Clan as a whole voted on whether to admit a newcomer to their ranks. They'd only been at Cassy's farm for about a week, yet this system and the others Cassy and Frank had put in place seemed to be second-nature now. Ethan once read a book in which that dynamic, where early leaders had a profound effect on the society they began, was called the "Founders Principle."

Ethan shook his head to clear his thoughts and realized Frank was talking to him.

"...so I don't think he's a spy, but Michael disagreed about releasing the little guy."

"Oh, the Asian guy the Marines knocked out, tied up, and dragged into camp? I don't think we're his favorite people after the handling he got from our noble defenders."

Frank chuckled. "Still with the anti-authority crap. I get it, I guess... The more self-reliant a man gets, the less he tolerates other people telling him what to do. But you can't blame our Marines. When you're a hammer, every problem is a nail."

Ethan nodded. "Yeah, but now if we don't just kill the guy they found, we'll have to work harder to get him not to hate us. I have a feeling it'll be worth the effort to make him a friend. He's the wrong race to get along with those red-raggers, and he didn't take part in the fight, he just watched. Didn't struggle when he was caught, either, though he had to be scared to death at the time."

"Well, that may be, son. But he's one of those monks, right? At peace with the flowers and so on? I don't think he *can* hate us."

"Buddhist, from what we know of him and the few things he's said. They aren't supposed to hate anyone or anything, but 'people is people,' as you like to say. Still, I'm told he didn't run when they found him, and he didn't fight back when the Marines knocked his skull with a rifle butt. That's promising."

"Hey, Ethan... Do they have Buddhists in North Korea?"

Ethan grimaced. "Yeah, I'm certain they do, but they'd be well hidden I imagine, like a Jehovah's Witness would have to be. They don't like religion there. Opiate of the people, didn't the Bolsheviks call it? But this guy seems like he's American, which meshes with his story about his parents immigrating here from South Korea. Michael isn't so certain, of course, but it's his job to doubt everything. Which, I think, would be a terrible way to live."

Frank laughed out loud at that. "Says the pot to the kettle! You doubt everything too, unless it's a conspiracy theory."

Ethan didn't reply. He couldn't tell Frank the things he knew, or suspected. And it didn't seem like the right time to point out that he'd been right about a lot of things, as confirmed by their present circumstances. Well, *one* of his theories had been right. Not exactly Nostradamus.

With a wave, Ethan headed to his "comm center," which currently was a bicycle with a car battery and HAM radio strapped to it and a big antenna sticking up from the back. Time to reach out and see how things were going in the bigger, wider world outside the farm.

A half-hour later, riding along a gravel road well away from the farm, he found a likely place with cover and rode toward it. Being away from the farm was riskier by the day due to the Red Locusts—those bastards needed to burn in Hell—but until it became impossible to ride out, he had to take the chance from time to time. Michael was at least a hundred yards behind him, on a low hill with one of Cassy's bolt-action hunting rifles, covering Ethan just in case. The man was *scary* good with that rifle.

Ethan put the thoughts aside and lugged his gear to the top of another low hill with some foliage on it for cover, set up the car battery, inverter, and HAM radio, and flicked it to one of the "prepper" channels. He was rewarded with bits of communication, mostly in code like his own transmissions were when he broadcast for the 20s. He did that with the other network of bigger antennas, of course, and got much

longer range than he tended to get with his bike setup.
When the chatter calmed, he went out. "Watcher One, Watcher One. Dark Ryder reaching out, conf 1-8-0-8-1-9-Delta-September-Romeo. Please respond. Over."

A few seconds later, he was rewarded with the sound of a familiar voice. "Dark Ryder, this is Watcher One, confirmation 1-8-0-8-1-9-Alpha-Sam-Tango. Over."

"Good to hear your voice, Watcher. I've been off air a bit. What's the latest?"

Watcher replied, "Can't reply too much over air. Check Comm Protocol Beta for additional, over."

Ethan frowned. Beta protocol meant logging on to his VPN maze and talking to the 20s via computer. Although it was easier and safer than HAM, it also usually meant he had to do a scramble-cast with updated info for Resistance groups, which carried its own risks, not least of which was the need to broadcast from the big antennas. He reminded himself he had only three more broadcasts that he could count on to be relatively safe; after that, the invaders could figure out his general area by triangulation and process of elimination, assuming they were monitoring the radio waves. He figured they almost certainly were.

"Dark Ryder, Watcher One: Roger that. Will check that soon. What *can* you tell me?"

Watcher One replied, "20s took a hit in the Big Apple but rebounding. Orlando OpFor, I mean, the enemy there, they've been drawn to a complete halt by 20s and Resistance operating from bases in the swamps all over the state. Invader buildup underway in Orlando, probable winter offensive coming.

"Mixed reviews coming out of Alpha-Kilo and November-Charlie, some say the invaders there are almost done consolidating, others say they're like Orlando, and still others say there was no invasion of the West Coast. 20s think the first option is likely.

"Last thing, check your Protocol Beta. Some juicy Two Zero India there."

Ethan felt a surge of excitement. 20s intel? Hells yeah. It was hard to sit there and finish logging radio chatter and so on—which he'd mine for intel and cross-collaboration of rumors later—when all he really wanted to do was ride like the Devil was after him, back to the farm to check his computer traffic. Also, Watcher One had just revealed, accidentally or otherwise, that he was tied into the 20s, himself. Ethan had suspected as much, of course, but now he was certain. Which, frankly, put a lot of their earlier conversations into a whole new light.

After a while, finally satisfied that he had enough chatter to dissect for the moment, he lugged the gear back to his bike in such a hurry that he almost fell down the hillside and then pedaled like crazy back toward home.

When he got back, Ethan immediately pulled out his laptop and plugged in his USB drive, loaded with goodies. It took only moments to set up his randomized proxy chain through the satellite backdoor, using still-online VPNs and such, and the familiar text box popped up. It downloaded a small .txt file in seconds, and Ethan opened it in a Virtual Machine, sandboxing the file in case it contained spyware or other nasty surprises. He ran some of his tools to scan the file, then the output, and found nothing alarming.

But, the file was in code. Another tool—which had automatically downloaded to his machine the first time he'd made contact with the 20s after the EMPs went off—quickly deciphered it. Oddly, there was still a big block of alphanumeric characters that made no sense. None of his tools knew what to make of it, either, so he stared at it for a long time, for the moment ignoring the rest of the message content.

Then an inspiration hit him; all the *numbers* in the jumble ranged from 0 to 26. What if this was a stupidly-simple cipher? He pulled up one of his tools, which he'd coded himself after putting together a framework made of snippets of open-source code available on the internet, and instructed it to offset each letter by a number of positions equal to the previous numeral. If a string of letters and a number read "3BHV," each letter would be offset by three positions, and decoded as "YES." When coded, Y would become #Y>Z>A>B.

Bada bing, money shot! The decoded message popped up. As Ethan read the hidden message, his eyebrows rose, and then rose again. So. Surprise, surprise... The 20s had a leader, and he was American. Apparently, a Lt. General with black ops experience. That was worthwhile news. Moreover, this general, named Adam Houle, was putting out a call for hackers and crackers to compile and improve on chunks of Unix code. It didn't say why, but Ethan suspected that, when all the chunks were improved and sent back, they would comprise some new program to use in the war against the invaders. No doubt related to the cryptic references earlier about "Operation Backdraft." Hot damn! Better than online castle raids. Almost. For the moment he put aside his curiosity about why Lt. General A. Houle had revealed his identity at this time. Heh, General A. Houle—that *had* to be a fake name, or the man's mother hated him.

"Well, then. Let's get this show on the road," Ethan muttered with a smirk, and opened a second attachment. As he suspected, it contained a large, discrete chunk of code for him to work on. Finally, something useful *and* fun to do. Sometimes, being in the 20s was worth the hassle. Even if he was now certain that he was working for The Man, any disappointment in that revelation was lost in the excitement of a new challenge to conquer. One that didn't involve digging dirt, tending to crops, or getting shot at.

* * *

1900 HOURS - ZERO DAY +19

Out of breath and covered in bruises and scratches, Peter straddled the man, who lay on his back with fear in his eyes. With his knife held blade-down, Peter gave his last ounce of strength to deliver a solid right-cross to the man's jaw—the blade left a deep slice in the other man's chest.

Then, face twisted with rage, Peter brought the knife point-first back across to his right, driving it deep into the other man's neck. Peter wrenched the knife hard and to his right, and the knife sliced its way out of the man's neck, showering Peter with blood and gore. The victim, whose blood now added to the crimson color of the shirt he wore, twitched and convulsed for half a tick, then fell still.

Peter struggled to his feet and looked around. Surrounding him were the bodies of the fallen—two from White Stag Farms, but most were these red-clad bandits. Peter and his two scouts had given far better than they got when, while scouting, they were leapt upon by six half-naked men painted in red warpaint, wearing red bandanas and red shirts.

But Peter was alive. Damn right, alive! No way God was going to let him fall any more than He had let Moses fall. Not when his mission was incomplete. Then the sheer joy of being alive—the *last one* alive—overtook him, and he raised his knife high into the air, heedless of the blood that dripped from it onto his face and hair, and let out a terrible cry of victory and rage. Fuck you, raiders! *God* was on his side. Who the hell could stand against *that*?

Peter saw the rest of his group, now numbering almost

seventy people if the stragglers he'd picked up were counted in, approaching. Their eyes wide with fear, anger, or a dozen different reactions that played across their faces, Peter's followers watched him with something approaching awe.

He liked the way they made him feel. This was *Peter's* moment. This story would grow in the telling and could only enhance his image and reputation. So much the better. Let's give 'em a show, he thought, and reached down, dipped three fingers into the hot blood still seeping from the dead man's neck, and reached up to paint three stripes across his face. He watched as his followers either looked away or stared, eyes wide. Let them look. He'd written his victory in blood for all to see.

Jim separated himself from the crowd and approached just as Peter heard a rough burst of coughing from his left. Reflexively, he lowered into a half crouch, knife between him and the source of the noise, lips pulling back into a savage grin. But there was no real threat, Peter realized. One of the red-clad men was regaining consciousness. His whole body shook from coughing, and despite a bit of blood bubbling from the man's mouth, Peter had no mercy or pity in his eyes.

Slowly, deliberately, Peter turned his head to face Jim. "You see? God has provided, and has been my shield and my rod, if you believe in such things. Jim, take this man far aside and get answers any way you want, but do get them. Find out how many of his people remain, where their camp is, and whatever he knows about their leader. If we can talk to their leader we will, but if he's not the talking sort, I need to know that."

Jim would pretend to hate the task, of course, but whatever. He was the only one Peter could trust to do the job right, and not to keep the info close to his vest—he'd tell Peter, no matter what the guy spilled to him. Jim was mostly a good man, pretty damn bent but loyal, and easily convinced that the unsavory things Peter tasked him with were necessary in this freakin' hell of a new world. He seemed to need the excuse, and Peter had no qualms about providing him one. Well, Jim's kind of loyalty was hard to find even before the shit hit the fan. It was more valuable than gold these days. As long as Peter kept giving Jim the noble excuses the twisted bastard needed to indulge his inner self, he would probably die for Peter if he asked him to.

Jim nodded, lips pursed as he mentally prepared himself for the task ahead, which might well get very unpleasant. He was good at this. He could be very, very persuasive when Peter ordered him to be. Peter knew he wouldn't have to wait long for the information.

Peter turned again to the growing crowd of his people, raised his knife into the air once more, and screamed his bloody, victory roar. None now dared return his gaze, and Peter allowed himself a satisfied smile. Why not?

It was all going the way it had to go. And he'd be a legend before this was over.

- 4 -

1000 HOURS - ZERO DAY +20

CASSY SAT ON the couch in her living room and looked at the others gathered there for this Clan meeting. On some level, she realized that their attendance was a sign of her standing as leader of the Clan, a position she didn't really want but that *someone* had to fill. And after all, it was her little farm...

Others attending included Frank, whose role had changed from Clan leader during their dangerous trek into something akin to a foreman or pit boss, with his ability to get people moving willingly on a task; people had begun to treat him as a liaison to Cassy, though she depended on him as an essential support, not a gatekeeper. Ethan, the geek who had saved them from an invader attack and sacrificed his underground bunker for their sakes, was now essentially their Intelligence officer. There was little of a technical nature that he couldn't mend, jury-rig around, or cajole into working. Mandy, Cassy's mother, didn't want to be there when decisions were made, but Cassy trusted her to provide a well-thought-out moral viewpoint as a balance against raw practicality or rage against the invaders and the renegade

Americans who threatened their Clan. And, of course, there was Michael, woodsman and former Marine, who had fallen into the role of head of security and defense.

The reason for the meeting sat in a kitchen chair against the wall opposite Cassy, the Asian they had captured the day before, just after the Red Locust raid. He sat regarding them calmly, looking more interested than afraid. The other Clan members sat in a semicircle, facing the prisoner, with Cassy.

At times like this, Cassy truly wished Frank was still the Clan's leader. The job sucked—dealing with this kind of crap was terrible. She didn't trust her own judgment, and she desperately wanted to hand the job off to Frank. She blew air out sharply, forcing herself to relax. Well, it was a damn job, and if no one else wanted the position, she'd just have to keep at it. Time to get the show on the road...

She cleared her throat, and everyone stopped what they were doing and looked to her. "So, your name is Chihun Ghim, and your friends call you 'Choony,' is that correct?"

Chihun nodded, seeming much more at ease than Cassy was. He smiled. "I have said this before, and I've answered all your questions truthfully. I will continue to do so. Dishonesty inspires a troubled mind."

Michael looked at Chihun intently and said, "You'll forgive us for not taking your word for that, sir. We may ask you the same question again later. And again after that."

Ethan said, "Your name is pretty common in South Korea, less so in North Korea. Where were your parents from, and where were you born?"

Chihun didn't seem at all frustrated by the questioning he had undergone since his capture. He calmly replied, "Mom and Dad were both from a village in Gangwon Province, east of Seoul. I was born in Mansfield but grew up in Scranton. I'm at Penn State, a fourth-year student majoring in chemistry."

Michael studied the young man for a moment and said, "That's plausible. It's also a good cover for a North Korean spy. We heard they're actually in charge of the Islamist invaders. We also heard the Resistance is giving the 'vaders hell all over the place. Seems to me that a lost Korean soldier might take some poor S.O.B.'s clothes and pretend to be American. So which is it really? Are you a North Korean spy, or a lost North Korean soldier?" He turned to Cassy. "I say we should eliminate him for our own safety."

Frank frowned. Cutting in, he said, "Michael, that's murder if he's an American. He sounds American. I won't kill our own if we don't have to in self-defense." He turned to Cassy. "What do you think?"

As Cassy started to reply, Michael interrupted. "Cassy, if we eliminate him, we eliminate the threat he poses, and if he's American then that's called collateral damage. It's unfortunate, but our top priority has to be our own survival. The best way to do that is not to show up on enemy intel reports. We want to stay invisible."

Frank looked angry when he shouted at Michael, "We can't kill him just on the off chance he *might* be an enemy. That's not the world we want for our kids, is it? Why can't we just, I don't know, send him packing?"

Ethan nodded enthusiastically. "Yeah, like exile. We could blindfold him and bike him out someplace, and let him go. Then we're safe whether he's the enemy or not, and we don't have to kill a guy who might be American."

Michael frowned. "If he's dangerous, you really want him running around out there knowing about us?"

Chihun sat with his mouth gaping, eyes wide, but shook away the shock. "Are you really talking about killing me, *right in front of me*? What kind of people *are* you? I told you, I'm an American. If you don't want me here, why'd you bring me here? Dying isn't so bad—it's just part of the grand cycle, it's death and rebirth—but I'm not eager for it and you — some of you—seem far too eager in my opinion."

Cassy held up her hand. "Stop," she said in an almost-whisper, yet the people in the room went quiet. She'd heard enough... Michael was a hammer and wanted to treat their captive like a nail. Frank was quiet, but he was honorable and wanted to send him on his way unharmed. Ethan was no real warrior and didn't have the stomach for killing, except to protect innocents or the Clan, but thought "exile" was workable. She hadn't heard from Mandy, and she'd brought her mom in for a reason.

"Grandma Mandy," Cassy said, using the name everyone called her these days, "you've heard the problem and the opinions. I know you aren't part of the Clan council, if that's what we are, but you know right from wrong better than anyone I know, and I respect your opinion. What should we do?"

Mandy was quiet for a long moment, looking uncomfortable. She looked at her hands, intertwined together in her lap, and said, "The way I see it, the Bible doesn't say we can't kill our enemies—do we truly love our neighbor if we allow the evil in the world to kill them when we could prevent it?—but murder is still a sin, and wrong. But if we exile this young man, will he not be almost certain to die? Probably at the bloody hands of the Red Locusts, if not every racist American or invader hiding in the woods? Besides, no one has asked the boy what *he* wants to do."

Michael shifted in his seat uncomfortably, but regained his usual composure. "Probably, ma'am. But I don't see how that's within my mission parameters. My mission is to keep us all as safe as possible, and he's a risk any way you look at it. Regardless of his preferences." Always respectful, that one, and Cassy nodded in approval.

Mandy replied, "Maybe not in your role as our protector,

but as a human being it's within *all* of our mission parameters." She looked around the group. "This man looks no more than twenty-one or twenty-two, to me. Question him about Penn State, perhaps; I'm sure we have someone on the farm who went there. They'd know if he's lying about being a student. And if he *is* a student there, he wouldn't likely be a spy or a soldier for North Korea. Not given his age and his fluency in English. He's got our local accent, even."

Chihun looked from face to face, but to Cassy's mild surprise he didn't look particularly concerned about what happened to him. Maybe he *really was* upset only by the things her people were saying, rather than fearing death at the hands of fellow Americans. Her gut had earlier told her to let Michael kill the guy, but her reasoning told her she was being a bit paranoid about trusting anyone she didn't know, especially after the things that happened before and after she joined the Clan. The Clan itself, and how it saved her life when it didn't have to, proved that some people were still good at heart, even while America withered and died.

Cassy slapped her knees, and stood. Facing Chihun, she said, "Alright. Firstly, there's reason to doubt he's one of the enemy. His age, his accent, the fact that he didn't run when we captured him. And you know, it seems weird that he was nearby when the Red Locusts raided us, but he didn't seem to be a part of them. Why would an enemy stay in the area with a raid going on, when neither side was *his* side? For that matter, why did *he* stick around?

"Secondly, I don't want to dump him off to die out there and pretend we didn't murder him. I understand why Michael felt he *had* to capture this man, but when we did that, we made him our responsibility. If we kill him, we'll do it with our own hands, not by sweeping him under the rug so we can sleep better at night.

"And thirdly. He's not begging for his life, and the only

thing that upset him as far as I could tell was that we were casually talking about killing him right in front of him. He seemed offended, not scared. Does that sound like an enemy? He sounds more like a philosopher or one of Ethan's RPG mages to me.

"So, if anyone has an objection," Cassy finished, "speak up now. Otherwise, I think we should take him in if he'll have us. Probationary, let's call it."

Mandy spoke up. "First, dear, why not ask him what he'd like to do? That counts, too, or at least it should."

Cassy looked to the others, each in turn, waiting for someone else to speak up. A compelling argument against letting him live could still sway her, and she was far from sure letting him stay was a brilliant idea, so it was important to let everyone be heard. But no one spoke against it. Michael looked uncomfortable, but he didn't argue. So be it.

"Very well." She focused in on the prisoner. "Grandma Mandy suggests we ask what you want to do, Chihun, and this is your chance. Anything you want to say?" Chihun smiled but shook his head. She continued, "Okay. By agreement of the Clan, Chihun, I invite you to stay with us here, at least for now. We'll see how it works out, and revisit this down the road if we have to." Chihun's smile broadened, and he nodded. "Frank, will you please untie him, and set him up with a place to sleep and put him on a job? Thanks. I guess that's all I have for now... Anyone else have something?" No one spoke.

Frank rose to untie the former prisoner and left with Chihun in tow, followed by Mandy and the others. Before Michael left, Cassy put her hand on his arm. "Hey, Michael. Can I get a word with you?"

Michael stopped and looked to the door, watching as the others left. Then he turned back to Cassy. "Yeah, shoot. What's on your mind?"

"I know we decided to let the guy live, but I'm not one hundred percent that it was the right choice. I just don't see an alternative I can live with, you know?"

Michael nodded. "Yeah, I get it. We all know you make decisions for the good of the Clan, even if it's just because that's the same thing as being good for your family. In all this shit coming down outside our farm, we all are the Clan, we have to be. And the Clan is us. Just how it has to be. I support your decision, Cassy. Even if I have my doubts, too."

Cassy smiled at him. He was a good man, that was damn sure. Thank God they had a warrior like him, instead of some bullet-happy Rambo type. "Good to know. I appreciate the trust. But, I want you to make sure we keep an eye on this guy, too. If it looks like he's going to make a break for it, or betray us in some way, your job is to protect the Clan. Do you understand what I'm telling you?"

Michael looked at her for a couple seconds, but she couldn't read his face. Then he nodded. "Yeah, I was going to do that anyway. Keep an eye on him, that is. I can't help it, but I don't trust people who look like the enemy."

Cassy shook his hand and thanked him, then watched him leave. She hoped she'd made the right choice. If Chihun really was one of the invaders, then the Clan now had a wolf among them. She expected that sleep would not come easily that night.

* * *

1200 HOURS - ZERO DAY +20

The New York cityscape rose up to either side, and Taggart was on high alert. His eyes darted to every corner, alley, car, and window they passed, looking for danger. "Eagan, get a status check on both our squads, then report back. We're ten blocks from that camp, and I want us wired tight before we engage these cannibal bastards. This is their turf, and they probably know it well. We can expect harassment and ambush, if they see us coming because some Militiaman is out of place."

Eagan nodded once and ran off leaving Taggart with his thoughts. Two of Black's gangbangers had gone missing that morning, and the soldiers Taggart sent to find them reported back with gruesome news. They found the gangbangers' bodies, or what was left of them. They'd been butchered, biggest chunks of meat cut away and missing, and their weapons had been taken too.

Worse, the scouts reported being ambushed by at least a dozen people, ragged and emaciated, who came at them with knives and didn't slow down when the scouts shot two of them. Taggart's people reported that they barely escaped and would never have evaded if the mob had guns.

Thank the Almighty, however, the scouts *also* reported that, as they fled, they saw a filthy, makeshift camp in a dark alley. They were positive it belonged to their attackers, and it looked like it contained a *lot* more space than a dozen people would need. Taggart wasn't sure why they were so certain it was the raiders', or saw it as a camp for many more than a dozen, but he trusted their instincts. They were Rangers, those two, with six years' fighting in the Sandbox between them. They had even been in Bagram Air Base in Afghanistan at the same time he had, once, but they hadn't crossed paths there.

Taggart did one last mental check of his battle plan—based off crude maps his scouts had drawn—when noise to his rear seized his attention. He spun on his heels and brought his rifle to bear, but stopped before pulling the trigger. It was only Mr. Black and a dozen gangbangers, half a block away still and making more noise than seemed possible from so far away and moving over a paved surface. Fucking civilians. If they screwed up this Op, Black better hope Eagan was around to talk Taggart out of just shooting him on the spot.

Finally, Black got within a dozen yards, and Taggart went to intercept him. Better to talk to them back there, where they couldn't gum up the works with his squads as they got ready to push forward. Taggart came to a stop, drew himself up to his full height, and looked Black in the eyes.

"What are you doing here?" Taggart's tone was the one he used when giving commands, very different from how he'd spoken to Black thus far.

Black's eyes were narrowed in anger, and Taggart saw that his men were tense, ready. Their body language was not promising. Black said, "Those were *my* homies who got killed, yo. That shit was messed up, homie. And you left without sayin' shit about where you were headed. That ain't right."

There were murmurs of agreement from the gangbangers at Black's back. One of them took a step forward to stand beside Black in solidarity. This could get ugly. Taggart read the situation and made a quick decision. The conversation would go better if he had it in private, to keep Black's pride out of it. "Black, will you come with me? I want to talk to you in private so we can work this out. Like a briefing." Like hell.

Black paused, glanced at his homeboys, and stood up tall, chin up. "Yo, lead the way, soulja boy. Yeah, we can talk. Don't wanna embarrass you in front of my homies."

Taggart didn't reply, but walked away from the group. Let him have his pride, it wouldn't change Taggart's decision. Black followed, swaggering. They got out of earshot, and Taggart stopped and turned to face Black.

"What up, puto? You can't take off without me like that, yo. This whole thing is *my* posse, my set, my dead homies. I saved your life, and you need my four-one-one. So you better recognize, and lay down before you stay down." Black's face was red, and the left side of his mouth twitched.

Taggart kept his face stoney, unreadable. "I have no idea what the fuck you just said, civilian. I respect what you've done, setting up a Resistance cell and saving lives where you could. That makes you a hero in my book, but make no mistake, Black. We *are* under Martial Law, and we *are* at war. You *are* under my command. The only reason I haven't drafted your men is that they respect you, they follow and listen to you, and we're on the same side. If they were under my direct command, their bullshit gangster crap would force me to deal with them like insubordinate shitbirds, and 'we ain't got no prisons,' as you once said. So, now, do *you* feel *me?*"

Taggart paused to let that sink in. When Black's face contorted in angry shock, he continued, interrupting whatever gibberish Black was about to spout. "Don't get me wrong, Black. You're a good leader, but you aren't a soldier. You don't have that training. You also aren't in the chain of command, so I can't allow my unit to take orders from you. What I can do, the *best* I can do, is leave you in charge of your men. But you might have fucked up my operation with all the noise your guys made coming in. If I lose people because you let the entire damn neighborhood know we're here with your civilian bullshit swagger, I'm going to hold you *personally* responsible. I promise you won't like that. And think carefully before you speak. I will take what you say seriously, and act accordingly. What do you have to say, and what do you intend, civilian?"

Black glared at Taggart, red-faced, but Taggart neither flinched nor looked away. After a long, tense moment,

Black's shoulders slumped slightly, and he broke eye contact. His fists came unclenched, and then he let out a long breath. "Taggart, I get what you're sayin'. And I know that we didn't have this talk sooner just because your mission was easier if you went along with the program, but then Spyder took my turf. Things are different now, yeah. But I gotta save face, homie. Those bastards out there, they butchered my homies like they was pigs. I'll get pushed out if I let that go unanswered, yo, especially after losing my turf. I'm on the ropes, man. It don't help none of us if I catch a nine to the head by one of my men lookin' to move up."

Taggart nodded, slowly. "I hear you, Black. Leading your men is *your* concern, so long as you follow my orders in my operations. Your operations are your own affair, if they don't interfere with us. We'll help if we can. And I'd much rather deal with you than with one of them, so what can I do to help?"

Black looked back into Taggart's eyes, but this time there was no rage, no threat behind the look. "Listen, Taggart, I'm a criminal. All I know is pullin' work for my set, and reppin'. But this is my country too, and fuck those invaders, and fuck that traitor, Spyder. That's why I tried to help people, yo. It was, like, my *duty*. And it's why I set up to be Resistance—I was the only one in my turf who *could* set that up. They're bleeding my country, man. I didn't know I even cared, until the ragheads started kickin' in doors. It put things clear for me. So, I'll go with the flow. You the man, now, El Jeffe. But if you want my set to do work, I need to be the one in charge of them, not some other esse. So, keep lettin' me front like I'm the top man, at least as far as the gangsters go. And, you gotta figure out how to let us get some fuckin' blood-red payback for the shit those pendejos did to my people."

Taggart paused, then allowed a slow grin to spread across his face. "Black, I respect you now more than ever. I'm reconsidering my decision to put a bullet in your head when this is all over with. Okay, so go tell your boys they get to have their payback. I need to think of a way to use them that won't fuck up the Op. We need to coordinate."

Black shook his hand, probably for the benefit of his gangbangers, and strode back toward them with what Taggart thought was a ridiculous swagger. He could only imagine the yarn Black would spin to his men about this.

Then Taggart saw Eagan running toward him from Team Bravo's position and awaited the report. Afterward, he'd figure out how best to use Black's team. Maybe Eagan would have an idea.

* * *

Dean Jepson looked up from the tractor and said, "Well, Frank, there's no way we'll get this workin' again. Not without parts we don't have. But I reckon we can still use the trailer."

Frank shrugged. "How? The horses don't have built-in trailer hitches. Maybe you have an idea how to get around that?"

"It turns out I do," said Dean. "The trailer's damn light, for being steel. I figure I can hack off this hitch end and work up some leather that'll act like a pulley, or a suspension. A come-along. If we attach that to a harness, two horses could easily pull it out loaded without hurting themselves. Then just pulling it without a come-along would be easy for a couple of horses. The same kind of rig would work for pulling stumps and rocks, too, and horses can pull a plow if we can beat one into shape somehow. Got a sword?"

Frank grinned. "Now Dean, I know I told you Cassy won't let us plow. 'No-plow farming,' she calls it. Not really a creative name, but not a lot of wiggle room either. And you can't have my sword, if I had a sword."

Dean grinned back and shrugged. "Not my call. But I figure we'll have to plow some of that soil we're taking over from the neighbors. A lot of it never did see a plow. It'll be too stony to dig in."

"Just do as she says. She got this place up and running, right? From what I see, she's got twice the output of any farm in these parts, with none of the inputs. No fertilizer, no chemicals. Which is kind of handy these days, seeing as there isn't a lot of that stuff to go around."

Dean shrugged again. "Yep. Just as you say, Frank." It was obvious he still felt skeptical but, if Cassy didn't want plowing, well that was her call. Her house, her rules. Maybe she'd show him something new. It wouldn't be the first new thing he'd seen in the short time he and Monique had been at the Clan's farm.

Giggling nearby caught Dean's attention. He watched as the kids ran around with faces beaming in joy, playing tag. His own son, Tyler, was just about the same age as Cassy's kid. Tyler and Aidan always did get along, even if their parents didn't always see eye to eye. The sight warmed him, and a smile crept over his face.

As if reading his mind, Frank said, "I reckon if they can get along, we can too. You know, that idea about the wagon was just like something Jed might've said. He was a redneck engineer, that's what I called it. He could figure out just about anything. Y'all aren't too different, 'least on the inside. Alright, let's figure out how to reinforce the stress points we'll have when we hitch it up."

Dean nodded and looked to the wagon, but he was thinking more about Monique and Cassy than about the job at hand. Maybe it was time to put that whole mess of women-in-conflict behind him. New world, new start, new friends. He'd have to talk to his wife about that later, when the day's work was done.

* * *

The shirtless man squatted, peering at the small homestead with so many meals walking around inside it. Over his head, he wore a red t-shirt, tied up like a shemagh over his face. In his right hand he held his necklace, with its ten teeth strung on it—one for every man he'd killed taking over the Locusts. It was a trophy, and a warning, but it wouldn't help in cracking this farm wide open.

Earlier he'd sent a few troublemakers out to raid it, to earn the right to challenge him for leadership, but half didn't come back at all, and the other half he called cowards. They tasted pretty damn good, and the stew his people made of their leftovers would last a week.

Still, they'd run out of stew eventually and needed to restock. This farm would do just fine. Not to mention all the glorious real food they had. Not one of his people would rather eat long pig than fruit, nuts, beef, and bread. It was disgusting, eating the locals. But, it was definitely better than starving to death like half the people they found as they scouted the region.

To his second-in-command, a burly man nearly twice his own mass but dumb as rocks, he said, "So, there's at least two dozen people in there now and a couple more every few days. The house is bulletproof somehow, too. They got some crack shots and a guard tower. How do you figure we should take this place, Ed?"

"I don't know, Max. You're the smart one. Shoot them, maybe?"

The shirtless man laughed. "Eventually, but that's the hard part. But in the meantime, maybe it would be better to go after that new group moving through the area. Those farmers with all those wagons. They've beaten two teams of scouts, so far. I don't mind, of course. Scouts aren't supposed to try to ambush meat on their own, but they wanted the glory and got the dirt nap instead. I think I'll have to gather all the Locusts to get that one done, but half of those farmers won't have the stones to fight if we offer to let 'em join us. The other half, who fight, we'll eat or use for entertainment. After that, we ought to have all the people we need to bulldoze right over this farm."

"You got a bulldozer, Max?"

The man frowned. What an idiot. But, a useful idiot. "We will, in a manner of speaking. Let's go."

The two slid away into the forest shadows, and Max noted with satisfaction that the guy on the watchtower hadn't seen them at all. When the time came, that fresh meat in the tower wouldn't see it coming. Nor would the rest of the meatbags at that farm. And every liver he ate only made him stronger. Those, he'd order the Locusts to set aside for him.

- 5 -

1000 HOURS - ZERO DAY +22

STANDING IN THE kitchen, Frank paused to think about Chihun before he answered Cassy, but he felt pretty sure of his judgment. "Well, he did every task he was assigned, without complaint and without taking his sweet time about it. Choony also found helpful things to do when he was done, before I gave him another task. If he keeps that up, he'll be fine by me."

Michael shook his head. "But Cassy, that's just what a spy would do. Same with a soldier trying to get in with the locals. He's *Korean*, for chrissake."

Cassy said, "Michael, watch that language. You know Grandma Mandy hates it."

"Sorry. It's just a habit. I'm working on it though."

"Thanks," Cassy said, "I appreciate it. Anyway, I don't know what to make of this guy. Choony is pulling his weight for now, but it's only been a day, and he knows we're watching every move he makes. Let's see how it goes after a week, and then the three of us will talk again."

There was a rustle at the entryway into the kitchen, and Frank glanced over. Mandy walked in with a smile for each of them. "Talking about the Asian man, Choony?" she asked, though obviously she knew they were. "I don't know why you don't like him, Cassy. Your best friend growing up was Korean, too, wasn't she?"

Cassy frowned. "Yeah, her name was Faith, Mom. Did you forget, after all the time she spent at our house? Her parents were immigrants too, and they ran that little shop by the tire place."

Frank shrugged and cut in. "So what's your problem with Choony, then?"

Cassy looked uncertain. "Well, I mean, I guess it's the circumstances. We're being invaded by Arabs and Koreans, so they're not high on my trust list."

Michael interrupted and said, "Well, to be fair, Cassy, no one is these days except us in the Clan. I gather you used to be the trusting sort, but a couple bad run-ins after the collapse have you doubting people. I get it. Keep it up—that'll keep you alive more than trust will."

"I disagree," said Mandy. "If you show people distrust, they won't be trust *worthy*. People live up to the expectations of the people around them, but they also live *down* to them."

Frank watched Cassy's face closely, but she was closed off and unreadable. Then she furrowed her brow, grimaced, and pinched the bridge of her nose with her thumb and index finger. "This all gives me headaches," she replied. "Alright, Mom. I'll try to keep an open mind. And we'll meet back in a week to discuss, like I said. In the meantime, Michael, keep him under watch like before, but maybe pull back a little. As time goes on, if he doesn't screw up, we'll pull back a little more and then some more. And if any of the Clan says anything about him doing something wrong, find me immediately. I guess that's it. Anyone else?"

No one else offered anything, and so Cassy broke up the meeting. Grandma Mandy was looking at Cassy with obvious concern, Frank noticed, and he was full of heavy thoughts of his own as he walked toward his current work detail.

* * *

An hour after their meeting, Cassy watched as Michael approached her. He wore a slight frown and held his head high with eyes darting around, which she knew was the man's sure sign of stress. "What's wrong now," she said with a smile that she hoped would set him a bit at ease. It didn't work. She saw Ethan following a short distance behind, and he too looked tense. Cassy prepared herself for whatever latest emergency had come up.

Michael replied, "We have a situation. One of our people couldn't hold his shit together and got drunk last night. Gary, I think is his name. He's one of the people in the tent enclave, he and his wife, Marla. Apparently they got to arguing, he pushed her, and she fell and jammed her wrist. Amber bound it up, but figures it'll be three days before his wife is fit to work with her hands again."

It was Cassy's turn to frown. "What the hell. I have nothing against drinking, but I have plenty against pushing each other around. And then there's the issue of her being unable to work the farm. We have too much to do and too few hands as it is."

Michael said, "I agree. It doesn't just affect the two of them, it affects us all. So, what do you want to do about this?"

"You talked to other people in the tent enclave, and the wife, Marla?"

"Yes," Michael said. "The story is pretty consistent. Guy's guilty."

Cassy inhaled deeply, then let it out slowly. "Okay.

Clearly we have to do something about this, but what? Got any suggestions?"

Michael shrugged. "Flog him in public. He'll behave, after that. Or confine him so he can't hurt anyone else."

"Michael, we don't have the resources to jail anyone, much less guard them. Confining will only mean we have *two* people who can't work, but who still have to be fed."

Ethan interrupted. "I'm not okay with whipping someone anyway, Michael. We're our own thing here, we can try something besides violence against our own citizens. I didn't care for it before the EMPs, and I don't think we should repeat the mistakes of the past. Let 'em fix their own relationship."

"Damn hippy," Michael said. "This guy cost us a lot of man-hours of work. That affects us all. We're on a deadline, literally. If we aren't ready by winter, some of our people won't make it."

Cassy said, "Let's go get Frank and Grandma Mandy. We have to figure this out now, not later, and they may have some ideas."

A few minutes later, the five of them stood together in Cassy's living room. Cassy repeated the problem and the suggestions she'd heard so far.

Mandy shrugged. "Why are their family issues our business? We don't have time to babysit everyone. I say leave it to them to figure out. What he did isn't right, but he didn't beat on her. It sounds like her falling was an accident, though a predictable one."

Cassy shook her head. "No, Mom, we have to do *something* because what he did cost us, what, thirty-six hours of work? Even if I were inclined to leave drunken assaults to them to solve—which I'm not—the fact that this Clan is supporting them and Gary's wife can't work is our problem, clearly. We have to set a precedent."

Frank, who had been quiet up to this point, spoke up. "Well shoot, let's get some of the Clanners together to be a jury, and Cassy can be the judge. He broke the law and beat up on his wife, after all."

Ethan rubbed his chin and said, "No... That won't work, Frank. Firstly, those were laws in the old world, with old world punishments. The only laws we have now are what we decide they are. And more importantly, where there are laws there is injustice. Law is about law, not justice. Ask any district attorney."

Cassy asked, "So what would you do, Ethan, ignore it completely? We can't. Got any better ideas?"

Ethan paused a moment. "Prison's not an option. We can't afford the people to guard it. Exile and whipping sound overly harsh for a squabble that got out of hand. Forget a jury or laws. I think the core of any law ought to be 'don't hurt anyone else' and 'don't be a burden to others.' Who needs laws for that?"

Michael snapped, "Then what would you do? We're running out of options."

Ethan replied, "Getting to that. We're small, right? Not a lot of people. But we have enough different views and personalities here in this room to fairly judge any situation. We can be like a panel, the five of us, reviewing Clanner complaints and judging based on fairness and the good of the Clan as a whole. You know, 'judge each situation on its own merits and rule for fairness and justice' rather than some minimum sentencing law."

Cassy considered that. It was fast, it was personal, and it didn't require trials and appeals and all the other things the old society had resources for, but which the Clan didn't. Much of the time, Michael and Frank would probably agree with each other, as would Mandy and Ethan, so having five people made sense. "Right. Ethan, you're a genius. But although I'll be there with you at the trial—or tribunal, whatever we call this—I won't cast a vote unless you four can't get a majority going. I'll be the tiebreaker and otherwise just keep things orderly."

An hour later, in front of anyone in the clan who cared to watch, they'd questioned everyone involved and decided he was responsible for the hours his wife was unable to work. For the good of the Clan, Gary would have to make up those hours diligently and without complaint unless he decided to give up the Clan. Exile.

Later, Ethan said he was happy that it set the precedent of "the good of the Clan" outweighing the good of an individual, even the victim. "The victim always seems to want to either sweep it under the rug or get their pound of flesh," Ethan said, "so focusing on what they'd cost the Clan seems like a great limit to state power."

Michael chuckled. "State power? What are we, the government?"

"Actually, yes," Mandy said. "You don't realize it, maybe, but what we've done here today is turn a homestead full of refugees into a real community, with rules and our own ways of justice. I don't know where all this leads, but I'm sure interested to find out."

They chatted for quite a while, and all in all Cassy figured it went as well as could be expected. It set the scales even with Gary for the Clan's loss and put the onus of staying or leaving on Gary himself. All that from a ten-minute conversation. The world was changing, and she resolved to change along with it, if she had to, for the good of her people.

* * *

1230 HOURS - ZERO DAY +23

Chihun sat with the others on their lunch break, and his tired muscles welcomed the relief. Lunch was a laden plate of potatoes, fresh bread, eggs, bacon, and sliced-and-spiced tomatoes. He didn't like to eat meat, but it wasn't a violation of his philosophy as it was with some of the monks he'd known. It just made him uncomfortable. He could deal with that. Even if it had been against his beliefs, the protein was needed, and animal meat was all that was available. Idly, he wondered what he'd have done if eating animal meat was in violation of his philosophy. Would he be strong enough to starve for his convictions? He toyed with the idea as the smoky taste of bacon melded with the sharp tang of spiced tomato, and he realized the complex flavor mix greatly pleased his tongue. He shrugged. His body knew what it needed.

Then his thoughts shifted to the situation he was in. He'd done everything asked of him and more, without complaint, and knew the others all did the same tasks he was given. Unpleasant chores were rotated. Some of the Clan seemed to avoid being around him, but that didn't bother him. It was like that even before the North Koreans destroyed America. Sure they watched him constantly, which at first irritated him to no end because, dammit, he was no spy. But he wasn't abused, singled out, or even given short shrift on the farm's unpleasant chores.

Since being watched irritated him, he decided to work on his perspective. He consciously tried out what he thought must be the "Clan" point of view and found that their caution made sense. Chihun also reminded himself that the "problem" was not so much the situation itself but his own pride and resistance to that situation. Once he let go of feeling indignant and, as his monk teacher put it, got "off his high horse," he felt centered again. The chores and constant supervision became a much lighter burden. He also then realized he could count himself lucky that the Clan treated him as well as they had. Other groups of fellow Americans had tried to kill him. Yes, perspective was the key to finding peace here, as in most places, he mused.

Once the all-too-brief lunch break was over, everyone took an hour of time to themselves. Most used it to mend or wash clothes, work on the house now under construction, or to do other useful tasks. Some simply took a nap, which was Chihun's preference. He began to walk up the hill toward the livestock paddock, which he found a great place to nap. It was warm, sunny, with a nice breeze, the lingering animal smells were comforting, and best of all it was quiet. But then he remembered that going up there would require someone to go with him, to keep an eye on him. That didn't seem fair to the other person, so instead he turned toward one of the various trees just beyond the market garden. It would be shady there, at least, and serene.

He saw that one of the Marines followed at a respectful distance. His afternoon escort, he mused, smiling. Then he reached the tree, a late-fruiting apple tree on dwarf rootstock, surrounded by comfrey, clover, and string beans that grew up the trunk of the mid-sized tree itself. A couple bees buzzed nearby, but they were more interested in the flowers than in the human invading their space. He settled down, leaning against the tree, and closed his eyes. The warm blanket of sleep gradually covered him. He dreamed of digging up potatoes, surrounded by smiling children.

Then one of the children walked up to Chihun, making a lot of noise. The boy shouted at him. "Get the fuck up," he screamed.

Chihun smiled at the boy and said, "But child, I *am* up. See? We're digging potatoes."

The child said, "What the fuck are you talking about, chink? *Get up!*" Then the boy kicked Chihun, and he fell to the ground clutching his ribs.

But when he opened his eyes, it was no boy standing before him. No, it was a man in a red t-shirt pointing a hunting rifle at him. Also, he was nowhere near the potato fields. Understanding came to him, and he muttered, "Dreaming..."

The raider bared his teeth and hissed. "No dream, gook. Get up, and be quiet if you want to die quickly instead of slowly. Tell me now, where are the others? What's the best way into the compound right now?"

Chihun saw that, behind the man with the gun, were a dozen others with rifles, pistols, even one guy with a nail-embedded baseball bat. He wondered where the Marine guarding him was, and hoped the raiders hadn't killed him. Martinez was his name, Chihun recalled, and he had been both diligent and polite, friendly even.

Chihun quickly replied, "They are on personal time. Some sleep, some wash clothes, some—"

"Shut up," interrupted the raider. "So they're scattered?"

"Yes," answered Chihun. He hated to tell this truth to the raiders, but lying wasn't something he could bring himself to do. Still, he didn't volunteer any information... And they hadn't asked *where* the Clan members were, after all. He was pretty sure the omission would leave his personal harmony intact. "Why do you attack now instead of at dawn, as in all the movies?"

"Talk again and I'm gonna break your damn jaw, gook. Here's what's gonna happen—you're gonna lead us through the maze of bullshit jungle they got growing out here, and if you be a good little zipperhead, I might not eat you when this is all over with. If you do *anything* to alert those assholes, I'm gonna ventilate your cranium. I hope we understand each other," growled the raider, prodding Chihun with the barrel of his rifle.

"That is actually not jungle, it's all food, or plants that—"

"Shut the fuck up," snapped the man, and he shoved the barrel painfully into Chihun's ribs. "Turn around, and move. I won't say it again."

Chihun obeyed and hoped that if he died today, his soul would decide his karma was in balance; it would determine in part the circumstances of his birth when the next cycle of life began for him.

They reached the outskirts of the market garden. The foliage was high and dense enough to block the view, so the paths were all that could be seen from inside. Those paths started out narrow enough that the raiders had to walk single-file behind him.

Ahead, he saw a small open circular area; other narrow paths like this one branched from it, and a single slightly wider path extended out of sight toward the homestead. It was beautiful how all the paths of the garden mimicked the veins of a leaf, branching and narrowing as they extended out from the homestead itself.

He wasn't sure whether the Clan meant to plant things in that way, but it made perfect sense. The pattern maximized crop area, minimized ground taken up by the paths, directed the flow of energy and the needed work in a peaceful and efficient way, and of course it was zen-like in its simplicity. How much else on this odd farm copied the patterns of nature? He would have to investigate, if he survived. Dying now would be a shame, with so much yet to discover about this interesting place.

As they approached the circular area ahead—a hub of branching paths—Chihun silently prayed: *Buddha, Dharma, and Sanha protect me if you will, and protect these good people of the Clan...*

Chihun entered the circle, a simple dirt-and-gravel affair, and turned toward the thicker of the five paths that branched from it. That was the path that headed toward the next circle, which would lead to a thicker path, and again, until eventually they'd come out in front of the buildings of the homestead. But there was more in the circle than dirt and gravel. He'd overheard others talking about the traps and warning devices Michael had hidden at these hubs. He frantically looked around, all the while keeping his head still and his body relaxed, yet poised.

There! A thin length of fishing line stretched over the entry to the thicker path, all but invisible unless one looked for it. He prayed this was one of the alarms, rather than something lethal, but it didn't seem likely the Clan would place lethal traps in a place like this, where work had to be done and children ran. If he was right, then the Red Locust would kill him, but the Clan would be alerted. If he was wrong, then the trap would kill him, and the Clan would be alerted.

In either case, his probable last act would be the protection of these innocents. Any people who could make a garden paradise like this, and treated a one-time prisoner like him with kindness—if not exactly trust—deserved to stay in this lifetime as long as their own natures allowed. Chihun thought about the karma this would bring to his soul, but that was a secondary benefit.

* * *

Cassy relaxed in the shade of the house under construction along with Frank and his wife, Mary. Cassy and Frank had spent the morning working on the house and were already covered in dirt and sweat. Mary had worked in the makeshift outdoor kitchen they'd built, getting lunch ready for everyone, and had brought food and plastic bottles of well water to the workers.

"So tell Mary how the defenses are coming, Frank," Cassy said between bites of stew, more for small talk than anything. She already knew the answer from their weekly meetings. It was amazing how small talk had changed so much in so little time. She only half-listened as Frank summarized it for his wife. The long-term defenses would mostly be "living fences," which were thorny, dense bushes planted along the perimeter. There would also be some willow trees that eventually would be coaxed to grow interwoven with each other, creating a durable fence. Right now they were only saplings, though, and the hedges would be solid long before. Still, Cassy noted wistfully how much the defenses were in keeping with the rest of the design philosophy of her farm, with everything impacting everything else in a dense web of life.

As he finished summarizing those details to his wife, Cassy nodded. "So we're still focusing on early warning devices from Michael and small sandbagged foxholes to fall back to if we're in the field when trouble comes?"

"Yep. The hard part is getting them emplaced without taking up good planting space. But we're going to put one in each of the larger hubs out in the Jungle and among the food forest."

The Jungle was what they'd started to call the sprawling intercropped intensive agricultural area, with the branching paths and so on. Cassy wasn't sure when the term had gone from being a joke to being its proper name, with a capital "J."

"Cool," Cassy replied. "What's the status of the chickens program? Did we lose those two chicks that hatched last week?"

"No, with the lightbulb and that nasty herb you soaked into their water bin, they came through. More will hatch any day. At this rate, we'll have a full flock by winter, but then we'll have to feed them. I'm going to recommend at the next meeting that we cull all the older ones and most of the hatchlings, keeping only the biggest and healthiest to start anew in the spring."

"The plant's called comfrey, Frank. Why can't you remember that?" She smiled. "Internally, it's mildly astringent and helps make for healthy lungs and intestines. The loose droppings have stopped since we began adding it, but I'm nervous to try a stronger concoction on little chickens."

Frank was about to reply, when a deep boom sounded from far into the Jungle, accompanied by a white cloud. One of their trip-wire early warning traps, which were shotgun shells filled with baking soda, had gone off.

Cassy scrambled to her feet, reaching for her rifle that leaned against the wall of the house under construction. Fear shot through her. None of the Clan would have set that off. Someone was out there, but who? The odds were against it being someone friendly. As she looked out over the Jungle, she heard the *bang, bang, bang* of several rifles being fired, though she couldn't tell if they were firing at the homestead. No ricochets, no tufts of dirt flying up.

She saw Frank grab Mary and dive over the low wall to take cover, and Cassy did the same. She peered over the wall even as she clicked off the safety of her M4. Once again, she was glad Michael insisted that rifles be issued and in the field at all times, though at the time—before the first Red Locust raid—it seemed like an unnecessary encumbrance. She glanced up at the watch tower, and just then another series of shots was fired by whoever was in the Jungle; the rounds hit the tower, but hit only the sandbags. The guard sensibly ducked behind cover, and she lost sight of him.

There was a pause in the shooting, and Cassy waited

anxiously. Then there was movement in the Jungle, just beyond the raised beds right outside the houses, and she took aim. She was about to fire, when Choony burst out of the corn sprinting for the homestead. Had he set off the alarm? Where the hell was his escort, Martinez? As he came closer, she heard him screaming.

"Locusts! Locusts!" he repeated, and then dove over the low, unfinished wall of the house they were building. It was closer to the fields than the original house. He landed spread-eagle in a heap near Cassy.

The thoughts whizzed by like bullets. Choony had set off the alarm, intentionally, to alert the homestead. Martinez wasn't behind him and was likely dead or injured out there somewhere. Because of the alarm, the Clan was armed and ready to face the threat, when they caught up.

She didn't have long to wait. In seconds, there was rustling all along the deep strip of corn that fronted the Jungle. She took aim where she thought a person must be and fired. She was rewarded with an agonized scream, but she had no time to relish the small victory as the raiders returned fire. Shots came downrange from seemingly everywhere; there must be a dozen or more raiders, damn it all.

Duck. Rise, fire, duck. Repeat. Apparently, however, the raiders didn't realize the houses were bulletproof, the sandbag-like construction offering all the protection the Clan needed. Thank God she'd built out of earthbags.

Cassy looked over at Frank, who frowned and nodded. She didn't know what that meant. Then he rose up, fired a couple of shots, and ducked. To her left, from near the original house, she heard Michael's clear, strong voice: "Mueller, Sturm, get eyes on our flanks! Tower, verified targets only! Eyes on, mister!" She heard him continue yelling, getting defenses at the house organized. But for now,

Cassy, Frank, Mary and Choony were on their own, and only Frank and she had rifles.

Cassy stared at Choony for a long moment. Because of him, they had time to get the children inside the house. They had time to take cover. "Thank you, Choony," she said with a single, curt nod. The young man had just earned his place.

* * *

1700 HOURS - ZERO DAY +22

Peter rode at the front with Jim, leading the wagons and a trail of people on foot. He had a new bruise over his swollen right eye and ad-hoc stitches in his left bicep. Those had come from attacking the fuckin' red-clad cannibals, thanks to information Jim had "obtained" from their prisoner. Poor bastard didn't survive interrogation, or maybe Jim had just killed him after questioning. Peter hadn't asked about that.

After they'd slaughtered half of those desperate, starving morons—they put their sentries in all the wrong places, and Peter's people picked 'em off one by one without even raising an alarm—their emaciated leader had called Peter out to single combat. Well, God was on *Peter's* side that day, as he knew He would be. Once the Red leader was disemboweled, Peter offered the rest food and life if they joined him. Join or die. They'd all chosen to join. Heh, killing the leader took the starch out of 'em, Peter congratulated himself.

Now, instead of four dozen or so people, Peter had about seventy people under him. And that turned out to be a good thing—divine providence, really—because the Reds had informed him that there was another band of Red Locusts to the west, fucking with some farm. From their description, it sounded *remarkably* like the homestead the spy had fled to back when Peter tracked her down. The difference now was that the spy's crew was building a fortified house, had three dozen people, and had just kicked the everliving *shit* out of the other Red Locust band. His new recruits didn't know how many Locusts survived that, but they knew it wasn't many. They couldn't agree whether the spy's group had lost one or two people, but either way it was a very lopsided victory. They unanimously blamed an apparently huge collection of early warning traps and alarms the farm people put up all around the property, scattered around for acres in every direction. Hell, that info was worth the couple friends he'd lost "recruiting" this band of Locusts to his team. Team Peter. Ixin's Immortals? No, too flashy. People of the White Stag... Now *that* had promise. Peter made a note to find someone who could sew up a banner for him. It'd give him a pretty sweet air of mystery, he reckoned, something to inspire his followers. Hell, they didn't even really deserve the salvation they'd get from this little modern-day Exodus. But, he needed someone to dig the dirt, because Peter Ixin, Chief of the People of the White Stag, would never have to break his back farming again when this worked out to the finish. How could it not end with victory? God Himself was on Peter's side.

"I'm coming for you, bitch," Peter muttered, "and Hell is coming with me."

Jim smirked. "Ain't that from a movie, boss? Yeah, that Tombstone movie. Man, I sure do miss movies."

"Seemed apropos," Peter said with a chuckle. "Besides, 'Let my people go' doesn't really work in our situation."

In a couple days, his scouts would return from the farm, and he'd have his people ready to get the revenge the bleeding world needed, realizing his destiny as the man who saved his people. Peter laughed out loud. Destiny was calling.

- 6 -

1000 HOURS - ZERO DAY +23

CASSY WANDERED THE homestead, checking on the work parties tackling various projects and crop harvesting. Frank stood in the shade of the guard tower with Michael, having what looked like a heated conversation. She wanted to check in with Frank anyway, so she went over and stood nearby, waiting without interrupting.

"...can't rely on just one obvious tower. We need a hidden observation post, too," Michael said.

"I already told you, we don't have the man-hours available to get that done," Frank said. "We need houses, we need the outdoor kitchen expanded to feed the new people, we need to tend the farm continuously. Harvest time is on us, and I'm just glad Cassy was smart enough to plant lots of varieties that ripen at different times or we'd be screwed." He turned to Cassy. "Don't let that comment about you being smart go to your head," he said, smiling.

Michael greeted Cassy with a nod, and said, "Why don't we build a little tree stand on the far side of the houses, away from the tower? That would give concealment to a hidden lookout and won't take long to set up."

Frank looked thoughtful and nodded. "That's true. I'll tell you what—if the location is okay with Cassy, you and whoever wants to help can build it on your own time. I'll reserve a couple of lanterns for you, so you'll have light after it gets dark. You won't have to stumble around out there. But that's the best we can do, man. We're just overloaded with things that need doing and can't wait."

"Defending ourselves needs doing, too," Michael replied, clearly irritated. "But alright, Frank. It's not what I hoped to hear, but I understand. Thanks for letting me draw on the stockpiles for this. It'll pay us back with better security for the whole farm." He turned and nodded to Cassy, then added to Frank, "I'll see you later. I need to go check in with the guard."

He left Cassy and Frank alone. Cassy didn't really like Michael going to Frank with such issues, dammit, because Frank didn't always have the latest information. She should have been brought into it automatically. They should have either come to her right away or put it on the agenda for the weekly Clan meeting. It was a little frustrating, but she couldn't manage everything, and Frank was, after all, supporting her. It was nothing to get angry about, so she shook herself mentally and put on a smile.

"Morning, Frank. How are the work projects coming? Have we found jobs for the newcomers?" There were a dozen new faces already this week, some brought in by Cassy and a few who heard about the farm and left their homes to join the Clan for the safety in numbers it could offer.

"Yeah, they're being productive. We have a couple chopping wood, like you asked, and the rest are either helping to harvest or working on the second house, depending on their skills and age and so on."

Cassy nodded. "How about the Jepsons—how're they doing? I was a bit hesitant to bring them in, but I couldn't just leave them out there to die."

Frank chuckled. "I get that. Well, Monique is using her skills at yakking and yapping to motivate the workers. She was a politician, after all. She's also written down a bunch of suggestions to streamline how we do things, which I figured I'd bring up in our next weekly meeting. Some look pretty good. She'll be an asset."

Cassy nodded again, a little surprised at Mrs. Jepson's pitching in like that. Frank continued, "Dean is another story. He's a damn hard worker, but impatient with the others when they don't understand his point or what he's driving at. I think he's probably a genius, though—his ideas for getting the house built faster all will work as he says. And he knows how to get more done in fewer steps. He got everyone to set one earthbag each time they come in from the fields. If they each put down one bag every time they come in for breakfast, lunch, supper, and the end of the day, that's around eighty extra bags a day, all without diverting any people or taking much time. I figure we're more likely to get sixty bags, because people will forget, or be in a rush, or whatever. Still."

"Wow, that's pretty smart," Cassy said. "So tell me, how are the two of them integrating with the rest? They didn't exactly want to be here, and they don't much like me being in charge. No surprise, all things considered." She smiled at him. "By the way, I don't think I've told you how grateful I am for all the support you've given me."

Frank nodded in acknowledgement of the thanks. "I know you have some rough history with them. But they're integrating fine, other than always coming to me. I finally told them both that you're the leader here, it's your farm and they need to accept that or find another Clan to live with. Dean seems fine with it, but he's the more practical of the two. Monique tried to talk her way around it, but I just kept repeating that it's your farm and your rules. Don't get me wrong; I like the two of them. I think they'll do alright here once they adjust. Like I said, they're already contributing even if they don't totally get how you've set this place up."

"Yeah, traditional methods are hard to avoid out here," Cassy answered. She spent a few more minutes talking to Frank about nothing much. He was easy on the eyes and had a great sense of humor. What wasn't to like about him? It kind of sucked that he was married, but those were the breaks. After a while, she continued on her rounds, checking the other work parties, patting backs, making suggestions. She never did like managing, but she guessed she could do it okay.

* * *

1200 HOURS - ZERO DAY +23

After everyone else had been served, Cassy filled her own plate with lunch. Today it was rice and kimchi with a little bit of meat from the night before, and hardboiled eggs, all of it served with fresh milk. It smelled good, and normally she would have demolished the plate in record time—everyone in the Clan seemed hungry all the time, with the current dawn-to-dusk workload—but today she didn't see Michael at lunch, and her uncertainty about the reason lessened her appetite. The three new Marines were also missing, and her anxiety rose.

Whatever those Marines were up to, it was probably important enough, and they could get lunch whenever they came in, so she wasn't panicking. She'd gained some confidence in them over the past several days, but she still didn't exactly like their unexplained absence. Michael was good at his job, she reminded herself, and he could handle just about any problem he came up against with the help of the Marines. Whatever kept him from lunch had to be pretty important. He never missed a meal if he had a choice, Cassy thought with a wry smile. A habit he learned the hard way, out in the field, she supposed. She had just eaten her last morsel of food, when the Marine Lance Corporal, Sturm, approached Cassy's table and sat down.

"There you are," Cassy said, putting on a friendly smile. "You don't normally miss lunch. Seen Michael? He missed lunch, too."

Sturm looked at her, face inscrutable, and said, "Listen, Michael and I found a pair of people on horses, scouting our position with binoculars. We caught one, and Michael needs to talk to you about it. He said to tell only you right away, so you could let the Clan know what you feel they need to know after the two of you talk. If you're done with lunch, he's waiting. He said to make sure you come back with me."

Cassy felt a tingle of anxiety and realized she was fidgeting with her silverware. She forced herself to stop and put her hands in her lap. "Red Locusts?"

"No, something new. Don't know. Michael can tell you more." She started to rise. "Shall we go?"

Cassy stood, decided to ignore Sturm's peremptory manner, and put her dishes in the first of three 55-gallon drums—it was full of hot, soapy water. The cleaning team would scrub each dish in one drum after another, getting the dishes progressively cleaner as they traveled down the line. Dishes cleared, Cassy followed Sturm. Weird that she didn't know Sturm's first name, but Michael had said they went entirely by last name in the military, though for some reason Michael was insistent that everyone call him by his first name—something to do with not confusing the Clan. Apparently, the young woman was more comfortable going by her last name. "Okay, Sturm. Let's get this over with."

Sturm led Cassy through the maze of raised garden beds, passing the now-empty fields of spring wheat starting to overgrow with clover, flowers, and nettles. They continued into the food forest that marked the edge of her original property. They had gone deep into the woods when they finally came to Michael and the other Marine, Mueller.

Near them was another man, stripped naked and tied hands-and-feet to a couple of trees, which forced him to stand spread-eagled. The man was unconscious, though still breathing, and covered in cuts and bruises.

"What the fuck is going on here, Michael," Cassy demanded. She heard her own voice crack, and even to her own ears she sounded almost hysterical. What the hell had Michael done? The man could be just an innocent passerby, for chrissake. And Michael had clearly *tortured* the guy. She felt a deep revulsion as she looked back to Michael. Michael, her friend. Her companion. Her *defender*. And now, apparently Michael the Torturer.

"Please, Cassy, keep it together until I've told you what I've learned. This could be vital to our survival. You can judge me later, but for right now I can only say that these measures were both reasonable and necessary, from a military P-O-V. Point of view. We needed intel fast, and I obtained it. It's not the most reliable method of getting information, because people will say anything to make the pain stop, but it is the fastest."

The words "vital to our survival" struck Cassy like a hammer. She winced as he said the rest. Time to calm down. Freaking out could come later, but for now it was time to be the leader the Clan had chosen her to be. Lord be merciful, she wished Frank was still in charge.

"Okay, Michael. I'm calm. See? Deep breaths, voice level. Forgive me if I beat the shit out of you when this is over though. *We* are not the *bad guys*, Michael. So, what did you learn from torturing a fellow human being?"

"Well, found out that he's a scout from a little farming community called 'White Stag Farms.' "

Cassy paled at the mention. That was where she'd been hunted before she found the Clan, and the memory haunted her. Faintly, her right shoulder suddenly ached, reminding her of the wound she'd received while fleeing those gun-happy bastards.

Michael nodded once. "I see it rings a bell. Good. Their community got hit by the invaders right after you encountered them, and they blame you personally. He didn't know your name, but described you. They just call you 'the spy.' Well, it gets better."

No flipping way. This couldn't happen, could it? Did those bastards really track her all the way here? A chill ran up her spine. "Go on."

"They're led now by the guy who hunted you. And, since he thinks you brought the invaders to them to divert attention from your own farm—obviously faulty logic, given the distance—he's determined to take what you have to make up for what they lost. He's got at least twice as many people under arms as we do, and they're on their way here *now*. Not to raid—they brought everything they could carry. They're migrating *here*. To *stay*."

"Oh my God… How long do we have? Can we bargain with them or something?" The terror was rising once again, and it came out in her shaking voice. Still, she looked Michael in the eyes. Scared or not, this wasn't the time to panic. It was time to be a leader.

"They'll be here in a couple days at most. And Cassy? Their leader's name is Peter, and he's built himself a little cult. They think of him as being like Moses, leading them out of bondage and into freedom to a land of milk and honey that they'll have to fight for. Peter would rather die than bargain. He's coming, and we can't prevent that. We can only fight and hope to survive, or flee and hope not to starve out there."

Cassy was silent for what seemed a long time. She closed her eyes and fought to rein in her racing thoughts. Focus, dammit. "Okay. I'll call an emergency Clan meeting. Some may leave, and then the rest of us will have to decide whether to stay and fight, or follow the others away from here. But I get the feeling this Peter guy won't ever stop following us. This is personal for him. What should we do with the scout?"

Michael's jaw stood out as he clenched and unclenched it. "Peter may be fanatical, but I doubt every one of his followers is so committed. My advice is to string this guy up on the path Peter's taking, and brutalize the corpse. PsyOps may deter some of his followers. It's unpleasant, and I've never done it before—not even to the Taliban assholes we killed in the Sandbox—but I recommend we hang him high, peel the skin on his face back like a damn banana, and shove his own junk down his throat. It will unsettle his followers, trust me. The Afghans did that to a British soldier we found too late. It sure as shit unsettled me, and I've seen a lot of fucked up things, Cassy." He looked grim. "Now I'm having to do some. It ain't easy."

Cassy felt the blood rush away from her head, and her cheeks tingled. Everything seemed to spin for a moment. The next thing she knew, she was in Michael's arms, looking up at him. "What the hell happened?"

"You fainted. I'm sorry, Cassy. I know it's unpleasant."

"That's not the fuckin' word for it. What kind of animal are you, Michael? Who would *do such a thing?* We're not the monsters!"

Michael didn't seem upset by her words—he had that eerie Marine thing going of looking utterly composed under stress. "Cassy, I know you're freaking out. But you and I can take care of this, somewhere away from the Clan. They don't have to see it—just Peter and his goons."

"Do you really think we should do that? No. No, I can't. Michael, it's not in me, even if it was necessary, which I'm not even sure of. But I can't think straight... I need time to figure this out."

"Dammit, Cassy, we don't have time. We need to spend every freakin' minute between now and then getting ready for this shitstorm. You get me? A world of hurt is coming downrange, straight at us. For all of us, Cassy, including Aidan and Brianna. Think of your kids, Cassy, and let's go do what's needful."

Cassy felt her stomach rolling, churning, threatening to unload everything she'd just eaten. "Michael, I can't do it. I'm sorry. Can't you just... I don't know, can't you just take care of it? Do whatever you want, but I can't be a part of that. I just can't!"

Michael again wore his stone mask, his battle face. "Cassy, you're the leader of the Clan. You gotta start making these hard decisions. I can only advise you."

"I never asked to be the damn leader, Michael," she spat. "I hate this. I only led because *someone* had to, and I'm the only one who knew how to handle this farm. I didn't sign on for torturing people and skinning their goddamn faces."

Michael's features softened, and he put his hand on her shoulder. "I know this is hard, and you're right. You're a civilian, and a good person, a good mom. You're a better leader than you give yourself credit for, Cassy, but this is war. You chose me to lead our defenders and see to our safety, and that's what I'm going to do. You can go back to the farm and get that meeting going, okay? Mueller and I will take care of what needs doing. It's a Marine's job to do terrible things so bad people don't do even more terrible things to the people we protect and love. And don't worry about the rest of the Clan finding out. Mueller and I will keep quiet about it, and we'll do this out of sight so no one else has to suffer nightmares, the way I do. But this is war. You only have to tell me I'm in charge of our tactics."

Cassy felt tears rolling down her cheeks, and her throat closed up. She tried to speak, but her voice was only a croak. She wiped the tears with her palms and nodded. And she realized that after this, she'd never be the same again. God forgive her for what she asked Michael to do, because Cassy doubted she'd ever forgive herself. Then she turned her back on the unconscious man, on Michael and Mueller, and on the grisly scene about to happen. She and Sturm walked back toward the farm. Back to the light, and back to the people she loved.

* * *

Capt. Taggart grinned and held up a bottle of 18-year-old Scotch from a case of other such bottles. His troops, soldiers and Militia alike, shouted and cheered. Around them lay the bodies of some twenty Arab soldiers and one Korean low-ranking officer. The walls of the small, corrugated metal warehouse let the light in, beams of bright and color illuminating the once-dark interior from the Swiss cheese they'd made of it during the firefight.

Firefight wasn't the right word, Taggart thought wryly. "Like fish in a barrel," he shouted, knowing it would raise morale. The cherry on top of victory, hearing their commander actually banter with them—something only Eagan was normally privy to.

Chongo and the other gangbangers weren't allowed to be part of the fight—Taggart needed discipline, not bravado, and had little faith in Black's gangsters—but Taggart brought them in after it was all over to help with the looting. *That*, he had confidence they could manage, and they proved very good at it.

The raiding party spent the next fifteen minutes looting the warehouse and planting demo charges; what they couldn't take, they'd deny to the enemy. Crates of grenades and ammo, dozens of AKs, Chinese-made MREs—all made their way out of the warehouse.

And best of all, a crapload of intel. Maps, a few laptops, USB drives... It'd take a while to go through it all, but Taggart's spirits soared at the thought of the juicy information they'd get. Maybe enough to start fighting back in earnest, not relying on the limited information the 20s provided them in dribs and drabs. The 20s were how he'd found out about this cache, and he'd been told there would be enemy operations-level intel here. The 20s said the intel cache would only be on-site for four hours, so that had been the window of opportunity for the mission.

As the looting phase wrapped up, Taggart found himself next to Chongo, who was trying to direct his "soldiers" in their looting. Chongo glanced at Taggart as Eagan walked out with an armload of rifles, and said, "Sure as shit, you just kicked a hornet's nest, yo. Hope it ends up worth it, *Jeffe*."

Eagan stopped, smiled, and said, "Yeah, but let 'em buzz. The more they're buzzing around looking for us, the less time and men they can send out to fuck with the fine upstanding citizens of New York City."

Chongo shrugged. "Don't bother me none. I'm just sayin', I hope you're right. They'll be looking for us hard now, *esse*."

Taggart interrupted their conversation. "Doesn't matter if Eagan is right or not. I have a mission to complete, and that's to liberate American soil and American citizens. I promise you we'll be doing this again, Chongo. And yes, they'll come looking. In fact, I'm counting on it. So get your ass in gear and help liberate some of this war materiel."

* * *

1600 HOURS - ZERO DAY +23

Jaz was on her way from the house to the top of the hill to feed the animals and check their water. Most peeps hated that chore, because it was kinda hard work getting all that feed up the hill from the barn, but Jaz didn't mind. The animals were, like, peaceful and quiet, and always happy to see her. Around them, she felt a little like she had when Jed was around. She smiled at the thought of him. It'd been long enough since he died on the journey to the farm that she didn't cry about it anymore. Mostly.

As she wended her way through the maze of the Jungle, however, she heard the clink of metal on metal and froze. A bolt of fear shot down her spine, but she forced herself to stay calm. Clanners on a chore were more likely than Red Locusts, but it paid to be careful. She listened carefully and then heard a muffled voice. It was the Marine they'd picked up, Mueller.

"So just say it, Sturm. What's on your mind, Lance Corporal?" Mueller said.

"Fine. Why is Choony still here with us, sir? He's the reason Martinez got fuckin' eaten!" That voice was Sturm's, of course, and she sounded pissed.

Jaz briefly considered getting on with her chore, or letting them know she was there—the polite thing to do—but instead she stayed frozen. What was this about Choony, the friendly little Asian priest guy? And Martinez eaten? This totally had to be Red Locust stuff, and it was news to her.

Mueller grunted. "As you were, Sturm. We're all high-strung about Martinez, and no one more than Michael. He's a Marine too, goddammit, and a good man. Place your blame where it's due, Sturm."

That was news. Mueller standing up for Michael? Far as Jaz knew, Mueller totally hated being under Michael in the command chain thing. And Sturm was always, like, playing mediator between them. Jaz had thought Sturm liked Michael.

"I know, sir, but I can't help feel like he's putting this hippie outsider before one of our own. And he's a Marine, sir! Michael's loyalty is wrong. He should be answering to you, not the other way around."

"I'm only going to say this once, Sturm. First, we're guests here, and unless you think you and I can force dozens of armed people to do what we want, it has to stay that way. Second, even if we could force them, how does that advance our mission goals? Third, Michael's retired. You may feel like he should be reinstated to active duty, but what officer is around to decide?"

"I guess that's true. I just don't like it. I know Michael's a good guy, but that's not the point. But I understand what you're saying. Aye, aye, Staff Sergeant."

Mueller then said, "As to Choony, he didn't get Martinez eaten. We don't even know for sure the Locusts got Martinez when they grabbed Choony, but if they did, then blame the Red Locusts, not the civilian. Martinez should have been more alert. That's what standing guard *means*, Sturm. And that hippie may refuse to defend himself or others, but he did risk his damn neck setting off that warning device. Without that, who knows the damage they could have caused before we got an effective counter-attack together?"

"Well," said Sturm, though she still sounded totally frothy, "there is that. And Michael didn't pull any punches when we interrogated the other scout, from that other group."

What the hell was this? Another group? Jaz felt a cold fear, a claustrophobic jolt. Enemies seemed to be everywhere. Why couldn't they just, like, leave the Clan alone? Would it always be like this in the new world?

"No, he didn't. It took a couple hours of working at him with blades and hot shit to get the intel out of him, but we're in a world of trouble. That guy, what's his name? Peter? He's some sort of Messiah-complex loony, and he's got an army of loonies following him. But don't fuck with Michael, Sturm. You didn't see him torture that poor S-O-B the way I did. Michael didn't seem to enjoy it, but I've never seen anyone so cold. I was almost relieved when Michael had me end the prisoner's frikkin' misery, war crime or not. I'll have nightmares, Sturm."

Jaz clenched her jaw. Rage rose up. Michael *tortured* someone? That bastard. The Clan was cutting people up now. She saw that once in Philly, hiding behind a dumpster. She felt her terror come back at the memory, a brief flash of complete paralysis. Well, she knew this much—there was no way Cassy knew about it. Jaz *had* to tell Cassy. She'd make it right, somehow. Jaz didn't really think about how it could be made right, but she was so pissed she couldn't think straight, and she knew Cassy always kept it cool. Jaz wished she could be like that. Yeah, Jaz had to tell Cassy, and Cassy would know how to fix it. "Fine," she muttered to herself, "let's see what Michael thinks after Cassy finds out." She crept quietly away, leaving Mueller and Sturm to their talking.

- 7 -

1630 HOURS - ZERO DAY +23

JAZ STOMPED HER way back toward the main camp, gnawing on the talk of torture she had overheard in the Jungle. Even she knew torture only produces whatever the victim thinks his tormenter wants to hear. As she went, her steps gradually stopped being quiet and cautious. By the time she stomped into the farm, Jaz was steaming and eager to see Cassy. Or confront Michael. It didn't matter which.

Judging by the sun, Cassy would be in the outdoor kitchen with Grandma Mandy to help get dinner ready for the kids, who ate first. The kids wouldn't be there yet though. She left the Jungle and passed the toolshed, a large structure they'd built from pallets and tarps to store all the shovels and stuff the Clan had gathered up. She went by the half-finished new earthbag house, which was way bigger than Cassy's own farmhouse, but refused to wave back to any of the Clanners there. She was on a mission.

Finally, she reached the outdoor kitchen, with its pole barn-style roof and adobe rocket stove griddle, burners, and ovens. Mandy chopped veggies into a stew. Oh man, Jaz was tired of stew, but apparently it was the best way to get the most calories out of food, or something. Better than field rations at least.

Jaz strode up to Cassy and, ignoring her greeting and confused look, said, "I need to talk to you, like, right now, Cassy."

"What's up? You look upset, sweetie."

"You're damn right I'm upset," Jaz said, then clenched her fists and took a couple deep breaths to steady herself. Then she stared into Cassy's eyes and, voice stony, said, "Cassy, did you know about Michael and some scout they captured? About Martinez missing? About what Mueller and Michael did to that scout?"

Cassy said, "Look, Jaz, I don't know what you heard, but sweetie, just leave this to me to—"

Jaz's face turned red and she interrupted, shouting, "Goddammit, Cassy!" She shot a glance to Grandma Mandy. "Sorry, Granny. I'm pretty upset. I *know what it's like* to be used and abused, and nothing I went through can compare to anything they put this guy through."

Without waiting for a reply from Mandy, Jaz again turned on Cassy. "They *tortured* that guy, Cassy. *Michael* tortured that guy. We aren't the animals here. This is total bullshit. Cassy, did you know?" she asked, venomously punctuating each word of her question.

Cassy stood stock still for a long moment, and then nodded once, curtly. "I found out about it after Michael had questioned him. I didn't like it either, and a month ago he'd be in jail. But, do we have a jail, Jaz? We can't imprison him, nor would I. Michael is one of us and matters more than a hostile stranger. The information he got, now *that* matters far more than anything Michael might have done."

Jaz felt her stomach churn. Cassy, their leader, was trying to justify torture. And if Jaz just quietly accepted it, then she was part of the problem, too. No flippin' way. "Did you believe anything he said? He'd have admitted arranging the invasion if he thought it would make Michael stop. People lie under torture. They'll say anything. The ends *can't* justify the means, Cassy. My messed up mom used to say that, and it was the only damn thing she was ever right about." Tears rose unwanted into her eyes. "What we do defines who we are. If we do monster things, then we're monsters. *I'm not a monster!*"

Cassy pursed her lips, and Jaz saw her eyes flash with anger. But so damn what. If their leader was signing off on torture, well, Cassy could just go be frothy. If she'd rather be pissed about the truths Jaz told her than about the Clan torturing people, well those priorities were just, like, bass ackwards. No. Just–no.

Cassy said, "Listen, Jaz. I get that you're pissed about this. I was too, when I found out about it. But the things Michael found out make me forgive him for it, and you might want to think about why he did it also. That scout wasn't a Red Locust. He wasn't just some nobody wandering the hills. He was a recon scout for an entire damn army marching straight for us, and their intentions are clear. They're going to kill or enslave us all and take our farm if we let them. So, am I glad we got early warning about this? You're damn right I am. You can afford to be all high and mighty about this Jaz, but I can't. Frank can't. Michael can't. And Amber can't. A dozen other people can't. We have kids to worry about, and I care a damn bit more about *their lives* than I do about *your feelings*." Cassy sighed. "Or about a self-declared enemy scout, not when it's defend ourselves or die."

Mandy, who had been stirring the almost-completed stew for lunch, turned on Cassy now, arms akimbo, fists planted on both hips. "Cassandra Elenore Shores, what is this I'm hearing? Are you really trying to rationalize torture? I can't believe my ears, Lord help me. So a threat is coming our way. Threats haven't stopped coming our way since the EMPs. And yet God has brought us through each and every time, always against the odds. You can't honestly believe all the times we survived was due to dumb luck. From the beginning to the end, God has protected you, me, and the kids every step of the way on our journey here, and watches over us still." Mandy was trembling with anger. "Have faith, and keep your humanity. Keep your soul, sweetie! Turn away from such worldly evil, and find a way to atone for what you've done."

Cassy snapped back, voice ragged. "No, Mother. No! This is the *end of the world as we know it*. You and Jaz both better get used to the damn reality of our situation. We're outnumbered and outgunned. We're committed to staying here—to staying in one place—where they can find us. They can attack when they choose. They can snipe at us, ambush us, pick us off one by one."

Cassy turned back to Jaz and said, "The only reason we have a chance in hell of surviving is because Michael did what was necessary, not what was easy. Now put on your damn big girl panties, and get on board this boat we're all in. Because the alternative is to die here, watch our loved ones die here, and let the new world start the way the old world ended—with evil people doing evil things to good people who didn't know any goddamn better."

Jaz began to reply, but Cassy spun on her heels and stormed out of the kitchen. The self-righteous woman had an answer for everything, but not this time—Jaz knew it was totally bullshit. Cassy was just making herself feel better for becoming the monster the whole Clan was trying to get away from. All the chaos and torture and murder and pointless death out there, out in the wasteland of so-called civilization among the hungry and desperate. Bringing it here was just wrong.

Jaz turned to Mandy. No way Grandma Mandy would side with Cassy on this one. Jaz wished she knew another word besides "monstrous" for what Michael did, but that was the only word she could think of, and it echoed in her mind.

Mandy said, "Jaz, I understand your feelings. I share them. But don't be too hard on Cassy. She bears the weight of all our safety, and she didn't find out about it until after Michael had done the thing, and she couldn't stop it. Look at it from her point of view. She can call Michael out for his crime, but evil people are still coming to kill us all. Michael will be needed more than we need justice, at least for now. We'll have to come to terms with what he did after we defeat Satan's minions—if we even survive it. And we need Michael for that."

Jaz paused, taking in what Mandy said. She was smart, and Jaz trusted her judgment, but then, trusting other people wasn't going so well for her lately. Jed's death and now this... Hope was in short supply. Jaz decided she needed to go for a long walk and figure out how to handle this pile of crap on her plate. She nodded absently at Mandy and walked off, head down, utterly absorbed in her own thoughts.

* * *

Cassy clenched and unclenched her fists as she stormed from one end of the barn to the other and back again for perhaps the twentieth time, railing at the walls. "Damn Jaz, who does she think she is? I didn't *ask* to be in charge, and I sure as hell didn't *ask* Michael to do what he did. But if he hadn't, we might all be dead in a couple days. He did what was *needed*, right? Hell yes, he did. And sure as shit we'll all be *grateful* to him when we survive Peter and his army."

A voice spoke from out of the shadows—Choony's voice, she realized. "Convincing Jaz, or convincing yourself? I don't see Jaz here."

Cassy spun toward the voice, fists clenched, and found Choony sitting atop a bale of hay set back on top of other bales. She grit her teeth and growled, and struggled not to lash out at him. It was a losing battle. "And who are you to judge me, Choony? You won't even pick up a rock to defend yourself, much less any of us. You have no voice in this. And that makes you *lucky*."

Choony shrugged. "I did not judge you. I asked a question. You're in turmoil, Cassy, and it doesn't come from the situation. You resist the judgment of others because what you did violates who you think you are, and it threatens your role as leader. You don't want to be leader, but you do want the best possible chance for your kids to survive, and someone has to be in charge. A challenge to your leadership is a threat to your kids' lives, your inside self believes. Please, don't turn your anger onto me. I am not the one you want to snarl at, am I?"

Cassy stopped mid-stride and froze in place. She looked down at her feet and took several deep breaths. Choony was right, dammit. And he didn't even have the decency to be smug so she could hit him, so she could rage and rain down fury on him. She was spinning, she needed to let some of that fury *out*. The rage was overwhelming. But not Choony's fault. Not Choony's fault. She repeated that a few more times like a mantra and felt her wrath begin to subside, if only a little.

"No, you aren't the one I should have said that to. Thank you for calling me on it and not taking it personally. I still want to smash your face in though."

Choony chuckled. He was safely out of her reach, she noted, unless she intended to climb up a tower of loose hay bales, which would make her look more foolish than frightening.

Choony replied, "You're welcome. But you should know,

I think you're a good leader in a really bad world. Keep it up, but be true to *you*. If you can do that, you'll truly earn the respect the others already give you. You can't force respect, Cassy."

"So, in all your wisdom, what would you do?" Cassy asked.

"To start, I would go see Jaz and apologize for whatever words were said. She may not apologize back—she seems like she has a personal history of some sort, involving torture. Obviously, she is shaken. But you'll feel better for apologizing for your own temper. Most importantly, she'll respect you for it, even if she's not ready to accept an apology just yet."

Cassy nodded. Choony was right again, of course. What, did he make a study of the people he was around? Anyway, it seemed he wasn't the complete tool she had figured him for. Without a reply, she brushed the bits of hay off her pant legs, nodded to Choony, turned and walked out of the barn to find Jaz.

Twenty minutes later, she still hadn't found Jaz and felt her self-control again being chipped away. Well, crap. She had other things to take care of too—not just babysitting a know-it-all angsty teenager. Screw it, Jaz could wait. She'd surely be at dinner, and Cassy could waylay her for a conversation then. Seething, she turned back to her rounds, seeking Dean Jepson to talk about the homestead's defenses.

Cassy found Dean talking to two Clanners about how to lay out sandbags around a couple foxholes they'd dug between the Jungle and the living areas. "Heya, Dean. Can I get a minute?"

Dean broke away from the two workers, and Cassy led him out of earshot of the others. She said, "Let me get an update on the defenses Michael tasked you to get built. We ready yet for Peter's army?"

Dean let out a long breath and ran his hand through his thinning hair. "Well, like I told you before, we got more work than hands. I reckon it'll take about a week to get this sorted out to my likin', unless you want to take everyone off harvesting."

"Dammit, Dean! I know I told you we need to be ready when they get here. How the hell am I supposed to protect my family and the whole Clan if we're wide open to them?"

"Now, Cassy, I got a feelin' you were a mite upset before you came to talk to me, so let's just settle that out right now. Deal with one thing at a time, girl." Cassy felt her rage rising again and tried to control it; she knew it was affecting her judgment. Dean continued, "Half-assed defenses won't stop a cow, much less an army. We gotta get it right, or it won't do us no good. I appreciate you're anxious, but you have to see that."

"My kids, Dean. They don't care about next week, and neither do I. We won't be here in a week unless we get our shit together *before* they get here."

Dean frowned. "Don't go swearin' at me. Your name ain't on my paychecks, and I don't have to take it from you. But you listen here, doing things your way put me in a mess of hurt once before, you recall. I almost lost my house over that pointless squabble between you 'n Monique, from the backlash of people who stopped shoppin' at my store for a while over it. Well, I ain't about to let you do that to me again, especially when the kitty on the table is my life, not just some mortgage."

Cassy felt like she was about to burst like an overinflated balloon. Too much hot air, most of it her own, was going to make her explode if she didn't get away. "I know you're doing your best," Cassy said. "We need the defenses to be as complete as possible when Peter and his army attack you, your wife, and everybody else in two days. I do appreciate you—I hope you know that. And I apologize for the language; you're right—I was worked up before I got here. It was nothing you did."

Jepson nodded in acknowledgement, but Cassy hadn't waited for a reply. She had already turned to walk away, her whole body feeling stiff, rigid. Like every damn cell in her body wanted to blow up. But that wouldn't help her kids nor the Clan, and dinner was about ready. She needed to clear her head before she brought this crap, this venom, to the table with her children. They deserved better than to see her like this. Heck, so did everyone else. Cassy headed slowly back toward the barn, half hoping and half dreading to see Choony there again. He was infuriating, but somehow he knew how to help.

* * *

Frank had eaten dinner with people leading various projects around the farm to get an informal update over food. Shared meals tended to lessen tension and stress, in his experience. Things stood more or less as he expected, which was to say, a day late and a dollar short all over the place. The fencing for the cows they wanted to bring up wasn't halfway done because he had to divert people to drilling a second well—Cassy's original well just didn't cut it with all the new people. It had already been strained taking care of Cassy's family and the bit of farming she'd done, even before the EMP hit. Now it was totally inadequate. He would've been glad to have a dozen more hands, but then he'd have to feed, water and house them, too. It was a damn vicious cycle. Thankfully, Cassy was ultimately in charge, so he didn't have to make the hard decisions anymore.

He was deep in those thoughts when a shadow fell across him, and he looked up to see one of the recent joiners sit down across from him. Frank couldn't remember the man's name but saw that he looked troubled. "Hey, how's it goin'? Got something on your mind?"

The other man smiled, but Frank thought it looked forced. Just polite, then. "I'm Gary, remember? From the tribunal? I'm still new, and I hate to bother you at chow, but I overheard something I figure you should know about. I'm told you were the leader of the Clan on the journey here, so you probably still have some weight. I think you should talk to Dean and Cassy."

Frank narrowed his eyes. He'd be damned if he was going to let people put leadership on him again, not when Cassy was doing just fine, thank you. "Maybe you should talk to Cassy then. No offense, but I don't make the decisions around here anymore, and that's kind of the way I like it."

"So I've heard. But this is something I can't talk to her about. I don't have the standing, yet, especially after what happened with my wife's wrist. Cassy would never listen to me. I'm hoping maybe you can actually do something. I overheard Dean and Cassy arguing about the defenses. It seems she wants them done before Peter arrives—and don't get me wrong, I'm here for that fight, this is my home now— and Dean basically told her to screw herself. He said it wouldn't be done in time no matter what she said, and he wouldn't 'half-ass' it just for her. I really thought she was going to flip her lid and eat his face right then and there, but she just got all stiff and walked away. Now, I don't know where she went or what's the history with those two, but they have some obvious bad blood between them. Either way, it's a hurdle we don't need right now."

Frank closed his eyes for a moment, let out a deep breath, and said, "That was worth bringing up. Thanks. I don't know what I can do about it, but I'll look into it, Gary. Go enjoy your meal, and thanks for looking out for the Clan."

After Gary left, Frank got up and sought out Michael, who was still out in the Jungle laying out traps more lethal than the alarms they'd originally set up. He greeted Michael with a smile and a wave.

"Hey, old friend. Listen, there's some discussion about whether we ought to half-ass the defenses to get them in place before Peter arrives, or do it right even if it means we won't be complete by then. You're our military guy, bro. I need to hear your thoughts before I jump into the middle, maybe chew the wrong asses. I'd better at least know whose ass to chew."

Michael threw his head back and laughed. It was flippin' amazing that the guy could find humor even with what qualified for an army these days bearing down on them. Frank raised his eyebrows expectantly.

"Frank, I'll tell you, I'd rather have something than nothing between me and Peter's bullets when he engages us. We have tons of concealment but precious little cover, if you know the difference."

Frank nodded, and Michael continued, "They can't shoot through the earthbags, so the kids and old folk will be safe at first. But we only have a day, maybe two, before it gets nasty around here. That's enough time to fortify a few entrenchments along their likely avenues of attack—and we can stretch barbed wire to try to funnel them into kill zones between our positions. We can set up a few sniper posts to triangulate fire on whatever leadership or other targets of opportunity present themselves during the fight. I wish I had some claymores, but we don't. We'll just have to adapt and improvise. So, I'm setting up makeshift explosives out here that will wreck a lot of growing food, but also a lot of the OpFor. We don't have to kill them all, just neutralize as many as possible. If we can give him enough casualties, he won't be able to penetrate our inner defenses. He'll have to call it off or lose everything, if he's even sane enough to care."

Damn, Michael was good to have with them. Frank once again had cause to be thankful he'd befriended his new neighbor two years ago, and it was a stroke of luck that their wives got along so well. "Okay, Michael. So I'll have Dean focus on the foxholes and sniper posts. Where do you want them?"

They spent the better part of twenty minutes going over where to put everything. Frank had a gut-churning feeling that whatever they did, it would be too little, too late.

* * *

0800 HOURS - ZERO DAY +24

In groups of two or three, the Clan filtered into the outdoor kitchen area for breakfast, coming in from whatever work they'd been doing for the first couple hours of the day. Cassy greeted them individually as they came in, following Frank's idea of greeting people personally and eating last. It had a great effect on morale—a fine thing, considering the psycho messiah who was bearing down on them all. Once again, she found herself wishing Frank had put his own steady hand to being the Clan's leader, though she understood why he declined it, given the situation. Her farm, her rules, and that trumped everything. But she still wished she could just hand it over to Frank.

This morning, she had another purpose in mind besides raising morale. Once she was sure everyone other than sentries on duty had come to the table, she strode to the head of the long, improvised seating area and raised her hands.

"Your attention please, Clanners," she began, and waited for the hum of conversation to stop. She looked from person to person, hoping this would make each of them hear her next words as though she spoke to them personally.

"You already know we will soon face off against the greatest threat so far, and we had some doozies during the trek here. This 'Peter' fellow and his people are coming, and if they can, they will take what is ours for themselves. But we're going to make sure he has a surprise waiting. Peter is about to find out that in this new world, not all people are content to sit back and watch or be victims. We are the Clan, and together we've beat every challenge to come our way. The 'vaders couldn't stop us from getting here, they couldn't stop us from settling here. The Red Locusts tried to take us as their next meal, and failed. Starvation, which has claimed so many lives outside the Clan, has been defeated here, by us, as well.

"I've heard some of you comment, half-jokingly, that you wish we could just call 9-1-1 like in the old days. But what do we need old-world police for? To protect us? Pah. Together we have more courage, more *grit* than any stranger in a blue uniform. *It's our fight, not theirs,* and we're not helpless. The way I see it, we don't need protection from Peter and his kind. No, *they* need protection from *us* if they are stupid enough to come to the party we have planned for them."

Cassy looked over the crowd of Clanners and hoped her pride showed. She saw little fear among them but lots of smiles and nodding heads, even a few cheers. Where there could have been fear, she saw instead an iron determination. They would defend the farm, its resources, and the Clan to the last man, woman, and child.

Having set the stage, it was time to reveal the true purpose of her stumping this morning.

"So every one of us can defend ourselves, our farm, and our families, I am going to ask Michael to train all of you with our firearms, our stockpile of M4s. That means everyone, right down to kids old enough to hold and use a weapon. In groups of ten, he'll cycle everyone over the age of ten through a simple shooting drill. Those who excel will partner up with those with less experience or skill shooting, so that *all of us are ready* when the time comes. Peter wants to take our land? Well, we need to make sure *we take his life*, instead. Are there any questions?"

She hadn't expected anyone to speak up—it seemed pretty straightforward—but to her surprise, a hand shot up. It was Choony, damn it. Cassy had a feeling this was going to be a problem, but she motioned Choony to continue anyway. Every Clanner had a voice and the right to speak their mind, even though it was Cassy and her council—Michael, Frank, and Ethan—who had final authority on things Clan-related. At times like this, that could be frustrating.

Choony stood and made a slight bow to Cassy and then to the roomful of people. "Cassy, I know that we all respect your wise leadership," he said with apparent sincerity. "And this plan is a good one, a wise one. But it is a *worldly* plan. I have a higher responsibility to my conscience. I'm sorry, but I don't feel I can pick up a rifle, much less kill another human being, even at the cost of my life. I will risk my life for all these good people, but I cannot take anyone's life even in defense."

Dammit. Cassy clenched her jaw, the muscles standing out as she struggled to remain calm. Screw Choony and his high-and-mighty morality. "Choony, would you really be willing to let other Clanners die at Peter's hands without lifting a finger to help defend them? Their children? Defend *my* children?"

Cassy was infuriated that Choony wouldn't lift a rifle, though the saner part of her knew it was just the end result of his principled stand. And then that touch of respect she felt for him pissed her off even more, though mostly with herself. Dammit, she had to take herself in hand before she lost the whole group. Time to get a grip and lead from strength rather than fear.

"Cassy," Choony said slowly, cautiously, "I would never put other humans at risk, especially those who are my family, and all the Clan is my only family now. My inability to kill people does not equal putting my family at risk. I—"

Cassy narrowed her eyes at him as he spoke, then interrupted him. "Yes, Choony, it *does* equal that. The Clan will defend itself, and I'm not sure I want to make room for someone who won't pull their weight. The others might not sit well with your decision, either, and this isn't the time for division."

Cassy felt a hand on her arm and glanced over to see Frank standing next to her, a concerned look on his face. She glared at him, then deliberately turned to face Choony with an iron gaze.

Choony replied, "I'll respect your wishes if that's really what you want. But please hear me, Clan Leader, when I say that there is much I can do to help without ever picking up a rifle. I have First Aid training. I can retrieve our wounded from the line of fire. I can ferry ammunition where it is needed when the battle is underway. In fact, I can even put together quite a lot of pipe bombs and wire them for remote detonation—I'm majoring in Chemistry, you know—and I can do it with the things we have on hand. I won't place the bombs or press the button to explode them, but I will build them, and you and Michael can place them better anyway. I can do that, but I won't directly take another life even at the expense of my own."

Cassy stood frozen, her mind racing. Not only was this newcomer not going to defend the Clan, which endangered all of them, but he was also directly refusing an order *in front of the Clan*. Damn him, why couldn't he just get a minute to talk when everyone wasn't around? The fight would be in a day, two at most, and he chose this time to get uppity in public, when unity was needed. Had he come to her separately, she could have talked through it to find a solution that used Choony to the best effect, conscientious objector that he was, rather than have to face down a refusal in front of everyone in the Clan right before The Big Battle. Life or death events left little margin for what amounted to mutiny.

"Choony, you leave me little choice," Cassy said. Her voice was tight, and if she relaxed her self-control for even a moment right now, she'd definitely regret what she said or did. This was the time for self-discipline, if they were to survive, and she was not about to lose it right now in front of everyone. But she couldn't stand for outright refusal in the face of an implacable enemy. "You will take up arms and train like everyone else, just as I have ordered, or you forfeit the Clan's protection, its resources, and its fellowship. We value you, Choony. Your insights, your skills—those are much needed assets. But our people are about to fight for our lives, and some will likely not make it through. I owe it to them to make sure we're fighting for people who want to be one of us."

Before he or anyone else could respond, Cassy spun on her heels and walked away with her back erect, head held high. Only her brisk pace now gave away her agitation. But as she spun, she caught sight of Frank, and the tight-lipped look on his face as he stared at her quickly turned her anger into worry. Please, Lord, don't let it all fall apart now...

Then a new anger rose, at Frank. He would have known how to handle that, but he refused to step up, leaving her to hold the bag. Well, she'd done the best she knew how, and that was all she could do.

Cassy motioned for Frank to follow and left the "chow hall." When they were out of sight, she turned and said, "Look, Frank. I know I'm blowing this. I don't know what to do. The only group I ever led before was a marketing focus group for a media marketing agency. You would have handled this better. I see you look at me with disapproval, and I get it. I disapprove of the job I'm doing, too. But since we both know you can lead us better, why not step up? I'll step down, willingly."

Frank looked down, refusing to meet her eyes. "I'm happy to be your right-hand guy, Cassy, but I can't lead this bunch. I did it on the journey because I had to. Now we're here, and this is your show. Please forgive me, Cassy, but I won't step into your shoes."

Cassy let out a long breath. Finally, she said, "Alright, Frank. I understand. Very well, then—go talk to Choony, and find us a way out of this mess. Then go talk to Jaz. She's hurting, and lashing out, and I don't really know why, but I don't like seeing her in pain. Let's get our ship squared away, as Michael would say, so that together we can all face what's coming."

Silently, she prayed for the first time in years.

- 8 -

1100 HOURS - ZERO DAY +24

PETER WAS DISTRACTED by a commotion outside of camp, and he sent Jim to find out what was going on. Two minutes later, Jim returned with one of the scouts who was supposed to be checking out the spy's farm, taking notes and drawing maps. Peter's irritation rose. "What the hell is going on here? Jim, why isn't this man scouting? Last time I checked, he was a scout."

Jim nodded. He stood with one hand on the scout's shoulder and the other held palm-out toward Peter in appeasement. "Yeah, boss. But it turns out those people—they call themselves the Clan—captured our other scout. Tortured him, and probably wrung every ounce of information out of him, before staking him out on the path we're to take. And boss... They skinned his face off and did some other nasty shit to him. I imagine they thought it'd scare us away."

Peter's face flushed red, and he swung his clenched fist through the air. "Goddammit, Jim! I bet they know every fucking thing about us by now."

The scout lowered his head, and his gaze. "I'm sorry, sir.

But it wasn't a complete waste. I caught one of them walking around alone and brought her to you." The scout turned to Jim and said, "I expect you'll appreciate some of her finer qualities."

Peter saw Jim perk up. Yep, Jim was easy to control. Feed his vice and tell him what a great guy he is, tell him his victims deserved it, and he'd follow Peter anywhere. "Jim, I'll need you to handle her questioning personally. She's with the spy and not only has information we need, she deserves much worse than anything you could think up. Use your imagination to get what I need out of her."

Then Peter looked around to evaluate the faces of his other nearby followers. They looked at the returning scout with doubt and at Jim with disgust on their faces but were careful not to look toward Peter himself. Peter smelled trouble brewing. The failure of the scout, he figured, was the first time these people had seen Peter fail in anything, even before the EMPs. Now they knew he *could* fail, and that was a monkey wrench in the gears unless he could flip it to a win in their eyes. No way he was going to let this fuck up his program.

"Jim, before you question her, I need this 'Clan' scouted. Understand? I need it done right, so I'm sending someone more capable than the last crew. You go and handle it personally. I won't allow their screw-up to endanger the rest of us."

Jim sidled up toward Peter and said in a whisper, "But boss, I don't have any scouting experience. What can I do that a scout can't?"

Aha. So that was it—Jim was afraid of failing him and screwing up a good gig. Very well. Peter smiled, his face full of pleasant goodwill. "It's good you know your limits, man! But I know you are well-suited to do this. And you'll have help with some of the tricks—I'll send the scout who made it back to us with you. He'll backstop you, and if you say he does well, then he'll earn his place back from his earlier failure." Yeah, he gets redemption, people. See?

Jim grinned. He seemed plenty happy with that solution. "You got it, boss. Just one more question, though…"

Peter grinned right back at Jim. So predictable. "You don't even need to ask. When you get back, of course I'll expect you to question our little Clan prisoner. Then we can put together what you see, and what she says, and get the full picture."

Jim nodded, and stood taller. More erect. "I won't fail you, boss," he said, shooting a warning look at the scout. "On my life."

Peter nodded his approval. Yes, Jim surely would put his life on the line to please him. "Before you leave, Jim, make sure our new prisoner is secured, but don't waste time questioning her. Scout first, then you can deal with her when you and the scout get back. Grab another prisoner too, if one stumbles by." Go see your prize before you leave, feed your delusion, and be useful, Peter mused. Call it motivational. Peter kept his face open, cheerful and honest as Jim and the scout left while the others looked on. Yeah. Smile at the nice little followers, let 'em bask in your confidence. He winked at the onlookers and turned away to his desk, pretending to have something to do. Obediently, they left, murmuring among themselves.

Peter wondered if God had just thrown him a test. Well, if so, he aced it. His smile turned genuine then, even reaching his eyes for a brief moment.

* * *

Mandy walked into the living room, empty save for Cassy, who was doing her daily inspection of the house. Good, because it wouldn't do to have this conversation in front of others. The Good Book was wise when it said that if another person acted in error, first discuss it with them alone. "Honey, I need a minute. I see you're doing your inspection, and it isn't time for lunch yet, so I know you have time. I'll follow you around if you like, but you need to hear me out."

Cassy paused, looked up, and let out a long breath. Then she nodded. Mandy was relieved; she hadn't relished having this conversation in public, but that would have been her next step.

Mandy continued, "I only have one thing that can't wait. It's Choony. I know you said he had to train with the rifle or leave the Clan, and I'm here to tell you, I don't think that's very Christian or the right way to approach this. People here like and respect that peaceful, brave little Buddhist."

Cassy clenched her jaw, crossing her arms the way she had done since she was a child when she was about to go on the defensive. "I won't let anyone in the Clan shirk their duties, Mom. I think the Bible has something to say about letting those who won't work also not eat. My house, my rules, and dammit, we're about to be attacked. Go ask Michael if we need discipline right now—you know what he'll tell you."

"True, the Bible says that, and Michael will give a military response." Mandy paused a moment before continuing: "No one here can say Choony doesn't do *more* than his fair share of the work, and they've all seen or heard about how he came through to warn us while bullets chopped at the plants around him. He works hard without complaint, doing jobs no one else wants. He earns his keep, Cassy, so don't cherry-pick Scripture to serve your own ends. God isn't fooled, and I taught you better."

"Mom, you're right about Choony. I already hit Frank up to see what we can do about him, about arranging it so he can stay here without driving wedges. But he didn't bring it to me privately, he forced it on me in front of everybody. Now I'm on the spot. And do you really think God is watching us? I think He turned His back on us a month ago. And I'm not sure He ever did watch over us. My husband died, and He did nothing. My job took a turn for the worse, and He didn't lead me to some milk-and-honey job—instead I had to work harder for less money and spend less time with the kids. Is that what the Bible says He wants? You got diabetes. Where was He when that happened? If He's watching us at all, He doesn't care about what happens to us."

Cassy relaxed her stiff posture and took a slow, calming breath. "Look, I admire your faith, Mom, I do, and I sort of share it, most of the time. But this isn't a time we should rely on God. We have to do whatever we can for ourselves and hope to survive—and maybe hope God gives us a hand, because that's the best we can expect."

Mandy felt her cheeks flush red and realized she'd clenched her fists. She counted to three slowly as she unclenched her fists, then took a deep breath. She'd seen Cassy try to tone down the disagreement, or at least her anger, and of course she should try to do the same...but to deny God like that? She closed her eyes, breathed deeply again, reaching for calm. Wrath wasn't the solution here, she knew, besides it being a sin. Cassy was watching nervously, waiting for her to reply, and looked to be trying as hard as she could to get this conversation right. That made it even more important not to falter, not to fail her daughter.

After a few more moments, she replied, "God watches over us more than you know. The evidence is all around us. Every plant on this farm is a testament to that—after all that desolation, it was your farm that didn't get sprayed. Me and the kids survived to get to Ethan's bunker, and that reclusive man risked it all to save us in the face of everything. All of that is proof. *You* surviving to get there just when we did is proof, too. We would all be dead on our own, but God put us in the way of meeting Ethan, and put Ethan in mind to help us, and in return we've helped Ethan continue his mission for our country. That is all in God's plan. How can you doubt it? I got diabetes from eating too much cake, not because God failed me. We have Free Will and I chose to eat badly. We make our choices in this life, and we accept the results. God didn't take your husband from you either—cancer did— but if He hadn't allowed nature to take its course, if the kids still had a father, however sick, you wouldn't have gotten that life insurance money when you needed it. You wouldn't have been able to buy this land. Your job wouldn't have given you all those months off on sabbatical, so you wouldn't have had this place set up right when it was needed, ready when *we* needed it."

Mandy paused then, giving her daughter a steely look, but Cassy didn't contest what she had said, so she continued: "Look. We would all have starved to death by now, like so many other people, without the unlikely chain of events that got us all here. So don't you *dare* try to tell me God isn't among us, turning men's evil deeds and nature's random works to His own good purposes."

Cassy sighed. "Mom, you see God's will, but I see luck. We're only one random event away from dying, even now, so you'd better stop relying on God and start to rely on your own smarts and hard work."

Mandy closed her eyes and let out a deep breath with a small, silent prayer. Sadness washed over her like a wave, drowning out the light—if her daughter couldn't see God at work here, nothing could ever convince her, and when the Lord called Mandy home to sit at His side, she wouldn't see her daughter again. Anything she said now would risk being said in anger or would mirror her sadness, and either way it would just make a mess of things. There was no point in arguing—she could only hope Cassy changed her ways of thinking before she stood before Him for Judgment. "Very well, Cassy. I love you, honey, and I hope you change your mind. Never mind God, letting Choony stay is the right and the practical thing to do. You know it or you wouldn't be saying such terrible things. I'll see you at lunch, sweetie. I've said what I came to say."

Mandy turned on her heels and walked out of the house, head held high and desperately struggling with her feelings, her anger, her disappointment, her grief. And another thing… Choony was clearly brought to the Clan by God's will, no other explanation for it would do. Too much luck wasn't luck at all, it was divine intervention. What would making Choony leave do to God's plans for them all? Surely, He couldn't be thwarted by the actions of one frightened woman? But in Mandy's heart, she feared. The Bible was full of stories about what happens when you turn your back on His wishes. Mandy prayed for His forgiveness, and for strength.

* * *

After lunch, Frank found Cassy talking with Michael about the various defensive positions Michael had directed Dean in building. As Frank approached, he heard Michael saying something about how they hadn't had time to put grenade sumps into the fighting pits, whatever a sump was. When Michael spotted Frank approaching, he nudged Cassy, and the two of them waved. Frank waved back and stopped a few feet from them.

"Cassy, can I get a word with you if you have the time?" Frank asked.

Cassy looked to Michael, who nodded and then walked back toward where Dean was still directing the construction of more foxholes on the other side of the farm. Turning back to Frank, she wore a warm smile as she said, "Sure, Frank. What can I do for you?"

Frank couldn't help but grin back. Cassy always seemed to have a smile for him no matter what else was going on. It was a good thing his wife trusted him so much and that he loved her so deeply. He'd never violate Mary's trust, but he did relish Cassy's smiles, maybe too much.

Frank said, "Well of course it's about how you've been leading us lately. You're a good leader, or I wouldn't have stepped down, but let's be direct: People think you're under too much pressure, and it's affecting your leadership. So, if I were the leader, I'd—"

"But you're not the leader, Frank. If you want the job, though, it's yours. I don't want it, never wanted it, and you can have it." Cassy's grin morphed into an unreadable mask.

Damn, this was not how the conversation was supposed to go. Why'd she think he wanted the job? He was her advisor, dammit. Or was she just saying to lead, follow, or get out of the way?

"Not a chance," Frank said. "I'm still on Team Cassy. You're our best bet for survival, and you visualize and bring together all these little sub-plans better than anyone I've ever met. You get the best out of people in a way that I can't, and you make it look easy."

"Then please don't bring up what you'd do if you led us, Frank. Just tell me what you think without stepping all over me. My confidence is pretty low right now, so support me—even if that means telling me what I don't want to hear—but don't let me ever think you might step up to the plate, or I'll hand it over and run whether or not you want the job."

Frank forced a smile. "Alright, Cassy, fair enough. So,

people are talking about this Choony thing and the scene with Dean Jepson. They understand the thing with Dean because they agree with you that no preps is worse than some. But Dean is just a bit too much of a perfectionist. That's a craftsman thing, and I think he's a genius, but it can get to the point where he doesn't quite think like everyone else. So ignore that, and look at the big picture."

"Yeah, I get that," Cassy said. "I delegated that situation to Michael, and now Dean's on board. Sort of. At least the work is getting done, finally. Michael took the choice away from Dean, which I couldn't do because Dean has a hard time listening to women, and because he and I have a history. I didn't hear a squawk out of Dean when Michael stepped in. I suppose it's a guy thing. He's getting used to the notion, but it might take him some time to get used to being led by a woman. Kinda ticks me off, but he is who he is."

"I can't argue with that," Frank said, nodding. "So, Choony... No one agrees with you there."

Frank watched as Cassy frowned, looked down, and let out a long sigh. Finally, she said, "I know that. I lost my head. He sort of cornered me by challenging me in public, during a crisis, instead of coming to me in private. But when I cooled off some, I remembered *this isn't a dictatorship*. I was treating it like one because I'm afraid for my kids, and I'll do anything to keep them safe. It's the mama bear in me, I guess. But I forgot that everyone else with kids feels the same. People without kids probably don't want to die, either," she chuckled, shaking her head at herself. "So I asked you to help."

A light went off in Frank's head. "So that's why you had me go talk to him. A bit of pride, a bit of practicality. Well, that's the real strength of your leadership—your ability to let go of *you* to focus on *the Clan*. Turned out to be a good call. He's actually quite reasonable. I don't think I've ever seen that man get angry. I think he just processes his emotions faster than the rest of us can and moves on. He never seems to dwell on the past. Anyway, he wants to stay if you're willing to keep him. He likes it here and likes the people, including you. And his medical and chemical knowledge is something we couldn't replace anytime soon."

"I hoped he'd be willing to stay, if we let him," Cassy said. "The problem is how to bring him back in without totally losing whatever perceived authority I have. Authority from the people, not Peter-like rulership. I'm not Peter, and we're the Clan, not White Stag Farms."

Frank nodded. There it was—this was the woman they'd put in charge. Frank spared a moment just to feel glad to have Cassy back. The real Cassy. Frank wondered if he'd have been as good at leading them as she had been, but in his heart, he didn't believe he'd come close. Stepping down in her favor when they got here had been the right choice after all.

Snapping back into the moment, he looked Cassy in the eyes and said, "I only see one way. You have to ask him to come back specifically to perform a dangerous mission. Something we *have* to get done if we're to win that doesn't require a gun. By asking, you show the Clan humility and pragmatism. They need to see that after what happened. And you leave it on his shoulders whether to return afterwards, so you aren't being a dictator with his future. He has the choice. That way, you restore the authority people have given you. You restore it just by not abusing it."

Cassy pursed her lips. "How very 'King Solomon and the Baby' of you. I like Choony, and while I think I know the mission you have in mind, I'd planned on asking for a volunteer. I don't think I can just order someone to take a mission I wouldn't want to try to do myself. Not if I want to sleep at night."

"Yeah, but this is your way out," Frank said. "You aren't forcing him to take the mission, you know. He has a choice. But if he does it, that frees up someone who *will* shoot a gun, kill people, defend the Clan. We need every shooter we can get, and we need them *shooting*. This is just the best, most practical solution with Choony. You don't have to do it that way, of course, but if you don't then you squander two people —Choony and the volunteer—and I'll damn sure be disappointed in you, Cassy. Either way I'll support you because we need unity right now. We'd still need you to lead, but I'm hoping you'll do the smart thing. It's the right thing, too."

Frank studied Cassy's face with an inward grin and saw that his blunt speech had the desired effect. She was going to make the right choice and invite Choony back, even if her feelings about Frank were the deciding factor. He doubted she even realized the feelings he thought he saw, and he wasn't going to point it out. Ever. Like Mandy told him often enough, Frank was a better leader when he wasn't the one openly leading. It suited him.

* * *

1400 HOURS - ZERO DAY +24

Taggart grinned. The 20s had found their operative. Whoever he was, he was now using a more secure broadcast system—something called a HAMnet—and one of Taggart's Militiamen knew how to interpret the signals. Taggart now had access to the broadcasts the 20s coordinated, so he didn't have to rely on that damned Mr. Black.

Taggart briefed Eagan, knowing he could be trusted with such vital information. Eagan might be a shitbird, Taggart thought with a wry smile, but he was hard as stone when he needed to be. "So their agent, Dark Ryder, is something like an intel coordination officer or C3 tech," Taggart said, continuing his briefing. "He's working with some shady character called Watcher One, who I think must be higher up in the 20s, and between the two of them they handle all the Resistance intel for the Eastern Seaboard operations area. That Dark Ryder operative is really good—nobody has a clue who he is and his broadcast locations are different every time. Nobody knows how he does it."

Eagan shrugged. "So, two people deep in occupied territory have to work together to give us the intel we need to throw up token resistance. Tell me again why you're excited about this, Captain?"

Leave it to Eagan to see through the hype. "Affirmative, shitbird. The system's fragile. But now we have it straight from them, instead of getting it filtered through Mr. Black. Remember the Operation Backdraft that Black mentioned nonchalantly? It seems the reality is that this is our best hope for pushing the 'vaders back into the ocean, where hopefully they get eaten by sharks, or maybe a Kraken. All the New York Resistance cells are to launch a coordinated attack at the opening of Operation Backdraft. Details are still sparse, but Backdraft is supposedly going to put us on a level playing field with them. Something about making their C3 infrastructure FUBAR just before we hit them hard wherever it'll hurt them the most."

Eagan broke into a vicious grin as Taggart got to the part about hurting the 'vaders, but then his face fell. "Yeah, Cap, but what happens if either of these 20s guys becomes a casualty before the Backdraft balloon goes up? It sounds like a lotta hope to pack into one little five-pound bag."

"Just follow orders, Eagan. I'll let you know what you need to know in plenty of time for you to get it all wrong, don't worry." Such questions were the reason he valued

Eagan for more than his rifle, but it could be damn annoying.

Eagan put on a mock Dutiful Soldier face, saluted, turned and left after looking back just in time to see Taggart hiding a grin. But Taggart's thoughts were troubled by the very questions Eagan had brought up. The future of America seemed like a lot of eggs to put in one fragile basket, especially when that basket consisted of two separate agents working far, far behind the front lines. "God help you both," Taggart muttered. "God help us all." He folded up his map then and reached for his rifle. It was almost time to go on another raid for supplies. Business as usual, for now. But he couldn't help feeling hope rise that soon the balance would change in their favor for once. Playing guerrilla had its place, but damn! He wanted to take them all down, every one of the foul, murderous bastards. He shook himself free of that useless train of thought and left to find his Militiamen.

* * *

1000 HOURS - ZERO DAY +25

Peter looked at the bodies. Four of his own were dead or clearly dying, but thankfully they were no one important. Eight of the second band of Red Locusts were dead too, so it'd be no trouble to tout this as his latest win to his sheeple. He didn't care about them personally, of course, but he did need them motivated and loyal. This victory would help with the motivation part, and some selective praise would do the rest.

"Jim," Peter called. Jim had returned the night before with news of both the spy farm and the location of this second band of Red Locusts. "Have the Locust bodies piled up, and arrange a burial detail for our fallen. They were heroes, all of them, and in death they deserve our honor and our respect."

Total bullshit, of course, but Jim would eat it up—giving out orders while he convinced himself he cared about those people. He was the King of Torture, but he'd fall apart without his delusions. Peter congratulated himself on his excellent leadership skills and turned to deal with the loyalty he required from his people. Or fear. Whatever. And he might as well boost his numbers a bit while he was at it, just as he had when he defeated the first band of Red Locusts.

"Citizens of White Stag," he bellowed, and all heads turned toward him, including the seven bound-up Red Locust prisoners. Peter fought down his irritation at their presumption and reminded himself that they were probably eager to find out if they were about to die. From what Peter had seen, most people seemed to worry about that a lot. As though their lives mattered. He shrugged and continued: "In recent days, we defeated the first Red Locust group, and today we completed that victory by demolishing the second. Now, when we take the land that is rightfully ours, we can rest easier knowing that we'll have no foul bands of cannibals waiting for us to slip up. We had three challenges, and now there is *only one left.*"

There was a half-hearted cheer from his followers, despite their battle weariness. And despite losing loved ones, Peter reminded himself. People were always mourning the dead when they should be cheering for their own survival. Certainly, Peter himself could barely contain the fierce joy he felt after battle. What would he do when all the enemies were dead or routed? He'd have to find another threat to face, to fight, to draw his followers together in fear and hate. Such useful tools, those.

"You see now the wisdom of bringing the surviving Red Locusts into our fold—they fought as bravely as those who were with me in the beginning and lost one of their own fighting this band of cannibals. Or I should say, lost one more of *our own.*"

Peter spat on one of the enemy dead. Circuses for the masses. Now for the bread... "We will bury our honorable dead, who gave their lives so that we could live. They honored you all with their sacrifice, and so we will honor them with a proper burial and three days of mourning and rest, to prepare for the struggle to come. But what of these dead enemies? Do they deserve to be buried? I say no, they do not. Our food stores are for citizens, yet these recruits need nourishment as well. I give them the enemy fallen, just as I would anyone who betrays us all by turning against their leader, and our God-given mission."

Peter looked around and saw, but did not understand, the horror in his people's eyes. Good. Let them remember the grisly scene that was about to unfold, and reckon in their hearts whether they really wanted to question his rule. They were sheeple, so without proper motivation they were always cowards. Love of each other and fear of consequences, now *those* were real motivation for a cowardly flock.

"Jim, invite the remaining Red Locusts to join us as their brethren did. Any that don't jump at the chance are to be shot immediately and thrown on the banquet." But Peter knew they'd all prefer to join him than die. People respected only strength, and now they had a leader they could really look up to. Peter resisted the urge to laugh, and his ears wiggled from the effort. Must keep up appearances, after all. The sheeple were easy to impress, but you did have to keep it up or they forgot. Always gotta pump it.

Just as important as the fear this cannibal feast created, feeding the Locusts to their own would save days of White Stag food stores. The Quartermaster was the only other person who knew that, unless they took the farm within a week, the White Stag people would go hungry. And he'd better damn well not let that happen.

- 9 -

0900 HOURS - ZERO DAY +26

JAZ SAT LEANING against the tree they'd bound her to, her hands tied up in front of her as well. It was hard to move around, but of course the bastards didn't care. They were total tools. Especially the one who stood in front of her. His name was Peter, she'd learned, and he was the leader of the people coming to take the farm away from the Clan. The enemy. And he was looking down at her with an all-too-familiar expression. He was pretty hot, but in that cocky, strutting kind of way that just screamed "douchebag." It would be best not to upset him, so she broke eye contact.

Peter said, "So your name is Jaz, and you're one of the original members of the Clan—one of the spy's first little followers. Seeing you now, I regret that I promised to give you to my lieutenant, Jim. I almost want to just take you for myself. Next time I capture enemies, I'll be smarter about it and look at them myself before handing them out."

Rage bubbled up inside Jaz. Could this freak really be, like, talking about handing *people* around like candy? Well, two months ago Old Jaz would have just played it safe and stayed quiet, trying to make the experience not totally suck by not resisting, just like her dad taught her, that sonovabitch. New Jaz decided that someday soon she was going to cut the dude's junk off and choke him with it. Him and Jim both. Fuckers. Just as soon as she got up the courage.

"So you don't have anything to say about that?" Peter asked. "Well, that's fine. It doesn't change your fate. You see, I'm going to take the Clan's lands for my own, to make up for what your bitch of a leader cost me. And the people of the Clan will be compound interest on that debt, because someone has to do the dirty work. I'd rather break all your backs in the fields than my own people."

Jaz seethed. She didn't expect any better from this prick, but it was still a jolt to hear him say openly that they'd all be slaves of one sort or another. On the other hand, most of her people might live through this, and that was totes amaze, because it would give whatever Clanners survived time to plot some freakin' payback. Surprise, surprise, fuckers—karma, beotch.

Peter grinned down at Jaz. "I see your wheels turning. Plotting. It won't do you any good, you know. I got you outnumbered, and I reckon outgunned, too. But hang on to your dreams, girl. You'll need them soon."

Jaz had the urge to lash out, tell him he was in for more of a fight than he bargained for, but stopped herself at the last second. That would betray the Clan's preparations. She'd already opened her mouth to speak, so she covered it up by begging. It almost always worked with the bad dudes. "Please, don't hurt them. Just let them go, they're no threat to you! I'll do...whatever... Anything you want." She forced herself to smile the timid smile that always worked. "I'm not, like, committed to them or anything. They just kept me alive, but you totally have more peeps, more guns. Maybe you and me, we can work something out."

Peter laughed, but it was forced, deliberate, taunting. "Oh girl. You are a smart one, aren't you? Well, I'm not falling for it. I don't *need* your permission to make you do 'anything I want.' You're a prisoner, not a guest. And soon, the rest of you vermin will be under my boot as well. But you did give me an idea, little liar."

There was a noise behind Peter, and Jim stepped up next to him, eyeing Jaz with a cold expression that sent a chill up her spine. "Boss, you said she was mine. I haven't questioned her yet."

Peter put a hand on Jim's shoulder. "You'll have the chance, but first I'm going to see if she can be used as bait to lure their leader out. It won't change anything for Jaz here, but if we can kill their leader before all this goes down, taking out her cronies will be a lot easier. Before you get to doing what I asked of you, I need to try to negotiate a swap. Jaz for Cassy. If the bitch is dumb enough to stick her head up, though, we'll have a sniper ready. Smile for the camera, wait for the flash. If it goes well, great. If not, we lose nothing. Either way, Jaz isn't going anywhere. *Then* you get to question her. Or whatever you feel is needed."

Peter turned and walked away, leaving Jim staring down at her. Jaz thought his eyes looked like a snake's, the ones that hypnotize birds before striking. Guess what, New Jaz wasn't some bird he could freeze. Not anymore. Then he said, "This pisses me off. I have a responsibility to my people to question you. To punish you for what you all did to our boss's people—"

Jaz snapped, and interrupted his monologue. "You're a piece of shit, Jim. Total douche. My people didn't do a damn thing to you, or him, or any of you White Stag losers. Maybe you'll win, but that won't make you right, and you're gonna have to live with what you do. You're a monster, just making excuses to do what you wanna do anyway."

"You deserve what's coming, Jaz. Hah! I made a joke and didn't even know it. Well, just know that when the questioning is done, Peter's told me I'll have to train you for your new duties after he raises the flag of White Stag over your bullshit little farm. You're too mouthy, Jaz. I promise you, when you get your 'training,' you are *not* going to enjoy it." He grinned, then added, "Well, maybe you will enjoy it. Either way, I know I will."

New Jaz immediately regretted lashing out. Dammit. It was gonna suck to be her real soon.

* * *

1100 HOURS - ZERO DAY +26

Cassy stood in the outdoor kitchen chatting with the day's kitchen duty people. She made a habit of checking on them at least once each day, talking to whoever was working about their needs, their triumphs, their concerns. It was a way to connect with them and make people feel heard, and let them see her acting like the leader they'd made her into.

Sturm, the Marine Lance Corporal, walked into the kitchen and came up to Cassy. Her brow was furrowed, lips tight, and it immediately set Cassy on alert. Sturm said, "Can we talk outside?"

Cassy nodded and led her outside, away from the others. "What's going on?" There were only so many things it could be, and none of those things were good. Cassy felt the effects of adrenaline beginning to hit her system and struggled to stand still and calm.

"It's that time. Peter and his army are finally here. And ma'am, he has Jaz. That's why she disappeared, and why Michael and I couldn't find her. We went to look for her yesterday but had no luck. Peter's on the far side of the food forest edge of the farm with a couple armed people, and Jaz is tied up a couple hundred yards further back. He says he wants to negotiate. Michael sent me to get you."

Cassy's jaw dropped, and her eyes were wide with shock. Those bastards have *Jaz*? "Oh God. Alright. Let me think. Get a half-dozen armed people together, and spread the word for the Clan to get their weapons and take up their assigned positions."

Sturm nodded, then said, "You aren't really going to talk to that psycho, are you, ma'am? He can't be trusted, you must know that. I don't think you should put yourself at risk, not for anyone here. Not even Jaz."

"Sturm, I'm just going to talk to him. We'll see what he has to say. Please, go do as I asked, and get our people in position just in case this goes south on us." Not try to save Jaz? Yeah, right. Jaz was Clan, and Cassy's mind roiled with curses aimed at the White Stag people.

Sturm sprinted away, and ten minutes later Cassy had her six people together. Sturm and the other Marine were busy getting the Clan in place and ready, so Cassy would have to rely on these six. "No one shoot unless they fire first," Cassy said. "That's Jaz out there, one of our own, and if she gets hurt because someone got an itchy trigger finger, it won't go well for that person. Stay alert. I don't want to lose any of you, either."

Cassy and her six walked in silence toward the food forest, and Peter beyond it. When she reached the far edge of the forest, she saw Michael standing behind a tree with his M4 held at the low ready.

"Cassy," Michael said in greeting. "They're over there. This Peter guy insists on talking to you directly, if we want Jaz back. Alone. Listen, I like that girl, and she's one of us and an original. But you matter more to the Clan right now than she does. Please, don't go out there. Let me run messages back and forth, or something. His sidekick gives me the creeps."

Cassy shook her head. "Sorry, can't do that. But get one of our guys here ready to put a bullet in his head if this goes wrong, okay? And Michael, we can't afford to lose you right now, either. You're our general, and we need you. Don't take any risks, okay?"

Once she was sure everyone was in good position, she emerged from the dense foliage, heading toward the man who must be Peter. Then she saw the man standing far behind him, next to a bound-up Jaz. Her jaw dropped, and a spike of fear and rage jammed itself into her heart. James…

She felt suddenly, terribly naked out there alone in the open. Exposed. Every shrub that rustled in the breeze looked like a sniper hiding and ready to take her out. She focused on keeping her back straight, head up. Now was not the time to show fear, no matter how badly she wanted to run back to the tree line. Which, she had to admit, was something she *really* wanted to do.

She locked eyes with Peter as she drew closer, focusing only on him, and avoided looking at Jim. She couldn't show fear, not now. Peter's eyes were sky blue. He showed no sign of being nervous either, his handsome face was relaxed. Even cocky. He raised an eyebrow as she approached, and he wore a faint smirk. Sonofabitch.

"You must be this Peter I've heard about," Cassy said. It took every effort to keep her voice steady, but dammit, her people were on the line. For their sakes, she steeled herself and felt a flood of courage rise up when she thought about the need to protect them, her new family. "I want that girl back," she added, and was proud of the steel she put into her voice.

"Yeah. I imagine you heard my name from the scout. Yet another murder on your head. Well, you'll soon pay for that, along with all the other people you killed at White Stag Farms."

He still wore that smirk, and it infuriated Cassy, but she tried to keep her face carefully neutral. What the hell was this guy talking about? "The only one of your people we've killed was your spy. I assume you found him on your way here. We won't let you, the Locusts, or anyone else terrorize us. We're done running from the Peters of this world."

Peter's smirk vanished, which gave Cassy a moment of pleasure until he said, "That's not so. When you led the invaders straight to us, most of my people died. It's ironic that you call my scout a spy, when all along the real spy is you. It'll be your people who pay the price for that treason."

Cassy clenched her jaw. This guy was a freakin' lunatic. Her, a spy? "I think you're misinformed," Cassy said. "I led no one to you. In fact, it was *your people* who fired first at *me*. I was alone on my journey then, but instead of helping a fellow human being you—or one of your people—tried to kill me. Followed me. *Hunted* me. I didn't lead the invaders to you, but I figure it was just a big dose of karma. You earned it, you bastard."

Peter put his hands on his hips, looked up into the sky, and let out a long breath through pursed lips. Then he said, "Well, I guess we'll have to agree to disagree. I suppose that very soon, we'll see who God deems right. I've led my people from the wasteland you helped create to this, the Promised Land. Or at least, that's how my people see it. God's on my side, so who can stand against me? You and your handful of people? You're leeches feeding on the corpse of America, and we're going to put that right."

Smug prick. Psycho nutjob. The world would be a better place when Cassy killed him personally, she decided. "We aren't just going to hand this over to you. This is *my* land, and they are *my* family. My people. We'll fight you tooth and nail to keep what we've built here, no matter what evil you do to that poor girl you captured. She's a good kid, and every harm that comes on her will be repaid, Peter."

Then Peter surprised her, by smiling and nodding. What. The. Fuck? "Yes, Cassy, if I may call you that. She's why I came to talk to you. I don't want to hurt her, but she's with you and that makes her my enemy. But there's a way to avoid that. There's a way to get Jaz back before my right-hand man indulges his impulses on her. Actually, you can save them all, Cassy. Not just Jaz, but every one of your followers can be forgiven for the sin of following you. It requires only an offering, just like in the Old Testament."

Cassy felt her skin go cold. Peter wasn't just crazy. He was *evil*. Behind his charming eyes lay the soul of a pit viper, and the sensation that she was his prey made her stomach lurch. After a few moments, she said, "Really, you don't say? I can only wonder what sort of generous offer you have for us. How 'bout you enlighten me, you wannabe Moses."

Peter shook his head slowly. "I don't want to be Moses. Because of his arrogance, he never got to see the promised land God led him to. I'm smarter than that. Everything I do, I dedicate to the Lord these days. Well, at least that's what I tell my people. The sheeple eat that shit up. Alright, I'll speak plainly, then. If you surrender yourself and half your supplies of every type, I'll have enough to feed my people until spring. Then I want half your winter wheat and so on. You get the idea."

"And what should my people eat, if you take half?" Cassy asked.

"The other half," Peter said. "If you don't agree, of course, we'll just kill you all and take both halves."

"Logical. I have two questions though. First, what will you do with me, if I surrender to you?"

Peter said, "Don't be stupid. I said God needs a good old-fashioned Old Testament sacrifice. That's a blood offering, if you haven't read the Good Book. Your blood, of course. But in a way you'll live on—I'm going to feed you to the Red Locusts who now follow *me*. Which is to say, all the ones I didn't kill. If you have ketchup, they might like some to go with your liver."

Peter seemed to freeze, his eyes revealing a smile that his face didn't show. Poker face. Whatever. This sick sonofabitch really thought the Clan would go for that? Cassy's mind raced.

Then Cassy said, "I acknowledge your offer. I have a second question, however, which is this: How do I know you'll keep your word? You are a psycho nutjob with delusions of grandeur, after all." Take that, you prick.

"Your opinion matters less than you know, Cassy. Whatever you think of me, the fact is that it is *me* you have to deal with if you want your people to live. But, to answer your question, I offer you a question in return. What would you take as reassurance? A couple hostages, perhaps."

"Yeah, right. You'd sacrifice your grandmother if you thought it'd get you what you want. I have a better idea. First, two of your lieutenants and their families. They'll live with us and be well cared for. Every few months we can trade out for new ones, so they don't get too comfortable among their betters."

Peter let out a sigh. "I'll think about that. It's not unreasonable, though you're still gambling that I won't sacrifice them to get the rest of your shit. But you said 'first.' What's second?"

Cassy steeled herself for the next part. If she had judged this guy correctly, this would be the harder sell—but the one that would most encourage Peter to keep his word. "Second, you send Jaz back to me *with your capo, Jim*. You must know what a devious little shit he is, but your scout told us he was your right-hand man. Your pitbull. I figure you manipulate him by letting him do whatever pervy rapey bullshit he wants and telling him it's justified. Is that close to the mark?"

"Yeah. He's useful though, and I trust him as long as I can feed his particular tastes."

Wow, this maniac didn't even bother to hide what he was doing, Cassy thought. Shoot, he was practically *bragging*.

"Well, he and I have some history," Cassy said. "You want to do God's will? He comes with Jaz to face justice for what he did, both to me and to however many victims you've thrown to your pitbull since then. And, he brings that Camaro with him. We won't use it, but you'll get it back if you honor your word. I have to talk to my people about it first. Give us time to decide."

For the first time, Cassy saw frustration in Peter's eyes, and the muscles over his jaw throbbed as he clenched and unclenched his jaw. Good—she'd gambled rightly by asking for Jim and his damn car. But hostages weren't much of a deterrence unless they included someone Peter actually gave two craps about. Peter stared at her for half a minute, and Cassy saw that his hands trembled ever so slightly. He was struggling to control himself. Well he'd better succeed, or her sniper would end his sorry ass, and then, well, they'd just have to see where the chips fell.

Finally, Peter said, "That... is acceptable, assuming you don't chicken out. And Cassy? Don't wait too long to let me know. You have two days. If you haven't delivered yourself and your stuff by then, I'll know your answer is 'no' and I don't think you'll like what I have in store for you."

* * *

1900 HOURS - ZERO DAY +26

Supper was over, and Cassy walked the property to check on the sentries. She carried a gallon of water and a tin cup with her and offered a drink to each sentry when she stopped to chat. They exchanged pleasantries, and Cassy made sure to encourage each one to stay both vigilant and hopeful.

After she had stopped at the last sentry, who declined water, she walked up the hill to where the animals were kept, went into the small barn, and sat on fresh straw in the back of the shed. It was both soft and prickly, but it was quiet, and no one ever came out here at this time of day. Right now, Cassy wanted peace and quiet to think things through.

The Clan-wide meeting she'd held earlier in the day had gone about like she expected. None of the original Clanners or those who came immediately after had wanted Cassy to go surrender to Peter. They were willing to fight for their community. Cassy supposed they mostly thought of the Clan as their family, nowadays. Of the newer members, only a very small minority had suggested that Cassy submit herself to Peter's cannibals, and they'd been soundly shunned by everyone else since then. This bothered Cassy. Right now, the Clan could die without unity. If she surrendered to Peter, she'd have to figure out a way to smooth those waters before she went. A fractured Clan was a vulnerable Clan. She'd trust her mother and many others in the Clan to raise her kids, but she wouldn't leave them vulnerable. She couldn't do that to them.

Cassy picked up a piece of straw and was about to put one end in her mouth to fidget with while she thought, when a motion to her left at the edge of view caught her attention. Her head snapped around toward the movement, and a flash of alarm washed over her, but then she realized it was Choony. Of course it would be Choony.

Cassy said, "You seem to have a knack for finding me when I'm doing some self-reflection, Choony. Did you follow me up here?"

Choony, ever honest as far as Cassy could tell, simply nodded but said nothing. He sat in the straw a few feet away from Cassy and picked up his own blade of straw. Cassy decided she'd sit in silence with him and wait until he spoke first, but after a few minutes she gave up. "So, tell me why you followed me up here. Bored?"

Choony shrugged and said, "I knew that if I had to make the choice you must face, I would want some company. Especially company that wouldn't tell me what to do."

"So you aren't going to tell me to stay and fight? At the meeting you said you'd like it if I stayed, but now you don't have an opinion?" Cassy smiled at Choony. The last few days had seen them speaking like this more often. Choony was a good guy to bounce ideas off of, it had turned out.

"Of course I have an opinion. I think you should stay, because I don't trust this Peter to keep his word. That being the case—and given the Clan's determination to fight back if needed, rather than flee or submit and hope it wouldn't end horribly—they need your leadership. On the other hand, if you believe Peter would honor a deal and you feel your life is worth giving to avoid more bloodshed, I would honor your decision. To give your life for theirs has great honor, and I'd earnestly hope to see you in my next life."

"But you don't think I should go. I can tell," Cassy said. "Otherwise, you would have said that. I don't always agree with you, but I believe you always tell the truth as you see it."

Choony said, "Peter's kind is poisonous on the inside, and their poison withers everything it touches. I don't think you believe his intentions either, not fully. And I think you came up here to talk yourself into going. You're telling yourself that it's for the good of your family—"

"It is," Cassy interrupted.

"But sneaking out in the night doesn't shout confidence," Choony said. "It tells me, if I'm right about how you process information and decisions, that you have given up. You despair of victory, so for the sake of your family you will surrender and hope it goes well. I think *you* think that some chance is better than none. You want to believe in wishful thinking, but you find it's harder than you expected. That's why you came up here. Though whatever you decide, I think you know the deep honor I will hold you in."

Cassy pursed her lips and furrowed her brow in frustration. "Dammit, Choony. You are as confusing as ever. What the hell should I do with that gem of wisdom? Of course I'd rather give my people a chance, any chance, even at the cost of my life."

Choony didn't reply at first. He chewed on his piece of straw, leaned back on both elbows, and sat in silence. Finally, he said, "Cassy, if you sneak out to surrender, coming from despair and fear, you only *think* you do it for your family. In fact, you would be doing it because you've given up, not because it was your Right Thing. If you do that, you only drive fear and despair into your people. You're their leader, and they'll follow your lead in whatever you do, but the fear that drove you to submit would infect them all. Do you suppose a man like Peter would miss such a change in their aura? If you don't believe in auras, call it their 'vibe' or 'energy' or 'body language,' whatever. The point is, you may delay their doom by submitting, but you will practically guarantee it comes, and soon. That's just how I see it, of course. What do I know? I'm just a chemistry major who won't pick up a gun."

It was Cassy's turn to sit in silence for a while. Damn that Choony, he was probably right. About all of it. It was really hard to think clearly through all the fear, uncertainty, and doubt she felt dragging at every thought. She really would be taking a coward's way out by surrendering, as counterintuitive as that felt. Would her people have the iron will to fight and persevere if she did what she'd intended? To be honest—and damn that Choony anyway for making her face it—she really had intended to sneak out and surrender with no one watching. Maybe she wanted to convince herself that her mind hadn't been made up, but in her heart of hearts she knew the truth. And of course, Peter would strike hard when he saw the fear and confusion among the Clanners, no matter what his intentions were originally. If he'd ever intended to keep his word. Choony didn't believe that and really, neither did Cassy.

She turned to Choony and smiled. "Thanks for coming up. I think I've come to respect your opinion, and your motives, despite our earlier conflict. Or rather, *my* earlier conflict. Anyway, let's go back down to the farm. I'm sure people will be wondering where we went if we're not back soon. I think maybe tomorrow we'll have a party, a celebration of life. It may be our last, after all, and I have a barrel of apple cider that we should drink while we can. I don't intend for those looters to have it if things go sideways."

She hopped off the haystack, waited for Choony, and the two walked side by side back to the homestead, leaving the animals asleep behind them. For some reason, she felt good now, better than any time since Peter's insanity arrived at their border.

* * *

0200 HOURS - ZERO DAY +27

Cassy woke to the sound of gunfire. It came from up on the hill where their chickens, goats, and hogs rested—when they weren't being used to intensively graze a plot of land—but it didn't sound like the shots were aimed at the homestead. Hard to tell, with the rifle reports bouncing off the hill, the trees, the buildings. She scrambled to her feet, grabbed the M4 next to her bed, and charged out of the farmhouse. Outside, a trickle of other Clanners was turning into a flood as just about everyone awoke and came out with their weapons ready. Cassy observed with a chill that they looked afraid. A lot would depend on how she acted now. Damn.

"Michael, get defenses organized! Mueller and Sturm, recon that hilltop!" Cassy shouted over the din, her voice rising high and clear.

The milling, frightened Clanners seemed to suddenly change gears at the sound of her voice directing them. People sprinted away toward their positions, determination clear on their faces, while others quickly but calmly herded the children into the bulletproof earthbag house. The rest formed a perimeter, prone in the dirt, and the sentry in the little guard tower sounded the airhorn. "A little late, whoever's on duty," she muttered to herself, then called to those who could hear, "That's great, people. Now let's make our practice pay off!"

She heard random shouts in return as she ran to her own position inside the farmhouse, at the upstairs windows.

A couple minutes later, her little hand-held radio crackled. Mueller's voice came through the static: "Scout team to base. OpFor has retreated. They've seized assets—our pigs and goats—and faded away before we could engage them. There is also a note here. Scout team exfiltrating engagement area, returning to base. Stay frosty, people."

Cassy heard two brief exchanges over the radio between Michael and Mueller, then her radio again went silent. She waited for Mueller and Sturm to return, and the two minutes it took seemed like two years. Finally, Mueller entered her upstairs room with a paper in his hand. She wouldn't leave her post until Michael cleared everyone to stand down, as Mueller knew, so he had come to her. He handed the paper to her, his face a neutral mask that Cassy couldn't read.

She looked down at the folded piece of printer paper and saw crude handwriting in blue pen. It read simply, "Consider this a warning. Decision is due by next dusk. If you comply with terms, we will consider these animals to be part of our half of your supplies. Those who stand against our just cause will be dealt as you'd expect. We are coming for the spy in any case. Lovingly yours, Peter Ixin, White Stag Farms."

A flood of relief washed over Cassy, and the room reeled. She'd almost surrendered to this monster, yet he couldn't even honor the time they'd agreed upon for the Clan to decide. Thank God Choony had talked her out of going... No, the die was now well and truly cast, and Cassy swore to kill that sonofabitch before this mess was over, even if it cost her life to do it.

- 10 -

0600 HRS - ZERO DAY +28

CASSY LISTENED AS Michael briefed the defenders. His voice was calm and level, yet it carried over the crowd, and Cassy again marveled at that military bark of his. "Remember, Clanners, if you have one of our M4s it's because you're a *good shot*, but this weapon will fire up to sixty times faster than its ability to cool down. What this means is that on burst, its *sustainable* rate of fire is only twelve or so per minute in a lengthy firefight. If you engage in prolonged intensive fire, then you must provide adequate cool-down time or it will overheat. Remember your training and fire deliberately. Your goal is to *kill the enemy*, not fire off all your ammo. Remember to use your pistol if your primary weapon gets hot! We can't replace those M4s. Any questions?"

A woman's hand rose. She carried a Remington 700 rifle—bolt action, slow, but accurate. "Are there any more of the M4s? This rifle is painfully slow."

Michael didn't even break stride to look to see who was speaking when he replied, "No, they all went to the top marksmen among us. But there's no such thing as a bad weapon, only bad warriors. No one here is a bad warrior, but we only have so many Mil-grade weapon systems available. Next?"

No more hands went up. It had been a lengthy briefing as Michael and Cassy went over every aspect of the defense plan with the assembled Clanners. Over a dozen with M4s, and two dozen with other weapons ranging from bolt-action hunting rifles to shotguns. Grenades were given to those with military training, but there could never be enough of them to make Cassy feel well supplied.

As Cassy ran through the plan and contingencies in her head, Choony walked up to her, a tense smile on his face by way of greeting. "Hi Cassy, got a minute?"

"Not really," Cassy said. "We have more things to do than time to do it in, as always. But what's up? Walk with me while I inspect the foxholes. Or 'fighting pits' as Michael calls 'em." Cassy walked toward the first of the pits, with Choony at her side. He seemed calm, not frightened, and she wished she had that kind of courage. He and Mandy both seemed to have it. Maybe it was a "faith" thing.

"While we still have the chance, Cassy, I just wanted to thank you for allowing me to stay. I know I disappointed you when I declined to take part in the gun violence, but I assure you I'll work hard and will be useful in other ways. Michael tasked me with running ammo to the field positions, if anyone runs out, and getting any wounded to our makeshift first aid station in the unfinished earthbag house. You can believe me when I promise I won't fail our people in this duty, so long as I still breathe."

Cassy stopped mid-stride, then turned to face a rather surprised Choony. The guy was rock solid, and here he was thanking her for putting him into what Michael said was one of the most dangerous roles in the coming battle. She spared a quick prayer of thanks that God—if He was up there listening—had put them in the way of meeting this amazing young man. Cassy put her hand out to shake his, and when he took the offer and shook, she gave him one slow nod of approval.

And then she was on her way again, with more things to do than time to do them in. Peter was coming, at an unknown time and with an unknown plan of attack. Michael had put their odds of survival at fifty-fifty, and Cassy hoped that wasn't overly generous.

* * *

0800 HOURS - ZERO DAY +28

Cassy stood with Michael in the guard tower, which gave them the best view of the property. They wouldn't stay there when the fighting started, of course; she and Michael would be in the loft of her house manning radios and issuing commands, keeping track of the battle's progress. They'd both swapped their M4s for bolt-action rifles, good for sniping from their position and freeing the more combat-effective weapons for the people doing most of the real fighting and dying. Hopefully more fighting than dying.

Cassy looked out at the vista of her property and the land beyond, and felt a certain solid pride at all she'd accomplished in turning the property from an overgrazed wasteland into a verdant oasis. The house sat halfway up the gentle slope that distinguished her property. The earthbag house now under construction, the guard tower, several sheds, and the tent enclave all sat with the main house in a roughly circular cluster on the gentle hillside.

North of the house, farther uphill, was a series of swales and berms where the farm collected and channeled rainwater, slowing it down so it could infiltrate the soil thoroughly before draining as runoff into the collection ponds. The entire area was a food forest—fruit and nut trees with dozens of companion plant varieties. Beyond that, at the top of the hill, were grassy paddocks for livestock, though the animals were now gone thanks to Peter's earlier raid. Normally, the animals' natural wastes would leech into the ground or flow down into the swales, keeping their nutrients in use as they meandered down the hill over time.

The problem with that setup was that the food forest blocked the view to the north and gave any approaching enemy excellent cover and concealment. Michael had constructed the sniper nest he wanted and also a second one, there in the trees. Those snipers would hopefully hold off any approaching attackers, who had to travel over open ground to get to the trees, and the trees themselves blocked the enemy from sniping at the farm's defenders from the hilltop. It was still their weakest area, however.

To the east and west of the homestead lay interconnected ponds with thick foliage growing on their shores, holding the soil together and incidentally making attack from those directions difficult. The sniper nests in the woods to the north each overlooked one of the ponds as well, and they'd create a high casualty rate for any enemy trying to swim across the ponds.

To the south, the other half of the homestead consisted mostly of the Jungle, that maze of growing things and food plants carefully balanced by Cassy to keep the soil renewed and healthy. Its seemingly arbitrary lack of pattern had been dictated by the curves, dips, and rises of the land itself and by the nature of the surrounding plants. Now the resulting Jungle would impede movement unless they followed the network of paths, which branched out repeatedly the farther from the house they went. Anyone coming through would be channeled into only a handful of exit points as they approached the house, and Michael and the Marines had densely booby-trapped both the paths and, especially, the growing areas between them.

South of the Jungle lay more food forest, stretched across the southern border of the homestead. Though it could provide Peter's attackers with a less disorienting route to the house than the Jungle, it lay downhill from the living complex and wouldn't be much real use as cover for the attackers, since the Jungle still blocked any clear line of sight between the forest and the complex.

So, as Michael had explained it, the enemy would likely be channeled to attack either en masse in a wave from the south, or haphazardly from the north. The foxholes—or "fighting pits"—lay mostly between the Jungle and the house, with a couple to the north as well for good measure. These would be the front-line defense for Cassy's people so it was strictly a volunteer posting, but Michael had no shortage of volunteers. He made sure all were well trained to use their M4s, and he often took Choony with him on these tours of the fighting pits, both to drill the small Asian on the routes between the pits and to make sure all their fighters knew Choony would restock them with supplies during any fight. Choony's support would be psychological as well as tactically necessary to the defense.

Roughly two-thirds of their fighting force was in the foxholes or other cover, while Michael held the final third in reserve at the house, where they could respond to threats and defend the house itself if Peter's people pushed that far through the defenses. The kids were hidden well inside the earthbag house, as safe as any place could be in combat, and a few people would stay there with shotguns as a last line of defense if it all went bad.

Cassy, without turning to look at him, told Michael, "Ethan should be in the bunker by now, manning radios.

That was a great idea, by the way, but he's a good fighter, too. I wish he could be more active in the fight." She sighed. "We have so few people, compared to Peter. But I guess we're as ready as we're going to be—now we wait." Then she turned to regard Michael directly and added, "I have huge respect for you now, knowing you did this every day in the Sandbox. It amazes me. It's torture. I almost hope Peter shows up soon just so we can get this over with."

Michael only nodded, and Cassy was sure the warrior knew just how she felt.

* * *

In an abandoned farmhouse not far north of the Clan, Peter stared at his scout's map, and his fingers dug into the edge of the dinner table where it lay. "So you're telling me," he said to Jim, "they're all wearing the same outfit? Hunting camouflage BDUs, with matching hats. We have no way to tell which one is Cassy when we start the fun."

"Sorry, boss, but no we don't. I can't tell her from any of the others, even though I met her before."

Peter saw Jim's slight shudder as he recalled his early encounter with Cassy. It had nearly cost him his life, and Cassy hadn't even toughened up yet before the 'vaders started killing their countryside. It wouldn't do to underestimate her.

Peter continued: "We know the southern route is booby-trapped, and we know they've added lethal stuff to the early warning devices they had already planted there. After that, we'll have to go through that weird overgrown crop area, which is also laced with traps, or follow the trails that lead through it. They might also be trapped, but those trails only let us approach from a couple places even without any traps. They're sure to have some sort of crossfire set up there by now, covering all those exits."

"Kill zones, yeah boss. I'm sure they do. But what about from north of the farm, where we snatched their animals?"

"I don't much like coming from that way, either. The wooded area has to be trapped, and we know they have some bunker-holes built up between the bulletproof house and the woods."

Jim said, "I hope you aren't thinking of crossing those ponds. There isn't much defense there, but there's zero cover. It would be a slow crossing right out in the open."

"No..." Peter said, voice trailing off. "I think we'll have to risk a northern attack. Come in through the forest and just expect some casualties along the way. If we can get through the woods and bum-rush the bunkers, we can overwhelm them and come right up to the house itself. I think if we take the house with all those kids in it, the rest of them will surrender just to protect the kids."

Jim nodded, a smile on his face. "Then we take all their stuff, not just half, and the farm is ours."

Peter grinned back at him. "You're an idiot, Jim, my friend. I was never going to honor that deal anyway. If she'd been stupid enough to surrender, all it would have done is thrown the defenders into some confusion. Made them less effective. I offered it just in case they'd fall for it, not because it was a real deal."

Jim smiled and nodded. Ass-kissing psycho. Still, Jim was useful in so many ways, and Peter didn't give two shakes what he did to the prisoners. Or to the White Stag people for that matter—the more scared they were, the more they followed orders without any back-talk. It was all coming together beautifully.

"Alright, it's almost time. Get our people together, groups of four, and line 'em up on the back side of the hill where we got the livestock off of. When I'm ready, we're gonna run their asses south, right through the woods and into those bunker things. I mean, they can't *all* get killed by two guys in dirt holes, right?"

* * *

0845 HOURS - ZERO DAY +28

Cassy sat at a window in her loft bedroom with Michael at another, each armed with a 7mm hunting rifle. Their roles during the impending attack would be primarily to direct the flow of battle via Ethan's radios, but also act as snipers for any "targets of opportunity," as Michael called them.

Michael said, "If they're smart, we'll get hit at dusk or dawn. But controlling the pace of conflict is hard enough in broad daylight, so we'll probably be engaged soon. Peter's a farmer, not a military man, from what that scout said. He might make some stupid mistakes."

At the mention of the scout, Cassy was flooded with gruesome images of Michael's handiwork, and shuddered. Michael was such a good person. How could she reconcile the man before her now with the savage warrior who could do such things? She fought back the images and reminded herself that Michael had been right. The information they got probably saved lives, and if they won the fight for the farm it would only be because Michael had stacked the deck in their favor with the knowledge he'd gained.

Cassy said, "I hope it's soon. The wait is killing me. But I'm terrified, as well."

Michael looked at Cassy intently, no doubt sizing her up. He must have been okay with what he saw, because he looked away and back out the window once again. "We're all terrified. Don't fight it, channel it. Use it. We feel fear for a reason. You *can* channel it so that it helps rather than hinders you. Adrenaline is a hell of a combat drug, and we all make our own," he said, and shrugged.

Cassy didn't reply. There was no need. She wasn't in the mood for chatter anyway, and Michael probably wasn't either, though he was too much the good warrior, loyal subordinate, to say so to the Clan leader. Cassy looked out the windows, gazing first out the north window and then the east, looking over one of the ponds. At least the pond was peaceful. Michael had the other two windows covered. She could focus on just these two.

Well, the window to the north didn't show much, just the foxholes and the patch of food forest between the house and the hilltop. The woods blocked her view farther uphill. So she found herself gazing east, at the pond. It looked so peaceful, like life used to be before the invasion. The foliage around the pond was beautiful; half were useful plants and water-loving things like foxtails, but the other half were flowers and little fruit-bearing shrubs. The water was still, save for the ripples left in the wake of three ducks, who paddled around looking for food. Good luck, little ducks.

Two loud bangs ripped Cassy out of her daydreaming. Adrenaline spiked for a second, and her mind reeled to catch up. Michael was saying something, but it just sounded like gibberish. He furrowed his brow in irritation and repeated himself, and Cassy understood this time. The enemy was coming, and from the north. Dammit, that was *not* what they'd wanted.

A radio crackled to life: "Sniper One to base. Multiple incoming hostiles, at least fifty, with small arms." There was another *bang* of rifle fire, and another. "Four down, they're still coming. Retreating to fighting positions November One and Two, request reinforcements *now!* Over."

Cassy moved to grab another radio, but Michael was faster and she heard his steady, hard voice saying, "All units, all units. September positions move to reinforce November One and Two, *even numbers only.*"

So, they'd bet wrong putting most of their defenses on the south side, and Michael was diverting half of the southern units north to back up the fighting positions there. Cassy knew she'd soon have plenty to shoot at.

Three seconds later, Cassy saw the two people who'd been in the sniper stands sprinting out of the woods toward the foxholes, and they literally dove into the positions, landing in a jumble of arms and legs with the people already in those foxholes. Just as they landed, Cassy heard what a real firefight sounded like when at least a dozen spots in the dark woods lit up from the muzzle flashes of Peter's people. She was in shock and stared for a few seconds, but in every second she saw another muzzle flash joining the first ones. So, they were keeping in cover in the woods, for the moment. Good.

Michael grabbed her shoulder. "Cassy! Engage the damn enemy!"

Cassy shook her head to clear it and then brought up her rifle. She scanned the tree line through her scope but saw nothing at first. Then she heard Michael's calm voice again. "Cassy, look for the muzzle flash. Fire at the flashes." Okay, that made sense even to her adrenaline-fogged brain.

There! A flash! She fired at it, but was either hasty or shaking—she couldn't tell which—because the shot went wide. But now that she'd focused on a flash, she could see the person behind it. She counted to three as she sighted in, took a deep breath, exhaled halfway and then held it. In that second, she lightly squeezed the trigger. *Just like hunting...* There was a deafening sound when her rifle went off, and the scope view jiggled from the recoil, but she saw enough to realize she'd practically decapitated an attacker. Holy shit. She'd never killed anyone before, and the realization that she had just ended a life hit her like a hammer. She'd tried to kill Jim in the first days of the EMP, but that was different. That was personal. This was just... some person following orders.

And then she was struck by the realization that, despite the shock of it, killing that man didn't actually bother her. Would she feel it later? She'd have to ask Michael about that when this was over, if they both lived through this. But for now she shoved the thought away and sighted in on another muzzle flash in the woods.

* * *

1100 HOURS - ZERO DAY +28

Peter walked with his people back to their farmhouse headquarters and fumed. It just didn't make any damn sense. How could a few dozen people hold off his army like that? They'd exchanged fire for maybe half an hour before Peter called the retreat. He could have kept going, of course, but once all those other Clan fighters had joined the battle, he knew a simple rush to overrun the foxholes would have seen his people slaughtered. He outnumbered the Clan three-to-one by his scouts' estimates, yet they'd held him off.

Worse, Peter lost half a dozen people—three to Clan rifles, and three were lost to booby traps in the woods. Another half dozen were wounded. He hadn't expected so many traps. The bastards had littered the woods with them. Time to reevaluate his strategy.

Peter caught sight of the prisoner, Jaz, tied to the tree out front. Normally her condition would have mildly disgusted him—Jim was a bastard, that was certain—but after the defeat he'd just suffered, it brought him a measure of savage joy. Her clothes were torn, nose probably broken, lower lip torn open, left eye swollen completely shut, and she was covered in dirt, bruises, blood, and other things Peter preferred not to think about. After Jim had finished "questioning" her the night before, he'd returned to the house full of smiles. All Jaz had done since then was sit curled up into a ball, back against the tree to which she was bound.

All the rage he felt toward the Clan for embarrassing him today was somewhat cooled by the thought of what Jim had done to Jaz. It was actually *satisfying* to see one of the Clan so thoroughly defeated, as long as he didn't think much about how she'd got that way. Yep, good ol' Jim. And he figured that his people seeing Jaz in that condition would help keep them in line.

"Okay, enough of that," Peter mumbled. He turned to Jim and said, "The plan didn't work. I figured we had the people to just smash through, and if we'd had another dozen, I might have tried. Even if we'd lost half our people, we'd still have had twice what the Clan has now. But you know what they say about wishes and fishes. We didn't have another dozen, and we have even fewer fighters now. We need a new plan, Jim."

Jim lowered his eyes, avoiding Peter's gaze. "We all thought it would work, boss. It isn't anyone's fault but the Clan's. Jaz says they got some Marines with them, and they must be the ones who figured out how to set up for a north attack like that. I wish we had some Marines of our own, but the closest we got is a guy who was a County Sheriff, an Army Reservist who was basically a file clerk, and a retired Navy guy. You know he never saw any ground action."

"Shit, Jim. I know what we have. That isn't what I asked," Peter snapped. "I need a new goddamn plan whether we have real soldiers or not. We have to figure out the Clan's weakness. Taking Jaz didn't make 'em surrender, so I don't think snagging more of them will work either. Put on your big-boy britches, buddy, and think this through with me."

Jim was quiet for a moment, and Peter let him think. Then Jim said, "Boss, what if we came at them when they couldn't see us? If they can't see us, they can't hit us. Yeah, this could work. What if we came at them in the middle of the night? I'm sure we'll set off some of their traps, but we can afford to lose another half dozen. At night, they won't know where we are until we're right on top of them, where our numbers will do the most good, and they can't use those freakin' snipers so well. Those are what got most of the hits on our people, you know."

Peter glanced at Jim again. Maybe he wasn't such a caricature after all. "I've considered that, too. Alright, let the sheeple know the plan, and get us ready. We move out tonight."

* * *

1300 HOURS - ZERO DAY +28

Ethan sat next to Amber, Michael, and Tiffany at lunch. All the various little knots of friends were eating together today, which was understandable. They'd just faced their first test of battle as a full Clan—more than just the group he'd saved at his old bunker—and come through the other side. They had a right to show some pride.

Michael said, "See how they're all smiling and laughing? We all know Peter isn't done with us, but this is the afterglow of surviving a firefight. It's as good as sex, and even better for some people."

"I'm glad we're all thrilled," Michael's wife, Tiffany, said. "Some of these people haven't seen a fight before. I remember what a high I felt after our first gunfight, and it's almost as good this time around. Like the time before that, too."

Ethan chuckled, and said, "Between the firefight at my house, the skirmish at the garage on our way to the farm, and the encounters with the Red Locusts, I feel like a real Vet now, and I'm still riding an endorphin high this time. Michael, does that ever go away? This intense thrill after surviving a battle?"

"Negative," Michael replied. "Nothing ever compares to the first time, but it never gets to be routine, either. Food will always taste better, flowers look prettier, all that stuff, after every battle you get in. I've been through dozens, if you include the crap storm over in the Sandbox, and I'm still in a rush. No, it never gets old."

"The sex is better after, too," Tiffany said with a smirk.

Amber giggled, and Ethan suppressed a grin. It sure would be nice to find out how much better the sex was after battle...

Michael looked Ethan in the eyes, wearing half a grin, and said, "So when are you and Amber going to find out for yourselves?"

Ethan was taking a drink of cider when Michael said that, and he nearly choked, some cider shooting out of his nose. Did he really hear that right? Holy crap! Maybe the Clan was ready to move past Jed's death now, in the face of this implacable enemy. "Leave it to the jarhead to be direct," he said, wiping his face with a cloth napkin. "We, uh, haven't really talked about that... There's been a lot going on lately."

Tiffany nodded and then rested her head on Michael's shoulder. "We've all been talking about it, and we think it's time to let you two do what you want. Frank agrees, by the way. We're not saying you have to get together, but if that's something you both want, we won't c-block you anymore."

Ethan said, "Thanks, guys. I know Amber and my

friendship has been hard on you guys and Frank, what with Jed's loss, and of course he's missed by more than just Amber. We've done as you all asked, to keep the peace in the Clan. But yeah, I'm glad we can move on now if she and I decide that's what we still want."

Michael's face grew serious then, and he said, "I recommend you don't wait too long to decide. We don't know when Peter will be back, but it will be soon. None of us are guaranteed to still be here tomorrow, so live for today while you can. Take it from me. I lost too many friends in the Middle East who planned to do something *tomorrow*, but then ate an IED *today*. I plan on making Tiff wake the neighbors, tonight."

"Good point," Ethan said. He turned to Amber. "I have some 20s things to do in the bunker tonight, with the radios and all that. I could use company."

Amber's face turned a little red. "Sounds good to me. That might be the only place around here to get any alone time."

* * *

0100 HOURS - ZERO DAY +29

Cassy couldn't sleep. She'd been in bed for hours but couldn't stay still long enough to doze off. Instead, she found herself kicking her legs, spinning in place, doing anything but sleeping. In frustration, she left out a long breath and sat up. Screw it. If she couldn't sleep, she might as well go be useful. She'd been sleeping in clothes since learning of Peter's approach, so she only had to slide on her boots and grab her rifle. Then she crept out of the loft room, through the overcrowded living room, and walked outside into the fresh night air.

She looked around for a moment, enjoying the relative quiet. There were only five people on guard duty at night, working in four-hour shifts. She could only see the guard in the tower, however; the others were hidden around the perimeter with radios to alert the Clan if Peter came in the night like the boogeyman. Ethan slept in the bunker with the central radio setup, maps, and so on, so in an emergency they had a communications center in a safe place.

Cassy couldn't see the person in the tower well, but they could probably see her. Dean Jepson had made a couple pairs of night vision goggles out of colored film, welding goggles, high-intensity infrared LED lights, and a glue stick. A darn genius, he was, even if he was as grumpy as anyone she'd ever met. One set was kept in the guard tower, and the other was in the bunker for safekeeping, to swap out with the tower set if needed. Cassy smiled as she thought of Michael saying, "Two is one and one is none."

With nothing else to do and nowhere else to go, Cassy decided to go keep the tower guard company. Besides, maybe an hour spent staring off into darkness would bore her to sleep. She walked slowly toward the tower, taking care not to trip on anything in the darkness. There was only faint moonlight that night, and it would really suck to be sidelined from her duties if she was foolish enough to sprain her ankle wandering around outside at night.

Cassy slung her M4 over her shoulder and climbed up the makeshift ladder, up to the guard tower's platform. It was barely large enough for two people, so the guard helped her up through the hatch. Cassy saw that it was Gary on duty at the moment—the man who'd sprained his wife's wrist, but he'd behaved himself since then. He and his wife had turned into good additions to the Clan since that incident.

"Hey, Gary. Anything moving out there?" she asked, voice nearly in a whisper.

Gary shook his head and gave her a thumbs-up. Good, nothing going on. Cassy didn't really expect Peter to brave the Clan's traps in the dark, but one never knew what a desperate and deranged lunatic might try.

Michael had said that a night attack was actually likely, but Cassy didn't really believe it. Without electric lights, such an attack by untrained farmers would be far too bloody for a guy like Peter, who had to rely on superior numbers to get what he wanted, rather than negotiating. Too bad because Cassy would have jumped at the chance to negotiate giving herself up in exchange for the Clan's right to be left in peace, if he could have been trusted to keep his word. If Peter wasn't such an evil prick. If it hadn't turned out that the guy thought he was doing the Right Thing, on a mission from God. You couldn't negotiate with someone like that except from a position of strength. The Clan was not in a position of strength.

"What's on your mind?" Gary asked quietly.

Cassy realized she'd zoned out, off in her own little world thinking about Peter and too many what-if scenarios. "Just wishing we had more options. More time to get ready for him, at least."

Gary shrugged. "I know. We all do. But it is what it—"

BANG.

A shower of blood sprayed the tower's wall behind Gary, the bullet punching through the center of his chest and exiting his back. Gary wore a surprised look on his face. He reached out toward Cassy and opened his mouth, but all that came out was a torrent of blood, and then he collapsed. He was a marionette whose strings had been cut.

Cassy dropped to the floor by reflex and spent half a second—a seeming eternity—staring into Gary's now-vacant eyes. Those bastards. Anger welled up within her, replacing the spike of fear that had sent her to the floor, and she burst into motion. First she scrambled over Gary's bloody body, reached out, and slapped a switch mounted to the wall. The switch was tied to an old siren they'd recovered. Connected to the battery power system of the homestead, the siren wailed into life.

Then she tore the night vision goggles from poor Gary's head and hastily donned them herself. Picking up her rifle, she peered over the edge of the guard tower's wall, glanced, then ducked back down. She knew the flimsy walls would provide no real cover, but they offered a bit of concealment as long as she stayed down. Bitterly, the thought crossed her mind that the tower had been one of the preparations she had argued with Dean about. If only she'd let him put up the structural reinforcements, and the sandbags... But no, there had been no time.

What if, what if, what if. Enough of that. There would be time enough later for soul-crushing guilt about Gary and what might have been if she'd listened to Dean. She shook her head to clear the thoughts.

A bright flash and a scream from out in the Jungle announced that another one of Michael's traps had worked, and Cassy grinned savagely. Now only some seventy to go. She brought her rifle up and, with her night vision goggles, saw two of the White Stag people making their way out of the Jungle and into the raised beds area. Deep breath. Aim. Exhale. Fire. The muzzle flash practically blinded her, but she did see one of the approaching enemy fall over backwards, head snapping back. There would be no victory feast for that bastard. She ducked back down and crawled to the tower wall's other end, over Gary's body. She hardly noticed him now, focused on the fight at hand.

Gary's radio crackled, and Ethan's groggy voice came out, sounding somehow both frantic and calm at the same time. "SITREP, Tower."

Cassy fumbled at the radio, but her hands didn't seem to work right. "Shitty adrenaline," she cursed, then made the damn radio work. "Clan One to base. Tower One is down. Multiple OpFor coming through the Jungle. Over."

There was a long pause, and Cassy imagined the chaos in the bunker right now as Ethan tried to manage a dozen radios, a dozen points of intelligence coming in so that the Clan could respond the best way possible. Odd to think the survival of the Clan might rely on Ethan's radio skills, honed only by years of playing online games.

Finally, the radio crackled to life again. "Clan One, you have a dozen enemy about to exit the Jungle. They'll be on top of the foxholes in seconds. Hit them hard, we can't let the foxholes get overrun! Over."

Cassy peered over the wall, and dammit if Ethan hadn't been right. She could see one person, then another and another, all filtering out of the tall vegetation of the Jungle. She took aim, but then lost the target, and glanced over the top of her scope. The enemy fighters were *sprinting* toward the foxholes! Thank God they were occupied. She saw burst after burst fired from the Clanners in those holes, but more and still more enemies came out of the Jungle. She took aim, and fired. Another of the assholes dropped. She aimed at another, a woman, and dropped her in her tracks. It looked like combined fire from the foxholes and those behind the earthbag framework of a house stopped the drive. The enemy took cover behind raised garden beds, and both sides began to pop off shots at each other—mostly ineffectively.

But where were the rest of them? Peter had seventy-odd fighters, and there were no more than a third of them attacking from the Jungle. A shiver ran up her spine. Something wasn't right.

- 11 -

0130 HOURS - ZERO DAY +29

CASSY ROSE UP to fire again, but with her night vision goggles she saw an attacker aiming his rifle right up at her, and she threw herself to the floor again. Part of her was horrified at the blood soaking into her clothes—Gary's blood—but the thought was gone as fast as it had come. She grabbed the radio again and shouted over the din of battle. "Bunker One, where's the rest of them? I only see a couple dozen!"

Ethan's reply came immediately. "No sign of them anywhere, Clan One. You have heavy movement to the south-west. They're focusing on just a few foxholes. We need supporting fire or they'll be overrun."

"Dammit! Where the hell are the rest of 'em?" Cassy knew the question deserved no answer, but an answer came anyway: "We'll tell you when we find out." She put down the radio, embarrassed that she'd wasted Ethan's time. Maybe Peter learned his lesson and was holding the rest in reserve. If those foxholes got overrun, there could be an onslaught of a few dozen enemies charging through the gap—right at the houses, kids and all. If only she'd stayed in the loft with

Michael. He would know what to do. But she *wasn't* in the loft, and Michael was probably as busy as she was. She heard his voice echoing in her head: "Any action is better than inaction."

Okay, well those foxholes had to hold. Everything could ride on it, and to the north all was quiet. "Bunker One, redirect everything but the snipers from the north side to reinforce the houses and the foxholes on this side. We have to hold them!"

Cassy leapt to her feet and fired at two White Stag people running southward, toward the foxholes there, and the noise of it blocked out Ethan's reply. Both targets dropped, and Cassy scanned for more enemies. It was a target-rich environment.

* * *

Choony's muscles strained under the weight of the man he dragged, but the adrenaline coursing through him made it difficult to tell if he'd have pulled muscles tomorrow. The Clanner had been shot in the shoulder. Those could easily be fatal, unlike in the movies, though the guy—whose name he couldn't remember right now—might survive. But Choony's job was only to drag the poor fellow from the foxhole to the house, where the Clan had set up a makeshift field medical unit.

He was maybe halfway across the open ground between foxhole and house when he noticed puffs of dirt flying up around him. Someone was shooting at him, he realized. Between teeth gritted from effort he muttered, "We take refuge in the Buddha, the Dharma, the Sangha..."

Fire streaked across his right arm and he glanced down, confused. Blood welled up through a small hole in his light jacket. His arm still worked, however. At least for now. There was no way to tell if he'd been hit or only grazed, but it didn't matter. The fear and adrenaline washed through him, cleansing him of thoughts of pain or danger, and he redoubled his efforts. In moments that seemed like lifetimes, he was through the doorway of the house and into relative safety. A big .50-caliber bullet probably couldn't get through those earthbags.

The "doctor," whom Choony remembered was really just a paramedic, scrambled toward him to take the heavy load. "Where's he hit?" the doctor asked while he and Choony got the injured man onto a makeshift cot. The doctor's voice cracked, and Choony decided not to comment on it. The man was probably scared beyond belief.

"Shoulder, where the blood is," Choony said. His words came out fast and clumsy, his tongue seeming to rebel at the fine control needed to make words come out. "Hey, doc. You got this." Then there was no more time. He left the paramedic to work on the injured man and dashed toward the door again. Someone screamed for more ammo, and Buddha be honored, Choony was damn well going to deliver it if he survived long enough.

* * *

Frank knelt with his back against the wall of the main house. He'd fired at two White Staggers coming toward the building but missed and had to duck back when they returned fire. He grinned savagely. It certainly was nice to have an M4 when his enemies had only hunting rifles. One, two, three; he popped his rifle around the corner, ready to fire, but saw that the enemies were only a dozen paces from him now, and running. Shock made him pause, but animal, hard-wired reflexes took over, and he fired at the man in front; his head seemed to collapse. Frank felt somehow detached from what was going on and was surprised to see two bloody blossoms sprout on the second man's chest, and he fell forward carried by his own momentum.

Frank felt frozen, confused. His mind wouldn't catch up. Abruptly, he realized he was pulling the trigger on an empty weapon. He'd unloaded an entire magazine into the two men who now had far more holes in them than he'd realized. He ducked back behind the corner and pulled out a fresh magazine. Shaking hands dropped it, but he fumbled for it in a near-panic and finally got the damn thing in and ready. Okay, it was definitely time to take a deep breath and get his shit together, he realized. By the time he counted to five, his mind was starting to catch up from its shock.

Frank heard the sound of gunfire rising in volume, at first as though it came from underwater, but then louder, and finally the cacophony of noise burst into full volume. Damn if it didn't sound like the intensity of the firefight was trailing off a bit. Maybe they were pushing back the attackers? His spirit soared. He swept his field of view with his scope, looking for another target.

His radio crackled, and he heard Ethan's voice. "All unengaged units move north, enemy forces overrunning sniper nests!" Ethan's voice was high-pitched, tense as a wire, and he was talking too fast. "Shit," Frank said, and turned to rush to the north end of the building. Ahead he saw a person falling from a tree—one of the snipers, now a casualty. The other was probably dead now, too. And then he saw it: a horde of people he didn't recognize filtering out from the food forest and headed directly south, right at the house, right at Frank. A new, cold terror sprinted up his spine. The children—all of them—were sheltered inside the house Frank was using for cover.

* * *

Cassy slid down the tower's handmade ladder, feet clamped to both sides of it to slow her descent. She hit the ground and sprinted toward the house. She reached for the knob at almost full speed and almost missed it, but at the last moment it turned, and she shouldered her way through the now-unlatched door. To the few people inside guarding the children she shouted, "North windows! Incoming!" but she didn't slow down.

She darted between the kids and the furniture to the loft ladder and scrambled up it. As her head rose over the edge of the loft floor, she spotted Michael in the window, methodically firing one round after another and aiming with expert quickness between shots. She heard him muttering, "Five..." BANG "Six..."

"SITREP," Cassy shouted as she unslung her rifle and took position next to Michael. She saw a field of enemies rushing out of the trees, over and through the unmanned foxholes, and across open ground toward the house.

"OpFor engaging with overwhelming force. South attack was a diversion, and it worked. We'll be overrun."

BANG.

Cassy fired a burst, but her target dropped down into a foxhole at the last moment. She missed. "Get the damn kids and take 'em south, Michael!"

BANG. "Negative, Clan One. OpFor engaging from the south still, they'd be cut down. Shut up and shoot."

The next twenty seconds seemed a lifetime, as so often was the case during a firefight. Cassy knew that now, and it seemed odd for her to know that. She steadied her breathing and began the rhythm of fire, breath, aim, fire. Time seemed to vanish altogether then. And every target she fired at was replaced by two more.

Click, and her magazine was empty. She automatically reached to her ammo vest for another, but found it empty as well. "What the hell…" It took a moment for her realize what this meant. "Michael, ammo!"

"Grab the weapon you left up here," he said, voice flat and tense. His battle mode. It would be damn nice to have that ability herself…

Cassy stumbled to the far side of the loft, where she'd left her scoped hunting rifle earlier when she had gone for her walk. When her world wasn't crashing down around her. Just as her hand reached the rifle she heard two thundering booms—the meaty report of shotgun fire from the defenders downstairs. This was followed by a staccato of different blasts. Shit, the attackers, armed with a variety of weapons, must have gotten inside and were firing at the children's guardians. Bile rose in her throat.

A silence fell across the farm for a second as every member of the Clan realized what those sounds meant. She glanced through the window to the north. There was little to see in the dim and dark of night, but with her goggles she saw a few enemy fighters; they too had frozen. Predator and prey, locked in time for one crystal-clear moment, awaiting the drama's grand finale.

A strange voice roared up to the loft from below, a woman's voice: "Order this to stop or the children die. Please don't make me do it. *Please.*" There was desperation in the voice, the sound of someone following orders they didn't like but would obey. Bitch…

Cassy took a deep breath and slowly let it out. Her mind raced, but every option she thought of ended with dead kids. Shit. Checkmate. So much for God being on their side.

"Michael. It's over."

* * *

0600 HOURS - ZERO DAY +29

Frank sat in the dirt with the rest of the men of the Clan. He squinted against the newly rising sun and avoided looking at the stack of Clan and Stag bodies that the losers had been forced to pile up, full of both enemies and friends. Frank's arm was haphazardly bandaged, at least. Peter had let the Clan's wounded get patched up, but not until his own people were tended to. In the time that had taken, two of the Clan had died from wounds that didn't have to be fatal. Frank tried to fuel a rage inside himself, but it was too damn tiring. The wind was gone from his sails, well and truly gone. He glanced around at the other Clan men and saw nothing but defeat and resignation on their faces.

Not all was a complete loss, however. He hadn't seen Choony among either the seated Clan men nor in the pile of bodies stacked in front of the assembly. Nor had he seen Ethan, so there was hope at least that the bunker was still in Clan hands. It wasn't much—Ethan was just one guy—but Frank held tightly to that tiny spark of hope.

Peter said, "Bring the women out one by one. Have them go to their man, if they still have one, or sit over there." He pointed to the right of the Clanners, over by the tower just to the north.

Frank looked at Peter for just a second. Long enough to see the smug asshole smirking. Then he waited with a mix of hope and terror as the women were led out. Would his wife, Mary, be among them? Cassy? Grandma Mandy? Slowly, the women filed out and sat next to their boyfriends or husbands, or those they just wanted to be near in this time of tragedy. Those without someone to sit with were roughly shoved to the side to sit together.

His heart soared when Mary came out and sat beside him, her plump cheeks fairly glowing red and eyes narrowed.

Maybe no one else could tell, but Frank knew his wife enough to know she was only barely keeping her temper under control. He took her hand and squeezed twice, rapidly. It was their "calm down" signal. He relaxed only slightly when she looked away from Peter and down at the ground in front of her.

Frank then watched wordlessly as the occupiers separated the unattached men to the far side of the attached Clan survivors, away from the unattached females. Peter then strode up and down the row of Clanners, looking at each face intently once again. Finally, Peter said, "Bring out the spy." Frank cringed inwardly at the steely voice. It sounded almost inhuman, totally lacking empathy or even enthusiasm. Maybe only violence and murder would fill whatever had eaten a hole in Peter's soul.

There was a gasp from the north end of the Clan lineup, which spread down the line toward Frank, until he saw Cassy and he too gasped. Almost every inch of her was covered in blood, although she didn't move as though she had been injured. Hopefully that blood belonged to some of the White Stag people. The vision of him mowing down two of the attackers brought a thrill, and he had to suppress the urge to grin, until he came back to reality.

Peter's goons dragged Cassy over to him. With a swift thrust of a rifle butt to her gut, they forced her to kneel in front of Peter. And Frank saw the slumped shoulders, the look on her face, and knew that his friend's spirit was utterly crushed. She'd failed them, she'd be thinking, and he wished he could go comfort her. She had made the Clan's loss horribly expensive to Peter; he hoped nobody missed how many more invaders the stack of bodies held than Clanners. She'd hardly wasted a bullet during that final, incredible firefight, and it was her first experience in battle. *She failed no one.* He wished she could see that, but of course she wouldn't. She wouldn't be Cassy if she did.

Peter stood tall and preened, the asshole, sneering at Cassy as his goons brought out a heavy chain and a padlock. He grinned as they put the chain around Cassy's neck and locked it on. Frank only hoped it wasn't too tight for her to breathe, but she didn't seem physically distressed. She hardly seemed to notice it at all.

"Well," said Peter with his voice pitched to carry. Even that prick's *voice* sounded cocky. "As I told my people, there was no way God existed in a world where this woman's crimes didn't come back to bite her in the ass. Karma, if you prefer. I'm happy to be the one to deliver her comeuppance, after what she did."

Cassy spoke in a low voice, but it was loud enough for Frank to hear her in the otherwise silent scene playing out. "I did nothing to you, Peter. Not to you, and not to your people. And they know it, even if you don't. Fear—"

Peter cut her off, a brief flash of rage washing across his face, which Frank thought was interesting and filed away for future use. Maybe his temper or pride could be used against him. Peter said, "Shut up, woman. I know what I saw. You fled from us, and then *they* came with their sprays and their missiles. Half my people were killed that day. Perhaps I couldn't get justice on them for what they did, but I sure could get justice for what you did."

"I fled because you were shooting at me, before you knew who I was or why I was there. You tried to murder me, and I fled. That's all that happened involving me," Cassy said. "And I know your people all saw the shitty things the invaders did all along the way. Or did you forget Lancaster? Were all of those men, women, and children also spies?"

Peter clenched his jaw, and then visibly forced himself into a relaxed, confident posture. "They died for resisting the invaders, just as my people did. And now, just like your people did for resisting me. You led them alright—straight to their deaths." Peter turned to Cassy's guard and said, "Go chain her to something, where everyone can see her. If she tries to run, then just shoot the bitch."

Cassy didn't respond. Her face just went blank, and she lowered her gaze to the ground again. Frank's heart went out to her. Clearly Peter's "you led them to their deaths" remark had scored a hit. It's what he thought when she called out her surrender, and she still must think there was some truth to what Peter said, but any Clanner would tell her it was total bullshit. Firstly, because many more of Peter's people had died than Clanners. And secondly, Cassy had done all she could, more than anyone had thought she could, and everyone knew it. She was being harder on herself than anyone in the Clan would be. Even Choony, with his insistence on total honesty, would tell her so.

He paused. Where was Choony, anyway? Frank tried to look around without being obvious about it, but he still didn't see any sign of their new Korean Clanner. Maybe he died. The thought made Frank somehow terribly sad. Amber and Ethan were missing too, but he suspected they were safe for the moment. Everyone else was present, either sitting down before Peter or laid out somewhere in the pile. A goddamn pile! Peter was a monster.

* * *

1300 HOURS - ZERO DAY +29

Ethan sat with his head in his hands, elbows resting on the desk. Amber sat next to him, staring blankly at the screen as it cycled through one camera view after another, over and over. Neither had said much all day, nor touched, though they'd fallen asleep in each other's arms crying, long after the battle had ended.

He didn't much believe in God, but he'd silently thanked Him for the blessing of having Amber in the bunker with him when the attack began. Otherwise, she'd be out there, either with the single women or in the pile. As it was, she'd tried to leave the bunker when bullets began to fly, but Ethan had remotely locked down the bunker door. She'd been more pissed than he'd ever seen her, but shit, there was nothing she could have done to help against those odds beyond catching a bullet for someone else. He'd worried she would stay angry since she wanted desperately to rescue her child, but as they had watched the Clan surrender, Amber, shaking, had reached out, took his hand, and started to weep.

Ethan was still in shock. How far things had fallen in such a short amount of time. One minute he and Amber were racking up sack time—and boy had that been amazing—and the next minute they were scrambling to the Comm Center naked, their interrupted lovemaking all but forgotten. Even now, their overly enthusiastic, much-repressed sex seemed like it happened long ago. Not exactly irrelevant, but his perspective had changed. There were definitely more important things than getting to lay some pipe with a gorgeous woman, even if he'd been more certain every day that he was in love with her. He still was in love, but now protecting her meant something different. Now it meant keeping her a virtual prisoner, hopefully without her realizing it.

"Anything new?" Ethan asked. His voice sounded strained and thin in his own ears.

"No," Amber replied without looking over. Her voice was flat, emotionless. She must still be in shock, too. "Cassy's chained to the basketball hoop out in the hot sun, just like before. I don't think that's her own blood, though, she's moving around just fine. When she moves at all. Frank has spent most of the day giving Peter the Great a guided tour, or in the house talking with Peter, I guess. The audio is partly out in the house, though, so we can't hear very well unless they raise their voices. They've been speaking quietly..."

"Super. Single men still in the livestock pen? Single women still in the second house? Families still working the fields under guard?" Ethan knew the answers, of course, but he had to ask. It was maybe the tenth time in the last two hours. He kept hoping for a crack in Peter's control. The situation was too unstable to stay as-is for too long. But when it broke, it might break in any direction, and that had him sweating.

"Yes." Amber's reply broke through his tension and she continued, "Michael's fine, but Sturm and Mueller are both in the singles groups. I hope they don't get singled out for their experience, but at least they were in civilian clothes. All of the kids are okay. Thank God for Grandma Mandy—she's been looking after them for the most part. Just knowing that is helping me not go crazy. And I haven't seen a visual on Choony yet, so that's promising."

"I hope he got out," Ethan said. "If he did, and if we can get some sort of communications to him, then we have an unknown X-factor to work with us in freeing our people. Too bad he won't kill these shitheads."

Ethan glanced down at the paper between his elbows. It was a list of the Clan dead, so far as he could tell, and his best guess at a tally of Stag dead. He was trying to get a force count, or whatever Michael had called it. It seemed the Clan had lost ten adults, but he couldn't be positive. Some might only be wounded, though he doubted it. His best estimate was that the Stag force lost at least twice that many. Good, the bastards deserved that and worse.

The problem, however, was that it left the Clan with *maybe* twenty adults, while the Stag people still numbered about twice that. No doubt about it, the battle had been bloody on both sides. But in the end, Peter had the numbers to throw warm bodies at the Clan knowing someone would get through somewhere, eventually. He didn't seem to care about his own dead. How could his control not be tenuous? The Stag people's fear must be pretty powerful.

Another thing Ethan had noticed was that the attackers had clearly known where the kids were, but he didn't want to think Jaz would have revealed that. Peter could just as easily have gotten that intel from a scout with binoculars. Hard to know. But Jaz was solid, she acted like someone who had finally found her family after a long search, and he decided to believe the scout theory.

Amber continued, "They've been bringing Clanners into the main house one at a time. I think they're questioning everyone. Only a few people even know there's a bunker here at all, so we should be safe in that regard. He's going to wonder what happened to all the stored food, I bet. Most of it's in here with us."

Ethan asked, "When the Clan people come out, do they look like they've been beaten up or anything?" Frikkin totalitarian governments everywhere, even now at the end of the USA...

"No. He'll probably get around to that, if we're right about the kind of person he is, but Peter's people haven't tortured anyone but Jaz so far, that I can see."

Yeah, Jaz. The first time Ethan had seen her on the cameras, he cringed. Not just because she looked so terrible, what with blood and scabs and bruises everywhere, but her body language. She had looked broken. Given what she'd been through before she came upon Frank's group when Zero Day came, it would take a lot to break such a resilient woman. But now Jaz kept her eyes downcast, her shoulders slumped, and from what Ethan saw she didn't bother moving at all unless someone prodded her or led her somewhere. And yet, when no one was looking, the camera caught her staring at the Stag people with a gaze that creeped Ethan out. It was cold, and deadly, and if there was any mercy in that stare, Ethan couldn't see it. That look should never have been forced onto Jaz, of all people. Good thing she was being careful not to get noticed when she did that.

"Okay," Ethan said. "Keep an eye out for Choony. If he lives, we'll need his help. He'll be a wild card—think a bit about how he can help. I'm going to go check my email and do a HAMnet broadcast. At least Peter's attack didn't take that away. As far as I can tell, the whole country's future has a lot to do with what I'm rebroadcasting."

Amber said nothing in reply. Ethan nodded, then turned and walked away. Yeah, she was in as much shock as he was and neither had spare emotional energy to give one another just yet. At least they still reached out for each other.

* * *

Steven Wallace sat in a cramped office at a desk that was too big for the space. There was little room to move around. But it didn't matter. His family was well-fed now by the 'vaders. He looked out the tiny, dirt-covered window and thought about the others like him, the ones who'd traded their freedom for slavery, to get food for their families. By the seventh day since the lights went out, only ten of Steven's original group of fellow slaves had survived. Steven shuddered as he remembered his old foreman blowing Mark's brains out for being too exhausted to work. It was a lesson Steven never forgot. He'd begun to take food from the other weary slaves that very day, so he could eat more. Keep his strength up.

And thinking of those other ten slaves, his companions, a

chill ran up his spine. He quickly stuffed the feelings it brought up deep down inside. They'd all died by now, of course, those other ten. Without enough food, it had taken only a few days to burn through them. But then more had come, prisoners of war or criminals or volunteers. As more people ran out of food, there was no shortage of people looking to trade work for food. And the foreman had eventually put him, Steven, in charge. Steven Wallace, the accomplice. Steven the traitor. He hated himself for it, at least as much as the other slaves hated him. But their hatred made it easy to do what the foreman asked. Whip this one, work that one to death.

Eventually he'd been ordered to beat someone to death with a rock, and he'd done as he was told. No way was he going to be the one taking blows from a rock, which was all that would have happened if he refused. The 'vaders rewarded him for that with a desk job.

Now Steven spent his days serving the needs of his old foreman's boss. Filing paperwork or running errands. Passing messages that meant death for someone, but Steven was long past the point where he considered doing anything about it. His fate was sealed. He was a quisling in everything but name.

The only bright side was that he had been able to quietly let the foreman's boss know about all the theft of "People's goods"—with a capital "P"—which the foreman had been managing to do for weeks. Yesterday was a good day. Seeing the foreman's boss—Lt. Chin or some such—get red-in-the-face pissed off, yeah, that was worth it. Screw the foreman. That one was for Mark. Because Steven had done nothing as the foreman murdered the young man, and that guilt had burned into his soul. Dropping the hammer on the foreman did a lot to heal that particular mental wound.

And then the door flew open. Steven looked up in

surprise, only to see several soldiers with guns at the ready. One had kicked in the door, but they didn't even wait for the door to stop moving before the next guy in line had darted in. The soldiers aimed their rifles at him. Steven tried to speak, but his throat closed up with fear and no sound came out.

"You betray foreman," said a young soldier in broken English. "You say for good of People's Army, but foreman your leader. Not the lieutenant. Foreman. Weak American mind, you don't know honor. Foreman is good... Sergeant. Good leader. He want us to tell you, before you die, you family. They now work for him, for your foreman. They good workers, not to be poison by you false loyalty. Goodbye, Steven."

Well, he'd known this day had to come sooner or later. You couldn't be an American and go up in rank without pissing off a Korean, and that rarely worked out. "It seems his boss doesn't know what my foreman's doing, yeah? Just get this shit over with, asshole. Someday your little cocksucker leader is going to take an American bullet right up his ass."

Yeah, saying that felt good. Real good. Might as well go out on a high note. He didn't have long to wait for their response.

- 12 -

1800 HOURS - ZERO DAY +29

CASSY SAT CHAINED all day to the post of the basketball hoop. Dinner had finished up, but from what she could see the Clanners hadn't been given much more to eat than she had—bread and a little bowl of stew—while the White Stag goons ate everything in sight, laughing and joking. It had been a rough day to be stuck there, people-watching.

The single women of the Clan had been paired off to men in Peter's group "for their own safety," which didn't bode well. The Clan's single men, meanwhile, were being kept in the incomplete house for now. They'd been brought food, but hadn't been allowed out, and Cassy was worried about their fate. Peter was the kind of guy who would have little patience for a group of hostile men with no kids to leverage. Meanwhile, the children were locked into the unused horse barn. It was visible but out of the way, and guarded at all times. Their parents would definitely give in to whatever Peter demanded of them. Right now that included serving all those new arrivals who came with Peter.

Cassy heard a noise behind her, footsteps, and she shimmied around to get a look. There stood Jaz, and Cassy nearly wept to see her again. Jaz had several bruises on her face, a torn lip, and a distinct limp. And yet, Jaz smiled when Cassy made eye contact. That poor, poor girl...

"I didn't see you at dinner," Cassy said simply.

"Your friend, Jim, was questioning me again," Jaz replied, and Cassy cried inside to see the traumatized, far-away look in Jaz's beautiful eyes.

"I stabbed him once. If only I'd finished the job. I just couldn't murder him in cold blood. Not back then. Different time, different world. How are you holding up, Jaz?"

Jaz slid with a grunt to the ground next to Cassy, wincing from pain. "It ranks right up there with the day I decided to leave home. I'll live, if they let any of us live. Don't beat yourself up about Jim. All of us have changed a lot since the lights went out. All your friend keeps asking about is where our stockpile of food is. They figured out we don't have enough out here to survive the winter, not with all these people. But don't worry, I didn't tell the bastard about your bunker—I figured Ethan was down there, like, doing something with his radios or whatever."

Well that was a bit of good news. The damn bunker might hold the key to winning the war, if what Ethan had told her was right. "Listen, Jaz, you mustn't tell them about it. You're one of only a few people who actually know where it is. And speaking of Ethan's obsession with those old HAM radios, he's a spy or something, working with some secretive group that's trying to beat back the invaders. What he's doing, it's probably more important than all of us put together. He doesn't talk about it much, but please promise you'll listen to me on this one."

Jaz leaned her head back against the pole. "I promise. Shoot, I wouldn't tell anyway. Screw them. I wouldn't roll on Ethan, either. I doubt Jim will stop if he gets what he wants, anyway. I'm 'too much fun,' as he puts it. Also, Choony's missing. Never found him or his body, Frank said. But I have some bad news for you."

Just great. What could be worse than that? After a long moment of silence, Cassy said, "So what is it, this terrible news?"

"I'm getting to it. It's not easy. They're asking about your kids, Cassy."

A jolt of fear and rage shot through Cassy. What would they want her kids for? Only one reason that she could think of, and that was to punish her. Steely-voiced, she said, "What are they asking?"

"Their scouts saw you and your kids together. They know you have two kids, but they don't know which ones are yours. I guess that scout didn't make it through the last battle, and I hope he burns in Hell. When they were asking about your kids, Brianna was about to step forward, but Gary's wife stepped up to them and put her arms around them, told them to shut up. I forget her name."

"Marla," Cassy said.

"Yeah. Well, she claimed them as her own children," Jaz said. "Frank told them your kids were in the house when the fighting started, and that they must have run off when it began. But Cassy, they're going to grill everyone about their kids, and then grill the kids. It might take a few days, but they're going to figure it out eventually." Jaz paused, her beautiful face stiff from Jim's brutal fun. "I'm sorry, Cassy."

"So Choony was right," Cassy muttered. To Jaz's confused look she replied, "When we wanted to exile Gary for hurting his wife, that one night. Choony was against it. He said it was bad karma, and we should give the man the chance to atone. Boy did he. I was there when Gary died—the first shot of the battle took him out. It's his blood all over me."

Jaz let out a low whistle. "If you'd exiled him or worse,

your kids would be in their hands now. Karma's something else, isn't it."

Cassy nodded. "Karma, or God. Mom says God doesn't control us because of free will, but that He puts bad actions to good purpose. If the incident with Gary hadn't occurred and we didn't face the problem head on, Marla might not have been so brave when my kids were at risk. It seems that since we had the chance to show Gary the mercy Choony wanted, she trusts us."

Jaz was silent a moment, and then said, "I never much believed in God, but after listening to your mom all this time and seeing all these stupid little things that have such a totally big effect on everything... You know? I mean, it can't be all chance. Like, too many bad odds turned into good endings for that."

Cassy chuckled, but then the memory of Gary's blank, dead stare flashed through her mind, and guilt washed over her. If only it had been her that died, instead of him. Why did she deserve to live and he didn't? She forced the image from her mind. "Well, Jaz, if that's how you feel then do me a favor. Say a few prayers for my kids, okay? And don't forget a couple prayers for yourself, too. You've turned out to be a lot stronger and smarter than I ever gave you credit for, back when you stole my granola bars. Things were so very different then..."

A sudden, barking laughter made Cassy jump, startled. She turned and saw Jim there and visualized choking the shit out of him. She realized she was flexing her hands like claws and forced herself to stop. "What are you laughing at, you deviant shit? If my knife had been another inch over, your days of fun in the sun with your 'little tiny buddy' would be over for good."

Jim smirked and replied, "All I heard was that she stole granola bars. The idea of someone getting over on you like that amuses me. Me and my 'little buddy.' And yeah, you did almost kill me. First you fuck me over and then you try to kill me when I figure out what you were up to? Man, I hope Peter treats you the same way you treated our scout. You know, the one you left out to rot. After what you all did to that poor guy, you call *me* a deviant?"

A little of the fire left Cassy's belly. She looked away, no longer able to match Jim's hate-filled gaze. "We were here first. Your people came to take it from us. Bad things happen in war, they say. But I know you don't give half a damn about that scout or what happened to him. You're using a terrible event to manipulate others. It's what you do. It's just your nature. I only have one good memory of you—it's you lying on the road, begging for my help." She tried to imitate his cruel, lazy smile and added dreamily, "Begging."

Jim curled up one side of his mouth in a snarl. "You think you know everything. Well, you don't. Everything I do is for a reason. Peter understands that. It's why he instructed me to handle Jaz *personally*. To make an example of her, and to pay her back for—"

"For what?" snapped Cassy, interrupting him. "She never did anything to you. You *kidnapped* her and did what you wanted, not what you had to."

"Of course you feel that way, bitch. Just like a woman to twist everything up. My wife used to do that, you know. You should shut the hell up now, Cassy. Be smarter than she was."

Then Jim turned on his heels to leave, but stopped. He looked over his shoulder at Jaz. "Don't think I'm done questioning you, miss thang. Tonight's gonna be a long, hard night for you. Maybe I'll even enjoy you for once." He walked away without another look back.

Jaz began to cry softly and put her head in Cassy's lap. The poor girl... Cassy wished for nothing more at that moment than a knife and ten seconds alone with Jim. God willing, she'd get a chance to correct the mistake she'd made on the road when she left Jim alive. Next time, she'd make sure he went down. Hard.

* * *

2300 HOURS - ZERO DAY +29

Choony stretched his legs and wished for the tenth time that night that his parents had sent him into the Boy Scouts when he was young. As it was, he'd made a wholly inadequate shelter that was based on something he half-remembered seeing on YouTube—a branch stretching unevenly between two trees, with numerous smaller branches set to lean against that cross-post. On top of this he'd added dirt, leaves, and even a few fresh branches that were still green enough to hopefully provide some camouflage. It looked terrible, and he was glad Michael wasn't there to see the dismal structure.

Still, it would provide some warmth and shelter when he returned. If he returned, he amended. Tonight he intended to raid the Clan's homestead for a few key supplies. Well, now it was in the White Stag's hands, but that didn't make it their homestead. Anger boiled up, and Choony spent a couple minutes looking into the night sky calming himself, praying for balance and wisdom. There was no use being angry at the world or the people in it. He could only control himself. Anger came when one resisted the world. Peace came with acceptance. But acceptance was harder when people did such evil things. He couldn't merely think "Accept it" and make it so—these were people he'd grown to care about, deeply. Good people, doing the best they could. The homestead was practically a monument to Buddhist philosophy in the face of chaos and collapse, and the Clan didn't even know it.

That thought made him smile at last, and he could feel the anger recede. There was nothing he could do yet to help the Clan, but he could take what he needed to survive and look for opportunities to aid his Clan, even if perhaps only in little ways. The Stag people had cleared out the Red Locusts, so the national forest he hid within was now safer than it had been since the EMPs had destroyed the power grid. The Stags had done him that small favor at least, although unwittingly.

Right. Time to move out. Move slowly and quietly, he reminded himself. Stay low. Stop often and listen. He remembered that advice from Michael, during one of their many conversations, and thought about his first encounter with the Clan under attack, and him wriggling snakelike up that rise to peek over and see what was happening. His recklessness hadn't killed him that time, but he had learned much from Michael. With skill, patience, and a bit of luck, he would be able to sneak in, raid the storage shed, get a good understanding of the Stag's defenses and layout, and get out without being noticed. Of course, one never knew what might be found in the shed, as it was only a way station between the Clanners and the vast amount of goods stockpiled in the bunker. He had no idea where the bunker was and hoped Peter didn't either.

Choony removed all his clothes except for his boots and underwear, to reduce the noise he made, and then it took only perhaps half an hour to find his way in the dark northward to the homestead. He then followed the southern edge of the food forest, heading generally east toward the pond there. He knew where the traps were, but he would have to swim across the pond itself; skirting it would mean a long, noisy struggle through mud and reeds and thorny hedges. The westernmost pond would have been easier to get to and get around, but the guard tower overlooked it and was surely manned now by the cruel occupiers. And the shed he wanted was on the eastern half of the property, in any case.

When he arrived at the shores of the pond, he squatted down to grab handfuls of mud, with which he painted dark lines across his arms and legs, his torso, and finally, his face. Michael had told him once that random lines broke up a silhouette better than simply painting himself all black with mud. Choony wasn't quite sure this was what that meant, but he decided to apply it to his own situation anyway. He had no better ideas to go with.

Choony then crept into the water, careful to avoid splashing, and inched his way in a slow, quiet breaststroke across the water. Arriving at the far side of the pond, he crawled cautiously out through the mud. He was colder now than he'd felt in a long time, but it was still adequately warm outside. He didn't think hypothermia would become a problem before he dried off.

Unfortunately, the swim had removed most of his carefully applied mud. Okay, so that was poor planning on his part, he mused and, shaking his head, set about reapplying a muddy striped camouflage. When it was as good as he knew how to make it, he'd already mostly dried off. "Now for the hard part," he muttered, adding a brief mental prayer for protection.

The trees on this side of the property were sparse; the food forests lay to the north and south of where he stood. Still, there were enough trees between him and the shed that he felt reasonably confident he could make it undetected, with care and a bit of luck. He moved out in a low crouch.

In seconds he made it to the first tree. It was large and old, maybe oak. He wasn't sure. He put his back against it and fought to regain his breath and slow his heartbeat, a calming that took longer than it had actually to move there.

Once he'd brought his adrenaline under better control, he peered around the tree. Two more trees lay between him and the storage shed, the door of which was on the opposite face of the building. He could count five guards, including one in the tower. There were probably more that he couldn't see. The one in the tower was shadowed such that Choony couldn't see him well. The other four, armed with rifles, seemed not to move in any orderly pattern, but then he realized they stayed within a specific and well defined area. They'd walk a set distance, turn around, and walk back, looking mostly at the ground or at the lit, warm-looking house. Choony could imagine them feeling envious of the others inside, relaxing or sleeping.

He rushed to the second tree and repeated his calming process. Now that he was much closer, he could almost make out the face of the nearest guard even in the darkness. That meant it wasn't really all that dark. The moon was almost half full, and there was some ambient light from the house, he noted. When the nearest guard was walking away from him, and the other guards were faced away, he sprinted to the final tree that lay between him and the shed, slowed as he approached it, and crouched down. The back side of the shed was tantalizingly close, only ten or so yards away. Thirty feet of open ground, but the guards were more interested in watching the farm buildings than the perimeter. They were more worried about their new slaves than outside attackers, Choony realized with some slight satisfaction. Good. That would work in his favor, for the moment.

Choony gulped, preparing himself for the most dangerous part—getting to the shed and inside without being seen. It took some ten minutes of waiting to find the right time, when all the guards were faced away at once. The moment he saw his opportunity, Choony crouched as low as he was able and rushed to the back side of the shed. He took deep breaths to steady himself and listened for any cry of alarm, but none came. He then crept around the corner to the south side of the building. One more corner to go and he'd be exposed fully, but only for the few seconds it would take to get inside the shed. He waited until the nearest guard walked by to the end of his route, turned, and walked back. When he was surely well past the shed, Choony gritted his teeth. It was time.

He moved to bolt around the corner but caught himself short at the last instant. Dammit, there was a guard he hadn't seen posted right in front of the shed, leaning on the door. He ducked back and counted to ten to calm himself. He had to think this through. Maybe a distraction would divert this guard? There had to be a way that didn't involve killing anyone. That, he could not do.

As he crouched by the south wall of the shed, however, Choony heard a deep, male voice. "I see you. Don't run. I ain't gonna hurt you, fella. But stay put, and wait. When I say it's clear, get your ass into the shed. Otherwise, I'm gonna raise the alarm."

Choony didn't reply. What the hell was this? That guard should have raised the alarm already. What could he have to say to a rogue Clanner? That was interesting enough in its own right that the trip could be worthwhile even if he walked away with no supplies.

His thoughts were interrupted by the deep, quiet voice again. "Move it, now!" Choony wasted no time. Blind to any danger, he sped around the corner and, finding the shed door open, he bolted inside, into the welcoming dark and cover.

The shed was old enough that the paint had begun to peel, revealing other paint beneath. It was a square of about sixteen feet per side. Inside, he knew, there were floor-to-ceiling shelves along the outer walls and cargo shelves in the middle running front to back, similar to a grocery store's. He resisted the sudden overwhelming urge to flip the light switch. Desperately, he wanted to see what or who might be lurking in the darkness with him. With horror, he realized that he couldn't see well enough to find supplies or locate the empty feed sacks he had intended to use to carry his liberated supplies.

Then a jolt of fear shot up his spine with an intensity that made his scalp tingle... He was trapped inside, if the guard decided to lock him in. Had he just walked stupidly into a deadly trap?

The voice came out of the darkness, the same voice from before. "I seen you peek your fool head around the corner. You're the Oriental guy our scouts saw during recon, right? The missing one."

"Yes. Well, I'm Asian, but yes, that's me. Who are you, and what do you want from me? Can I help you somehow?" It might be foolish to demand information from a man who could be his captor, but there wasn't much time, Choony knew.

"My name's Joe Ellings, mister. What's yours?"

It felt dangerous to say his name. But he had to give an answer, and he just wasn't going to lie to a direct question. Lying caused too much disturbance to his inner peace. He'd learned that long ago. "My friends call me Choony," he replied.

"Okay, Choony. The thing is, you're a Clanner on the loose. You could stir up a lot of crapstorm if you wanted to. I'm askin' you not to though. If you rile Peter up, he's liable to start shootin' people again willy-nilly. Your people. A lot of our people hate that bastard, on account of killing one of our supervisors—the one we most liked—and then keeping them disgusting cannibals around. They're super loyal to him, so long as he's looking, but they don't really give two shakes about any of us. Neither does Peter, I think. But you people, you seem like good folks."

The voice stopped, and it took a second for Choony to realize the guy wanted a reply, now. And yes, this conversation surely was as interesting as he'd hoped. "They're the best people I've ever met, at least among those who aren't Buddhists. I'd risk my life to help them. It's what I'm doing here, going for supplies so I can find the right time to do something. Anything."

"That's a piss-poor plan, Choony," Joe said. "It's gotta be a sudden all-or-nothing, otherwise Peter will just start killing folks. Listen, take my little Stinger flashlight. I got it off one of your military guys, bright as hell and lightweight. Waterproof. Get what you need in there for yourself, and get it quick. Then I'll make a diversion for you to get away the way you came in. But if I want to find you again, me and another guy I think you ought to talk to, where can we find you?"

Wasn't this just a curious development. The wheels turned in Choony's head. "I'm south of the farm, about half hour on foot. In the second copse of trees beyond the farm's forest. There are still a few live traps out there, so be careful."

"Tomorrow," Joe said, "I'll ride out with another guy who doesn't much care for Peter. We'll bring all the supplies we can nick from storage and whatnot. And then we can talk, okay? I reckon you'll just have to trust me on this, if you want to help your people. Stay hid until then."

Choony didn't have to hesitate to make a decision this time. "Thank you, Joseph. I will do as you say," he said, and added under his breath, "Thank you, Buddha." With the small tactical flashlight to help, he went about the shed locating useful things to liberate.

* * *

0400 HOURS - ZERO DAY +30

Taggart grinned at the soldiers—now including a lot of Militia people—who were lined up before him. They wore stolen uniforms for this mission, all of them, and they looked about as close to the OpFor's Arabic troops as they could manage. They were about to take the fight to the enemy in a very real way, and it felt good to finally have direction, a mission to embrace, and an enemy to finally strike back at. Even if it was indirectly, this would be an outstanding PsyOps raid if they succeeded.

Beside him, Eagan said, "Still no word on launching Operation Backdraft, Captain?"

"No, none yet. But the last intel we got from our friends in the 20s via HAMnet said that the Koreans here weren't getting along well with either their Islamic allies or their American minions. Our old friend Spyder in particular is supposedly thinking about his best options for survival, and it may not include continuing support for the invasion forces."

"So, the 'vaders pissed off their gangbanger buddies. And we're going to help that along, right, boss?"

"Captain," he corrected his assistant out of habit. "And yes we are, shitbird. We also hear that the Arabs are beginning to take their Koreans' title of 'advisors' too seriously and aren't rushing to obey orders. This'll screw with the Koreans' program even more when they blame their Arabs for conducting unauthorized operations. Now get the unit moving. We're going north through the tunnels again, and we're going to give Spyder a nasty little surprise."

Eagan walked away whistling, heading toward the assembled troops, and Taggart suppressed another grin. Eagan was nothing if not reliable, at least once the shit hit the fan. He'd talk a lot of smack and drive a self-important

Pentagon pogue insane with his attitude, but he'd get the mission done come hell or high water. When they left Spyder with some fresh corpses and stories of Arabs ambushing his men, it would speed up Spyder's growing schism with his Korean masters. Only good could come from that. And if they were lucky, that schism would also put the Korean-Arab relationship under even more strain. All of which would make everything easier for the people working on Backdraft, whoever they were.

* * *

0800 HOURS - ZERO DAY +30

Grandma Mandy forced a smile at the kids she passed as she moved along in the line for breakfast. They were tired and hungry, scared and uncertain—but they all loved Mandy, and she did her best to bring a little reassurance to the poor dears, despite her condition.

The others had already received their food, and she saw that breakfast this morning would again be that constant stew. She was grateful the occupier gave them even that much. The White Stag leaders were angry, she'd heard, because they couldn't find the Clan's main stockpile of food. They knew there must be one, but few in the Clan knew where it had been hidden, and the rough questioning they'd all been through hadn't revealed the stockpile location. If any Clansmen here knew the location, they had managed to keep quiet. Eventually, she knew, between the fear and the fatigue, someone would let slip that they knew. She prayed it wouldn't happen soon.

Michael's wife, Tiffany, was approaching and Mandy gave her a friendly nod as Tiffany smiled at her. But Tiffany's brow was furrowed ever so slightly, her lips tight—she looked worried.

"Good morning, Tiffany. How's your family?" It wasn't an idle question these days. Michael, an obvious leader, had received rougher treatment than most during the questioning.

Tiffany's worried expression didn't change. "Michael will live, but he's having a hard time keeping up in the fields. They worked him over pretty bad. He's hanging in there like everyone else. But that's not why I'm here."

Mandy darted her eyes around, seeing who was nearby. She could hardly trust anyone with really important information, not when their overlords were beating people and threatening children to get information. "I gather he had nothing useful to tell them," Mandy said. Tiffany would know what she meant. Michael hadn't told what he knew.

"No, he doesn't know anything either," Tiffany said, but Mandy saw that she wasn't really paying attention to the conversation. Something else was chewing at her.

"So what's really on your mind, Tiff? You seem a bit distracted, and I suspect you aren't here to talk about the weather."

"No, sweetie. We've all been talking. Even the kids are concerned. Honestly, you look like hell. We need you, we all do. Is there anything we can get for you? Are you sick? We might be able to find some antibiotics or something, among the Clanners."

Mandy let out a long, slow breath. She'd tried to hide her failing condition, but apparently she looked worse than she'd thought. "Alright, Tiff. Don't spread this around, okay? I'm diabetic. I ran out of insulin a few days ago, but Cassy... found some. A couple bottles. The problem is, she can't get to wherever she'd found it." Mandy raised an eyebrow and hoped Tiffany would catch her meaning. The rest was in the bunker.

"I see." Tiffany's expression went from concern to irritation. "I'll ask around and see if anyone has some more. What are you doing in the meantime? You can't go more than, what, a day or two without insulin? I'll let Michael know how urgent this is." Tiffany shook herself then and added with tentative, clearly false good cheer, "We've gotta keep you around, you know."

Mandy forced another smile, but it was an effort. She wanted to lie down and sleep. It was getting harder and harder to keep going. "No, sweetie, don't talk to Michael about it. Promise me! He's liable to go do something stupid, if you know what I mean, trying to get more insulin for me. Somehow. You've got to keep him around, not me." She again raised an eyebrow and hoped it got her point across. They simply couldn't risk revealing the bunker's location to Peter's goons. "Anyway, I'm taking quarter-doses for now. I have a few days I can hang on like this. But you must never risk the Clan for me, do you hear me? I'm content to stay here or sit with Him, as He wishes, but I could never live with the guilt if, you know, bad things happened to the Clan because it tried to help little old Grandma Mandy. I've had a wonderful life, and I won't spend my family and friends for more, not when I could be sitting with Him instead. Do you understand?"

Tiffany gave her one grim nod, clearly not happy. "But I'll still ask if anyone has some squirreled away from when we were scavenging the nearby empty homes. Who knows, we might luck out." She threw Mandy a helpless look and added, "Either way, I promise I won't press Michael about it."

Meaning, Mandy knew, that she would not ask Michael to risk a sneak trip to the bunker. Ethan was still down there, doing his secret mission things, watching the Clan suffer on camera and helpless to do anything about it. Yet, his spy mission was more important than all of them. She'd figured out that whatever he was doing, it might be critical for America's survival. Mandy would not let anyone risk that just to save her.

Then she watched in revulsion as the servers scooped a ladleful of thick gruel into her bowl. Constant stew, indeed. None of them would survive the winter on these tiny rations.

She prayed silently for God to send them help, and though His will be done, if He wished it she asked that He save her people and deliver them from Peter's yoke. In Jesus' name, Amen.

- 13 -

1300 HOURS - ZERO DAY +30

CHOONY SAT UNDER his lean-to, scrubbing his aluminum plate with some sandy soil. It would get the food grit off. Next to his makeshift bed lay the items he'd acquired during last night's farm raid. Other than some MREs—which had been a great find—he'd picked up a water filter straw, new in the wrapper. It wasn't needed for the farm's clean water, but Buddha, Dharma, and Sangha had been kind to him to provide the filter just in case. He also got a compass and a pack of batteries for the flashlight Joe Ellings had given him to assist Choony's stealthy raid.

A small, high-quality backpack filled with what Michael would call a "72-hour kit" topped it off. It held a couple knives, two bundles of paracord, a BIC lighter, a weird little fire starter that worked by making sparks and would never run out of butane, an aluminum cookware kit, a waterproof five-gallon canvas bag, a tarp, and a wool blanket. He was especially happy with the tarp, which now lined the ground inside his lean-to for keeping ground moisture in the soil and for adding to the blanket's warmth at night.

As he finished scrubbing the plate, and rinsing it with a

dash of water from a gallon jug, he heard hoofbeats in the distance. Not long ago he wouldn't have recognized it right away, but horses were in common use on the farm, especially by foraging teams. Choony crept to the edge of the dense copse of trees that hid his camp and peered out; three riders approached. He was almost certain that one was Joe Ellings, though he hadn't gotten a good look at the man in the darkness the night before. The other was a taller man with light brown hair, and he rode tall in the saddle as though he'd been born to it. The third wore the red shirt and headband of Peter's Red Locust troops.

What the hell was this? Choony decided that Joe must have betrayed him. And he'd told Joe right where to find him! Not everyone was as honest as Choony. What a damn fool he'd been. Choony ran through his options. Hiding wouldn't do, because he'd told Joe where to find him. Nor could he outrun three men on horses. He wouldn't fight another human, even at the cost of his own life. The Locust could possibly be friendly to Joe's cause... Choony's only remaining option either way seemed to be to wait patiently and see what the universe had in store for him.

As they got closer, Choony caught drifts of their loud conversation. "...haven't checked these woods..." and "...you it was clear..." reached his ears in snippets. The men reined up near the edge of the woods, and then Choony clearly heard the tall man say, "Well if you want us to check it out, let's do it. I'm tellin' you no one is in there. Lead onward, red man."

All three dismounted, and the Locust took the lead with Joe and the other man behind him. Just before they reached the tree line, however, Joe took something shiny from his belt—a rather large knife—and, catching up to the Red Locust, Joe grabbed the man's hair and thrust the knife through his neck until the knife tip protruded from the

Locust's throat, dripping blood. A few seconds later, the Locust's legs collapsed, and Joe let him fall, let the momentum tear his knife out of the man's neck. He wiped the blade on the Locust's pant leg even before his victim's corpse had finished its macabre twitching.

Choony stepped forward, right up to the edge of the woods, but was careful to stay half-hidden by a tree. No use standing out in the open. Who could say if someone else was watching Joe's group? Choony wouldn't put it past a sociopath like Peter to send watchers after his own men. Hesitating at first, Choony said in a whisper, "Hello, Joe. Did you have any trouble finding me?"

Grimly, Joe shook his head. "Nope. But we had this tag-along to deal with, too. Peter likes to send these eaters out along with his own people. He thinks it'll keep his people loyal, and it mostly does. We'll have a bit of explaining to do when we get back yonder. How you holdin' up?"

The other, taller man stepped forward. Tall, fit, short sun-bleached hair, the picture of a corn-fed farmer. And he had a direct gaze. He certainly looked self-assured. This must be the supervisor Joe mentioned. "I'm Dennis, sir. Dennis Blake. It's a pleasure to meet you. Joe told me all about your risky little raid. I haven't decided if it was stupid or smart, but it was brave. A man has to respect that kind of grit, right, Joe?"

Joe grunted in affirmation. "Let's get in them woods with the body so we can talk in private." Then he and Dennis each grabbed a leg and, Choony thought, rather unceremoniously dragged it right into the woods. No measure of pity for the dead man. These were hard men, Choony decided. Right now, he needed that kind of "sand" on his side. Once the body was well inside the dense copse, they covered him with dirt and leaves and came back to Choony's camp, where they squatted on the dirt.

"Let's talk," Dennis said. "Peter knows about you, but he figures you ran straight for North Korea. He can't get his head around it, 'cause you're Asian, he thinks, so not an American. So he won't be looking for you, Choony. And I brought you some binoculars, so's you can scout the farm better and safer."

"Thanks," Choony said and took the offered binoculars. The rig was smaller than he'd imagined, from what he'd seen in movies. Lightweight. Good. He looked back up, smiling thanks at the man. "So, aside from this kind of support, which I badly needed, what can we do for each other, Dennis? Joe here risked himself to help me out last night, and I respect him and am grateful for it. If he trusts you, so do I. I won't kill anyone, but I'll do anything else that I can to help my friends in the Clan against your monster of a leader."

"Good thing, because we need you to do something for us tonight. It so happens it'll help your Clan, too. You see, your friend Jaz, she's not giving in to ol' Jim like the good little tart he figures her for. He isn't feeding her now, and with all the beatings she takes from him—body and soul, I reckon—she's gonna waste away fast. I don't cotton to men beating on women like that, and Jim's raped our women before. So, me 'n Joe here, we're gonna bust her out tonight. She don't know where to go and she's getting weak, so we need you to pick her up and hightail it the hell out of there before Jim posse's up and comes looking for her."

Choony considered for a moment. It sounded wrong, he decided. "Tell me, sir, why you'd risk both your lives to save one of ours? What does it accomplish for you? I want to know the truth before I'll agree to risk my life on your word."

Joe chuckled. "You're a smart fella, Choony. Turns out we got another sympathizer who's a crack shot. She'll be waiting out in the shrubs to ambush his punk ass. One shot to the chest when Jim is far enough out so the camp can't hear it too good. Peter's a great tracker and so are some of our people, and they'll pick up you two's tracks pretty quick. Jim will chomp at the bit to come after Jaz. Peter will let him, so his little minion can redeem himself. But once Jim's out of the picture, that makes Peter weaker. Jim's half the reason any of us follow him—better to follow him and screw you people over than to get tossed to Jim, and then the Locusts. But we're countin' the days until we can wipe Peter off the face of God's green earth. He don't belong here."

Choony nodded. That did make a cold sort of sense. Of course, it also made Choony and Jaz into bait for their trap. Their only hope of getting out alive hinged upon one sniper being able to get to the right place at the right time without being noticed, getting a clean shot, and hitting her target. Very long odds, it seemed to him. Still, Jaz deserved a chance to get away from whatever it was Jim was doing to her—and he had a pretty good idea of what that was. It would greatly weaken Peter to lose Jim. Perhaps the karma of saving Jaz would outweigh that of aiding in the murder of a man. Perhaps.

"Very well," Choony said with what he hoped sounded like iron determination. "When and where do I play my part in this drama?"

* * *

1630 HOURS - ZERO DAY +30

Choony lay in the tall post-harvest aftergrowth, now thriving dense and tall in one section of the Jungle. He was covered with bits of chaff and other foliage and looked through his newly liberated binoculars, scanning the homestead, simply observing. From what he could see, there had been no change in schedule, no increasing of the guards. Peter's people must not have noticed the items gone missing during Choony's raid the night before. That was good because in a few minutes Jaz would escape if all went well. Peter would hunt her, but with the unalerted White Stag people somewhat off guard it might take them an extra few precious minutes to get their act together. It had to happen fast or it wouldn't happen at all.

In his binoculars, he saw Jaz sitting on her heels, knees in the dirt, not far from Cassy but probably too far to talk to her unnoticed. In the guard tower, a single sentry seemed alert. But Joe had assured him she would be another sympathizer, eager to take revenge on both Peter and Jim for her own reasons.

To his right, off to the east a bit from Jaz, the outdoor kitchen was in full swing and a crowd had gathered, just as expected. Everyone was still on slightly reduced rations until Peter could locate wherever the Clan had hid its food. Apparently, neither Cassy nor Jaz had broken down and told them, at least not yet. Cassy was a strong one, and it was a little sad that she didn't realize her own inner strength. He'd tried to help with that in his own way, much as his elders had taught him by leading him to his own conclusions when he was younger. But she was stubborn too, and it had almost turned into a game between them back before Peter arrived. It had touched him deeply when she had said she trusted him.

He swung the binoculars back to Cassy and zoomed in as close as the little field binoculars would allow. Her face was covered in bruises, he saw, and one of her eyes looked swollen shut. Her hair was matted to her head in one large spot over her left ear, and he hoped it was mud, not blood. Buddha, Dharma, and Sangha, watch over her! If only they could free Cassy as well as Jaz... But things were what they were, he reminded himself. "Bend to life's misfortunes like the reed in the wind," he muttered, more for Cassy than for himself.

Choony checked the sky with a clinical eye and saw that the sun was about 35 degrees above the horizon. This time of year, that made it roughly 4:30 or 5:00 p.m., he decided after doing a few quick calculations in his head. Then he smiled, realizing Michael would have known what time it was at a glance—no geek math required. Well, whatever worked.

It was almost time for Jaz's karma to save or doom her. If she died, he mused, she'd surely come back as an eagle so she could soar above the terrible earth she'd had to endure during this lifetime and would see only its beauty. He shook his head to clear his thoughts and began mentally chanting the calming mantras that would empty his mind and heart so he would be ready to play his part in what was about to happen, without hesitation or fear. *Om tare tuttare ture soha...*

* * *

Mandy stood at the outdoor kitchen's counter chopping carrots, Brianna beside her washing more of them. So many carrots. Still, it was the Lord's blessing that they even had carrots to eat.

Brianna let out a sharp breath and practically tore out the rat nest of hair that fell over her face as she struggled to somehow push it out of her eyes. "Dammit, Grandma, why can't I at least wash this mop of straw on my head? My hair looks so terrible, I can't stand it."

"Dearie, stop messing with your hair. I know you don't like it, but right now it's time to get dinner ready. I suspect the Clan will think that is more important than your hairdo."

"But Grandma, it keeps falling over my face and I can't

hardly see."

"Can hardly," Mandy corrected. "And that's your new hairdo until the White Stag is gone, honey. Some parts of life go on—like making dinner—but with your hair a mess and your clothes looking ratty, I feel a lot better about the... intentions... of the White Stags. You know you are a beautiful young girl, and you have to learn to dress down to avoid getting the wrong kind of attention. Just like when you were in school and your mom wouldn't let you wear makeup or miniskirts. It's not that you shouldn't wear those things, but it's smarter to avoid unwanted attention."

Brianna exhaled sharply through her nose and furrowed her brow. "I guess, Grandma. But this is stupid! I hate this new world. I can't even do my hair nice."

Mandy shrugged. "That's true, dear. Not yet. But the Lord has a plan for us, you mark my words. Our fate could have been much worse, you know. Peter needs us until he figures out this whole permaculture thing. What worked before can't be done anymore, so it's either learn or die. God willing, you'll be able to do your hair however you want soon, but we need to get through this tribulation first."

"Yes, Grandma," muttered Brianna and she rolled her eyes. Mandy pretended not to notice and was soon lost again in the steady *snick, snick* sound of chopping carrots.

* * *

Damn those bastards. Look at them, like, totally eating food and just looking at her like nothing was wrong. Jaz fumed but it did no good. No one, it seemed, would risk Jim's wrath by bringing her food without his say-so. She glanced at Cassy, who was near enough to see—and to pity, in her current condition—but not close enough to talk to. Someday, she swore, Peter and his asswads would pay for what they'd done to Cassy. She was too nice, too smart, and too strong to be treated like that in a just world. But, it wasn't a just world anymore, she reminded herself. It never had been, not in her memory. Even with that said, a lot of her illusions about humanity's basic decency had fallen away in the last month.

Briefly, Jaz wondered why she was so focused on Cassy's buckets of trouble, when she totally had enough troubles of her own. Maybe it was easier to be inside her own skin, with everything Jim had done to her, if she focused on someone else's craptastic life. Or maybe she just really liked Cassy. The poor woman hadn't ever had to deal with this kind of stuff like Jaz had for her whole life. Cassy had never been on the streets like Jaz, so how could she know? If the two of them ever got out of this alive, Cassy would need someone to cry to, someone who knew what she had been through. Jaz wanted to be there for her when the time came. Decent people had been rare in her own life and, for Jaz, it was too late to hope for better, but she wanted better for Cassy. By God, she'd help provide it if she got the chance.

Jaz decided she had to survive to be there for Cassy when that day came, and the result dazed her a bit. She felt the anger flow out and away, replaced by... Something. Something "do or die." She wasn't sure of the right words for it. Resolve? Determination? Yeah, maybe that was right. Whatever. She just suddenly knew she'd better be ready if an opportunity came to strike back at these White Stag pricks. Pay attention, study their weaknesses. Every dude had them, but now she'd just be looking for a different kind of weakness. And then she was going to kill that sonofabitch and get her and Cassy the fuck out of Dodge. Bide her time. Stay alert. Strike quickly when the time was right. That would be her new mantra.

A voice behind her jolted her out of her thoughts. It came from the Jungle, to which she had her back. "Jaz, don't say anything or move. I'm a friend. You're getting the hell out of here in just a few minutes, so stretch those legs while you can, and get ready to run, but don't look all excited. Reckon you can handle that?"

It was a pleasing, deep voice that sort of rumbled in her ears and felt warm and reassuring. But go where? How? Well, whoever he was, if he was legit then he'd have the info when she needed it. Jaz carefully unwound her legs and stretched them, grimacing as the blood flowed back into them after sitting on her heels for so long. She felt a bit disoriented at first, having been lost in her own thoughts seemingly forever.

When her head cleared and the pain in her legs had subsided, she murmured, "Ready when you are, Mister Growlyvoice."

"Good. We have only a couple minutes more before your opportunity shows itself. You'll know it when you hear it. I'm going to cut your ropes first. When I tell you to move your ass, you sneak into the Jungle with me, and we'll run to the southwest, toward the whatdoyoucallit, the Food Forest. I'll lead you, but you gotta keep up, sweetie. The timing's as tight as a frog's ass. Then a friend is waiting with a stolen horse. He knows what to do from there."

The unknown guy behind her cut her ropes while he spoke, and she forced herself to sit still and avoid looking around. Whatever the guy had planned, she was onboard. Anything to get away from Jim. Sorry, Cassy—rescuing you would have to wait. For a moment Jaz considered not going, so she could stay with Cassy, but in the end she couldn't really do anything to help her. Not here. Not now, not when she was constantly bound and watched, just as Cassy was. Jaz promised herself that she'd come back, and when she did she was totally gonna come down on Peter and his dickwads like the fist of God. Biblical asswoopings were coming Peter's way, just as soon as she figured out how to do it. Once she made that promise to herself, she felt a lot better about leaving Cassy. It would only be for a little while.

The outdoor kitchen began to admit the Clanners for dinner—what little of it there was—and the area between and near the two houses became, as usual, somewhat chaotic. The guards kept things orderly, but only barely. These were hungry people, and the guards' attention was completely absorbed in the effort of forcing thirty-five desperately hungry Clanners to form up in lines and wait their turn. For their part, Jaz's Clansmen were friendly and polite to one another, but when pressed forward toward the servers, they resisted any sense of order.

Amidst all that, over the din Jaz heard the staccato *CRACK! CRACK! CRACK!* of several semi-automatic rifles fired as fast as the shooters' trigger fingers could pull. Half of the dozen guards dove for the ground and began to low-crawl toward cover, which effectively took them out of the fight for the moment. The other half charged east, rushing toward the source of the shooting.

"Now! Move it!" said the voice behind her, and Jaz wasted no time. She sprang to her feet and charged after the man, of whom she could see only his back. He was faster than her, but never let himself get out of her sight among the dense overgrowth of the Jungle.

As they ran, Jaz heard a back-and-forth gunfight going on to the east, behind her. The thought of those rifles being turned on her kept her adrenaline pumping and her feet moving. Through the Jungle they went, sprinting. The man in front of her ran in a straight line, but then suddenly jinked to the right, then back to the original course, and she realized he knew where the traps were. That made her feel a little safer, at least.

Jaz's lungs ached and her legs began to burn as the lactic

acid built up in her poorly nourished muscles, but her guide didn't slow. Abruptly they were out of the Jungle and sprinting across the narrow stretch of open ground to the food forest. Jaz stumbled from muscle fatigue a couple of times but somehow kept moving. Then they were in the woods! Still they ran, though slower due to the dense interplanting of trees, bushes, and other plants that made up the food forest.

And then they were on the other side, just as Jaz felt like her legs couldn't possibly keep up the pace any longer. Her guide slowed to a brisk walk, and Jaz gratefully slowed as well, her eyes darting all around.

And then she spotted Choony. Good ol' Choony, and with a horse no less. Mister Growlyvoice was telling the truth! Go figure. She saw Choony wave to her, and a broad smile blossomed on her face.

Choony called, "Joe, amazing, thanks! You know where we're heading, so if you must run from Peter, head our way. Okay, brother?"

The other man, Joe, grinned and then said, "Yep. I reckon I'll be fine though. Let's do this."

Jaz watched as Choony first nodded and then slammed the heel of his palm straight up into Joe's chin. Joe's head snapped back, and he fell backwards like a tree falling.

"Let's get out of here, Jaz," shouted Choony, and he swung up onto the saddle. Then he reached his arm out for her. She grasped his wrist and jumped upward as Choony swung her back and up. She landed in the saddle behind him as he shouted "Hiya!" and tapped his feet into the horse's flanks. It bolted, and Choony leaned forward as the pace quickly picked up.

Jaz felt wind on her face and smelled the fresh air. It totally smelled like freedom. She wanted to yip like she was in a cowboy movie but then asked, "Why'd you knock Joe out?" She had to shout to be heard.

"Peter had to believe it," he shouted back over his shoulder. "We're headed deep into the National Forest. My gear's there. Wait. When we're safe, we'll talk." Choony's words traveled back on the wind in fast, staccato bursts.

Jaz kept her grip tight around Choony's waist and wondered whether he'd learned to ride a horse as a child or since coming to the Clan. She didn't bother to ask—questions could wait until they were safer. Instead, she buried her face in his neck and hung on for dear life. But was that joy she felt? She realized she was laughing.

* * *

1700 HOURS - ZERO DAY +30

Peter Ixin knew his face was flushed, but it wouldn't do to lose his self-control in front of his peons. He rested both hands on his belt and heard the leather squeaking beneath his crushing grip. He forced himself to relax his face into its usual stony mask. "So what you're telling me, *Scout* Ellings, is that you didn't find any trace of Jaz. You looked, with your outstanding tracking skills, and found... What? Nothing. Is that right?"

Joe Ellings looked at the ground, eyes boring holes into the dirt. He looked pretty frustrated, himself. "No, boss, I found some tracks. They head southerly. First set of tracks must be Jaz's. The second set started a fair ways away, past the Jungle, and they was horse hooves. Somehow she got herself a horse and rode hell-bent for leather south toward the National Forest."

Peter watched his scout carefully. No flinching, but no stubborn pride, either. Good. It seemed likely then that he was telling the truth. The whole, incompetent truth. "Get out of my sight, scout."

Then Peter turned toward Jim, who stood nearby. Jim, dysfunctional little psychopath that he was, didn't bother to hide his anger. Good. His pet got away, and he ought to be pissed. "So, Jim. How is it that you allowed a bound and beaten prisoner to escape in the middle of the day?" Peter forced a smirk to show on his face, the better to piss Jim off.

"Now, boss, that isn't fair. You know damn well we were under attack. She got away in the confusion. It's not my fault. You had a dozen other guards on watch, and they didn't see her leave either."

"True," Peter said. "But Jaz wasn't their responsibility. She was *yours*. What's more, that attack was a diversion. Not one person got hit when they opened fire. And the soldiers of our so-called army failed to hit anything, either. No blood, nothing. Very few tracks, not enough to know how many there were, where they came from, or where they went."

Peter paused long enough to pick at some imaginary bit of food stuck in his teeth. Let Jim stew for a minute and he'd be easier to control... Finally, Peter continued, "So. My property has escaped on your watch. You're my right hand, but you let yourself get humiliated by that little tease of a woman. You and I both know she loved your 'questioning' even if she pretended to hate it, right? Because she's just a woman, and you're a hell of a guy. She'd be crazy not to love it. But now she's gone, and I don't think I can give you the responsibility of questioning these Clanner women anymore. You're done, Jim." God, Peter felt disgust even saying the words. It was too bad Jim was so useful, or he'd have killed the man long ago.

Peter almost smiled when he saw Jim's face, full of outrage and near-panic, but Peter hid it well. Jim practically leapt forward, and then said, "Peter, no! You know I'm your guy. I'm loyal, dammit! Just give me a chance. I'll make this shit right, boss, I swear. Give me three guys and some horses and I'll ride that bitch down and bring her back. You'll see, Peter. You gotta give me the chance. Who else is gonna have your back the way I do? Just let me try."

Peter watched as Jim nearly lost his self-control. Inwardly, Peter grinned as Jim's voice cracked while he begged. Good. Begging was good. It showed who was running the show. Maybe he'd been a mid-level whatever in the old world, but here he was a *king*. "Very well, Jim. She's been gone maybe fifteen minutes. Get three guys and your horses, and get the hell out of my sight. And Jim? Don't come back without her. You get me?"

Yep. Peter knew that a little added motivation would do Jim a lot of good. Don't let the minions get lazy, that's what his dad had always said, and it was even more true now. Only order kept the chaos at bay. And Peter knew just how to get the best out of a tool like Jim so order could be restored—at any cost.

* * *

1830 HOURS - ZERO DAY +30

Choony guided the horse into the forest depths, far away from the tree line. Although the woods had more foliage to mark their passing, it also reduced line of sight to a few dozen meters or so. Moreover, there would be other animals in these woods making their own tracks, which Choony supposed could only help his cause by confusing whoever Peter sent after them. He was under no illusions—Peter would definitely send people after them. A man like that could not abide the embarrassment of losing a prisoner.

But the best part about moving through the forest, instead of along it, was that his horse had to carry two people while their pursuers would likely each have a mount. It made sense, then, to get into an environment where his own horse could keep a top speed that matched theirs, and which his own horse could sustain for a long time. Charging at full speed across open ground would have quickly driven his mount into the ground, as loaded up as the animal was.

As the pace slowed within the woods, he felt Jaz's grip relax a bit. Not that he minded having Jaz clutch onto him, but it was getting painful in his ribs. He took a deep breath. "You alright back there, Jaz?"

"Yes, I'm good. I totally can't believe you pulled this off. Who was that dude that helped me?"

Choony guided the horse around a large tree and tried to keep heading roughly southeast. "He's one of the White Stag people, but it seems they're not all fans of Peter. It seems Peter's rise to power didn't happen without some bloodshed, and most of the White Stag people were just farmers and farmhands before the EMPs."

"They can go screw themselves," Jaz said, and Choony heard iron in her voice.

"Remember, Jaz, they don't care for Peter or Jim. It seems they're mostly decent people in a very bad situation."

"Maybe, but I do wonder if their sniper ended up killing Jim. And one of them did help me get out, so I guess not everyone there's a complete tool."

It was good that she could see that, Choony mused. Even if she didn't like it. Dehumanizing others was the sort of thing that led to people like Peter, and he'd hate to see sweet Jaz go down that dark path. It was how wars got started and how people in different groups began to hate each other. The results at the end of that path were always ugly.

"Your harmony is improved by realizing they aren't all monsters, Jaz. No, they didn't turn on him, but only because they value their lives more than their morals. Most people do. You certainly didn't shoot Michael for what he did to Peter's scout, and your life wasn't even in danger from him. These people fear Peter. Dwell on this while we ride. We'll be going well into the night, so if you must sleep, hook your hands into my belt so you don't fall off."

Jaz didn't reply, and Choony rode on. He was both glad she must be considering his words and uncomfortable at the pleasant feeling of her behind him as they both moved to the horse's gait. Worldly distractions, he told himself more than once over the next few hours. This was not the time for such thoughts.

* * *

2100 HOURS - ZERO DAY +30

Taggart nodded and said, "I understand," for perhaps the tenth time. He stood with Mr. Black—Angel—a bit away from the others, who were cleaning their weapons and tending their wounds after the raid. And what a raid it was! Too bad this P-O-S, Black, wasn't happy with the results, but he knew that was going to happen.

"So you see," said Mr. Black, "I know you putos put me an' my crew in the hard spot, fool. I don't like you using my people like that."

"Listen, Black. I had no idea that tunnel through the rubble wall would be so well defended. You're the local with the local contacts, remember? You should have known, and told me. We could have adjusted our operational parameters to reflect the new intelligence."

"Don't think you can spout that military shit and I won't know what you're saying, holmes. This ain't my fault. You got ten of my peeps killed. Those were people I knew, fool. People I grew up with."

"I understand," Taggart said again. "But it wasn't intentional. I—and by extension, the U.S. Army—both appreciate and value our civilian partisan assets. You're a part of Team U.S.A., Black. I would never misallocate my forces for personal gain. You should have had prior warning from your own intel; I did not. I had to rely on what you told me."

Like hell, Taggart thought. This little maggot was always getting in the way of the mission, and he was a loose cannon. With all Taggart's new soldiers recently, including the Militia people, it had become expedient to reduce his risk exposure from Black. He sure as shit did send that trash, Black, through the kill zone. Defended tunnels were choke points, and deadly. But it hadn't worked out quite as planned.

Taggart continued, "However, I congratulate you on quick thinking in service to the American cause. It was a sign of good leadership that you recognized the squad of Spyder's men and could claim a higher loyalty from them. Convincing them to defect mid-battle was a primary factor in the success of our little mission to frame the Islamists for attacking their traitorous allies, Spyder and his men."

Capt. Taggart watched as his words were deciphered by the gang leader. He'd just said that Black was instrumental in having such an overwhelming success with the mission—which was true—and reminded him of all the new gangbangers he now had under his command. Also true. Dammit.

"Yeah... Yeah, puto. That's right, G.I. Joe. You need us, we don't need you. Remember that, fool. And I got more people than you, now. This is our 'hood. We know the place, every corner and tunnel. Fuck with me or my people like that again, fool, and you ain't making it back from the next mission. We clear, bitch?"

Taggart let out a long breath. This was not going to work

out. It would soon be necessary to part ways with Black and his gang, one way or another. Very soon. "It wasn't intentional, but yes. Crystal clear, Black. I understand you perfectly."

But Black had huffed and turned away before Taggart replied, so he never saw Taggart's half-hooded eyes or marked the cold, almost venomous anger on his face.

- 14 -

2200 HOURS - ZERO DAY +30

FRANK LOOKED AROUND at the other assembled Clanners, surrounded by what looked to be almost all of Peter's people. They were armed and very quiet, which set Frank on edge. This wasn't a good sign. He had a feeling something bad was about to happen. He spotted Michael nearby and began slowly scooting toward him. Not that Michael could do anything if something bad happened. Still, he'd feel better being near the Clan's ace defender.

Peter strutted back and forth in front of the Clanners, looking puffed up and cocky, the bastard. "It appears that one of you Clanner pieces of shit managed to escape today. Now, I've tried to be nice to you people. I've given you productive work to do, so that all of us—White Stag and Clan alike—will have enough to eat for the winter and into spring. And I've given you all food, even though rations are low. But despite my kindness, one of you has fled your responsibility, no, your *duty*, to care for one another."

Peter paused, feet apart and shoulder width, left elbow resting in his upturned right hand, left hand stroking his chin. It was, Frank thought, a rather melodramatic pose, and ridiculous. Peter must have sensed his audience starting to drift because he broke his "camera opp" pose and continued: "I would normally punish all the Clan for allowing this to happen. But instead, I think I will allow one of you to suffer the consequences for all of you. That's a kindness you don't deserve, but we are all in this together despite your treachery. I hope eventually you'll learn that."

Then, pointing at one of his White Stag guards, he ordered, "You—fetch me Cassy. I'm tired of her eagerness to make everyone starve rather than reveal the location of the food storage. Tired of her stubborn refusal to answer my simplest questions. You all can rest easy tonight, knowing that in the end, she redeemed herself through personal sacrifice." The guard started to leave, but Peter called, "And guard? Get me a machete."

Frank finally managed to squirm in next to Michael just as Peter finished his speech, and grunted a welcome.

Michael nodded and muttered, "So are we gonna let him do this to Cassy?"

Frank frowned. "What can we do? If we try anything we'll be mowed down. You hear how quiet his people are? They're tense. It's bad, man. It feels really bad."

Michael said, "At least Jaz escaped. Someone has to live through this. Remember when help was a three-digit phone call away?"

Frank said nothing. A reply wasn't needed. Then Peter smiled, and Frank followed his gaze. The guard had returned with Cassy, still chained about the neck, and carried a black machete in his left hand. He handed both chain and blade to Peter, who smiled down at Cassy like the sick bastard he was.

"Hear this, Clan," Peter said with a grin that got nowhere near is eyes, with his chest puffed out as if he had too much personal power to contain it all without making extra room. "Your leader means less to me than you do. She has failed to tell me where the food is stored, though that would have given all of us full rations. She has failed to tell me where the gear is stored, so that all our lives could be made a little easier. And now one of you fled. On foot. Cassy was there, yet she did nothing to stop the escape or alert my guards. The guards are here for your protection and ours. They needed to know. Should the sentence be death?"

Peter walked up and down the line of sitting Clanners, staring at each in turn, as he led Cassy on the chain like a leash. No one spoke up, and Peter's grin grew.

"None of you want her to die? Not one?"

Still there was silence.

"The alternative is easy. I can show Cassy some mercy. I can spare her life, despite her treachery. But it's up to you, because she's one of you. And the choice is simple. One of you only needs to volunteer to take Jaz's place beside her. One of your so-called leaders. You take Jaz's place and end up like Cassy here, taking her extra punishment onto yourself, or she dies. Anyone brave enough or loyal enough to do that? Are you all cowards and vipers? There's got to be one who would step up to spare Cassy." Peter pointed the machete at the crowd, sweeping it back and forth at them all.

No one spoke up and even Frank was stunned into silence. He didn't have the right words to describe how he felt about Peter at that moment.

Peter laughed out loud, a forced sound, like a polite laugh at a badly told joke. No one mistook it for humor. "Very well. Since none of you want to take Jaz's place, Cassy's sentence is death. You Clanners will get what you asked for. Hey Cassy, how does it feel to know that no one here will step up for you to save your life?"

Cassy spat on him, her face a mask of anger. "You didn't give them a real choice. You're a sadistic bastard, and someday you're gonna reap what you sow, motherfucker."

Frank felt a jolt of shock. Cassy almost never swore, not like that. But Peter didn't bother to wipe the spit from his face. He smiled again, and said, "Defiant until the end. It's why you have to die, you know. So be it. Cassy, bend over so I have a good shot at your neck. I'm gonna be as quick as possible, because mercy is a virtue. If you don't, it won't go well for the rest of your people. I think you understand what I'm saying."

Cassy stood tall and proud, Frank thought. "You'll kill me either way. Let's just get this over with." She spat again on the ground and bowed at the waist as low as she could. "I hope you're good enough with that knife to get it right the first time."

Peter moved to Cassy's left side to put her between himself and the crowd and placed the machete blade on her neck. "Let's find out," he said, and raised the blade up over his head.

Frank's mind finally caught up to what was happening, the shock flowing away like the tide. "Fuck this," he muttered to Michael, and leapt to his feet. Michael tried to pull him back, but Frank shrugged him off and shouted, "Stop! This isn't right, Peter. I'll take Jaz's place, just spare Cassy's life. Chain me, instead," he shouted.

There was a collective intake of breath from the other Clanners, and Frank's wife, Mary, let out a strangled sob. But it was too late to back down now, even if he'd wanted to.

"Only one among you is brave enough. How sad. Very well. I told you I'd spare her, and I'm a man of my word. I respect you, what's your name? Frank, right? Then get over here and let's get this over with so everyone can go to bed."

Frank wove his way through the crowd. He kept his gaze on Peter, but it was more to steady his nerve than to show bravery. That, and he couldn't bear to meet his family's eyes. He reached Peter and stopped a few feet away. Looking at the ground, Frank said, "I'm ready for the chain."

Peter motioned a guard, who walked up to Frank and put the chain around his neck. The guard then put on the lock, closing it with an audible click. Frank fought the urge to shake from all the adrenaline pumping through him. What the hell had he just done? Well, Cassy was worth it, he told himself over and over.

Once the chain was clasped, Peter furrowed his brow and pursed his lips and with his left hand tapped his chin. After a moment he said, "Something is missing. Let's see..." He continued with his bullshit showmanship, and Frank felt dread growing in the pit of his belly. Then Peter's face lit up into a happy smile. "I know what's missing! You see, Jaz fled, leaving all of you here to deal with the results. I can't have anyone else running off willy-nilly, now can I?"

Peter then turned to his nearest guards. "Grab him by the hands and feet and stretch his stupid ass out. He'll bear Jaz's punishment, just like he wanted."

As the guards piled onto Frank, he struggled, landing one solid elbow into someone's nose, but it did no good. In seconds he was buried under a mound of White Stag people, and his arms and legs were pinned, spread-eagle.

Peter, still grinning, walked to Frank's left side, putting Frank between himself and the Clan. The better for them to see whatever he had in mind. Frank stared at Peter and considered terrible ways to kill the sonofabitch. Peter looked him in the eyes, and grinned again. "I'm going to enjoy this," he said quietly. Then, louder, he said, "Jaz's replacement will never run away. Ha! He'll never run at all, after this. You Clanners, watch this and remember. This is the penalty for disobedience."

Frank watched in horror. Peter put the machete blade on Frank's ankle and rested it there. Then Peter turned his head enough to look Frank in the eyes. "Brave, but stupid."

Peter raised the blade high over Frank's ankle and then brought it down with all his might.

*　*　*

0500 HOURS - ZERO DAY +31

Grandma Mandy sat near the pitiful fire with Michael, Sturm and Mueller. They were discussing ways to escape or turn the tables on Peter. Mandy had come to the fire after being unable to sleep; the terrible vision of Frank's foot laying in the dirt with blood spurting everywhere wouldn't leave her mind. The sound of Frank's scream when they cauterized his wound would haunt her dreams forever. She shuddered and forced herself back to the conversation.

"If we could get to the stockpile," Michael said—they never referred to the bunker by name, fearful someone might overhear it—"then we could arm ourselves. Maybe engage the enemy at their weakest, just before shift change."

Mandy shook her head. "But if Peter somehow followed you, wouldn't that be the end of Ethan? And with our stockpile, who knows what use Peter would put the Clan to."

Sturm shrugged. "If we're armed we can defend that bunker all day."

Mueller said, "Stow it, Sturm. We will not abandon the civilians we're entrusted with just to get ourselves to safety."

Michael nodded and looked like he approved. "Oorah. But we're overlooking some operational assets that we didn't know about before Jaz's escape. Someone was shooting at the guards, a feint that distracted the Stag fighters. They didn't hit a single guard or civilian. We were all accounted for. I think we have sympathizers among the White Stag people."

There was silence for a long while as that sunk in. Mandy

finally spoke up. "God works in the hearts of all good people, strengthening them through the Holy Spirit. I think He is working toward our eventual triumph over evil."

Michael nodded. "That may well be. But I know God, and He told me we have to help ourselves first and *then* He will look after us as He did Jaz. What were the odds she'd escape? Pretty small, I think. Yet it came together just right for that to happen. More and more, I believe in Mandy's God."

"All of our God," she said with a smile. "He loves all men and wants them to be saved, even the ones who don't love Him back."

Sturm snorted. "Maybe. But here and now, we're outnumbered. We can rally maybe twenty fighters from among the Clan. Sympathizer numbers are unknown and can't be factored in. We're looking at twenty fighters at best, facing at least twice that many enemy forces."

Mueller nodded. "A direct engagement is out of the question. And, we're unarmed. We can get armed, but only if luck—or God—goes way above the call of duty to get us into the bunker undetected. Would twenty people even fit in the bunker?"

Mandy felt a wash of resignation flow over her. "No, only about ten people, including whoever's in there now. At least Ethan, and hopefully Amber as well. So eight of us."

Michael's head snapped up to look at Mandy, and he frowned. "And then there's Ethan. From what I know, his mission matters more than every living person here. He's kept operational secrecy, so I don't know exactly what he's doing, but something to do with coordinating partisan and guerrilla activity."

Sturm shrugged. "So, nothing. Nada. We can't arm, we can't sneak out, we can't engage the enemy directly, and we lack assets to go guerrilla. What's left? We sit here and rot."

Mandy stared into the fire, and the others grew quiet. Each was lost in thoughts they didn't share, of course. God didn't put obstacles into the path of the righteous that they couldn't overcome, was Mandy's thought, unless their loss served a greater purpose. She could see no great purpose to their enslavement and probable death. Therefore, God had a plan for them. His ways were unknowable though. She had to remember that it wasn't necessary for her to know, just to keep her faith. Sometimes, she thought sadly, it's hard.

But then she remembered that the others looked to her for guidance, and she rallied. "You folks are Marines. Christ's Soldiers. Do not lose faith, brothers and sister. God has a plan for us even if we don't yet see it. Keep your eyes and ears open. When God presents us with the opportunity, we have to be ready. Tell all the Clan we can trust to be ready. Everyone needs to start to gather and hide whatever supplies they can. We must be ready when He calls us to action." She turned to Sturm. "What's your motto? Always Faithful?"

"Semper Fi," the Marines muttered in unison. They still looked down into the fire, Mandy noted, but she thought she could see their shoulders rise a little higher, their backs grow a little straighter. Okay, *Semper Fi,* she had to remember that and trust God's power was in it.

"God bless Marines," she murmured, seeing the others look briefly surprised, then lower their heads. "And God, watch over Frank, if it be Your will, for he needs You now more than ever, and so does his family. So do we all. In Jesus' name, Amen."

* * *

Taggart inched his way into a sitting position, his back aching from a night on the cold cement floor of the tunnels they used as a basecamp. Other than the light of one rechargeable camping lantern in the tunnel nexus outside what had become his sleeping chamber, no light penetrated down here. The lantern cast eerie shadows that seemed to crawl toward him from the dark beyond. Glancing at the wind-up watch he'd acquired in a raid, he saw that it was barely 0500 hours. He'd only fallen asleep a few hours earlier, and he muttered a curse. Someone probably got up to hit the head, but these days even someone moving quietly to the bathroom would wake him up. He was about to lie back down when a slight sound caught his attention.

He felt an adrenalin surge as he sat in silence, straining to identify the noise. It was soft and repeated, but didn't come in any regular pattern. Then it hit him. He was hearing shuffling footsteps and whispered voices. What the fuck? He slowly lifted his rifle off the cement and rose like a phantom from his makeshift bedding. With a toe he nudged Eagan, who hadn't woken but was beginning to stir. Eagan sat bolt upright, but Taggart held a finger to his lips, and Eagan nodded. Taggart touched his ear with his left hand, then pointed out toward the nexus, and beyond, toward the tunnels that led to other little chambers.

Once he knew Eagan was alert, Taggart moved out with his rifle firmly welded to his cheek, finger lightly on the trigger guard. His posture low, almost a crouch, moved with the fluid, noiseless grace of a panther prowling. Just before the nexus, he paused and spared a moment to curse the lantern; it was ruining his night vision now that he was within its warm glow.

Directions weren't clear down here, but the nexus had five intersecting tunnels. One went to the chamber where he and Eagan had slept, opposite a tunnel that stretched away toward another nexus down the line. To the right, a short tunnel led to a larger chamber where several more of Taggart's people slept. The left-hand tunnel led to their "supply depot," and between it and the entry came another chamber where more of Taggart's forces slept.

Again, he listened carefully. To the right, no noise. To the left, one person softly snoring but nothing more. Staying low, he moved across the chamber to the tunnel entry that stretched away toward another nexus and paused. Ahead, he barely heard the faint scuffling of feet. Eagan caught up to him and placed a hand on Taggart's shoulder to let him know where he was.

Taggart moved forward again and noted Eagan's hand remained on his shoulder. Good. They arrived at the next nexus, again pausing just before they entered it. All was blackness there, as not even the faint light from Taggart's lantern reached within. They paused once again, searching for any noise, but all was silent. He couldn't hear the scuffle of feet anymore. But where was his guard? He'd posted a guard in this nexus to guard the tunnel they'd come down. Then a familiar stench—the smell of blood and of bowels released in death—reached him in the dark.

After a few seconds to marshal his reactions in the utter silence, Taggart felt secure enough to turn on his flashlight. He pulled out the little Stinger and covered the lit end with his fingers, then flicked it on. Only a little light seeped out between his fingers, and he spent a three-count sweeping the light around the nexus. Then he turned it back off. The brief time had been long enough—he'd spotted the sentry. She was sprawled on the floor in a pool of blood, face down. Someone had changed everything with this act and had to be stopped, but first Taggart needed to know the situation. It had to be Black's doing. This was a complete Charlie Foxtrot now.

Taggart muttered, "We return to base. Sentry down. Move out." He and Eagan then moved somewhat faster back down the tunnel toward their chambers. Taggart led, with his rifle covering their advance; Eagan covered their retreat.

Soon they had returned to their own nexus. The two set about waking the few soldiers in silence. Once everyone was roused, Taggart went to check the supply depot—the chamber where they kept their stockpiles—and gasped. Most of their gear was gone, only a medkit and their comm gear remaining. Ammo stockpiles, enemy weapons, Arab "uniforms," food and medicines—all gone.

"That fucking civilian sonofabitch," growled Taggart, no longer concerned with silence.

Behind him, Eagan said, "Captain, we have another problem. Black may have taken off with our supplies, but he was also the only one who knew these tunnels very well. Until we find a hatch to topside, we're stuck down here."

"We'll have to organize a search pattern to find our way out. We can assume Black has left this operational area as fast as he can, but I still want our people moving in pairs. Get them together, Eagan, so I can brief them. We'll find an exit point soon enough, and then we go hunting for those traitors. We need that gear to survive, but most of all *we need that radio*. Without it we can't receive intel and instructions from the 20s and our effectiveness is degraded. We can't let him do that to us."

Eagan grinned. "You mean we'd be blind and hungry? Good call, boss. We're under Martial Law, right? What's the book say about treason, looting, and stealing military supplies during times of war and enemy occupation?"

Taggart clenched his jaw. "You already know the answer, shitbird. A short trial followed by execution. No appeals. Now stop dicking around. The mission window is closing while we chatter."

* * *

0800 HOURS - ZERO DAY +31

Jaz and Choony faced a small ravine. She saw no way across, and the White Stag pursuers could only be an hour behind them at most. More likely twenty minutes... "Choony, what do we do?" she asked, and she could hear the panicked tone in her voice.

Choony seemed calm. "We turn left. Go deeper into the woods. And pray."

Choony turned the horse and urged it to move faster, but it refused to charge through the dense foliage. As they wound their way through the underbrush, the trees grew denser, further slowing their progress. Minute after tense minute, they tried to urge the horse forward until they came to an impenetrable barrier of brushes stretching to the left, away from the ravine.

"We'll have to double back," Choony said, and Jaz now heard an edge to his voice that was very out of character. He must be totally freaking out inside, she realized.

Jaz cried out, "No! If we do that we run right into them. The horse is trapped, but we're not." She slid off the horse and grabbed Choony's backpack. "We can get through on foot. *Come on, Choony!*" She grabbed his arm, half-panicked, and nearly yanked him off the horse.

Choony nodded and slid down to join Jaz on foot, then took the backpack from her and slung it over his shoulder. "Go! I'll be right behind you. I'm sending the horse running—it might lure them away from our tracks."

Jaz didn't hesitate. Growing up on the streets, she'd learned that standing still never helped and death could come quickly. Doing something was better than nothing and, as much as she wanted to argue with Choony to stay with her as frightened as she was, she was more afraid their pursuers would catch up. Besides, if Choony could spook the horses, it might actually help. Screw it, she decided. She would totally not ever go back to being Jim's plaything. "I'd rather die," she muttered to herself, and sprinted toward the dense bushes. Behind her, she heard Choony smack the horse's rump and shout at it like a real-life TV cowboy. She had to smile at the thought even as she ran.

The bushes in front were thick now, covered in thorns, a tangled bramble. There was no way through. Then, looking around for an idea, any idea, she saw what appeared to be a small opening in the bushes to her left. On a closer look, she realized it was some sort of animal passage and already growing over. There seemed to be no way through there, either. Her heart fell, and she struggled to control her rising panic.

Choony appeared next to her and grabbed her arm. "No time for panic, Jaz. Let's go check the ravine. Maybe there's a trail, or maybe we can climb down somehow." He tugged at her again, and she found herself following him. At least someone was giving directions. She felt her cheeks flush, ashamed of her panic and indecision, but Choony spared a smile and continued on toward the ravine, moving quickly. And she felt better. Choony had a way of doing that for people.

Behind her, Jaz heard the faint sounds of hooves muffled by the forest soil, and voices raised in alarm. Their pursuers were closing in. If the White Stags hadn't seen them yet, they soon would. Jaz redoubled her efforts. Clinging to a cluster of tree roots that grew out of the soil at the edge of the ravine, she tried to shuffle along the ledge, feet planted on the ravine's wall like one of those cool SWAT guys. Only unlike those guys, Jaz wasn't doing so well at keeping her feet planted on the ravine's wall. The dirt kept falling away, making her scramble to keep from falling, and she wasn't going very fast. The slower she went, the faster her heart raced. In her mind, Jim and Peter were right behind her, grinning, leering, laughing at her feeble attempts to get away. She could never get away.

Choony penetrated the fog she'd fallen into, saying "They are coming through the foliage now, Jaz. I urge you to move faster if you wish to escape." His voice sounded far away, and she realized adrenaline was screwing up her perceptions.

Okay, deep breaths. Concentrate. Focus. Move right hand. Move right foot. Move left hand. Move left foot. Always keep three points of contact, move only one part at a time… She repeated the mantra in her mind and it helped. She let it cycle through her mind as if it were a dance step she was learning. She may have only moved at a snail's pace, but she managed to make some real progress along the cliffside.

The bushes stretched away to her right, but the end was in sight and knots of exposed roots were there to grab for the entire distance. If their predators took only a few more minutes to find them, then she and Choony just might make it…

Then a familiar voice boomed out. "Jaz, my sweet, stop moving or I'll blow your pretty little head off. Now, freeze!"

In her panic Jaz almost lost her grip. Once she'd flailed for a moment, she managed to get both hands on the roots and struggled to bring her feet up again. Then she looked to her left, and sure as shit, Jim's bastardly face was leering at her, just like she'd imagined earlier. He stood at the edge of the ravine with his rifle pointed directly at her, and another man had Choony covered.

The seconds ticked away like hours as Jaz considered her options, but when Choony let out a deep sigh and closed his eyes, jaw clenched, she knew it was over. The nightmare would continue if he didn't just slit her throat and leave her in the woods. She tried to reply, to say something witty, but no words came to her. Her mind struggled to string words together but came up blank. She realized she was in some kind of shock.

Jim laughed, and Jaz felt her cheeks flush. She visualized herself plunging a knife into his neck, watching him bleed out and smiling at him as the light left his eyes. It was a nice dream.

Jim said, "Don't just hang there staring at me, honey bunch. You and your Korean should get your asses back up here, or let go. I guess the choice is yours, but I'd sure rather have you back. Ten… Nine…"

Jaz felt her fear turn to rage. That fucking animal. He needed to die. Thoughts of letting go fled before the heat of her anger. If she just let go, her torment would end, but Jim would just find another Clan victim. She'd be passing the buck for the easy way out, and well… Fuck Jim. Fuck that. She'd bide her time and take the abuse for a while, but when the opportunity came—and it would come, eventually—she'd kill the sonofabitch and shove the only thing that rapist really loved right down his damn throat while he bled out. She'd make sure he knew what she was doing to him. The thought made her savagely happy, and she realized for the first time what bloodlust felt like. It drove out all thoughts of fear or self-preservation, and her soul sang to the tune she heard playing to the rhythm of her heartbeat. Jaz realized she was the wolf, now, a hunter being invited into the sheep pen. Some detached part of her mind watched the change in herself with fascination and a savage joy.

"We're coming back, Jim. Don't shoot, please," she said, forcing herself to sound timid and scared, just the way Jim liked his women. She saw Jim's rifle barrel lower just a bit, his shoulders relaxed a tad. It had worked. She and Choony slowly worked their way back along the ravine's edge toward Jim and the other hunters.

When first Choony and then Jaz climbed back up from

the ravine, Jim and his people backed up, keeping their rifles at the ready. Jim shouted, "Get on your knees, hands behind your heads," and Jaz felt an irrational urge to giggle. The bastard sounded like he'd watched too many bad cop movies. He probably had, along with a bottle of lotion and box of tissues. He was dangerous, but he was pathetic. And she knew first-hand just what he was compensating for.

Once Jaz and Choony were on their knees, one of the men approached Choony and raised his rifle over his right shoulder, holding it with both hands. Choony closed his eyes, but did not move, as Jim's flunky smashed his rifle butt into Choony's head, sending her friend sprawling. He didn't move. Jaz's rage flared up again, but she controlled it. Mustn't let Jim see that. He had to think she was defeated and broken. Hopefully Choony lived through that.

Jim laughed at the scene, a full belly laugh. "Did you see that?" he asked his partners. "Oh my God, the look on his face. Fucking priceless." Then he turned to look at Jaz, and his eyes roamed over her from bottom to top, lingering on her face. The bad men had always done that. Her face was her power and her Achilles heel, drawing the predators who always seemed to find her but helping her deal with them, too.

Jim continued: "Hey, cover us. I feel like she needs a little discipline put back into her before we go back, if you know what I mean." He chuckled.

Jaz saw that the other men looked down, looked away, looked anywhere but at Jim. Even those bastards realized what a monster Jim was. She knew they wouldn't stop him though. They turned away, focusing on Choony and binding him. Cowards. Then Jim approached her. He ran his fingers through her hair, then clutched a handful in his fist painfully.

"Oh yes, you do need discipline," he said, and his voice was breathy. If he was true to form, next would come the beating, and then he'd start in on what he really wanted from her. She braced herself for it. She'd been through it now more times than she could count. This was just another day with Jim, and she added it to the tally of reasons he needed a slow, painful death.

The sudden impact of his open hand across her face sent her sprawling, seeing stars. One. He always hit her five or six times before the really bad stuff began. She heard the hum of Jim's voice, but her ears were ringing too much to understand what he was saying. Not that it mattered much. She braced herself for the next blow, but Jim went off pattern. Instead of another slap, kick, or punch, she heard the rattle of a belt buckle being undone. It just figured the chase had excited the pervert.

An instant later, the staccato sounds of gunfire. Jaz jumped. Had the bastards killed Choony? Other voices. Jaz cautiously opened one eye, and the effort was greeted by the sight of people with rifles, moving like Michael did in battle—gliding like some deadly cat that spat lethal venom, a monster striding over the battlefield. She didn't recognize any of them, and they wore green camouflage. "What the hell?" she said aloud, without realizing it.

Then one of the green giants was standing over her. She saw his mouth moving, but it all sounded like gibberish. Her mind just couldn't make sense of the words. And then with a sensation she could almost physically feel, like a car shifting gears, her mind caught up. Holy crap—his hat. It had a symbol on it she now recognized. A symbol she'd learned to love. It was the Marine Corps eagle, globe, and anchor emblem.

"Miss, I say again, are you injured?"

Jaz looked over her shoulder and saw Choony, still unconscious, being looked over carefully by another Marine. A half dozen more were checking bodies. Jim's men. They were dead and gone, and Jaz said, "No, I think I'm all right. You're, like, my heroes."

The man smiled. "I'm sorry we didn't intervene earlier, miss. We had to see who the bad guys were first. They say your friend will live, but he has a significant concussion. We'll have to stay here until he's awake on his own. How many men were chasing you, miss?"

Jaz nodded. She'd figure out later how she felt about these people waiting, but it didn't really matter. They'd saved her, and Choony as well. "Four."

The Marine stood bolt upright and pointed at two of his people. "Single enemy has escaped. Pursue and capture if possible, otherwise terminate. If not found in twenty mikes, rendezvous here."

That got Jaz's attention. She sat up and looked at the bodies. Damn and hell. Jim wasn't there. "Oh my God," Jaz said and bolted to her feet. A wave of dizziness hit her, and she toppled over. The Marine grabbed her and eased her down to the ground. "The one that got away, his name is Jim, and he's the frikkin' devil. You have to get him! If he makes it back to the farm, he'll warn the other assholes."

"You're not making a lot of sense, miss, but don't worry. My people will probably find him before he can get very far. Now tell me, what farm? Intel on this area is sketchy."

"The Clan's! My people. Survivors with children and families. Good people. We beat the odds and set up paradise, but there's worse things than starvation these days. We fought, but lost, and now my people are slaves. Frikking slaves! You have to help us," she shouted.

The Marine turned to his people. "Alright, Marines, listen up! This woman and her companion are from the Clan. Get this man moving, build a stretcher if you have to, but get it done. Clanholme isn't far." Jaz didn't know what Clanholme was, but she could guess.

A female voice shouted, "Oorah!" and this was quickly followed by many other voices repeating the word. Michael's word. Right now, it was Jaz's favorite word in the world.

The Marine turned to Jaz again and grinned. "Miss, we were sent here to rescue you. Welcome to Echo Company, two twenty-fifth of the Fourth MarDiv. Oorah." Again, the chorus of gleeful repetition by the others.

Jaz grinned and whispered a thanks to God, or Buddha, or whoever had sent these men. "Where's the rest of you?" she asked, still smiling.

His face fell. "Making green grass grow, miss. We're what's left—twelve men and women, including me."

Jaz froze. Twelve against forty. But these were Marines, not farmers. They would find a way. They just had to.

- 15 -

1100 HOURS - ZERO DAY +31

JOE ELLINGS STOOD with two other sympathizers, discussing how best to overthrow Peter. The little cabal had ten people in the inner circle and another dozen known sympathizers that they had not yet actively recruited for security reasons—that recommendation had come from Michael, the Clanner. The things he knew about "OpSec" went beyond what one expected from a regular Marine, but Joe hadn't asked questions.

He heard a sudden commotion and snapped his head toward the noise. That little pissant, Jim, came tearing through the Jungle underbrush, and as soon as he emerged, he started hooting and hollering for Peter. "Cheese and crackers," Joe said to the other two. "I thought he got taken care of when Jaz escaped. Shit."

Joe trotted toward Jim and saw Peter emerge from the main house as well. Joe caught up just as Peter got to him.

"What the hell, Jim. Where's Jaz? Where are my scouts?" Peter crossed his arms and stood ramrod straight. Joe could see him clenching his jaw; Peter was dangerous when he was like this, but Jim seemed oblivious. Good.

Jim said, "We caught them, boss—Jaz and that damn Korean. We were about to bring them back when someone started shooting at us. I'm the only one that got away." Jim panted as he said it, out of breath from running back to the homestead.

"Who the hell shot at you? There's no one out there anymore. Did you see them?"

"No, dammit. All I saw was a bunch of people in green. There were more than a couple—they looked like they were all over the place. Dodged bullets long enough to get the hell outta there. They chased me for a long time before I ditched 'em."

Peter frowned and shook his head. Joe noted he was still clenching his jaw. Hopefully, he'd kill Jim out of frustration. He was that kind of guy, always had been even back at White Stag Farms where you could tell he often wanted to kill people. It's why the good boss had detailed him out into the field as a so-called scout. Too bad it hadn't worked. Then Peter started talking, jerking Joe out of his reverie.

"Let's hope they were bandits and took care of Jaz for us, but we sure as shit aren't going to count on that. Go double our guards on every shift. They could be right behind you still. And make sure those idiots have full clips."

Joe mentally corrected Peter. They're magazines, not clips. Then he interrupted, "Boss, you want us to round up the Clan from field duty?"

Peter turned his head toward Joe sharply, eyes narrowed. "You have to ask? Get your ass out there and round them up! Fucking idiot."

Joe turned and ran. He had to get the Clan together, not to help Peter, but so they could act in unison if the opportunity came—and so he could keep an eye on them all at once. All except Cassy, of course. There was no way Joe could get her off her chain right now. He reckoned she'd have to take her chances, but he did send up a quick prayer for her safety while he ran.

* * *

1200 HOURS - ZERO DAY +31

Frank lay in the shade of the second house, half-delirious from the pain in his left foot. Leg, he corrected himself—the foot was gone. Cauterizing it had knocked him right out from the pain, and it still burned. Hurt worse than losing his foot had, if that was even possible. Even now he faded in and out of consciousness as pain came at him in waves. Thank God Mandy had hidden away a supply of antibiotics. An infection would be the end of him, he knew. Mandy had also lightly wrapped the end of his leg in clean cloth to keep dirt out of the terrible wound. Grandma Mandy was an angel, and she'd looked like hell the last few days. Frank didn't know what was wrong with her, but she looked so bad that he didn't expect her to last long. He'd seen his own mother die from cancer, and Mandy had that sunken, drained look of his mother in the months before she died. He knew if Mandy died, it could knock the spirit right out of a lot of his Clanners.

He sent a short prayer for her up to her God and passed out again as the next wave hit him.

He awoke to a riot of sound all around, and as his senses came back, he realized the entire Clan was being herded into a knot of people centered on him. Herded like cattle. And the White Stag assholes were running back and forth around the homestead like bad guys in some '80s action movie.

"What's going on," Frank asked, trying to raise his voice above the din, but it came out sounding faint and weak. He wiped a layer of pain-sweat from his forehead. Disgusting, but sweating was the least of his problems.

Frank felt a hand squeeze his own, and he looked down in confusion. Someone holding his hand... He looked up and found his wife, Mary, looking at him intently. She wore her "I'm worried" smile, which Frank usually found charming and pretty but in his current condition, it was only alarming.

Mary said, "All the Clanners are being rounded up from field duty and herded together here. But we're making sure no one bumps you, love. The paramedic guy said you look like you'll pull through."

"Why bother? Even if I pull through, I'll only be a burden to everyone. I can't *work*, dammit!" Frank had spent his entire life working hard, from the day he turned fifteen. First he helped his dad at the garage, and then took over when his dad passed away. He usually held down a second job as well, moonlighting as a welder for local jobs when the work was available. "No more crab and steak dinners for us, baby," he said, trying to smile. He failed. "I'm just going to be a burden..."

"You hush now," Mary replied. "I won't hear any of that defeatist garbage from you, mister. Hunter and I need you. The Clan needs you, for a lot more than just harvesting wheat. Even Cassy listens to what you have to say before making a decision. She's weaker without you, honey. We all are."

Another voice came from his other side—Michael's voice. "Take it easy, Mary. Right now, we all need to stay calm, including you and Frank."

Mary nodded. "Doing the best I can."

"Remember, all is not lost," Michael said. "There are people among White Stag who hate Peter as much as we do. They help us, giving us extra water, bits of food, that sort of thing. They helped Jaz escape. And that leads to the best intel we've had in a long time."

"And what's that, Michael?" Frank asked. "What great news? We're slaves, all of us."

"Maybe not for long. Our assets within the Stag have told us that Jaz lives—she escaped with the help of our sympathizers and, get this, Choony. He's alive out there and with Jaz now."

That news brought Frank his first smile in many hours. "I'm glad," Frank said. "At least two of us might survive this. But they can't free us on their own, Michael. You're military. You know that. What do you call it? Insurmountable odds?"

"OpFor numerical superiority. But maybe not, Frank. Jim chased out after Jaz with three of their scouts, and a while later he came back. He was alone and running for his filthy little rapist life."

"What happened?"

"Well, it seems a group of soldiers in American camo came to Jaz's rescue and killed three of Jim's scouts. Jim escaped, and that's why there's all this buzz around camp. It's why they're rounding us up. Rumor is, at least a dozen soldiers were in the rescue party."

"You think a dozen soldiers can do much to help us here?"

"Hard to say, Frank, but I'm thinking that against these damned Stag farmers a dozen could well be combat-effective. Especially since Peter has made a lot of his own people into our secret allies." Michael paused, his expression tightening to steel. "Peter's about to fall, and hard. I'd like to be first in line at his execution, but Frank, you've earned that privilege."

Frank stopped to consider this new information. On the one hand, Jaz and Choony would certainly try to get those soldiers to help against White Stag, but there was no guarantee they would help. They might be on a mission, not just wandering survivors—of which there were damn few decent ones left around here. And far too many like Peter and his crew.

Even if the soldiers did agree to help, they would be outnumbered at least six-to-one. Those were long odds. They'd only stand a chance if they had total surprise on their side, and that was impossible now that Jim had warned Peter. Unless they had help from inside. Michael said some of the Stags were secretly working with them already. With soldiers firing from outside, the Clan and their Stag sympathizers really could turn the tide—but only if they could all coordinate action, and that was impossible.

Frank's frown relaxed a little and then one eyebrow lifted. Impossible... But was it really? Ethan hadn't been found, nor had Amber. He was certain they were holed up in the bunker, with cameras and radios and everything. The Clan could use that, if they had time. It'd still be long odds, but at least it was a plan, something for them to work toward.

His eyes came back into focus, and he looked up at Michael. "Listen, Michael, I think Ethan's in the bunker and staying out of sight, like Choony did until he got Jaz away. Now if we could get Jaz one of the radios the Stag took from us, Ethan still has cameras all over camp. He could coordinate us without anyone being any the wiser. We could get ready to spring something, or at least disrupt the hell out of Peter's plans at a moment's notice. But we *need* a way to communicate on our side. Look—talk to the sympathizers about getting us two radios—and figure out how to get someone out of here with one to give to Jaz. It's not much, but it's something to tip the odds a bit."

Mary smiled and squeezed his hand again. "God, I love you, Frank. That's a great idea."

Frank turned back to Michael and saw him grinning. He stepped in then where Mary had stopped. "Frank, you're a genius. It could make all the difference. I'll work on it. Worst case, it gives our Clanners the hope they need to keep going."

* * *

1700 HOURS - ZERO DAY +31

Peter nodded approvingly at Joe Ellings. "Yeah, that's a good idea. Take two scouts, and all three of you stay apart but keep eyes on each other. Ride north to the national forest, and find some tracks. I want to know how many, where, are they on foot, where are they headed, any input you can think of. If you can, get a firm location for me. If we can find their camp, we'll end this right now. We might even get the Oriental and the girl back."

Peter kept his face carefully neutral, but studied Joe's face intently. If anyone was going to turn traitor, this crisis would be the time to do it, and Peter didn't know who he could trust. But he had an ace up his sleeve. "Leave your brother here though. He's got good eyes, and I want him in the tower. He's smart, and he'll keep an eye on shit." And Peter could keep an eye on him, too. Nothing like a hostage to make people loyal. For a moment, he thought he saw disappointment on Joe's face, but he couldn't be sure. If that's what it was, Joe quickly squashed it. Anyway, Joe always liked to have his brother by him so if he was a little disappointed it didn't mean he was plotting. They worked as a team, is all, Peter told himself. So why did seem spooked? Peter was taking no damn chances.

Joe shrugged and broke into Peter's thoughts. "You got it, boss." Joe gave Jim a quick glance before continuing: "Should we take Jim with us? He knows where he first saw 'em, and that's the best place to pick up their trail."

Was that a hopeful look? Again, Peter couldn't be sure.

He usually read people better than that, and it bothered him. Well, if it was hopeful, it made no sense. No one liked Jim, not even Peter. He was just useful. "You want to take Jim?" Peter asked, his eyes narrowing as he watched Joe's reaction.

Joe didn't show anything though. "Well, I reckon he can bloodhound us to their trail. Once we find it, we can send him back if you want—we have good scouts, we just need a place to start."

That did make sense. Okay, so Joe was probably loyal. A little paranoia was healthy for a leader, but no need to see an enemy where there wasn't one. But no way would he send Jim off unsupervised with scouts right now. Too much temptation to get rid of the cunning little viper, especially with such a ready-made excuse. Maybe that was Joe's plan...

"Nope, I need Jim right here. With him and your brother partnering to keep watch, nobody's gonna sneak in or out. Plus, they're two of our best shots. I need that team in the tower. We're doubling the watch, remember? I can't afford to send Jim off on a goose chase. Get your two scouts, make 'em good trackers, and go. If you don't find a trail by noon tomorrow, get back here pronto. We'll need your guns in the pits if they try a surprise attack. I don't think they'll do it tonight. Tomorrow night, maybe. Right now Jaz is spilling her traitor guts."

Jim made a face and spoke up for the first time. "Bitches can't ever keep their mouths shut when you need 'em to, and then they bitch about it when you do want 'em to talk."

Jim sounded like he was working himself up to one of his little private parties. For a moment, Peter lost his composure at the thought, but he quickly hid it and snapped his gaze over to Joe to see if he'd caught it. A leader shouldn't show his feelings like that. But Joe was looking at his shoes, no doubt disgusted. So he probably hadn't seen Peter's slip. A good leader stood behind his men, and Jim was without a doubt Peter's creature. "Better get going, Joe."

Peter watched Joe scurry off to obey. Peter couldn't shake the nagging feeling that Joe couldn't be trusted, and he couldn't put his finger on why. But it didn't really matter. As long as he had Joe's brother under his thumb, that redneck would stay as loyal as Peter needed him to be, problem taken care of. That was the good thing about farmers—they understood the value of family, and it made them easy to control. Peter once again had cause to thank God he didn't have any family of his own, not since his asshole daddy beat on him that last time. He smiled. It had been just before Peter left while his daddy lay bleeding out under his own truck's wheels. Family only made people weak. Peter knew that from personal experience.

* * *

After draining his bladder into the "cathole" the Marines had dug for him, Choony hobbled back to the rock they'd set up for him to sit on. Every slow step was a misery that made his face and head throb. His eye was so swollen he could see the side of his own head. Choony sat with a thump and almost fell off the rock as dizziness washed over him again. A concussion, the Marines had told him. They tried to make it seem like some minor injury, but he saw how they glanced at one another every time he flopped over from dizziness. Now they only let him stand if he had to use the luxurious facilities they'd dug. They showed a gentleness for him that he had almost forgotten existed in this new world. Good men, even if hard, he reflected as his eyelids began to droop.

Jaz set her hand on his shoulder lightly in a comradely gesture, and it sent a jolt up Choony's spine. Beaten and battered as she was, Jaz could still take one's breath away, she was that beautiful. And where once he had seen only a damaged, ignorant street girl, he now understood that this was a mask. Inside, she was made of steel, though she might not even realize it herself. A survivor. And she was smart as a whip. Education and intelligence were not the same thing, he reminded himself. The lesson came home to him time and again just from watching Jaz walk through this brutal, magnificent world. It humbled him, which was always good.

"So, like, how's your head?" she asked, with a tentative smile. He smiled back, struck by how quickly the street in her speech had brought him back to earth from what he recognized as a drifting kind of internal chick flick, gushing all unicorns and rainbows. He blinked. He had to stop this drifting, stay alert. But Jaz would surely stun the Buddha Himself, he thought, as she continued happily, "Your eye isn't all the way shut now, so that's totally a good thing, right?"

Choony nodded, wincing at the motion. What an amazing universe, he thought. "The Three Jewels watched over me as I had asked, Jaz. It could be much worse. I'll live, if I make it through the next seventy-two hours or so. If I wake up in the morning, then my odds go up tremendously. It will be seventy-two hours more than I had any right to expect, actually. Thank you for your kindness and your help though. You don't know how much I appreciate you bringing me food and everything. I can sit up now, but standing erect is still...problematic."

Jaz giggled, and Choony was struck by how her face lit up. He wasn't sure what he'd said that she found funny, but he was glad that she did, and he smiled back. "Don't worry, Choony," she said with a wink, "every guy has that problem at least once in their lives."

"Statistically, concussions are rare, Jaz. Still, thanks for the encouragement."

Jaz giggled again, but before he could ask why she was

laughing, she got up and, with a backward wave and a smile, headed over toward the "food rock." It was what they called the large, mostly flat stone where they'd laid out their meager supplies. For lunch, they'd finished off the dead scouts' foodstores. Choony knew it had been a three-day supply, enough to provide a light meal for the Marines and their Clan rescues.

Suddenly, a Marine burst through the foliage and ran up to the one with the two silver bars decorating his collar, and Choony turned his head at the noise. He immediately regretted the sudden motion and had to lean forward to rest his head in his hands to avoid falling over. The world spun around him, making him dizzy.

"Sir," Choony overheard, "we spotted three riders leading their horses through the woods. It looks like a search pattern, sir."

"From the farm?" asked the captain. He hadn't jumped when the other Marine came sprinting into the camp.

"Sir, unknown. They're following the elephant path left by the one who got away though."

"Possible coincidence, but that seems unlikely. Very well." The captain then shouted, "Marines! Grab your gear and ammo-check yourselves. Do it now, *move!*"

The result amazed Choony. Every man and woman in the unit seemed to be suddenly moving at blinding speed, all at once. No hesitation. They were like a machine, each of them going through the same motions at the same time. In under a minute, all twelve were armed, ready, and assembled. Eleven of them faced the captain. This, thought Choony, was discipline. Under the circumstances, it was a very welcome sight.

* * *

1830 HOURS - ZERO DAY +31

In under an hour, the Marines had returned to camp, but with two others Choony didn't recognize. Jaz seemed to recognize them, though; she stared at them with open hatred. The two had been blindfolded and gagged with what looked like strips of a torn t-shirt, and their hands were somehow restrained behind their backs. The Marines shoved them roughly to the ground. Choony saw that one bled from his arm as they struggled back into a sitting position.

"Miss," the captain said to Jaz, "do you recognize these two?" Everything went silent, and Choony already knew the answer from Jaz's expression.

"Yes. They're from the White Stag bastards at our farm," she answered. "They turned us all into slaves." The steel in her voice made Choony flinch. Such anger from one so young. She clung too tightly to the past, which could never be undone but could be left behind where it belonged. Buddha help her...

One of the Marines let out a sharp, sudden shout that to Choony sounded like a dog bark. The other Marines then made the same sound, several times. When they all barked that way, it became a rather scary noise, Choony decided.

The captain nodded. "Line them up against those trees. Murphy, White, front and center."

Two Marines grinned and stepped toward the captain while others snatched the two prisoners to their feet and shoved them at barrel-point over to stand in front of two of the nearby trees.

Choony struggled to his feet. This was wrong. All wrong. It would be murder. "Captain, you can't just—"

"As you were, civilian," the captain shouted, interrupting Choony. It was a hard, sudden shout, and Choony found himself involuntarily taking a step back. "Understand that this is a military unit, and we—and you—are all under the jurisdiction of military law. Banditry is a capital offense."

The captain motioned to the two who had prodded the prisoners into place. "Remove their gags," he said. "You may each make your peace with God now or make a final statement." He glanced to Choony. "It's the best I can do for them under the circumstances."

Choony turned wordlessly back toward the prisoners. In his mind he urged them to say something that might spare their lives. Anything. He pushed out with his will, as if by effort alone he could change the reality of the situation.

The first—a thin, blond man with shoulder-length hair—began to cry. Sobbing, really. "Look, mister, we ain't done anything wrong, I swear it! We got a crazy leader, and he'd kill us if we don't do as he says. I don't got no bad feelings for them Clanners."

The captain nodded at the man's guard, who shoved the gag back into his mouth. "Guilty," said the captain. "What about you, mister? Last words?"

The other man was silent for a moment, then shrugged. "Sir, my name's Joe, and I done as you said. We bandited those Clan people and took their farm. We stood by while the Devil's crew did them harm, more scared for us than for them people. I reckon I deserve what you're about to do. But not all us White Stag people are like that jackass, Peter. Sir, some of us been trying to help them Clan people as best we can without getting ourselves murdered. That don't wash the stink off me though. Do what you will."

Something about the man puzzled Choony, but he saw the gag shoved back into the second man's mouth, and the two guards stepped well aside. The two who had been called up by the captain, whose names Choony couldn't remember through his fog, raised their rifles and waited for the captain's command. Choony clenched his eyes tightly. He had no interest in witnessing the murder of helpless people, even bad ones.

To his surprise, though, he heard Jaz shout at the top of her lungs, voice shrill with panic, "Wait! Don't shoot!" Choony opened his eyes and looked at Jaz. She was practically hopping up and down. "I know this one's voice," she yelled.

The captain made a motion with his hand, extending it and lowering it, and the two shooters lowered their rifles. "What's your point, miss? Make it quick." There was no sympathy in his voice.

"When I got set free, one of them helped me. He risked a lot. *I know his voice*. This is the one who freed me. He's telling the truth, dammit, so you can't just shoot him. He's on our side, he's been helping us for God's sake!" Jaz was frantic.

The captain glanced at Choony, then back at Jaz. "Well, this is a new development... Very well. Marines, get that man over here for interrogation. For the other prisoner, you have your orders."

The captain turned away from the scene and strode toward the main encampment, and if he flinched when the execution squad fired, Choony didn't see it.

Choony muttered a mantra for the dead man, the best he could do for him, and wobbled uncertainly toward the remaining prisoner, who was being tethered to a tree. He doubted this captain would use much restraint during "questioning."

Unable to see properly, he wondered if this was the man who had handed him a flashlight when he tried to raid the storeroom in the total dark. The man who asked to be knocked out so he could return safely to the farm and help other Clanners. Choony couldn't remember clearly. His mind felt detached but he had to look closer, to find out, to... he wasn't sure, couldn't think, and then he felt himself caught by one of the Marines. He must have wobbled too much, he thought, as the Marine lowered him gently to the grass and stepped back, murmuring, "You have to take it easy, sir. You're hurt. Moving around ain't good, it can hurt you more." Choony blinked again. He had to stop this drifting, he thought, as Jaz sat down and held his arm to steady him. He had to be here. Had to be present, not drifting somewhere, and he wondered if it was getting dark early today or if he was just passing out.

- 16 -

1830 HOURS - ZERO DAY +31

ETHAN CONFIGURED THE file and re-encrypted it. He'd added multiple bits of intel that had been filtering in lately online via HAMnet and from Watcher One, whom Ethan was now positive was a member of the 20s and probably his handler. While the encryption program ran, Ethan gazed at the maps on the bunker wall next to his workstation. Large yellow circles now showed confirmed EMP-blacked-out areas, which covered virtually all of America, Canada, northern Mexico, and the North Atlantic. Hawaii was also blacked out, which was new information but not unexpected.

Red pins with flags showed different invader unit headquarters. Pink pins showed suspected units. These pins were thick throughout the eastern seaboard, the west coast, and southern Alaska. Hawaii, too. But, there were also now a lot of blue pins of different shades, representing known U.S. military and partisan units. Every day it seemed he had to add more blue pins, and remove a red or pink pin or two.

That sounded promising, but Ethan, an expert at online military games, knew better—the invader troop movements showed they were reacting to American units effectively, and if they hadn't crushed resistance by midwinter they surely would when spring rolled around. There were too many, and they operated in a well-coordinated way. The Americans, unfortunately, relied at least in part on Ethan's intel, and disseminating that information took a long time. Much of it was passed on by word of mouth to units without HAMnet access—which came to at least half of 'em.

Ethan kept his spirits up by thinking about Operation Backdraft though. The details were hazy, but he'd pieced together enough to know that it would totally screw up the bastards' communications net, and therefore, their ability to coordinate their efforts or react quickly to new threats. It would be a game changer, if it happened as planned. D-day hadn't been announced, but the chatter he'd intercepted from Colorado Springs suggested it could happen at any time. Which was awesome, but it made waiting a difficult exercise in frustration and patience.

Amber's voice snapped him out of his musings. "Your computer is almost done. Can you click on the thing before it makes that damn dinging noise when it finishes?"

Ethan turned and saw her leaning over his chair to peer at the computer to his left. She was right, of course; she'd seen the cycle before. There wasn't much to do down here beyond going through his intel notes for the Nth time. When not working, all he could think about was how hard he was falling for Amber, though he kept his mouth shut about his feelings. It was neither the time nor the place. Time enough for emotional vulnerability later, when and if this whole Peter nightmare ended. First, they had to survive the crisis at hand.

Ethan went to the terminal to wait for it to finish compiling, with his hand on the mouse. "A lot of great intel going out to the Resistance today. The guys in Virginia were almost surrounded, but I found them an exit route to West

Virginia. They can hide among the partisan camps in the Appalachians through winter at the very least. I had almost written them off."

Amber frowned. "Wouldn't the 'vaders know they left a hole open? Could it be a trap?"

Ethan let out a long, frustrated breath. "Of course it could. But if our people don't take the chance, they won't be around to see winter anyway. I've been having partisans in Maryland step up guerrilla raids, so the 'vaders are sending some of their Virginia units up there in response. They can't draw troops out of the cities, at least not yet—they're barely hanging on in the big cities as civilian survivors and partisans get more desperate and violent. So there's at least a chance it isn't a trap. They'll have to move at night to avoid all those damn helicopter patrols down there, but most of them have a good shot at making it through. As soon as 'vader reinforcements start to arrive, I'll warn the Maryland partisans to fade away again."

Amber nodded in approval. She'd learned basic tactics fast, and Ethan had been keeping her briefed as things developed on the ground out there. She'd been a very quick study though she was still learning the fine art of guerrilla strategy. Still, she had learned enough to be dangerous to the 'vaders in her own right if the two of them ever got the hell out of the stupid bunker. Ethan's successes against the 'vaders had built his confidence. Real-world results proved how sharp his sense of strategy and on-the-spot tactics had become. And Amber's recommendations showed she was catching up fast.

Ethan sighed. "I can't wait to see daylight again," he said, his brow furrowed. "It's getting to be an overpowering urge, and twice I've barely stopped myself from leaving. The last time, I had my hand on the locking wheel before I talked myself out of it." He put another red pin up on the map, showing a new 'vader field HQ.

Amber frowned. "Yeah... Well, we'll both go nuts from cabin fever pretty soon, and that'll put you at risk of making mistakes and hasty decisions. We have to figure something out soon." She wrung her hands as she spoke, lips pursed in frustration. Clearly, she felt the same way he did.

"I've been working on that. Supposedly there's a Marine Reserves company still operational, originally based out of Harrisburg. I've sent word to them to head this way to help deal with Peter's group and set us free. Harrisburg was a total loss to the 'vaders anyway, so the company was already on the run. They might as well have something useful to do besides dodge and hide."

"You sent them this way, instead of west toward Gettysburg? But I thought those Michaux Militia folks and the 'vaders in Gettysburg were stalemated? Can you imagine what a whole company of Marines could do for us down there? It could open up the entire front."

Ethan put his hand to his face and pinched the bridge of his nose, eyes closed. "I know, Amber. I know. Not that there's really a 'front.' But the Michaux Militia can always retreat into their National Forest if they get overrun. If I can't send them the intel they need to be effective, though, they'll be overrun anyway. It was a tough decision with no right choice—just the least wrong one, I hope. The good they can do here is real and immediate, and not just for you and me." God, he hoped he was right.

The computer beeped, loud and annoying. Ethan made an apologetic grimace and Amber rolled her eyes. Their conversation had distracted them both. He grinned at her and turned to the terminal, where he prepared to send out the day's batch of messages. It took only a minute to get everything set up. Then he hit "Enter" on the keyboard and waited. The damn hourglass came up, of course. No surprise.

But then it kept going. And going.

"What the hell?" he muttered, and pulled up a diagnostic routine he'd coded during their copious free time. It took only seconds to find the problem. "It's not connecting to the main relay antenna. I can't send out the HAMnet."

Amber smirked and said, "Isn't it just a fancy HAM radio? You need a *main* antenna? What about the little whippy antenna you see on trucks, don't you have one of those?"

Ethan shook his head. "This isn't some trucker CB. I need a real antenna, with enough power to reach dozens of other relays all over the region—other people who disseminate the intel I send, even though they can't make sense of the message. But they know it's important. If I can't get the message to them, they can't rebroadcast it."

Amber nodded. She knew how important Ethan's broadcasts had become. But then her jaw dropped, and the color went out of her face. She put a hand on the table to steady herself, and then sat down abruptly. "Ethan, you sonofabitch, don't you *dare* go out there to fix this thing. There has to be another way. If they catch you, you won't be able to send the message anyway, right? Think about this. Please, they might be waiting for you there!" She snapped her jaw shut, realizing she had started to sound desperate.

Ethan gave her a smile, mostly to show he appreciated her caring about him. For some reason, she seemed to be getting mad at that, so he dropped his confident smile. Anyway, he felt no real confidence. He just knew he'd have to "bravo it up" to get her to go along with the plan, and he'd need her to help if he wanted to get it done. Whatever was wrong with the antenna, he'd need her to look up the checklist and run him through it while he was out in the field, looking for damage or failures. If he even made it to the makeshift tower alive in the first place, that is. He had no illusion that a skill at strategy would translate into success in an action like that.

"I'll be careful. We have cameras everywhere. I'll need you on the radio, both to run me through the checklist to fix the antenna and to keep an eye on all our cameras and get me safely through the maze of assholes with guns. This is going to happen, because it has to. Amber, I'm going out there, and I am going to fix it. But it doesn't have to be Mission Impossible. Help me, and it'll be easy as raiding Blackburrow with a fiftieth-level Shaman."

That got the reaction he wanted. Despite her inner turmoil, she snorted back a laugh and then let out a long sigh. She always thought his online gaming references were funny, not to mention adorable. "Fine, you win. Just wait until it gets dark if you want me to get involved. It'll hinder them, and the cameras see just fine at night. Tell me what you need me to do so you can get back in here with me to keep doing your 20s magic."

Ethan immediately saw the irony of the situation. Before, he could barely get a moment with her as Frank was a constant wedge between them. Now they had all the time in the world together, and of course something else had replaced Frank as that wedge.

Ethan said, "Sounds good to me. Let's 'get 'r done,' shall we?" He pulled up four PDF documents on the computer and squared his shoulders. "Alright, let's go through these while we wait. They're manuals on the principles and operation of HAMnet broadband. They show how I connected our routers to the bigger network out there."

* * *

1900 HOURS - ZERO DAY +31

Taggart looked at his scout, one eyebrow raised, as he considered the man's report. "So we found another entrance to the tunnel segment they encamped in? That's excellent. We'll have to keep eyes on them, soldier. Send two scouts ahead to make that happen. It's imperative that Black's forces do not become aware of our presence though. When the trap springs, I want them caught flatfooted."

* * *

2200 HOURS - ZERO DAY +31

Ethan waited at the entrance of the bunker, listening through his earbud to the radio as Amber kept him updated on his surroundings. "Okay, the last guard is passing you right now. In ten seconds you can sneak out and go north for twenty yards. That'll put you in the north food forest. Good cover there."

Ethan acknowledged, and then slowly counted. At ten, he pushed gently on the wooden wall of the escape hatch, swinging it upward. The hatch was really a wooden box with a mass of vines growing over it, carefully trimmed to let it swing open but still look like the bramble bushes that grew randomly all over the farm when it was down. He crawled out and swung the hatch shut again, restoring the illusion.

"You have ten seconds before the next guard comes around the corner. Get moving!" Amber said through Ethan's earbud. Perfect; he'd only need about four seconds to make it to the woods, even loaded down with tools and such.

Half crouched, Ethan jogged to the edge of the woods, holding his gear close to keep it as quiet as possible. Then he slowed to a walk and disappeared into the food forest and out of Amber's direct view until he got to the hilltop paddock beyond. "I made it to cover," he said simply.

He focused next on crossing the woods in the dark without setting off any Clan trap. The White Stag people hadn't bothered to risk finding and disarming them, so many traps were still in place, waiting for an enemy. He knew where they all were, in theory, but in the dark, things looked different. It was slow going. He'd move a couple steps, then stop to reexamine his surroundings, comparing small visible details to his memory of trap locations. "Rinse and repeat," Ethan muttered as he struggled to keep his attention on the task at hand. That had always been a challenge for him, but the terror of being seen and shot, or stepping into a trap, or falling over roots while his tools clattered to the enemy, helped to keep him focused. Mostly. After what felt like forever, he looked up and, to his surprise, found himself almost at the tree line. He looked at his watch and cursed—it had taken nearly twenty minutes to cross the roughly one hundred yard span of the north food forest. He was already badly off schedule.

"I don't know how special ops people manage this over and over in training. My brain is fried from searching so hard for the traps, and I think I could have crawled just as fast," Ethan said into the radio.

"Yeah, that took forever," Amber replied. "I thought maybe I lost you. I think I see you now on the edge of Camera Fourteen's view. Stay put for a while. Their guard is awake and looking around. Wait until he ducks down for a smoke or something."

Ethan shook his head. Screw that. It could be quite a while before the guard had to take a leak or light up, and that wouldn't take long enough to keep him out of view anyway. He had to neutralize the guard without firing a shot. Ethan felt at his hip to reassure himself the taser was still firmly in place. Good, he hadn't lost it in the woods. He set down his pack and other gear. He'd have to sneak up on the guy, tase him, tie him up, and blindfold him. He wasn't sure if people could still yell when tased, but he didn't think so and they were pretty far from the nearest sentry. Then he could safely repair the directional antenna.

"Where is he now, in relation to me?" Ethan asked.

"Inside the paddock, facing toward you. Oh wait, he turned around. He's walking to the far side. Now he's staring down the north face of the hill. He's sitting down now, and lighting a smoke. Good time to move."

Perfect. With only his knife, pistol, some zipcuffs, and the taser, Ethan moved out of the tree cover and speed-walked up the hill. He didn't dare run, afraid of drawing the guard's attention if he made noise, but it didn't matter; in only moments he was at the simple three-strand cattle fence that faced the food forest, and crawled through. He crept to the small barn with the animals' feed, keeping it between him and the guard, and caught his breath. Adrenaline had him panting. "Status," he panted into the radio.

"He's still smoking. Sitting down, leaning back on his elbows, staring at stars or his bellybutton or something. You're clear. Be careful. Beginning radio silence."

He appreciated that. He'd need to focus and didn't need Amber trying to talk at him until this situation was dealt with. He spared a moment to consider how hard it must be for her, sitting in safety, watching him attack the guard and being unable to help.

Ethan drew the taser and moved out, sliding first to his left, to position himself directly behind the guard, then crept forward. He took a step, paused. Took two steps, paused. Then another, and another pause. The guard took a languid draw off his cigarette, held it, and slowly exhaled. Ethan kept moving. Now he was ten feet from the guard. Six more feet and he could reach the man with the taser. Three more steps...

Ethan's foot hit a small rock and it skittered across the dirt. Shit. He rushed forward.

The guard's head whipped around and he leapt to his feet, bolt action rifle in hand. He swung the rifle barrel toward Ethan, his eyes wide with surprise.

Before he could bring the rifle to bear, Ethan grabbed the barrel with his left hand and thrust the taser at the guard with his right. The guard let go of the rifle and jumped back, narrowly avoiding the menacing *click click click* of the taser, and then raised his booted foot and thrust it into Ethan's undefended chest. Ethan flew backward, and the rifle went flying as well. The guard rushed toward his fallen foe.

Ethan sat upright and thrust the taser forward. The guard must have seen the move because, without losing momentum, he kicked with his right foot and connected hard with Ethan's wrist. The taser, too, flew away. Pain shot up Ethan's arm, radiating from the wrist; his whole arm felt heavy and refused to obey.

Ethan instinctively clutched his wounded hand to his body. The guard didn't lose a beat, however, and taking a step forward he drove his knee into Ethan's face. Ethan felt his nose break and blood flowed freely as he saw stars. The force of the blow knocked him backwards so he lay on the ground grabbing his face with both hands, heedless of the pain in his right wrist, while the guard stood over him. Ethan rolled over, panicked, trying to get away from his foe and clear his rattled mind. He crawled to get away, trailing blood behind him.

The guard laughed. "I don't know who you are, but you done screwed up. Dumbass." He followed Ethan, kicking him in the ass every other step, which knocked him to the ground. His wounded hand just couldn't hold him up.

Ethan felt the guard grab a fistful of his hair and cried out as he was yanked upright, onto his knees. "Please," he begged, and spit out a mouthful of blood. He moved his right hand toward his boot, where he kept his knife—a Ka-Bar fighting knife. The pain in his wounded wrist made it hard to undo the snap holding the blade in its leather sheath, especially with his pants leg in the way, but he fumbled at it while he spoke: "Why are you doing this to us? We never hurt you…"

It worked. The guard paused, and Ethan discreetly tried to free his knife.

"Your leader led the invaders to us. My family was wiped out," he said, panting, his words pushing into the back of Ethan's head. "She's on all your heads. Say goodbye, Clanner."

Success! The knife slid from its sheath, and Ethan drew it around to the front of his body, and his mind raced through the fog, trying to figure out what to do with the damn thing. Then he felt the guard shift his stance. With a jolt, Ethan realized the man was forcing his head forward and down from behind to put him into a prone position, the perfect position to simply grab Ethan's jaw with his free hand, twist with both hands, and snap Ethan's neck.

Ethan felt a surge of adrenaline course through him as his final moment ticked closer. The world seemed to slow down, and his vision crystalized. Every detail of the dirt and pebbles toward which his face was being thrust became clear. Two ants crawled through the dirt, oblivious of the life-and-death struggle taking place over their heads. Somewhere, a mockingbird chirped and the happy sound was completely at odds with Ethan's situation. It was surreal.

With the knife held like an ice pick, point down, Ethan drew his strength and then, in a sudden burst of effort, let his left arm collapse and flipped over in one fluid movement. He felt his hair tear away from his scalp, a huge clump left in the guard's hand. He whipped his other hand around at the same time, and felt a thrill of victory as the deadly knife point plunged into his attacker's right hip. His momentum continued, and Ethan landed on his back with a solid thud that knocked the wind out of him.

The guard screamed, eyes bulging in surprise, and his right leg buckled. This left him straddling Ethan. His hands went to the knife and Ethan's wrist and pried at them with a strength Ethan couldn't believe.

Ethan felt the bones in his wrist grinding and fire shot up his arm, and heard the "pop" of the cracked radius bone separate from the scaphoid, ligaments tearing with the sound of shredding paper. He lost his grip on the knife.

The guard snarled in pain and fury, face red and contorted, and pulled Ethan's knife out of his hip. With total clarity, Ethan saw blood ooze from the wound in pulses, in time to his heart beat, and knew he'd bleed to death soon—but not before he could ram the knife down into Ethan with the full weight of his body, and with Ethan's wounded wrist there was no way to stop it. The guard raised the knife over his head and held it in both hands, point down, and screamed.

Ethan saw his opportunity, his one chance at life. His legs were pinned under the man straddling him, but the rest of him was free. He grabbed the man's shirt with his left hand and pulled as hard as he could, at the same time sitting up with all the power left in him and tilted his head down. With the combined force of his sitting up while pulling his enemy down toward him, he smashed his forehead into the guard's nose. Ethan's face was immediately covered in blood, which geysered from the guard's ruined nose.

Then Ethan wrapped his right arm around the guard's back, pulling him down toward him as Ethan fell backward.

The guard fell on top of him—and the knife missed.

The guard's leverage was gone, but he tried to swing the blade toward Ethan's head anyway. Ethan grabbed his wrist with his left hand, but the guard's full weight was on him, and he found himself pinned. The guard strained to drive the knife into Ethan's face or neck. Somehow he got his wounded arm in front of him and used the length of his forearm to thrust at the guard's neck, trying to shove him away. For an eternity, the two sat locked in that deadly embrace, both wounded, both growing weak from blood loss, shock, and exhaustion.

And then Ethan felt his strength fading. The guard atop him might be bleeding out all the faster for their exertions, but he had the leverage and body weight to wear Ethan down. Ethan squeezed his eyes shut and put every ounce of strength into one last attempt to shove the guard off him, but it was futile. He knew the HAMnet would fail. The 20s would fail. America would burn before its implacable enemy. All because of one fucking rock that he hadn't seen in the darkness. God had a funny sense of humor. They would die atop that hill together, first Ethan and then his mortally wounded enemy.

The knife moved inch by inch inexorably toward Ethan's head, and the insane guard grinned down at him like a wolf over its prey. Ethan's arm shook from the effort of holding the bloody blade at bay. It was about to give out, and then it would all be over.

A bolt of lightning passed through both Ethan and the guard. What the hell? The faint light of the moon faded in an instant as consciousness fled him. The last thing Ethan saw was another man standing over both of them.

* * *

What the crap? He was alive. Or, he felt alive. He hadn't left pain behind, at least. His arm throbbed with fire, and his face was a pit of agony. Ethan fluttered his eyes open, trying to see, but he could sense only darkness. Then he remembered it was the middle of the night. He forced his eyes to stay open, and his sight slowly adjusted. A light to his right... There was the moon! Hello, moon. How beautiful it was—he'd never truly noticed that before. He decided to just lay there for a moment, reaching out with all his senses while he tried to decipher what the hell was going on, what his situation now was.

A rich and beautiful voice spoke up, a woman's mezzo voice, an angel's voice no doubt. "Bunker man, I see you live. Thanks for the taser, it sure did work."

Ethan turned his head toward the sound and saw an attractive woman couched nearby, sitting on her heels with a rifle across her lap. "What happened?" he asked, and felt stupid for doing so.

"For someone who avoided getting caught by Peter, you sure are dumb, mister. You were fighting. I picked up the taser. I tased him and it knocked you both out." She laughed, and it was the sound of a choir singing. It had the moon's beauty in it.

Okay, that was the after-effects of still being alive after a fight; he'd felt it before, after the ambush where Jed had died. Survivor's High, Michael called it.

"Why?" Ethan croaked, keenly aware that his own voice sounded ragged at best.

"Why did I save you? That's complicated I guess. But mainly because you're a Clanner I don't recognize, and so you must be working against Peter somehow. And this guy here," she said with a motion at a tied up guard, "is a total scumbag. One of Peter's creatures. Now my turn to ask. Why are you here, and what are you doing? Why shouldn't I just kill you and turn your corpse in to Peter?"

A chill washed over Ethan, but then he remembered that she hadn't bound him. She'd bound the guard instead. So, she must want to spare him. This was his game to lose, at this point. All he had to do was not screw up. Hopefully. "Well," he began, "I have a big tin can I'm going to use to fix an antenna, so we can save America..."

* * *

Captain Taggart watched as Eagan ran up to him in the tunnels. The unit had been searching for Black and his goons for half an hour, and the grin on Eagan's face told him volumes.

"Cap, we found them. Black and his men are holed up in an alcove waiting for an enemy unit to pass overhead before they go up through a manhole cover. It's a really big unit, sir. Been going by for ten minutes already. Even has a couple of tanks. So Black can't escape us, yet. We still could have tracked him if he hadn't been blocked in, but this let us catch up faster. It could have taken days to find them if they got out of the tunnels before we found them."

Taggart saw Eagan was babbling with excitement and smiled. "No kidding," he said and smiled wider. "Alright, get our troops in position to open fire into the alcove once the upstairs 'vaders have left the area. We can't engage until the troops are gone, unless we want to rush into hand-to-hand, and we'll take unacceptable losses if we do that. We have to ambush them. For that to work, we can't let them know we're there until we engage them with small arms. Once the troops pass overhead and they seem to be starting to go for the manhole ladder, engage them with everything we have. I want it over before it even began. And search the bodies for hidden weapons."

"Yes, sir. I'm on it," Eagan said, and rushed off to implement the plan.

Taggart watched him sprint away and allowed himself another smile. Eagan was a terrible trooper in barracks, but in the field? He lived for this. And Taggart liked having him at his back. Maybe it was time to promote the kid, if he'd even accept a promotion. He had always enjoyed his lack of responsibility a little too much to ask for promotion, but maybe he'd take a higher rank if Taggart made it an order? Or maybe not. Well, time enough to think about that later—the invaders would pass by soon. Taggart thought of the men in his unit who would become casualties in the ambush, and frowned. In a just world, he wouldn't lose anyone at all.

* * *

0600 HOURS - ZERO DAY +32

Jaz kneeled behind a bush next to Captain Boise, the CO of what was left of Echo Company. Choony had awakened during the night but, being Choony, he stayed well behind the unit, unwilling to participate in the killing. That had pissed off the Marines until Jaz explained that he was a very conscientious objector but a damn fine, courageous man. She had suggested they have Choony ferry ammo to the fighters if there was a battle and it was necessary, and told how he had done that under heavy fire during the fight for the farm. The Marines had warmed up again after that. It would give them one more trained Marine on the firing line. It didn't take a genius to see that would make the small Asian into an advantage to them.

Jaz now shifted her rifle to be ready to fire, as below them, at the bottom of a shallow gully, ten of the Arabic troops and one North Korean walked single-file toward them. She couldn't see the other Marines, but she knew they were out there, deadly ghosts waiting for a slaughter to begin.

Boise whispered, "We have triangulated fire on the ravine, so there will be nowhere for them to hide or run to. They don't have a point man in advance, so as soon as their lead soldier reaches the tree stump to our west, my unit will open fire without a command to maintain surprise. We've done this a dozen times in Iraq, so don't worry, miss."

Jaz nodded and merely waited. She felt calm, which surprised her a bit. There was no way she'd panic or run—not anymore. Die, bastards, die. Totally ready for this shit. Her therapy would begin once the shooting started. "Not worried," she grunted. "We totally got this, Captain." Jaz saw the captain look at her appraisingly, and nod. Oh, yeah, she was ready for this.

As the enemy in front approached the tree stump, Jaz bared her teeth and grinned the grin of a feral wolf. It promised blood and violence.

- 17 -

0600 HOURS - ZERO DAY +32

ETHAN STRUGGLED DOWN the ladder in the tube to the bunker. It was rough going. The simple metal ladder wasn't easy with his injuries, and he was worn out from both fighting the guard and repairing the antenna. He had bruised ribs—maybe cracked—that hurt with each breath, his right wrist seemed fractured, his nose had been shattered, and he had a huge clump of hair missing along with a lot of his scalp. He was covered in dry blood but thankfully had quit bleeding hours ago with some help from the White Stag sympathizer.

The instant he hit the ground at the bottom of the ladder tube, Amber pounced on him like a wild spider monkey, embracing him and burying her face into his chest. All of which hurt quite a bit. Ethan winced in pain. "Not so tight!"

Amber quickly released him. "Sorry."

Taking a step back, she looked him up and down, her gaze lingering on the visible wounds. Then her eyes met his and she said, "Next time, duck when a knee comes at your face. You look terrible."

"I'll keep that in mind."

"Well, whatever you did to get that woman to help you, it worked. All your computer stuff is back online, and your message went out. They replied, but I can't decode anything."

"That's good news. It wasn't anything I did though. She wanted to help me. She said there's a small group of people working to undermine Peter and help the Clan whenever they can. They're the ones who helped Jaz escape."

"Good, at least they aren't all monsters," Amber said. "I hope Jaz is okay out there alone... So how did you fix the internet, with a tin can and some dryer duct? You're like MacGyver with that stuff."

Ethan tried to bow, but it hurt too much. "Well, I call it a cantenna. If YouTube was up, you could see it for yourself. I used the tin can and some duct work to create an insulated tube for the signal and then mounted it where the messed up dish was. It took a while with a signal meter to get the damn thing aimed manually, but I finally got it connected with the rest of the HAMnet after a miserable hour at the top of an antenna with a broken wrist and my face swollen up like this. I could barely see."

Amber looked concerned, but her voice was playful. "You complain too much. Stop playing Call of Duty and do some real work around here. Maybe then you wouldn't get winded climbing an antenna."

While he appreciated her humor, now wasn't the time. Too much pain, too many aches, too close to death. "I need to check the messages now. Give me an hour or two to clean myself up and go over the files, and then we can get some rest. And Amber... Thanks for staying up to watch me on the cameras. Couldn't have been easy staying here, but it was vital. You did good."

He turned without another word and went to the mini-shower to clean the blood off him. The fact that some was his and some was someone else's made him shudder, and he spent a half hour scrubbing himself down before he finally emerged, red and raw, and got to work on the files.

An hour after coming back to the bunker, Ethan had decrypted and read the files. The cover message came from Watcher One, with a bunch of attachments—scans of documents, copies of emails, even a few video clips. The message itself was brief: "Review and decide. You're vital to America, and we feel you deserve to be brought into the fold and join us."

Ethan let out a low whistle. What the hell was going on? He clicked open the scanned documents and skimmed them. They were copies of the Presidential declaration of Martial Law and the terms imposed. The President's and Vice President's death certificates—that was terrible news—and a vote tally of what remained of the House of Representatives, appointing General Houle as interim Secretary of Defense *and* the sole remaining member of the Joint Chiefs of Staff "for the duration of the crisis."

Amber, reading over Ethan's shoulder, let out a muffled cry and then said, "They're really dead? And this general is in charge of...what, the whole country? Were there enough representatives left for the vote to even be legit?"

"No, but without new elections, that's what we have. It doesn't bode well for later, when we kick the invaders out, does it? I mean, canceling elections is legal under Martial Law, or at least that's how this could play out. Damn them for saying it's for the duration of the crisis. That's a dictator tactic. How frikkin' long is the duration?"

"Let's watch the video clips," Amber suggested. "Maybe they'll shed some light."

The very first clip, a scant ten seconds long, showed a satellite image of North America, which then zoomed in repeatedly until it showed the Clan's farm. Ethan shivered. It meant they knew his location, despite his HAMnet precautions. But that also confirmed Watcher One was legit and loyal to the U.S. "I suppose if Watcher was a Korean agent, the farm would already be gassed or bombed, right? So that more or less proves he is who he says he is, a loyal American."

Amber squeezed his shoulder. "It's also a bit of a threat, or at least I feel threatened. A power play. We know where you live...so do what we say. And why haven't they sent help, if they know where we are?"

The next video answered her question. It was a shaky cell phone video of a soldier with a headset on, with a joystick. He sat before a computer monitor that showed an aerial view, and it streaked by at fantastic speed. A young male voice on the video said, "Sir, we're receiving Dark Ryder's updates. The asset is still operational." Another voice replied, "Very well, abort mission. If he's alive, we won't risk collateral damage to his infrastructure." Then the video ended.

The third video showed General Houle standing before a few dozen well-dressed but frightened-looking civilians. Ethan recognized a Virginia senator among them. It was a long video, but the gist of it was to confirm just what Watcher One had said. What remained of the U.S. government had voted Houle into the position of ultimate power, if only temporarily. It also showed that, wherever Houle was, he'd gathered up enough surviving Congressmen and Senators to his location that he felt confident holding such a vote. Were they coerced? Impossible to tell.

The final video was a close up of the same man from the last one. General Houle. It looked as though he was in an office at a desk. Ethan hit the play button.

"Hello," the General said. Even sitting, he was an imposing figure. He was built like a Marine, Ethan decided.

He had a square jaw and buzz cut, high cheekbones, and eyes that showed no emotion. Dead eyes in a caricature of what a capable officer should look like. Ethan disliked him immediately. "If you are watching this, then we've succeeded and you are alive. Many of the coded orders you've been sending out have put a large number of American loyalists and soldiers in harm's way, to draw the enemy away from you. This is why your region is so devoid of strong enemy presence."

The General coughed, and it sounded wet and more like a gurgle than a cough, but when he spoke his voice was again clear and strong. "Sorry about that, Ryder. I got a whiff of their Pea Soup—that's what my boys and girls are calling their defoliant fog—and this is the result. Do avoid that fog at all costs. Anyway, the reason we've devoted irreplaceable resources to keeping you as safe as we're able is that you are connected to both the U.S. military via Watcher One, and more survivor and Militia groups than we can count. Also, if we go wide from our location, the Korean hackers will track us down and we can't have that. Not yet."

Houle then smiled, and Ethan noted that the grin seemed to reach his eyes this time. Ethan's tension level fell a little—at least the caricature's grin seemed genuine. "Soon it won't matter though," the General continued. "Operation Backdraft is nearly set. And we need you to make it happen. One of the Militias—unknown which one—has some sort of tight-beam communication with a surviving nuclear submarine in the North Atlantic. You'll re-send orders for us that no one but the brave men and women on that submarine can decode. Likewise, you'll pass on information to Watcher One, who will relay additional orders to an isolated Air Force control center. I can't tell you their orders, unfortunately. Need-to-know, you being at risk in the field, and all that. But I can tell you this, Dark Ryder: if you decide to cooperate, this war will change forever. We'll be back on an even footing with those bastards."

He straightened his collar, buying time while he collected his thoughts. "Ryder, our civilian leadership let us down. We knew something major was coming days before their EMPs hit us, but it was politically inexpedient to respond, to take proactive measures to protect our citizens. Those politicians are largely dead now, but that's a mixed blessing. On the one hand, we'll get around to replacing them, and their replacements will be people like you with the will and flexible mindset necessary to survive and operate uncaptured. On the other hand, it means I'm running the whole show for now, and that is not a position I desired. I do it for the love of our country, just like you, but I don't have to like it."

The General steepled his hands in front of him, fingertips resting on his chin, looking pensive. After a long moment, he continued: "Within seventy-two hours, you will receive our coded information through a relay network of terminals we've established. We'll use it once and then never again. The enemy will have no way to track it back to you or to the source of the orders. That coded information consists of the go-orders for Backdraft. You need only to distribute it as you have been doing—the right people will see it, recognize what it is, and proceed accordingly. I don't exaggerate when I tell you that the future course of the world likely depends on the success of your mission. It goes without saying that we'll be in an untenable position, in the long run, if you fail. Good luck and God bless, son."

Ethan stared at the monitor, riveted to the now-frozen face of General Houle. His mind raced, a jumble of thoughts and feelings he couldn't yet sort out but he noted revulsion in there somewhere. Air Force control stations and nuclear submarines? Equalizing the strategic situation? Houle hadn't spelled it out more than that, but Ethan felt a raw, roiling pit in his stomach as he drew the obvious conclusions from his limited information.

"My God, Amber. They're going to launch EMPs at the enemy. Or worse. I wondered why it hadn't happened yet, and now we know. No one was left to push the button, until now." He looked up at her with dismay. "They want it to be me!"

Amber narrowed her eyes as her own mind raced along parallel tracks. Then she raised an eyebrow and shrugged one shoulder. "Can't do more damage than it has already, right? I mean, we've already been hit with EMPs. Knocking out all their equipment and communications seems like it really would give us a fighting chance."

Ethan nodded, but the knot of dread tightening in his gut refused to hear her logic. He spent the rest of the day brooding, deep in thought and nursing his wounds.

* * *

0900 HOURS - ZERO DAY +32

Cassy forced a smile through cracked and scabbed-over lips. Grandma Mandy had hobbled up to her, as she did every day for as long as the guards would let her. Usually only a few minutes, but lately they'd been letting her stay longer. Probably because Mandy looked like hell. Cassy's eyes roved over her mom, noting every feature. It could be the last time they spoke, after all—her mom looked that bad.

"Good morning, darling daughter," Mandy said. "How are you finding the accommodations?" She chuckled, but it sounded so very feeble that Cassy winced.

Cassy leaned against the post to which she remained chained and tried not to be embarrassed by the terrible smell of her own urine and feces. Toilet visits for Cassy weren't on Peter's agenda. And yet Mandy made no mention of it, ever, and never wrinkled her nose. She was surely the best mom on the planet.

"I'm fine, Mom. They haven't questioned me today so far, so I think I'm not even bleeding anywhere at the moment." She peered at her mom still, through the eye that wasn't swollen shut. "You need insulin. Let me tell someone where the... Where they can find more for you." She didn't want to mention the bunker by name, just in case they were overheard. "If you don't let me, that's like suicide, and last I heard God hates suicide. Please, I'm begging you."

Mandy cut her off with an upraised hand. "No. Stop asking. I didn't come here to argue with you, honey. I come to talk to my daughter while I can. If you tell people where *it* is, then Peter could find out. Ethan's doing something more important than me."

Cassy's gut churned. Her mom could die while a huge stock of medicine sat only a few hundred yards away. She liked Ethan, but this was her mom after all. "Mom, we need you. Brianna and Aidan need you more than they ever have before. What will they do without you to look out for them? You have to let me do this!"

"Jumping crackers," Mandy exclaimed. It was her version of swearing and Cassy usually found it irritating, but not these days. Mandy said, "God has a plan for me, honey. If that plan is for me to come sit by His side in Heaven, I'm okay with that. But I think He has more in store for me than that. Be patient and have faith. God's will be done, whether we like it or not. I won't have Ethan's death on my conscience when I die. Cassy, I love you, but if you risk Ethan —maybe America—just for one person's life, even mine, then I'll never forgive you. Do you understand me?"

Cassy certainly did understand. Mom had never said

anything like that to her before. She'd never threatened to turn her back on her daughter, not once. Not even when Brianna came out looking nothing like Cassy's husband, nor when Cassy then confessed to that one infidelity at a business conference in Vegas. In fact, Mandy had been Cassy's biggest supporter and had paid for marriage counseling out of her own limited income. Mandy's church friends had shunned her for supporting Cassy once word got out, but Mandy never wavered, not once. And now she was threatening to turn her back. Cassy realized her mouth was hanging open and hastily took back control of herself.

"Yes. I get it. I do. I promise I won't send anyone to get more insulin without your permission. But I love you, Mom, and I don't want to see you go."

Mandy placed a hand on Cassy's filthy knee. "I love you too, sweetie. Thank you for understanding. I suppose I should go help with cleanup. Breakfast is about over..."

"Mom, I don't know how much time you have left. Considering where I am, I'm not sure how much time I have left, either. They'll kill me eventually, if God doesn't save us all first. Can we just sit here awhile?"

Mandy nodded, quickly enough that Cassy knew her end must be nearer than she let on. They chatted together for a long time, talking about old times, the births of the kids, Grandpa, Disney World. All the things that made the old world so much better than the new one. Cassy hoped it wouldn't be the last time they got to sit like that.

* * *

1100 HOURS - ZERO DAY +32

The guards had gathered the Clan together before lunch, and Peter walked out of the house to talk to them. He had his well-practiced grim look on his face as he approached the crowd, who turned to look at him. "Well, here we all are. Another day, another problem." Peter changed his expression to one of pain or grief, also clearly practiced in front of a mirror. Nothing ever really looked spontaneous about him, except acts of violence. "And it's a big problem this time, friends. As you know, I've taken it on myself to protect you all, to keep White Stag and Clan both safe from the chaos that's right outside our door. But, despite my generosity, you *still* refuse to tell me where the food and other gear are stored."

Peter paused to let that sink in and watched their dread grow. By now the Clan knew that whenever he talked to them like a sorrowful uncle, something horrific was about to happen. As the Clan's faces grew apprehensive, Peter suppressed a smile. It would ruin the effect. Instead, he turned sideways to them, bowed his head, and pressed the bridge of his nose with thumb and forefinger and then let out a long, frustrated sigh.

"Well, I've done some calculations. It seems that if we continue on half-rations as we have been, we won't have enough to last the final couple weeks until something is ready for harvest or we can hunt up more meat. But, if we go to quarter rations, no one will be strong enough to last the cold winter, much less sow and harvest. To protect my flock, a couple sheep need to be thrown to the wolves. But I'm not totally heartless, my friends."

Peter gazed over the crowd and embraced the rage he felt at those ungrateful, uncooperative little shits. He kept his face a mask of pained determination—or what he thought showed that—and enjoyed the feeling of impending doom a moment longer. Then he said, "So, I'll let you decide. My guards will split you into five groups of seven, and each group will have a mix of ages from thirteen on up. Then, each group will select one from among them to make the ultimate sacrifice so the rest of you may live. Unfortunately, I can't allow you to refuse a decision, so any group that declines to make this hard decision will be taken in lieu of all the other groups' choice. I'm sure they'll thank you for your noble sacrifice. That is all. Guards, split them up, right now. Give them an hour to choose and then come get me. Oh, and if they share where the stockpile is, let me know—we can stop this whole mess. Then when we're done, whoever's left will get lunch."

Peter turned on his heels and strode into the house. Let the bastards sweat it out. If they give up the stockpile, his plan would work. If they didn't, then the group would get rid of the least useful members among them, which would suit Peter just as well. Either way, his own people would eat just fine this winter.

Jim stayed right on his heels and closed the door before speaking. "Boss, are you sure this is a great idea? I mean, why don't we just kill off Cassy, her mom, and those three Marines? And someone did kill one of our guards on the north post. What happened there? I think our Marine guests did it."

Peter smiled. "Listen, Jim. Cassy is the only one who knows where the stockpile is. She's also the only one who knows a lot about this 'permaculture' thing she has going on at this farm, and we need her knowledge. This farm outproduces anything I've seen with the usual farming methods. And those three Marines, they work harder than any six other Clan people combined."

"But they're dangerous, boss."

"Of course they are, but until spring planting is done, we need them. And about the guy we lost, I suspect he had some personal beef with one of our own people. He was kind of an asshole, you know. Remember—the simplest answer is usually the right one."

Jim grinned. "You're the boss for a reason. But hey, when it's time to pop those Marines, can I do it? I always wanted to kill some of those cocky asshats."

Peter laughed out loud at that, the first real laugh he'd had in a while. "Sure, Jimbo. They're all yours when the time comes. Cassy too. You deserve some payback for what she did to you."

* * *

1230 HOURS - ZERO DAY +32

Jaz and one of the Marines, Cpl. Reed, belly-crawled toward "Clanholme," approaching from the more distant eastern pond. It wasn't as well guarded as the other ponds when Jaz ran away, and it offered a good, if distant, view of most of the homestead.

"So, like, do we just swim the pond?" Jaz asked as they reached the muddy edge.

The other woman nodded. "Aff. Take off your blouse and shorts. They slow you down and make noise. Once we get across, follow my lead. We are only here to scout, remember. Our orders are to get eyes-on and report the situation so we have operational intel about the enemy."

Jaz followed instructions, stripping to her bra and panties, and the two women inched into the water, careful to make no splashing noises. It was slow going, but some five minutes later they were across the pond, face-first in the mud of the far shore.

Reed carried a small pair of sporting binoculars on a lanyard around her neck and used it to scan the encampment. She pursed her lips and let out a short, sharp breath, then handed the binoculars to Jaz.

Jaz felt a knot in her stomach but made herself look anyway. She immediately wished she hadn't. In the courtyard by the outdoor kitchen, it seemed every one of the Clan and White Stag people was gathered. The Clan was clustered in the middle, surrounded by armed guards. Peter stood before them all, strutting and talking. Behind him were five of the Clan, facing away from the crowd, on their knees, with hands bound behind their backs. There were two teen boys, one adult woman who looked very frail, and two of the oldest Clanners. She searched, but it didn't look like Grandma Mandy was among them.

Then Peter drew a pistol from his belt and turned to face the kneeling five. He put the pistol to the back of one of the teens' heads, and Jaz looked away. Without a word, Jaz handed the binoculars back to Cpl. Reed. "Let's go."

Jaz turned away and slithered on her belly toward the water, but Reed wasn't behind her. Jaz glanced back and saw the Marine peering through the binoculars. Jaz shook her head and kept going. As she made her way across the pond with a slow dog paddle, she heard the slow, steady boom of a pistol going off every few seconds. Jaz clenched her jaw and reached the other side. And she made a decision. When the time came, she was totally going to kill every last damn one of those White Stag bastards.

In the back of her mind, she wondered why she wasn't crying about all this, but she shoved the thought away. Grief wasn't useful right now. She needed her "streeter" now, not the softer Clanner she'd learned to become. And that carried its own grief.

- 18 -

1230 HOURS - ZERO DAY +32

ETHAN WATCHED THE cameras in horror as Peter sorted the Clan into groups. His stomach lurched as Peter the dictator had one person from each group bound and shoved to their knees before the assembled Clan. Beside him, Amber gasped, and he could hear the faint sniffles of her crying, though she wasn't sobbing. They'd been through too much for sobbing anymore, Ethan thought somberly.

Movement on another camera caught his eye. The eastern pond camera triggered only when there was movement, so it was hard to miss the screen lighting up. "Whoa. Is that Jaz?"

Amber gripped his shoulder tightly. "I think so."

"Who's she with?"

"Looks like a soldier. A woman. Did one of ours escape?"

"No, and she's certainly not Sturm," Ethan said. "Look, it's someone new. They're scouting the settlement. God, I hope they have a plan to stop what's about to happen. Jaz must have hooked up with the unit I sent her way, some Marine reservists."

"Where's the rest of 'em?"

Ethan scanned the panel of screens and flicked through the even longer list of cameras, but nothing else was amiss. So, just scouting. They could do nothing to help the Clan, not yet, not in time. Now his worry was that Jaz would do something stupid once she figured out what was going on at the farm. He let out a breath he hadn't realized he'd been holding—Jaz turned around and was leaving. The other woman stayed behind for a while—long enough to witness what came next—and then she too turned and both left to the south after crossing the pond again.

He didn't watch the executions; too painful. Instead he focused on flicking through cameras, trying to again catch sight of Jaz, but she was out of view. "Dammit. I lost her."

Amber said, "Why are you trying to find her again? She got away, right?"

"I was hoping to see where she went, but yeah. Their camp must be way outside my camera range. If I could see the unit and maybe see how many there are and where they are, I could…I don't know, try to get in touch with them and coordinate." Maybe it was a silly idea, but Ethan wanted to feel like he was doing *something*, because after what just happened, he felt pretty damn helpless. "I gotta do something, Amber."

"Why don't you hack that satellite again?" Amber replied without conviction. It was obvious she was as messed up over the executions as he was. "Maybe it's got a camera in addition to all the communication stuff."

Ethan jumped from his seat and wrapped his arms around her, kissing her cheek. She looked pretty surprised, but he didn't care. "Genius. Not that comms bird, but I can get into another one that *does* have cameras. It's an older satellite, but it'll work for this. I'm not supposed to know about it, but I have my ways."

Ethan sat back down and kept busy for the next half hour

trying one data tunnel after another. Most would be fried, he knew, but something would be up... Bingo. There it was. He focused on getting access through the backdoor he'd learned of, but it was slow going. A lot had changed since it was put in, but nothing a Virtual Machine running on networked computers couldn't handle—he only had to get backwards compatibility. He didn't know how long it took, but eventually he got in.

He found the general area of the farm through trial and error and then began the laborious process of defining a grid and sequentially checking each "square." Normally, he'd have had to upload a rider program to leech the signal and passively check, but he doubted anyone on the ground was monitoring for hackers on old satellites these days.

It took longer than he would have liked, but eventually he found what he was looking for. Well to the north of the farm he spotted two riders, one in military garb, heading into the wild woods. He tracked them to an area well inside the woodlands and simply observed for the next half hour. He counted fourteen people, twelve in uniform. The other two were almost certainly Jaz and Choony.

Ethan turned to Amber and said, "I count twelve soldiers. Not as many as I expected from an entire company, but beggars can't be choosers. So, it's confirmation. Now we need to get in touch with them. I'll radio Joe on our channel when the camera shows he's clear, and tell him to bring another secure radio with him and to scout to the north. He can drop the radio when no one is looking, and when I have the coordinates, I can send a coded message to the Marines to go pick it up. We need to be able to talk directly to them if we're going to coordinate and share information."

Amber frowned. "Alright, then. I guess I'll keep my eyes on the cameras for a while, and you go take a nap. You've been at this forever, and you're hurt. If I see him alone, I'll come get you."

Ethan nodded and without a word walked toward the bunks. He was still healing, and the emotional toll of the day—not to mention the tedium of hacking and searching via satellite—had drained him completely.

* * *

1700 HOURS - ZERO DAY +32

Taggart was in a chipper mood. Black escaped but he'd been defanged, and the gear had been recovered. A lot of it was shot up, but the radio still worked, along with the two computers among other things.

Eagan entered the alcove they were using as a temporary command post and saluted him. "Cap, all the bodies have been dumped down to a lower level. The invader unit kept right on going after we ambushed Black, but I have a couple people keeping watch in case more come through. The radio and laptops are set up, and we have intermittent WiFi from another HAMnet antenna we focused our tin can on."

The "tin can" was a directional antenna, useful for setting up a direct data connection that didn't bleed signal all over the place like a beacon. The downside was that if you moved it, you'd have to spend an hour refocusing it before connection could be re-established.

"Very well. Turn it on and let's see if the 20s have sent us any more intel. We retrieved the cipher book so we can still decode. Have someone notify me if anything comes in. Put half the unit on duty, and put the rest on personal time. No one is to leave the base, however."

Eagan made a sloppy, almost insolent salute, grinned, spun on his heels, and left Taggart alone again. Taggart gratefully eased himself down against one wall and tipped his helmet forward over his eyes. Like soldiers everywhere and in every time, he fell asleep in seconds.

He thought he heard his name. Taggart opened one eye and saw Eagan standing in front of him. "Captain," Eagan said looking apologetic, "you wanted me to wake you if we received a transmission. One has come in."

Taggart yawned and struggled to his feet, then grabbed his rifle and the cipher decoding book they had retrieved. "When did the message come in?" he asked.

"Timestamp says hours ago, but it only just finished downloading. Weak connection, Cap."

Taggart followed Eagan to the cul-de-sac they had set up for the electronics and walked to the terminal. To the Militia tech at the computer, he said, "Thank you, private. You may go. Eagan, you're with me." Taking the chair, Taggart opened the book and began to decipher the message. It would have gone fast and easy on a capable intranet, but they had to do things Old School, and it took a while to get the decode sequence correct. Once he had, though, the message popped open quickly enough.

Taggart read and then reread the message. He looked at Eagan, a grin spreading across his face. "So, shitbird. It seems this Operation Backdraft is a go any time in the next seventy-two hours. No idea what it is yet, but the message ends by saying, 'Precaution: faraday' and repeating it three times. It must be important. Any idea what a faraday is?"

"Yeah, I know. Why don't you, Cap?"

"Eagan..."

"Okay, fine. You have no sense of humor these days, Captain. Faraday means 'faraday cage,' which is a fancy way of saying we should put all our electronics into a metal enclosure so that the energy of an EMP will move around our gear, rather than through it. This spares our circuits from the effects of electromagnetic pulses. They're gonna EMP the enemy by EMPing everybody." He frowned. "There are a hundred ways this could backfire on us."

Taggart eyed Eagan warily, but he showed no hint of insubordination. "So, we need to find metal enclosures... And where do we find those?"

Eagan grinned. "Throw 'em in the trash, sir. Metal trash cans with tight-fitting lids will work, especially down here. Or a working microwave—just put the gear inside, and it'll keep the EMPs out just like it keeps the microwaves in. I read that somewhere."

Taggart nodded. "You know some weird things, Eagan. Very well. Send a detail for one of those. Now another problem. We have received coordinates from this 20s guy, Dark Ryder, and he says the straight poop is that our old friend, Spyder, is bunkered up at that location. Apparently, he and the Koreans are on unfriendly terms and internal conflict between them is considered imminent."

Eagan shrugged. "Yeah, Cap. We got those two dogs barking at each other with our little PsyOps raid. Glad to see your brilliant idea worked. Sir."

Taggart ignored the private's attempt at banter. Some other time, maybe. "I'm thinking we need to organize another raid—"

They were interrupted by a fresh-faced private, one of the survivors of another unit that he'd picked up some time ago. "Sir," the private said as he saluted, "we have a situation at Beta Portal."

"The south manhole cover?"

"Yes, sir! At least a dozen soldiers requesting entrance. American, sir. One has a radio, and they said they were directed to us by the 20s."

"Very well. Show me." Taggart followed, and they arrived in minutes at an entrance.

Twelve Army soldiers—regulars, from their insignias—

stood in the alcove in formation at attention. "Why were these soldiers granted access before I was advised," Taggart said to Eagan.

"They came down while we were in conference, sir. Security breach—coulda been a total FUBAR, and I'll deal with that later."

Taggart nodded, then strode into the alcove. One soldier in front of the others saluted, and Taggart returned the salute. "So you've been reassigned to my command?"

"Sergeant Beaudoin reporting for duty, sir. I have eleven surviving soldiers. They're yours now, sir, if you can use us."

Taggart smiled. "I certainly can. Very well. Put your men at ease, Beaudoin, and we'll get some chow for your boys and girls. I'll return after you've all eaten, and we can debrief you then."

Taggart turned without waiting for more saluting silliness and walked away with Eagan on his heels. He still hadn't gotten used to people saluting him and really didn't like it much even in this subterranean safety where no enemy could see it and mark him as an officer.

"Shitbird, as I was saying. We need to organize a new raid. Obviously, we have to leave our electronics down here, but we have what, forty-five people now? Roughly. God bless the 20s for that. Have someone map those coordinates we received, and let me know where it is."

"Happily, Cap. Time to crush the Spyder. If we can hit him in time, we can probably use his bunker as a COP."

"If it's in a good tactical position, then yeah, we'll definitely use it for a combat outpost. The area's bound to be highly kinetic, so we'll need something to fall back to anyway. Then, when this Backdraft op goes up, we'll press the OpFor and their Korean masters from their own lapdog's base."

"Sir, I thought the U.S. Army doesn't fall back, sir. Don't

you mean retrograde?"

"Don't be an oxygen thief, shitbird. Enough of the milspeak. Now go follow my orders, pretty please and with cherries on top, before I bust you back down to private."

Eagan didn't bother to make his usual reply—that he was already a private—before veering off to follow orders. Taggart was a bit disappointed. Maybe Eagan was actually getting used to Taggart's field promotion being essentially permanent. He hoped not, as Eagan gave him his only real sense of camaraderie these days.

- 19 -

2200 HOURS - ZERO DAY +32

JAZ STOOD ATOP the hill and, though the intervening food forest blocked her view, she stared down toward the farm with narrowed eyes and a clenched jaw. "Soon I'll kill every last damn one of them," she muttered.

Choony frowned. "So much hate will eat you from the inside, my good friend," he commented. It was a shame to watch Jaz growing harder, colder. Of course, he'd never met "streeter" Jaz before, the hard-eyed survival-first young woman she'd had to become in the city, so he feared this new world had destroyed the girl's innocence. But Choony still saw the beautiful person inside her, and he did his best to nurture that, to keep it alive in her. She deserved better.

Jaz exhaled a long sigh. "I know, Choony, and I hate that, but not as much as I hate Peter and his goons. They totally deserve the whirlwind that's coming for them."

Joe Ellings, on Jaz's other side, shrugged. "It is what it is, Jaz. But with these knives and pistols you've brought, me and my friends reckon we can arm up your people. When the time comes, Peter won't know what hit him."

Choony said, "So how are you going to deliver these

weapons to the Clan? You said you had a plan."

"Easy," Joe replied. "We'll stash them behind the outhouses, in the reeds."

Choony considered this for a moment. The farm had three outhouses, which led to 220-gallon concrete cisterns. Worms ate everything that went in, and their castings—along with urine and any water—drained into a long, gravel-filled trench that acted as a grow bed for some sort of swamp plants. Overflow went into a second trench, which in turn overflowed into a swale and soaked into the ground. He'd seen the water as it left the trenches, and it was crystal clear.

"So the Clan will pick up the weapons as opportunity allows?" Choony asked.

Joe nodded and opened his mouth to respond, but his radio crackled: "Hey, Joe, status check."

Joe clicked the button on his radio and it chirped, letting him know he was broadcasting, but then the little red power light went out. He tried again, but nothing happened. "Battery died," he said to Choony and Jaz, "so y'all best hightail it out of here afore someone comes to check on me."

Choony nodded. Yes, that sounded like a great idea. "Alright, Joe. Good to see you again, and I thank you for the help you're providing to my new family down there."

Jaz motioned to one of the two Marines who had accompanied them to the farm. "Alright, let basecamp know we're heading home."

The young man pulled out his handheld, but frowned. "No power on it. When we get back, I'm definitely going to square away whoever was on charging duties."

Choony felt a tiny spider of doubt in the back of his mind. Both radios? At the same time? That didn't bode well, but nothing was yet certain. "Alright, Jaz. Let's get back and grab another radio so we can let Ethan know the plan."

They shook Joe's hand, and then they headed north

while the White Stag sympathizer walked south toward the farm.

* * *

Taggart stood with his command staff—Eagan, another soldier, and one of the Militia members—looking at the operational area map. It was just a folding paper map from a gas station, but it showed the streets around Spyder's base. Six pennies were spread around to show the general location of each squad under his command for the current operation. An unused stack of nickels would be used for enemy positions. Eventually. So far everything was quiet, and that made Taggart nervous. "Where the hell is the OpFor?" he asked Eagan, but it was rhetorical.

Eagan, ever the smartass, shrugged and said, "Maybe they realized what douchebags they are and, overcome with remorse, they all killed themselves."

Taggart fought the urge to grin. "And deny us the satisfaction of killing them ourselves? That would just be adding insult to injury. No, they're in there somewhere. Those few blocks are a maze of rubble now. We just have to figure out where they are."

He looked again at the map. Spyder's three blocks—no, now five, the bastard—were outlined in red pen, and his outposts outside the red zone were noted with X marks. "We've already cleared his outposts, all four of them. They were empty. Eagan, status checks."

A minute later, Eagan returned and nodded. "They're all now in position at the perimeter and awaiting furthers. Still no contacts. Maybe Spyder's guys are at the dee-fack."

Taggart kept looking at the map, but replied, "Neg. It's after 2200 hours so they aren't taking chow. And our latest intel said Spyder is once again being a good little lapdog, so I doubt he's been wiped out by our Hajji visitors and their DPRK masters. Do we see any civilians?"

"No, sir. No reports of civvy contact. But RumInt says Spyder has a dusk curfew for civilians, so that's not out of order."

"RumInt? Eagan, rumors are not intel. But you're right, he does have a curfew. Still, I don't like how quiet it is. Advise all units to maintain a slow op tempo. Slow and steady, stay alive, converge on the objective together. I need live soldiers, not dead heroes. Something ironic about using the enemy's own radios against them."

Eagan grinned, saluted, then moved aside to get on the radio leaving Taggart to his worry and his map.

Taggart's radio, tuned to the all-units channel, crackled to life. "Zipline, Zipline, this is Bravo One. We have visual on six Hajjis, small arms only, twelve meters east of Oscar Four, unaware of our presence. They're in a bagged emplacement."

Taggart glanced at the map. Second Platoon, First Squad had visual on six Arabs in some sort of a firing nest east of a major intersection—objective four. But that intersection was a poor tactical location. Spyder's HQ was thought to be at Oscar One, and this intersection was only of secondary interest. Something felt wrong.

Eagan's voice interrupted his thoughts. "Cap, that doesn't make any sense. Why would they put troops there? And why Hajjis instead of Spyder's gangbangers?"

Taggart stared at the map, and then it came to him. "Crap. Yes, it does make sense. Look, if we had just made a beeline for Spyder's HQ we'd have had to go right through that intersection. They'd have flanking fire on our guys. So, there have to be other enemy positions there. And stationing Hajjis there means Spyder's either been reinforced or replaced. I'm betting on reinforced. If I'm right, it's a trap."

Taggart picked up his radio and clicked. "Bravo One, this

is Zipline. Take cover and hold in place... Bravo Two, Bravo Three, divert east toward Oscar Four to scout for additional enemy positions. Go easy and avoid contact. Something's not right; keep your asses wired tight. Alpha, did you copy?"

The Alpha commander acknowledged, and then the next ten minutes seemed to tick by at a snail's pace. It felt like the seconds hand on Taggart's mechanical watch moved in slow motion.

Finally, his radio came to life again. "Zipline, this is Bravo Two. We've got eyes on another emplacement, corner November Echo at Oscar Four, second floor window emplacement." Immediately after, Bravo Three squad reported in the same information but at November Whisky corner.

So. Three emplacements at that one intersection. One on the ground just west of it, one in a building to the northeast, and a third in a building to the northwest. Anyone walking into that intersection would have been cut to ribbons. But why there? Taggart had deemed it the least likely objective they'd have to assault, which is why it was objective four.

Eagan returned and saluted annoyingly. Any time they weren't outside, Eagan went through this stupid routine, forcing Taggart to salute him back. Damn shitbird. "As you were. What now?" Taggart snapped, not bothering to return the salute this time.

"Sir, Alpha One reports all units have found nothing. They've scouted the other three objectives. Oscar One was clearly Spyder's HQ, but no one is there. There's even chow there, still warm. They must have left in a hurry. It's a bug-out."

Taggart clicked his radio again. "Alpha, this is Zipline. Converge on Oscar Four, but recon each block en route. How copy?"

Alpha's commander acknowledged, and Taggart nodded.

Their commander would be breaking the squads into fire teams right now to speed the search, probably, but that was her decision. Taggart didn't care how she got it done, as long as they swept the area and converged on objective four.

Eagan suddenly grew serious, losing his usual smirk. "Captain, I gotta tell you, the little lizard part of my brain is screaming 'danger!' at me. I don't like this one bit."

Well, no shit. "Yes, Eagan, I know. I feel it, too. But with those outposts empty, we had no one to question, no chance of getting paper intel. We're blind. They know we're here, somewhere. They left their little self-styled castle in a hurry. I don't know if they had scouts or if the Koreans are using their satellites or spy birds, but whatever they're doing we know, we don't have surprise anymore. We have to assume it's a trap."

"So why don't we just retrograde the hell out of there?"

"Eagan, I hate that word. It's 'retreat,' not 'retrograde,' got it? But the reason is simple. We need information. Those are Hajjis down there, at least some of them are. We need intel."

Taggart then clicked the radio again. "Alpha and Bravo, this is Zipline. SITREP."

Both units reported their situation, but nothing much had changed. Bravo was in place, and Alpha was sweeping through Spyder's now-empty turf to converge with Bravo. Alpha thought they'd be there in ten mikes. Taggart waited. And waited.

His radio chirped. "Zipline, this is Alpha. We are rendezvous at Oscar Four, with eyes on two emplacements." She then gave coordinates that put her squad covering the gap Bravo had left to the west of the intersection and two squads to the south and west to reinforce Bravo platoon.

Despite the late hour and cool night air, Taggart felt himself begin to sweat. Adrenaline was a bitch, but it could be controlled. Not stopped, but channeled into something useful. He took a moment to gather himself. It was time for his troops to either 'get kinetic,' as he thought of it, or get out. But they badly needed intel—the situation had somehow changed dramatically, and he was in the dark about it. Changing that would require someone to question, enemy locations, paperwork... Intel. Very well. Time to get kinetic.

"All units, this is Zipline. I have TOD 2247 hours, repeat, 2247... mark. Bravo One, at 2250 engage. Repeat, 2250 engage. Alpha One, hold position unless you see another emplacement or Bravo needs support. Alpha tune Tac 2, Beta tune Tac 3. How copy?"

Both platoon commanders confirmed the orders. Then there was again nothing to do but wait. Taggart frowned. War time was like being in garrison: Nine-tenths of the time was just waiting. The difference was that final tenth. On base, it was spent training. At war, it was spent in terror, screaming, killing, and dying. This war was no different than the Sandbox had been, except bloodier and harder.

"Eagan, thirty seconds. Get to the radio room. Grab our Militia guy to relay if you need to. I'm on channel Tac 1 still."

More waiting. Seemed like forever. Again. But really it was ten forever-long seconds. This part of war always sucked, but this time it was worse—he was the captain, now, in the rear with the gear. Before all this, he would have been Alpha One's right-hand man and in the thick of it. More dangerous, but better able to keep an eye on his boys and girls in the fight. Back here, he was helpless to do anything of much use except stay alive so his unit could maintain command integrity. What a damn oxymoron *that* was. Command Integrity. Being an officer officially sucked balls, not that he'd ever talk like that around Eagan again. Shoot, that was a tragedy in its own right. He and Eagan had been friends before. Weird, dysfunctional friends, but Eagan was like his own lost little brother, and Taggart suspected Eagan thought of him as a father figure. Eagan's dad, he knew, had skipped out when the boy was seven—

DING! Taggart's alarm chirped. 2250 hours, and time for his people to live or die. He heard the abrupt chaos of unit chatter emanating from the "radio room," and Eagan's steady voice droning in reply, though Taggart couldn't make out the words. If anyone needed him, his radio would sing; until then, Taggart was just ornamental.

For long seconds, he heard the faint chatter from Eagan's room, a steady back-and-forth of lifesaving information. Abruptly, Taggart's radio squawked into life, making him jump. "Zipline, Zipline, it's Alpha One," it screamed, though Taggart didn't recognize the man's voice. So, their commander must be dead or pinned. She was effective, and he hoped she was just pinned down. "We got rumble in the jungle, sir! Armor coming down the main road from north and south toward us." There was a pause and then the voice screamed, "Are you sure? Goddammit!" He'd obviously been too stressed to remember to stop transmitting. "Zipline, we got three, no *four* birds inbound to the west, and the Hajjis are going full retrograde, sir. They're squirting all over themselves!"

Taggart cursed. Tanks or some other hardened vehicles were coming in from both sides like hammers. The enemy was "squirting"—running the hell away—and four enemy helicopters were coming in from the side. Helicopters were his worst fear as a soldier.

He reached for the radio, but as his hand touched it, it chirped again: "Zipline, Alpha One. Bravo One has overrun, um, Tango One"—that'd be the first enemy position they'd found, on the ground level—"and got their fitty! He's chased off one of the birds—"

The voice was cut off mid-sentence. Two seconds later,

the same voice clicked through on Taggart's radio. "Zipline, Alpha One. Bravo One dropped a Hajji bird with the fitty, but we're being overrun. Tanks are almost on us, and the birds are banking east and west of us. They'll have us lit up in moments. I've ordered everyone to bug out, but there's nowhere to go. God bless America. And, sir? God bless everything you've done. If we win, find my fam—"

The radio went silent. Taggart ground his teeth, his lips raised in a snarl. His left eyelid wouldn't stop twitching, and he felt his face flush red with rage. His men. His *people*. America. Taggart clutched his radio and strode toward the radio room. He couldn't save his people, but he could hear them at their last. They deserved to have someone with them when they died, to remember their sacrifice. As he entered the room, he saw Eagan sitting at the table with one of the platoon-channel radios.

"...say again?" shouted Eagan. The Militiaman stood to Eagan's left with shock on his face.

The radios were silent. Actually... Not even a crackle came from them.

Taggart shouted, "SITREP," and stared at Eagan's radio, willing it to come to life. To show that any of his troops still lived.

Eagan spun in his chair and stood tall. He always slouched, except in combat, but not right now. The boy was rigid with tension. Eagan saluted—crisply, for once—and said too loudly, "Sir, I had multiple reports that the birds were taken out, someone shot them down or something. They were falling from the sky. The armor—it was APCs, sir— stopped in the middle of the road. We got that SITREP from both Alpha Two and Bravo One. Then the radios died. Not even static."

* * *

The slant-eyed *pendejo* had told Spyder that his satellites found a "rebel" nest with both soldiers and armed civilians, but they couldn't find out exactly where before he'd gotten satellite access because Ree's drones kept getting shot down by—get this—other drones whenever they went out looking. When Spyder's crew caught one of Angel's gangs scouting his territory, Spyder learned that Angel and his soldier tagalongs planned to invade and that they'd been behind the mystery raid on his turf by Ree's raghead pals. Spyder passed all that along, repairing his "loyal servant" status, and Ree had come up with the plan for this ambush.

Spyder stood in the slant's "T.V. Tent," as he thought of it. It was a command center that General Ree had set up just north of Spyder's turf. Ree stood with his back to Spyder, watching the ambush unfold with obvious glee.

Next to Spyder was the hulking, reassuring presence of his pitbull, Sebastian. They both watched the many monitors —and Ree himself—with fascination and fear. Fear because this setup showed him how stupid his idea of taking Ree out had been. Oh man, so fuckin' happy he hadn't found the right time to try, because it would *definitely* not have been the right time. There would never be a right time. He might be able to kill the man, but he'd never get away alive. His crew, scattered around the 'hood waiting for the signal, would have swarmed the command center as soon as he fired off the flare gun he'd hidden outside, but in seeing all Ree's power, he decided he'd never pull the trigger. Better to be a live servant than a dead rebel.

On the screens, Spyder saw swarms of Americans with serious hardware—M4s, M16s, a few AKs—rushing all over the intersection where General Kimchee and his sand-eating followers had tried to set the ambush. Ree's men were getting overrun right before his eyes. A glance at Ree showed that the bastard didn't give a crap about his soldiers.

"*Huelebicho,*" he muttered and saw Seb nod in agreement.

Four blank monitors lit up, showing a rising aerial view. "The helicopters have risen," Ree said in English, then began spitting instructions in Raghead.

Spyder said almost under his breath to Sebastian, "*Perro que huele carne.*" Like a dog smelling meat...

"Yeah, man. Angel's gonna get his ass handed to him."

On the monitor, the helicopters banked dizzyingly, moving into a circular pattern. Like sharks closing in. Spyder's heart beat faster in anticipation, and he licked his lips.

General Ree turned to face Spyder, grinning. "You are here because your information was correct, and this is happening in your kitchen. My units are about to engage the rebels. You will see what happens to American traitors to Great Father's noble cause."

Spyder watched enraptured as Ree turned back to the monitors and raised one hand. A moment later, he chopped down through the air and spat a single word in Sand-eater.

And everything in the tent went dark and silent. Nothing on the monitors. Nothing from the radios. Spyder looked around in confusion, but saw that everyone else was doing the same. That couldn't be good. "What the hell is going on," Spyder demanded, and felt—rather than saw—Sebastian grow tense and wary. He could almost feel his man's aura change from calm-but-alert to "mothafuckers are about to die." Spyder put a hand on Seb's arm. "*No te rochees,* Seb," he said almost under his breath.

As the people in the command center—a canvas pavilion tent—quieted down, Sebastian nudged him. "*Bichote*, listen to that noise."

"What noise?"

"Yeah. The generator outside is quiet. The vehicles Ree kept running? They're quiet. All is quiet. We've heard this silence before, yes?"

Spyder froze. Seb was right... The man was a meathead, but cunning. He'd never miss seeing advantage when it showed itself. Spyder hissed, "*Ése salió por lana y llegó trasquilado,*" and Seb stifled a chuckle. *Ree had gone out looking for sheep but came back sheared.* Asshole.

Seb nudged Spyder and tossed his head toward the door flap. "*Si se puede. Que ahora Motín,* bossman."

Spyder felt his lips pull back into a snarl. *Time to riot. Yes we can.* Seb was right. "Send it up," he said simply, and Seb left the tent like a shadow, almost seeming to disappear. More loudly, he said, "Stepping outside, General Ree. It's pitch black in here."

Without waiting for a reply, Spyder stood tall and proud as he walked out of the tent. Overhead, a single flare drifted lazily with the faint breeze casting flickering, red light over the small compound. It made everything look coated in blood. Totally appropriate for what was about to happen. Ree could try to run, that little slant-eyed bitch, but the gang was coming for him and his lapdogs. Spyder felt the edge of adrenaline and the serene, peaceful feeling he always got when killing time arrived. He took his time walking the twenty yards where he had hidden his AK behind a crate.

From somewhere inside the compound, the first shot rang out, followed by a guttural cry of pain, and Spyder grinned.

* * *

Ree looked around the darkened room, and a shiver ran down his spine, leaving his scalp tingling. He took a deep breath and put the fear into a box deep inside. Fear accomplished nothing and didn't serve the Great Leader's purposes, unless that fear belonged to the enemies of the

People. Ree ignored the American gangster leaving. It hardly mattered now.

"Check your watches," he commanded. All were electronic—and all were as dark as the monitors. Now what? Obviously, he'd have to get back to base to be of any use to his Leader, but none of his vehicles were likely to be operational if this really had been a retaliation EMP.

He pointed at one of the now-useless radio operators. "Go and get the American gangster's car. He didn't have it the last time we summoned him, so he must have found it."

A single shot came from somewhere fairly nearby. Ree recognized it as an AK, but had no way of knowing whether it belonged to his own men or someone else. The barbarian Americans had more firearms among their lazy, selfish citizens than in all of the DPRK's mighty military. They only lacked the conviction to use them, despite their absurd "mightiest nation" empty rhetoric before the war.

Then another shot rang out, and someone screamed in Arabic, calling for their god. As if there was a god who might help him. Fool. "Everyone up. Move together. We take the American gang member's vehicle, if it remains where it was. If it is gone, we will move northward, toward our base, and pick up our soldiers as we find them. Do not slow for the wounded. The Great Leader requires your obedience in this! We do no good for anyone if we become trapped out here in this urban wasteland. *Move!*"

As one, his soldiers rose and moved toward him. They stepped outside the tent, and his people surrounded him, providing cover. Eight soldiers against the hordes of barbarians who lived here. He noted that light covered everything; a flare still drifted downward. He used the last of the light to look for the car and found it still parked. It was beautiful, black, mean-looking. Clearly what the natives had once called "American muscle." He wasted no time before moving toward it.

All around came the noise of firefights. Small clusters of men fighting and dying. Ree sneered. Whoever engineered this disorganized attack was no soldier, that much was certain. He skipped a step as a realization struck him, but kept moving. "This is the American gangster's work. Kill anyone who is not one of us. For Korea!"

The men cried out, repeating that most noble of words as they rushed with him toward the vehicle. All around him now was the noise of battle. How many barbarians would it take to overrun the sons and daughters of Korea and their Islamic allies? Americans were like rats, always scurrying around. And they all had guns. If they saw a weakness in the invasion forces, there were more than enough to overrun every base the Liberation Forces had set up, but only if they could muster half the courage of a Korean farmer. If they perceived weakness, well, Americans could be brave if they thought they had the advantage. Bah.

They were ten feet from the car now, and Ree began to hope they wouldn't have to fight their way back to the main base in north Manhattan. His rising joy was cut short when a half dozen of the American gangsters rose up on the car's opposite side. They fired their rifles without hesitation.

All around Ree, his men fell. He felt something large and heavy strike him from behind, forcing him to the ground. The breath was knocked out of him when he landed, with the heavy weight still on him. He tried to roll over to see his attacker. It turned out to be a loyal Islamist on top of him, now dying and bleeding out. He mouthed the name of his god, but no words came out—only a bubble of blood.

Damn. His men were dead or dying, patriots every one of them. He looked around for a way out, assessing the situation, but any hope of escape was crushed. A circle of American criminals was slowly closing in on him from every direction, with rifles and pistols pointed at him. Damn Spyder, and damn disloyal allies...

A mechanical hum was suddenly heard. Ree looked for the source and saw that his attackers also looked for the cause. A moment later the source became apparent; dozens of small drones whirred in every direction. Each had a tiny weapon under it that looked like the gun mounts on a helicopter. The drones stopped abruptly, hovering in place. Then the drones' weapon barrels whirred into life, spinning like a Gatling gun. All around him, the gang members cried out and fell where they had stood, each becoming a bloody mess. There had been no sound of gunfire. Ree wondered what those weapons were and marveled at how they had torn up the people surrounding them. They looked like they'd been flayed.

The drones moved as one toward the car, and stopped. Ree watched, confused. Why was he still alive? The drones moved back toward him and then back to the car where they rose up to twice the height of a man and simply hovered. They all faced outward, their weapons covering every direction.

Ree wasted no more time. He sprinted the last ten feet to the car and vaulted into the driver's seat. The keys were in the ignition. Spyder must have wanted a fast way out if his treachery failed. Well, it had not failed, and this was no time to wonder about unexpected gifts. He shifted hard into Drive, slammed the gas pedal down, and the wheels spun for a moment before catching. Then the car vaulted forward, and Ree cheered in his heart. He wove back and forth, avoiding people, supplies, and anything else in the way. The little drones kept pace and pulverized anyone nearby whether American or Patriot. It would have felt good to run down some of Spyder's people but returning to base was the priority.

A minute later, he was clear of the battle and screaming down the broad, empty boulevard headed north toward the main base, the sounds of battle petering out behind him.

Those drones had not been his, nor Islamist—too small and too armed—so there was someone out there helping him. And whoever they were, they had to know the EMP was coming in order to keep the drones hidden until it was safe to bring them out. He'd escaped with his life, he realized, but whose drones had made it possible? To whom did he owe his life?

Ahead of him, the rubble walls of his base rose out of the darkness, lit by his approaching headlights. Inside the base, beyond the wall, all lay in darkness.

- 20 -

0230 HOURS - ZERO DAY +33

CAPTAIN TAGGART WALKED through the building, staying as quiet as possible. The enemy units had been defeated quickly once their birds had gone down in fiery glory. None of the soldiers they'd captured spoke English, so Taggart gave them a short trial and shorter execution. He'd spent the time since then tending to his own dead and wounded the best they could under the circumstances. He'd sent Eagan and some soldiers to retrieve the big radio and such, which had been left in the tunnel system, and they would return soon. Taggart owed a debt to this "Dark Ryder," whoever he was, for alerting him of the EMP. It had come sooner than expected, and the "Dark Ryder" warning was the only reason the radio hadn't been fried again, this time probably for good. He'd lost his handhelds, but they were acceptable losses.

Now he found himself in command of five squads of able-bodied soldiers and a squad of the dead, dying, or wounded. It didn't really matter that he'd inflicted terrible losses on the enemy—some thirty bodies and who knew how many wounded—because they had more, and more, and still more. He had only his squads and there wouldn't likely be reinforcements soon. Six to one, seven to one, it didn't matter. Each of his own soldiers was irreplaceable.

He walked into the room Spyder had set up as his office and closed the door. After checking the heavy drapes to ensure no light would escape to give away their location, he lit the cheap oil lamp they'd found on the desk. He sat, put his feet up on the desk, and let out a weary sigh. Looking around the room didn't cheer him at all. Spyder had kept his office Spartan at best, preferring to keep his loot and trophies elsewhere, no doubt.

A light knock on the door roused him. "Enter."

Eagan came in and closed the door behind him. He looked weary, but then, so did everyone right now. "Sir, the comm is secured. Two more dead since I left. The medico thinks the other four wounded will live, but one might lose an arm first. Watches are in place, I checked on them myself. The fires north of us are spreading northward, not toward us, so we don't expect a horde of freaked out civilians fleeing through our positions."

"At ease, Eagan. Sit." Taggart pulled out a pint of Wild Turkey—his favorite whiskey—and two plastic cups. "One drink, to mourn our dead. Then hit the rack."

"Yessir. But I wasn't done with the SITREP. We've had radio contact on the big comm, Captain. Two other Army units have come out of hiding to where they can hear our signal, finally. They were holed up in the subways and sewers..."

Taggart grimaced. The whiskey looked really good but would have to wait a minute. "Very well, Eagan. Out with it."

"One unit is well south of us, a reinforced platoon in size. They have a lot of food in wagons, sir, but they're black on ammo." Taggart frowned, but Eagan kept going. "The other unit is to the east of us, and they're about our size, but under a lieutenant. They're good on rations and supplies. Both units are moving to rendezvous with us, sir. Platoon should be here by dawn, the squad by about 0700 hours."

"Alright. Pass it on to the others. We don't want any accidents. I think if we can convince them to join my command, we'll be far more combat effective."

"You could just order them to take it and grin, Cap."

"Technically, yes. But you know damn well that right now—"

Bang! Bang! The sounds of weapons firing interrupted Taggart. Eagan sprinted out of the office. Taggart grabbed his rifle and was close behind. The shots came from the roof, on the north side of the massive building. Eagan darted away to rouse the other troops, and Taggart vaulted up the stairs three at a time. When he reached the top, he went straight to the window of the nearest north-facing room, heedless of the slowly-rousing soldiers sleeping within.

In the distance he could see the still-raging fires caused by some of the falling helicopters earlier, and the backlighting let him easily see what the soldiers on the roof were shooting at. Not a block away, there were a dozen figures. Most were armed with pistols, but a couple of them carried rifles. They were clustered together and had clearly not expected to be engaged with small arms fire—they had only just started scattering for cover when Taggart got eyes on them. Slow. So, not soldiers. Gangbangers, then. Which meant they were likely to be Spyder's goons. That suited Taggart just fine; Spyder was everything wrong with the world, as far as he was concerned. And he was owed some payback for past wrongs.

Out the window, Taggart saw a stream of his own soldiers pouring from the building, moving by twos as they flanked the now-pinned gangsters. Heh. This wouldn't last long… He watched as the gangbangers were whittled away.

His troops set up crossfires that eliminated their target's cover and gunned them down one after another. The enemy's return fire was chaotic, with no fire discipline; they shot at everything and nothing in their panic.

In only a few minutes, it was all but over. His troops strode through the carnage, finishing off the merely wounded—he hadn't ordered that, but he would let it go. The scum down there deserved their brutal end. Taggart reminded himself that these were the people who had sided with invaders, kidnapped, raped, and even sold into slavery the civilians they so ruthlessly controlled. He turned away, determined to reconcile later the mixed feelings he had about his troops' brutality.

When it was over, Taggart straightened his uniform and then walked downstairs and out the door, heading toward the scene of the massacre. When he got there, it looked as bad as anything he'd seen in the Sandbox, though minus the severed heads lying on the ground by the dead. Would his troops get to the point of committing atrocities themselves some day soon? He hoped not.

His thoughts were interrupted when he spotted four troops with their backs to him, rifles aimed at some survivors probably. He approached and barked, "Hooah, soldiers! What's going on here?"

A trooper, who looked like he was barely old enough to shave, looked up but his rifle never wavered. "Sir! We have two survivors. These two, we figured you'd wanna see 'em, sir."

Taggart drew even with the soldiers and froze. His eyes narrowed. It was Spyder and his top henchman there. Spyder lay on his back, hand over his liver in a failed attempt to stop the blood and black ooze leaking out of the wound. He was a dead man without high-tech emergency surgery, Taggart realized. And crouched beside him, between the soldiers and

Spyder, was Sebastian. Spyder's pitbull.

Spyder's eyes were wide with pain and fear. "Please... You have to—"

"Shut your mouth, traitor," shouted Taggart and the four soldiers tensed. They wanted nothing more than to blast that piece of garbage, and he'd let them do it.

When Spyder fell silent, Taggart straightened his posture. "You are Spyder and Sebastian. In addition to crimes against humanity, you've committed acts of murder, rape, and looting in a war zone while under Martial Law. And finally, you're damn sure guilty of treason. Have you anything to say before I pass my judgment?"

Other soldiers, finished slaughtering Spyder's goons, began to gather around the scene as well. Spyder, voice weak and shaking like the coward he was, cried out, "No, man, you got it wrong! I'm not Spyder. He's dead, yo, and I was just following orders. You got to go along to get along, right? A guy's gotta eat!"

Taggart looked down on Spyder and Sebastian, lips pursed, jaw clenched. "I need six volunteers," he barked, and had more than enough troops step forward. He picked six at random. "You're guilty, and you're going to pay for it," Taggart said. His voice was almost a whisper, and he hissed it out between clenched teeth. "Detail, take these traitors two blocks north. Put signs around their necks, Sharpie 'traitor' on them, and then hang them by the neck until dead. It's fitting they should hang in the neighborhood they terrorized. Once they're strung up, report back to me."

Taggart turned to the rest of his troops. "Hooah. Listen up, soldiers. Get back to your posts. This fire may get some 'vader attention. Get your sorry asses back to your posts! This ain't no vacation, Joes. And tomorrow... Tomorrow we're going to begin 'vader hunting. We're going to push those sorry sonsabitches back into the goddamn ocean."

There was a resounding chorus of "Hooah," and Taggart turned away from them to watch the work detail force-marching two traitors down the road. "See you in Hell," he muttered, and then headed back toward their temporary base. He had a lot of planning to do, and there wasn't really any way his small command could end the war. But for the first time in a month, he had a spring to his step. They could give the enemy serious hell. Payback was about to begin in earnest.

* * *

0630 HOURS - ZERO DAY +33

Cassy leaned against the pole, heedless of the urine and feces that practically covered her. The parts of her in pain seemed to outnumber the parts that weren't. Worse, she felt chilly even at midday—she couldn't look in a mirror to check, but she was pretty sure the cuts and scrapes on her face were infected. She had scabs on top of scabs, to the point where even the motion of eating made her face hurt all over.

If Jaz and her new friends didn't make a move soon, she wouldn't make it much longer. She might have given up already if she hadn't heard through the Clanner grapevine that help was on the way, but once she'd heard that, she resolved herself to stay strong, not to give up... To survive, for her kids.

The smell of the meager breakfast meal cooking wafted to her, and her stomach rumbled. That was another issue altogether; she got to eat only rarely, when Mandy managed to collect enough bits and bites from the Clanners' half-ration meals to smuggle some to her. Cassy's strength was waning.

A shadow blocked the dawning sun, and she looked up

only to see Peter and Jim standing nearby. She hadn't heard them approach. Peter faced her, his stare unflinching, and he wore a smirk. Jim, ever the damn lapdog, appeared to be paying rapt attention to Peter.

"So, Jim. Any luck getting her to talk about their stockpile?" Peter asked, but his gaze never left Cassy.

"Nope, sorry boss. She's been in questioning for part of every damn day, but she just won't tell us."

"Did you explain to her that if she tells us, the questioning will stop, and she'll go back on normal rations? She might like some bacon."

Cassy's mouth watered at the thought, but she kept her face a stony mask. Screw those bastards.

"Yeah, boss. It's like she doesn't give one crap about her own people starving. Why don't we just kill this waste of oxygen? It's not like she's useful anymore, if she won't tell us."

Peter shrugged. "Because, Jim, we need the knowledge in her head, too. The way she farms is weird, but actually grows more than our farms back at White Stag ever did."

"Yeah, maybe..." Jim said. Then he cocked his head to the side. "On the other hand, Frank seems to have picked most of that permaculture crap. And, he isn't exactly going to run away any time soon." Jim grinned, and then laughed.

Cassy turned her head inch by inch until she was looking at Peter directly. She stared at him for a long while, face unreadable. Finally, she said, "I've been teaching several of my people the principles of how I farm. And there's my farming journal—it has all the information on what grows on the farm, when to plant, how to harvest, how to seed... So yeah, you don't really need my knowledge. Oh, sure, there is a lot they couldn't have learned yet, or which isn't written in the journal, but they got most of it."

Peter smiled again, and the grin reached his eyes. "So, I

reckon we can just kill her. She's got nothing we need that she'll ever give us. She'll let her people starve come winter, rather than let us share in it. I figure she's earned some sort of punishment. You reckon?"

Jim only nodded. Cassy eyed Jim warily. That little prick would do whatever he was told and never lose a night of sleep over it like a real human being would.

Peter clapped his hands together as if he'd just come to some brilliant idea in his stupid, empty head. He'd look better with it rammed up Jim's ass, she decided. And the image made her laugh aloud for the first time in God knew how long.

"Alrighty, Jim. Let everyone know we'll be having some entertainment tonight with our evening meal. Oh, and find me an axe. No need to sharpen it—it'll cut through eventually."

Cassy watched as Peter and Jim walked away laughing, and her hatred for those two monsters seethed. She closed her eyes and muttered, "Lord, if you really do exist, I don't care if you let them kill me. I've served my purpose and saved a lot of good people. But Father-God, I'd sure appreciate it if you let me live long enough to see those two sonuvabitches dead, burned, and in the garbage heap."

There was no response from the heavens, but then, she didn't really expect one. If there was a god out there, they'd damn well better hurry with whatever their plan for them was. She knew she couldn't last much longer.

- 21 -

1200 HOURS - ZERO DAY +34

JAZ CROUCHED IN Jungle overgrowth along with four of the dozen reserve Marines who had joined her—well, okay, she had joined them. She was going to get some of those White Stag bastards, and if they wanted to help, she'd use 'em like she'd had to use Big Strong Men her whole life. And that warrior woman they had with them—she liked seeing that. At least these Marines were brave, and they knew right from wrong. So okay, she'd use them or they'd use her, who cared? So long as those bastards down there died on the farm they stole.

Jaz knew the layout of the farm, but the Marines didn't—or at least not all of them, and those who did, not so well—so she'd suggested a scouting mission first. Their officer dude totally thought it was a good idea, so there she was. Jaz was to explain the farm's layout and point out supplies, foxholes, traps, and where the original Clanners stayed. All sorts of details. Whatever, it totally didn't matter right now. Not anymore.

What did matter were the things going on at the farm. Peter had Cassy off her pole, standing in front of all the Clan with her hands tied behind her back. Jaz sighted in through the scope of the rifle the Marines had loaned her and saw that the White Stag dude standing next to Peter and Cassy had an axe slung over his shoulder. Meanwhile, Peter was totally grandstanding in front of the Clanners. She couldn't hear what he said, but she could see that his mouth just kept on yammering. The prick loved speeches.

The Marine next to Jaz also looked through a rifle scope. "Bastard's gonna chop her head off." He paused. "Damn, I'm sorry. I didn't think before I talked."

Jaz's jaw dropped and she reeled. Chop her head off? Who the hell did that sort of thing? But it took only a moment for her to decide that Peter Ixin was indeed that kind of monster. She couldn't deny that's what the scene looked like.

"Damn, he must have got tired of waiting for her to spill the beans." She pleaded, "We can't let this happen. We have to stop it!" She almost cried it out but held down the volume at the last moment, her voice cracking. She could feel tears coming on. Rage and helplessness. If the radios still worked, she'd have begged Ethan to just come out and give up the supplies, but they were still silent. This Marine was the only one now who could hear her. "Please..."

* * *

Peter Ixin showed the audience his carefully rehearsed Grief Face, but inside he felt... nothing. "My people, my Clan friends. I'd like to thank all of you for being so patient, despite the half-rations, the hunger, the nightly cold. I have tried so hard, for all you, to get Cassy to tell us where the food is stored, where the blankets are. All the things we need are here, but she will not share them with you. With us—*all* of us."

Yeah, right. None of these Clanners seemed to embrace his vision. But so what? Someone had to be the slaves if his own people were to enjoy the fruits of his labor, the results of his God-given vision for the future. Two months ago, slaves were called "immigrants," but now he didn't need a nicer label. Sure, this would horrify his own people too, especially the ones with kids of their own, but hell. Terror trumped outrage every time, in his experience. Besides, if he had to kill one of his own people, that could be interesting. Less boring afterwards, at least.

Peter glanced at Cassy, but she just stood stiff and upright, annoyingly proud. Bitch. Well, he could afford to forgive her personally, since she was about to get her comeuppance, so her attitude just didn't seem to matter anymore. He caught himself about to smile at the thought of her head flying from her shoulders, but forced Sad Face to stay etched on his face for his slaves' viewing pleasure. The Peter Channel always delivered quality entertainment. Hah. The best was yet to come.

"Soldiers, please take your positions." He watched as they obeyed and then readied their rifles. He turned back to Cassy. "You know, I was just going to have you hanged, but I don't think that delivers the same... impact. You're a traitor not only to America but to your own people, and they deserve to see justice done in spectacular technicolor three-dee. It's my responsibility to be sure they get what they deserve."

Peter shifted his patented Sad Face to his patented Iron Determination Face. He spoke loudly, "It pains me to say this, but I need every one of you Clanners to watch as we deliver Cassy to the justice she has earned. So, if anyone looks away—yes, even the children—I've instructed my people standing around you to simply shoot that person. No questions, no exceptions. You either watch and learn, or die.

Burn it into your memories, my friends, because if the lesson doesn't stick then you'll be watching more of this down the road."

* * *

Joe Ellings shifted his weight from foot to foot as Peter droned on. Joe's anxiety level was just about through the roof, so it was hard to stand still. Damn it all if Peter hadn't jumped the gun with this sideshow! A couple more days and Joe's people would have been ready to do something more. Well, he reckoned that plan was deader 'n Jesse James now.

He exchanged a nervous glance with the man next to him, another of his "group of ten" trusted collaborators plotting against Peter. There were more sympathizers, Lord knew, but he figured ten was about the right count to keep the plan under wraps. Every person they let in on the plot risked revealing everyone. The other nine were all with him on the west side of a crescent of guards that half-surrounded the Clanners.

Shoot, doing anything for Cassy would blow the show early, too. Well, it sucked for Cassy, that was for sure. Nothing he could do to save her now, not without starting the Gunfight at the OK Corral—with all them Clanners smack dab in the middle of it.

Joe's gaze slid to Frank, the other Clan leader. Great guy, but not much use anymore on account of his cut off foot, bless his soul. Another thing they could all thank Peter for. Joe cursed himself for a fool even thinking about Frank doing something to stop this madness. Nope, there wasn't anyone who would stop this craziness. Nice knowin' you, Cassy.

Something Peter said got his ear's attention. "...yes, even the children..."

Joe's head whipped back toward Peter. What in the hell did he just say? Shoot *children* for not looking? He reeled and almost stumbled as he realized that Peter had indeed said that. What kid could be made to watch this crap? Then an image crystallized in his mind: his own dearest child. In his mind's eye, he saw his son's small head shatter like glass into a thousand bloody pieces, Peter's inhuman laughter in the background.

This was too much for Joe to swallow, and damn the plot to hell. He'd be going to hell himself if he sat by and just watched this, the way some of the others had during the last executions. He froze for two seconds as he steadied himself. His hands didn't shake anymore. In one fluid movement, Joe raised his rifle to his shoulder and swung the barrel toward Peter. Fuck it.

Two shots rang out.

* * *

Grandma Mandy was kneeling next to Frank, trying to distract him from the pain these monsters had caused the man when they dragged him from the makeshift infirmary to watch her daughter's death.

That thought brought up a surge of grief that threatened to overwhelm Mandy's senses, and her heart began to race. In her pocket, she clenched the grip of a 9mm pistol that some of the White Stag people had smuggled in to her. They'd brought guns and knives to a lot of the Clan, in fact.

She recognized most of Joe Ellings' co-conspirators in the circle of guards around them. The Lord would surely bless men like Mr. Ellings and the people who supported him, people who did all the good they could in this evil world.

Mandy whispered to Frank as Peter put on his show.

"Tell me something, Frank. Do you feel in your heart that the Lord can forgive someone who kills another human being? I mean, if the reason is great enough? Can even Jesus wash that bloody stain of sin from a person's soul?"

Frank looked pale and his breathing was shallow, but his low, deep voice was steady when he answered. "Mandy, you believe the Lord forgives those who kill in cold blood, through Jesus, yes? How much more, then, will He forgive someone who kills to protect His flock? Do you love your neighbor more than yourself, like the Bible says, if you just let the ravagers have their way with the innocent? Yes, I think if there's a God, then He will sure forgive whoever kills this bastard. I just hope someone has the guts to do it soon, or there won't be any of us left come spring."

Mandy was shocked by his words. Frank was no preacher, not much of a believer in fact, but what he said rang true in her heart. God would forgive her when she rose up to smite Satan with her pistol as her daughter died. It would be her only opportunity, more than likely, and there was no way she'd squander the chance. Even if it did cost her soul, it would be worth it to save the Clan and avenge her daughter.

And then she heard Peter say the Clan children would be shot if they didn't watch. How could anyone... No. The Lord Himself had said that anyone who harmed a child had a special place in Hell waiting for them. Maybe this was why she hadn't died from her diabetes yet. Maybe she'd been spared in His wisdom, so that she could be the one to sacrifice herself for all their lives. Their retribution could be spent on her and her alone, but it was no loss. She was half dead already.

"Lord, forgive me of my sins," Mandy said with a trembling voice, "and spare the righteous here today." Then she pulled the sleek blued pistol out of her pocket. It didn't have a hammer like her .38 had, but Michael had told her this brand, a Glock, didn't have a hammer you could pull back.

Why was she thinking about that right now? How odd. In fact, everything looked odd. The sky was blue as Heaven, and birds chirping nearby were a choir of Angels singing. She'd never felt this sort of serenity before. The Lord was with her—she had no doubt now. She would be forgiven, and the Lord would give her the strength to pull the heavy trigger despite her declining condition.

Without another word, she raised the barrel and aimed at Peter's chest for as long as she dared—half a second—and knew God would guide her aim. Surely He would.

She squeezed the trigger twice.

* * *

Jaz saw sudden movement among the Clanners—Grandma Mandy raised a pistol toward Peter. She cried out as the older woman fired. Just as suddenly, a riot of noise from multiple gunshots and people screaming reached her ears. Jaz scanned the area through her scope and then froze. A cluster of guards were firing at the Clan, but what shocked her was the sight of a cluster of guards firing *at the other guards*. It must be Joe Ellings and the sympathizers. Clanners ran in all directions.

Damn, Mandy had forced the resistance's hand when she'd shot at Peter. Cassy was face down on the ground next to Peter. Mandy may have saved Cassy's life, but the several bodies that remained when the Clan members had scattered showed that the price was steep indeed.

Then she saw that a half-dozen of the Clan, including Michael, Sturm, and Mueller, were also armed, and firing at the loyalist guards from their position behind and to the south of them. Jaz sighted in on the unfinished house; a guard's head was visible. *Bang!* Jaz's shot took him in the face.

She became aware of a bass-heavy barking noise from all around her. It reminded her of the Hellhounds she'd seen in a horror movie and for half a second she almost panicked, until she realized the noise came from the Marines she was with. They were charging toward the farmhouse, barking, moving in a peculiar leapfrog kind of way; one knelt and fired while another advanced, took a knee, began firing, and the first Marine then advanced. It was brutally effective; the White Stag loyalists outside were mowed down from the onslaught of Marines, Clanners, and Joe and his sympathizers.

Jaz swept her rifle around seeking a target, checking windows for snipers on the earthbag buildings. She moved back to Cassy and Peter, but Cassy was nowhere to be seen, nor was Peter.

* * *

Peter Ixin cursed. His bulletproof vest had stopped the old lady's bullets, but he'd been out of commission for a bit. When he came to his senses, there were gunshots all around, and everyone was scattering. Some of his guards were firing at other guards, but he had no idea why or who were the loyal ones. There was a chaotic barking sound all around that freaked him out.

He pulled his .45-caliber M1911 and searched for a target, but the Clanners were darting around like rabbits fleeing from a fox. His gaze then settled on Cassy; she lay motionless, face down in the dirt, hands still tied behind her back, but she was alive and breathing.

Cassy had led the invaders to the White Stag farms,

killed his people, evaded him, embarrassed him, and refused to say where she'd hidden the food stockpile. The bitch's mom had shot him, and he was pretty sure he had cracked ribs from that, despite the vest. Enough was enough. Peter staggered to the still-twitching body of the would-be executioner and picked up his axe. He walked over to Cassy as he holstered his pistol and kicked her savagely in the side. She cried out and curled into a ball. So the bitch still lived. Peter smiled and then bent down to grab a handful of her hair. He forced her to her feet, and she hardly resisted. She must have been too worn down from the treatment she'd received during her captivity. Good. He resisted the urge to slit her damn throat with the axe. She might deserve that, but it wouldn't serve his purposes.

Peter looked around again. A handful of Clanners stood with a few of Peter's own people and a cluster of soldiers, firing at the unfinished farmhouse. They were prone or in cover, and Peter had only ten rounds in his pistol, so he didn't bother firing at them. Inside the building, loyal White Stag people popped up into the windows, returned fire, and then ducked down again. Peter wished he could help them, but they'd dug their own grave by getting holed up in a building with one exit. Stupid. There was no room for stupidity in this dark new world. At least they'd distract the attackers long enough for him to escape, so it wasn't a total loss. Maybe the defenders would even win, but he doubted it.

By the main farmhouse, however, he spotted Jim, who waved at him frantically and held the door open. An ally was just what he needed right now. Peter pressed the axehead to Cassy's throat with one hand, still gripping her hair with the other, and forced her toward the farmhouse. "Let's go, bitch. Jimbo and I are gonna hightail it out of here, and you're our exit visa. Your people might get the farm back, but they'll be celebrating without you."

* * *

Cassy struggled against Peter's iron grip, but not too hard—the sharp axe blade against her throat prevented more than a token resistance. It was maddening—and terrifying. Peter certainly wouldn't hesitate to cut her throat if it suited his purposes.

She considered drawing the knife a sympathizer had slipped to her, but she didn't dare to draw a hand away from Peter's. Not with that axe against her throat. In the back of her head, she was convinced that if she moved one hand away, the sudden slack would make Peter cut her throat. For now, the game was to play along and look for an opportunity to strike.

Adding Jim to the picture was a complication she didn't need but could do nothing about.

Peter rushed through the doorway, and Jim slammed it shut behind them, then Peter roughly shoved Cassy into a wall. Peter and Jim were now between her and both the front and back doors. The overwhelming sounds of a massive firefight continued unabated.

"Anyone else in here with us?"

"No, boss. Two Clan kids ran out the door before I could nail 'em. How long you think we need to hold out?"

Cassy was struck by the irony of these two pompous asses hiding in *her house*, still believing they were in control of the situation. Her terror and fatigue slammed up against the hilarity of the situation and shattered. Someone began to laugh, rising louder and louder, and whoever it was sounded completely hysterical. She realized the two men were staring at her. She was the one laughing. She tried to stop, but just couldn't. Screw it. She was going to die anyway. Might as well have a little fun first. "You two..." she said between torrents of laughter.

Peter's eyes narrowed, and he strode up to her in two steps to tower over her. His face was flushing, turning red. "Shut up! What the hell are you laughing at, bitch? You're gonna fuckin' die here, you know that?"

Oh man, he looked a little like Santa Claus now, with his jolly nose all red. A skinny cowboy Santa with no beard. Hilarious. She struggled to catch her breath, but managed to stammer, "You two! You're funny. Little Santa Cowboy and his little Helper Elf!" She lost the battle with herself and burst into fresh laughter.

Peter turned to Jim. "Get upstairs. I'll deal with Crazy Girl. Get on the rifle and start sniping anything not White Stag."

"What about the traitors? How will I know?"

"Moron. Our people are in cover. Anything moving around is fair game. Kill everything you can."

Cassy, cackling madly, watched as Jimmy the Elf ran upstairs to help Santa deliver deadly presents to all the good little boys and girls. Then Peter faced her again and raised the axe. He grunted and thrust the axe's eye—the nub of wood protruding from the top of the axe—straight into her left cheek. Cassy felt the bone crunch beneath the blow, and in only seconds, she could no longer see from her left eye.

As the pain burst throughout her head like fireworks, she gripped her knife tightly to the side of her leg. She had a present for Santa, and it wasn't milk and cookies. Again she was overtaken with a fit of mad laughter. Some part of her knew she was losing her mind, yet there was a part of her—clinical, detached—that allowed the madness to rise. It was useful. One step closer, Santa...

Peter was screaming at her, she could see his cheeks puff and his face turning a beet red with rage, but she couldn't make out his words. It just sounded like "womp womp," like the teacher in a Charlie Brown Christmas Special. The detached part of her understood he was about to kill her, that he somehow thought that if she died, he could regain control of the situation. Fool. No matter what happened in the next few seconds, his time on earth was nearly done.

Axe in his right hand, Peter reached down with his left to clench a fistful of hair. He lifted her head up so that she looked directly at him and raised the axe high. And then the look on his face changed. Anger turned to confusion and disbelief. The axe fell from his hand; he reached across his body and then held the now-empty hand in front of his face. It was dripping crimson. His blood, the color of Christmas. Slowly, he tilted his head to look down to the left, and when he saw the knife handle sticking out from his armpit, his gaze snapped to Cassy's eyes.

"You... bitch..." he managed, before he fell over. Cassy's hair slipped from his grasp as he fell to his side and lay there moaning in agony. Peter still had that idiot look of disbelief on his stupid asshole Santa face.

The clinical part of her mind decided it was time to get her shit together, and slowly, her laughter subsided. She grinned down at Peter and wiped laughter tears from her eyes to her chin. "Peter the Great, my ass."

Cassy struggled to her feet. Her body felt suddenly heavy, like her legs were full of lead. Adrenaline crash. Her hand shook uncontrollably when she pulled her knife from under Peter's arm; he groaned, but didn't move. Experience told her the shakes would last several minutes, but with Jim on the top floor sniping from the window, lives were in the balance. There was no way she could run out even if she'd wanted to. Jim would see her and shoot her in the back once she got outside.

Instead, she'd have to kill the bastard or die trying. Even if she lost, the time he spent away from the window to deal with her would save lives. Hopefully, she'd have another shot of adrenaline when she confronted Jimbo the Elf. If only she had one grenade, but she'd have to make due with Peter's own pistol. If there was a God, then He would see to it that she killed the pig upstairs with his master's gun.

With a sigh, she turned to face the stairwell and steeled herself for what must come next.

* * *

Cassy took a tentative step toward the stairwell, pistol in her good right hand and knife in the left with the point down like an ice pick. She vaguely remembered that Michael once told her not to do that unless she was a master knife fighter, but in her mind's eye she envisioned Jim leaping at her from the left side of the stairwell when she went up. She'd have no leverage with the standard grip Michael had taught her if that happened.

Or maybe her wits were just addled by fatigue, pain, injury, starvation, and raw seething hatred. Either way, she had no time to over-analyze it. Enough already—it was time to go upstairs. Her people needed her, even if her help came at the expense of her own life.

Creak. Cassy froze and listened. The first stair wasn't quite right, dammit, and she should have remembered that. Maybe Jim hadn't heard it over the din of combat and the thick earthbag walls in the house. It only took a couple seconds for her to realize that Jim hadn't stopped firing, however. He hadn't heard. She continued to creep upstairs, but she was careful to avoid the loose fifth step. It was the only other creaky stair.

As she continued up the steep, narrow stairwell—almost a ladder—more of the upstairs room came into view. First, the bed in the middle of the room, but Jim wasn't there of course. Then the north wall with its window—she wasn't surprised to find Jim wasn't there, either. Disappointed—she could have caught him unaware and exposed—but not surprised. The sadistic, little weasel was careful of his own welfare—always.

Finally, she was far enough up the stairs that her head was almost visible from anywhere in the room, but not far enough for her to see Jim. The last couple steps would be the biggest risk. She'd be the one exposed and unaware. She paused as a shiver of fear ran through her, but then that sweet, sweet adrenaline kicked in once again. The fear fell away.

She could get up the steep stairs faster and quieter with her hands free. It might cost her a half second to draw her pistol again. But the element of surprise would give her that time, whereas if he realized she was coming up, then he could get the drop on her... Cassy decided to tuck the pistol in her waistband and to clench her knife between her teeth like in the movies. It was a small room, so it was entirely possible she could kill him faster with the knife than by drawing her pistol again. She hoped so—it would be delicious to end Jim with her own knife as she had almost done with a small pocketknife a month ago right after the EMPs hit.

Cassy's hands reached the top of the stairwell railing, and she grabbed hold tightly. She brought her feet up a few more steps, forcing her to crouch. She was ready—it was showtime. She pushed up with her legs like pistons and pulled hard on the railing, vaulting her over the last few steps. As her head shot up and out of the stairwell, she caught a glimpse of Jim crouched at the south window with his rifle thrust outside; a shot went off, and he smoothly moved to cycle the rifle's bolt to ready another shot.

As she noted all of that, she landed a foot beyond the stairwell edge and snatched the knife from her mouth. Jim must have heard her despite the battle din, because he began to turn away from the window toward her, swinging his rifle around with him.

Everything seemed to be moving in slow motion, including herself, but Cassy knew that was only a side effect of the adrenaline that again poured through her system. Knife in hand, she pushed off hard with her right foot, propelling herself at the bastard. The surprised and suddenly-fearful look on his face as death came for him was satisfying in a way she hadn't felt before. Bloodlust... With savage joy, she realized she would reach Jim before he could bring the rifle around to fire.

Pain shot through her left foot when it landed, and the hardwood floor rushed up at her. There was the sound of a rifle going off and an odd metal *ting* noise. Cassy brought her knife up in a vain, instinctive attempt to put it between her and Jim—but her hand was empty. She stared at it dumbly, uncomprehending. Jim's hyena laugh echoed through the room.

Cassy looked down. Why was her foot bleeding? Was that a bone sticking up through her shoe? It looked more like a nail...

Jim spoke: "Caltrops, bitch. Pretty great shot though, huh?"

His voice snapped her out of her shock, and time sped up again. So it wasn't her bone, it was the sharp point of a caltrop. She realized there were several of them scattered at the top of the stairwell, made from filed-off soldered nails. Her knife was broken in half on the other side of the room. He must have hit the blade with his panicked shot.

Cassy looked to Jim again and saw him work the bolt. Reloading. Well, she might be about to die, but at least Jim was no longer at the window killing her friends and allies. They had a good chance now to get into the house before he could get back to the window. As Jim took aim, Cassy smiled

—content with her small victory—and waited for him to shoot her.

"What are you smiling at?" Jim asked, voice harsh and demanding. "Sure, you got me once by surprise, but that was the old-world me. I was trying to be *merciful* with my punishment, and you were just too stupid to take your lesson and move on. But even after you stabbed me by surprise, like a coward, you were too weak to finish it. Weak, Cassy. For all your high-and-mighty bullshit about being some powerful 'Clan leader,' in the end you're just a woman. Did you really think some *woman* could kill me? I'm all man, babygirl, and you never had a chance."

As he delivered his monologue, Cassy propped herself up on her elbows—which put her right hand tantalizingly close to the pistol in her waistband—and pretended to listen to his every word. Her smile didn't fade, though—this blowhard stood there gloating while justice rolled inexorably toward him. Without him sniping in the window, the other loyalists would soon be overrun. Dying wasn't so bad, knowing that her kids and her people would again be free of people like Peter and Jim.

Cassy said in her sweetest voice, "You know, Peter might still be alive if you weren't so painfully stupid—"

Jim fired his rifle—the noise and smoke briefly baffled her senses. Pain flooded through Cassy's left leg, but not from the nail in her foot. She cried out and glanced down reflexively. The bullet had struck her in the thigh, and a pool of blood was growing rapidly. It didn't hurt as much as she'd imagined a gunshot would though.

Jim cycled his rifle's bolt and then stood motionless, staring at her through half-closed eyes with a smile on his face. The same smile he'd had when he first tried to "punish" her outside of Philadelphia.

Cassy knew he'd never let her tie off her leg to stop the

bleeding, so what the hell. Now or never. She drew the pistol from behind her hip and shoved it toward Jim. He was so enraptured by the sight of her bleeding leg that he didn't even seem to notice. This time she didn't hesitate. She barely heard the pistol fire, but she saw clearly the spurt of blood that erupted from his right shoulder. Jim fired back reflexively, but the shot went wide, and the recoil caused his rifle to fly from his hands. He was already moving toward her when Cassy pulled the trigger again, but she couldn't tell whether the round struck him.

Screaming in pain and rage, Jim leapt into the air and dove toward her. He landed on top of Cassy, knocking the wind out of her. The pistol skittered away. Cassy struggled to catch a breath as Jim raised himself with his good arm, and then he drove forward so that his forehead smashed into her nose and swollen left eye.

As Jim raised himself up again, Cassy cried out from the pain and frantically struggled to get out from under him, to no avail. He dove forward again, but Cassy held him off with her outstretched arms. She felt her thumb slide into the wound on his shoulder, a sickening warm, wet feeling, and Jim screamed in agony. His left arm gave out, but he used the momentum to roll away—anything to escape that agony.

Cassy rolled onto her stomach and struggled to get away, but her left leg was just dead weight. She clawed at the floor to pull her body along, away from Jim. Away from death. She couldn't help it; the almost serene acceptance of her fate had vanished amidst the pain and terror of fighting for her life. But then her hand struck something metallic—one of the caltrops. She grabbed at it like a drowning person reaching for a life vest and managed to get ahold of it. It felt like a miracle, a gift from God.

Jim got to his feet and, with a quick shuffling step to get closer to her, whipped his foot forward, kicking Cassy in the ribs. She screamed, pain exploding in her side as she curled into a ball just as Jim kicked her again. And again. He laughed maniacally as his blows rained down on her. After the third kick, she stopped moving; try as she might, her body refused to obey her.

Jim kicked her twice more in the side and then stopped, panting. His shirt was covered in blood, and Cassy found herself wondering how long it would take him to bleed out. Not long enough, she decided.

Still unable to move, she could only watch as Jim looked around the room. He'd find his rifle, or her pistol, and she knew it would all be over quickly after that. But then he stopped looking around and stared at the floor. She followed his gaze and realized with horror that he had found her broken knife. Four inches of good, sharp steel remained, and the jagged edge where it had snapped in two looked plenty sharp enough to stab her with. Or maybe he would just slit her throat with what was left of the blade. Jim bent over and groaned with the pain, but managed to pick up the knife. He was talking, but she couldn't make out the words through her pain and fear-clouded mind.

Cassy forced herself to take deep, even breaths. She had only moments to get herself together, get her body to obey her again, but it wasn't working. Abruptly, she heard Choony's voice in her head almost as though he was there talking to her, and she had a vision of one hot summer day when they'd met in the barn to talk and banter. "Your pain and turmoil is a product of your will," he'd said. "You cling to what *should* be and so you don't see *what is*. Change doesn't hurt, Cassy. You change your socks, and it never bothers you. It's the resistance to change that so greatly disturbs your peace."

And then she knew what to do. She'd been fighting for her life, ruled by her instincts, ever since she leapt out from the stairwell. But she didn't have to fight for her life. What truly mattered was the Clan. She had given birth to the Clan, and if it lived, then a part of her would live on and not only through her children. Her *idea* would live on. She only needed to delay Jim as long as she could. Her pain and fear slipped away. She focused on moving her finger, and it obeyed. It obeyed! Her whole body tingled as she regained control. She opened her eyes.

"—cut your head off and put it on a spike," Jim was saying. "You die before I do, Cassy. Ladies first," he said and then laughed.

As Jim staggered toward her with the knife, she took one last deep breath to brace for the pain that was about to come and then rolled from her belly onto her right side. At the same time, she lashed out with her left leg, thrusting it with all her might. Her foot smashed into Jim's knee, and the exposed nails from the caltrop embedded in her foot punched deep, crunching and grinding against bone. His leg caved backwards with a sickening wet, tearing noise, and he fell forward screaming. It was unlike any scream she'd heard before.

The monster crashed face-first into the floor next to Cassy, still gripping her knife. She clenched her hand tightly around the caltrop she'd retrieved, heedless of the nails that sunk deep into her hand. However she gripped it, it was still a caltrop; one spike must always point away. Cassy screamed and swung it with all her might at Jim's head. The blow landed just over his right ear, the caltrop spike sliding through the thinner part of his skull with ease. She felt something warm and sticky spatter over her hand.

Cassy struggled to her feet. Her left leg wouldn't bear weight so it was difficult, but after almost falling over once, she made it. She looked down at Jim, and for the first time she felt nothing. No hate, no outrage, no fear. Part of her wondered how she could look at that monster without those feelings, but she knew that was just her analytical side trying to make sense of things.

The simple truth was that none of it mattered. Not anymore. Her Clan would live, under whatever conditions, or it would die. She would do all she could to ensure it lived, but she could only do what was possible. More than that was beyond her means and so not her responsibility. Peter's conquest wasn't her fault. Jim and his tortures weren't her fault.

Even killing Peter and Jim wouldn't be her fault, though she accepted that responsibility gladly enough. They had sowed the seeds for this showdown, not Cassy. The fierce joy she'd felt at killing Peter melted away even as her nagging little feelings of guilt did, disappearing down some needed drain like wastewater. None of it was her fault, including Peter; he'd tried to kill her, and she had done what was necessary. That's all.

Cassy looked around the room and spotted Peter's pistol. At her feet, Jim cried and whimpered, unable to move, begging for mercy. First, she realized she probably couldn't save him even if she'd wanted to. Without trauma surgery in a hospital, he'd die regardless of what she chose. She wasn't bothered by that fact.

She'd seen the monster he truly was outside of Philadelphia, but she knew she'd spared him out of cowardice—a resistance to the idea of killing that made it too emotionally painful to finish the job. Because of that lack of will on her part, so many good people had suffered or died at Jim's hands...

No, their blood was on her hands. If he lived and she exiled him—the worst punishment the Council had agreed to take responsibility for—he would only prey on others. Then their blood too would be on her hands. She knew now what mercy for Jim would cause for others. Ending him was her responsibility. Cassy picked up the pistol. Jim saw it, but could do nothing about it. Couldn't move. Destiny was coming full circle for him.

"Jim, the terrible things you've done are as much my responsibility as yours. I let you live once. It was a mistake. I want you to know that I no longer hate you. God made people good, and Satan made them evil. We're both, Jim. All of us have good and bad within us. God doesn't make us do evil things, but He doesn't force us to do good, either. We have free will, even when people harm us. You choose evil every time."

"You... could spare me," Jim whimpered. "I did... what I was told..."

His breathing was shallow and rapid, and Cassy recognized that he was in shock. It didn't matter though.

"I could leave you to live or die, but that would only avoid my responsibility again. I did that once, and look what it brought. Not again. We all have free will, Jim. I chose to fight you, to put you in this state after you made many people suffer. Your suffering here is because of me. And now, I choose to end your suffering. And ours too, you see, because today's survivors will be better off if I kill you before they get here than if I simply leave you in pain awhile longer before you die. Choony would call it 'realizing your Karma,' but I call it justice. This world needs that right now. And I am responsible."

Cassy raised the pistol and, reaching forward, placed the barrel against Jim's forehead. His begging was only the pain and fear that came from resisting *what is*. Hanging on to *what was*.

"Burn in Hell, Jim."

* * *

Cassy felt faint. Blood loss was taking a toll. She managed to pull herself to the bed and sat leaning against it. Outside, the shooting had almost stopped. Soon, the victors would find her and either kill her or save her. Either way she could die satisfied knowing that she'd taken out Peter and Jim. Whoever was in charge after this would be better than those two sociopaths.

She recognized the symptoms of shock settling in and felt more exhausted than she'd ever been before. Maybe she could just...rest a minute. Her eyes drifted closed.

A noise. Cassy's eyelids snapped open. Blearily, she saw a ghost; Peter stood at the top of the stairs, axe in hand, swaying on his feet. He was covered in blood.

The ghost said, "You almost got away with it. Almost."

So, not a ghost. He wasn't as dead as she thought. Not like she'd been able to check carefully while Jim was picking off her people. Her gun—the one she'd taken—was on the floor nearby. She tried to move her arm but just didn't have the strength. She focused and slowly moved toward the weapon—her arm weighed a ton.

"It doesn't matter, Peter. You're done."

Despite the blood trickling from his mouth, Peter chuckled. It must have hurt, from the way he clenched his jaw, but the bastard never passed up a chance to gloat. He staggered toward her and kicked her pistol aside. Of course he'd want to kill her with the axe, not the gun. Showoff.

"God Himself sent me here, bitch," Peter said with a wheeze. "Was gonna start a new society, like Noah after the flood. This hippie bullshit you had here has no place in this new world. Surviving will take iron balls, not a group hug."

Peter raised the axe and rested the hickory handle on his shoulder to catch his breath the best he could. "You may get another day or week of peace. But sooner or later, someone like me will come along and take your pretty little farm. Let that be your last thought, bitch."

Peter flexed his fingers to get a better grip on the axe, took a deep breath and, still grinning, raised the deadly blade over his head.

So this was how it would end. She was surprisingly okay with it. Peter was a dead man, and whoever won the fight for the farm would be better than this monster. They'd do everything they could to secure the farm. There may be no true safety for her family anymore, but this was as good as it got.

Cassy said, "Get this over with so you can fucking die already." She glared into his eyes as he began to swing.

A deafening BANG! flooded the room, and Cassy winced, taking what she knew was her final breath. A sudden darkness overtook her, and time seemed to stand still as her heart pounded in her head.

When her eyes shot open, she saw the left side of Peter's head had disintegrated, covering the wall and part of her bed in gore. Peter collapsed like a dropped sack of flour, the axe clattering onto the wooden floor at Cassy's feet.

Ears ringing, Cassy saw the figure behind where Peter had stood. Then the figure became clear—at the top of the stairwell stood Jaz with a rifle in her hands. Behind her, still on the stairs, Cassy saw Choony's eyes wide with surprise.

Jaz looked down at Jim's corpse and shook her head. "Dammit, Cassy. You couldn't leave Scumbag Jim for me to finish off?"

Cassy smiled, a wide grin. Thank goodness they'd survived. God—or perhaps Buddha?—must have watched over those two. "Sorry, Jaz."

Then the grin faded, as it just took too much effort. Still, she was happy to see them. "Welcome back, you two."

Choony and Jaz approached her, Choony with a medical kit in hand. It looked Mil-grade. They knelt beside her, and

Choony began to cut away her pant leg while Jaz moved the hair out of Cassy's face and peered intently at the swollen mess Jim and Peter had left.

"Don't worry," Jaz said impishly. "Dudes dig scars."

- 22 -

1400 HOURS - ZERO DAY +41

CASSY SAT WITH the other members of the Council and gazed out over the rapidly browning fields of the Jungle. Winter would soon be on them, but this was still a time for the Clan to celebrate, and heal—at least for those who weren't on the Council.

Originally, the Council had included Michael, Frank, Mandy, Ethan, and Cassy. The Clan had grown now though, between the original Clan survivors and the White Stag sympathizers who had earned an honored place among them. Cassy had summarily added Choony, as well as Joe Ellings, to the Council. Despite the urgent nature of this ad hoc meeting, it was good beyond words to see them all again, free of fear and tension and even looking tranquil, if only for the moment, after the total chaos of last week.

Cassy's eye was still swollen shut and her nose would never be the same, but they'd both heal. She'd carry a scar from her forehead down across her left cheek for the rest of her life, and the shattered cheekbone wouldn't let her face recover quite the same as before, but she considered all that to be small penalties for saving her family from Psycho Santa and his Evil Elf. Remembering that moment of crazed laughter could still make her smile. She needed a crutch to get around, but the infections in her leg, hand, and foot had been checked by antibiotics brought back from the bunker, and she felt stronger every day.

The others were doing well, too. Frank's amputated foot was healing much faster now with the antibiotics. Michael had somehow managed to avoid injury in battle, despite striding fearlessly back and forth across the battlefield, giving orders as combat ebbed and flowed around him. Mandy's health and vitality had recovered much since getting insulin again, though her eyesight was fading as a result of her diabetes going untreated during the occupation. Ethan had been stabbed in the side during some brutal hand-to-hand combat toward the end of the battle, but the vet who had been among the sympathizers was sure he'd live, even though he'd have to watch what he ate from now on due to damage to his gall bladder.

Cassy decided to scratch a curiosity itch while she had the chance. "Choony, will you miss the people who died? I mean, being a Buddhist, I know you aren't supposed to grieve about such things, but I'm curious."

"I didn't know most of them, I'm sorry to say. I would have liked to. My destiny was not to be among you during the occupation though."

Frank nudged Choony with his elbow. "Your destiny was to avoid capture, rescue Jaz, and bring those Marines to us. Without you, what were the odds against them all showing up just when things went off the rails like they did?"

Ethan, still setting up his laptop for his urgent, couldn't-wait presentation, answered for Choony. "Mathematically, the odds were effectively zero in 100. Common sense, Frank. Try some."

Frank grinned for the first time that Cassy had seen since

the occupation began. "Mandy has a different theory. Right, Granny?"

"I'm Mandy, or Grandma Mandy, not Granny. You do like to egg me on, Frank!" She grinned. "But you aren't wrong. Bad things happened to us because of decisions other people made, but God turns bad events to His good purpose. The odds are meaningless for the Lord. Not just the help arriving right when we needed it the most, either. Ethan reaching those Marines. Choony escaping. Jaz finding him. Them finding the Marines. My amazing daughter's survival... Too much. The Lord's hand was with us."

Cassy didn't know how to reply to that. She couldn't prove it either way, but Mandy had a point. It all seemed extremely unlikely, the way everything folded together at the end.

Ethan interrupted with, "Alright, let's get this going. This is mostly bad news, I'm afraid, but things are what they are, and we have to take them into account when we make plans. I haven't been able to do much of the labor around here on account of my excessive iron intake." He chuckled, pleased when Cassy politely groaned. "So instead I've got our power system up again with spare parts Cassy had, and I've been lurking on the internet, radios, anything I could monitor. The short version is, this is the apocalypse, or close enough. And our side caused it."

Michael grunted. "How bad are things, and how bad will they get?"

"I'm getting to that. San Diego and Camp Pendleton weren't hit by EMPs. Not theirs, not ours. Every other industrialized nation was blanketed during Operation Backdraft. Not just the Middle East, China, Korea, and Russia. *All of it*, including our allies. I guess General Houle didn't want to leave anyone able to take advantage of the situation. Also, most second-world nations are blacked out.

Basically, only the Australian Outback, rural Africa, and the Amazon Jungle were spared, but it isn't really sparing them either."

"Why not?" Cassy asked. "They didn't need all that infrastructure to begin with, so why does it matter?"

Ethan said, "Because except for a few truly Stone Age tribes, almost every place on Earth relied on goods and raw materials being trucked or shipped around. Some of them could make it on their own by going primitive or self-sustaining like we have here, but unfortunately, it isn't working out that way for most."

Frank nodded and frowned. "Because all the millions of city people from Baghdad to Buenos Aires are about to be real hungry. They'll go where they think the food is."

"Yes," Ethan said. "The rest of the world will suffer between seventy to ninety percent casualties within twelve months, depending on how industrialized they were and how harsh the winter. And forget about east Asia—half the world's population lives in a circle stretching from Indonesia to China, Japan to Pakistan. Once the cities disperse, they're almost all doomed without infrastructure, not to mention imports and exports. Same with Europe from France to the Ural Mountains in Russia. Britain may survive if they have the will to cordon off the big cities." He scowled. "General Houle made a brutal response against people who had nothing to do with the attack. Brutal."

Michael clenched his jaw and spat. "What does that mean for the U.S.?"

"We're actually okay compared to them. So far, casualties are only about ten percent, but winter and disease will skyrocket that. Stuff we haven't seen in a century or more, like plague and typhoid. Third World diseases, man. Cholera and worse. By the time it all settles out, the General's estimates average out to seventy percent dead, globally. They think we'll have ninety-seven million survivors, which is about what we had at the end of the first World War."

Frank replied, "Nothing we can do about that, people. But Ethan, didn't you once tell me it would take two years for us to order, import, and install the power grid's big transformers? What happens to that with the rest of the world gone dark?"

"LPTs, or Large Power Transformers." Ethan nodded. "Yeah, they almost all had to be built overseas and shipped in, and the U.S. only had thirty or so rail cars even capable of transporting them. We threw away our own industrial base when the corporations went global. None of our railways are running again yet, but I'm sure the General will have steam engines running by springtime, if he can find any. But if not, who will build them? There might be a couple factories left that can make those beasts here in the U.S., and I imagine the General will make it a priority to occupy those locations. If we're lucky, parts of the power grid will be up again in three years. By then, we'll be a mostly rural nation with small, busy cities that are easy to control, if you see what I mean." He was still scowling.

Cassy banged her crutch on the ground, and everyone looked to her. "Ethan, you could have told us all that without dragging us away from our responsibilities. What's the real issue?" She didn't like to sound harsh, but Ethan had a way of dragging his feet getting to the point, and her leg hurt too much to humor him. "Let's get on point, shall we?"

Ethan looked crestfallen, but a moment later he had dropped back to his geeky Presentation Mode. He closed the images of the world, with their population forecasts, and opened a new graphic. This one showed the U.S., covered in different colors.

"I've hacked into Colorado Springs again—"

"Freakin' NORAD? Really?" Michael asked, eyes wide

with surprise.

"Yes. Well, not 'hacked,' but that's just semantics. More like intercepted. Here you see a map of the U.S. Note all the colors scattered around, but it's mostly gray. These are apparently what the General anticipates will be various 'zones of control.' Green areas are American under Houle's command. Gray areas are uncontrolled, like us. The red, brown, and yellow areas are what invader remnants control. As you can see, they still have the Eastern Seaboard."

Ethan tapped a key, and the image changed to a different colored map of the U.S. "This is the forecast for a year from now. The invaders lose control of most of their holdings but remain firmly in control of a few remaining areas. The briefs call those areas 'cantonments.' The invaders will firm up their control of eastern New York and Virginia, southern Alaska, and everything from Vancouver B.C. to Eugene, Oregon.

"Houle's green zone, however, expands greatly. All of California's west coast and Central Valley, and the Gulf Coast from Corpus Christi in Texas to Mobile, Alabama. They'll also have dozens of outposts throughout eastern Colorado and Western Kentucky, the area between Oklahoma City and Dallas, and around the Mississippi River from the Gulf to Memphis.

"Those are all some of the best agricultural lands in the country, so I think what they don't control directly will be in some sort of medieval feudal system of landholders as semiautonomous nobles who will give forced tribute to the General by way of those outposts. The whole area is almost wide open, with a well-developed system of railways, so enforcement won't be a big problem."

Michael had watched intently, and Cassy could see the wheels turning in his mind. Abruptly, Michael said, "What about that light blue area from southern Michigan to northern Ohio and Indiana? It's not that far from us, Ethan."

"Now *that* is the real reason I called you all. If the General is right, that whole region will be controlled by the locals, at least at first. The intel reports I've seen are pretty clear that Houle will support a faction out of Fort Wayne, Indiana, which will hold off the urbanites from Detroit, Chicago, and Indianapolis long enough for the cities to wither away, and will then expand by gobbling up the nation's second most productive agricultural area bit by bit. Including us. You know how the Romans had subject nations that were independent internally, but had to pay taxes to the Romans, give military support, and so on? It'll be like that, if Houle has his way. Make no mistake, they'll be under the General's control. And they'll end up stopping just west of us before next winter. No forecast after that, but I think you can see where that's going."

Cassy slowly stood, using her crutch for support, and smiled to the other Council members. "Thank you for the update, Ethan. We lucked out more than we could have ever known when we met up with you. But I think there's not a lot we can do about any of that right now. We'll have all winter to think about it, plan, and prepare. Whatever we do, I don't think we can do it on our own. By spring, we'll have new neighbors, people like us who struggled and triumphed on their own. I think we'll have more in common with them than some rump empire out of Indiana propped up by a wannabe Roman emperor. For now, though, I'm tired. Still fighting off those infections, you know. And the farm still needs running until spring, so don't you all go getting lazy, my friends!"

The Council members chuckled politely and broke up the meeting. Cassy waited for Ethan, last to leave. He had to pack up his computer, of course. Amber approached from nearby. She had changed a lot during her exile in the bunker with Ethan. More mature, less impulsive, less angry, more thoughtful. All good things.

"Ethan. A minute?" Cassy said, and smiled at Amber as she drew close. "Actually this involves you too, Amber. I hear you two are thinking about making your relationship official. Everyone knows, of course, but it's maybe a bigger deal for the Clan than you know. It's a neon sign that life goes on, that we're still alive. Really and truly alive, not just passing time waiting to die."

Amber slowly nodded and smiled. "I'm glad we have your blessing—I know Frank and everyone else are okay with us being together. And Kaitlyn says she really likes Ethan though his online gaming references go over her head."

Cassy laughed. "And I just want to say, I'd love to hear wedding bells in the near future, but I know it's too soon for that. But when the time's right, I know we'd all enjoy a big celebration."

"One step at a time," Amber said, and Ethan nodded in agreement.

Cassy said, "Well, in the meantime, everyone will be busy settling down and getting to know the new neighbors from the White Stag and others straggling in. And there's plenty of work to do to keep us all busy until winter. Speaking of, I have another meeting with Frank soon—more planning and politicking. Stay out of trouble, you two."

"No promises," Ethan said with a wink before he and Amber strode off, hand-in-hand.

Alone, Cassy reflected that there was still a lot of work left to do by winter, and a lot of healing both physical and mental, but she knew that if they could joke about things again already, then everything would work out in the end. Or at least for now, and that was all she could ask for.

For the first time in a long time, Cassy felt hope, and happiness. She hobbled toward the house, whistling and thinking about the apple cider that would soon be ready. Now *that* would be cause for a celebration. She glanced around and, just for a moment, watched the bustle of work going on as her new family was doing needful tasks around the farm, the kids all pitching in, adding happy noise to the pounding and the shouting as the Clanners rebuilt their farm.

She was smiling as she entered her house... her home.

# # #

To be continued in
EMP Backdraft (Dark New World, Book 4)

About the authors:

JJ Holden lives in a small cabin in the middle of nowhere. He spends his days studying the past, enjoying the present, and pondering the future.

Henry Gene Foster resides far away from the general population, waiting for the day his prepper skills will prove invaluable. In the meantime, he focuses on helping others discover that history does indeed repeat itself and that it's never too soon to prepare for the worst.

For updates, new release notifications, and more, please visit:

www.jjholdenbooks.com

Printed in Great Britain
by Amazon